Neil Gibb was born i                                        t
Kent University he has                                      ,
worked in drug research, and now makes a living as a copy
writer. He lives in East London.

# Blood Red Sky

## *Neil Gibb*

PIATKUS

Copyright © 1999 by Neil Gibb

First published in 1999 by
Judy Piatkus (Publishers) Ltd of
5 Windmill Street, London W1P 1HF

This edition published 1999

**The moral right of the author has been asserted**

*A catalogue record for this book is available
from the British Library*

ISBN 0 7499 3115 9

Set in Times by
Wyvern 21 Ltd, Bristol

Printed and bound in Great Britain by
Mackays of Chatham, plc

I'd like to thank Andrew Carrick, Christine Kell, Bruce and Sarah Scriver, "Sammy" Wilson, Andy Darling and Rose Gunne for their support. Especial thanks to Karen Gibb for her support, ideas and diligent proofing – it made a lot of difference.

# 1

The wall ran straight down the back of the terrace; eight feet tall, eighteen inches thick, and a hundred years old. Its stained bricks were the same dark red colour as the dilapidated Victorian houses behind it – a deep, muddy red that looked damp in all but the brightest of sunlight. On the inside, Eddie Giles – Fat Eddie to most of his neighbours – was trying to nail some trellis to the ancient brick, so he had somewhere else to wind his Russian vine. On the other side, about twenty yards down in the dip in the alley where all the rubbish collected, Paula slowly choked on a mixture of vomit and blood.

Eddie was struggling. He needed another hand. He could just about hold up the trellis and balance the nail with one, while he swung the hammer with the other. But every time he managed to hit the head, the trellis lurched, causing the nail-end to skid across the surface of the compressed brick.

This time, though, he was sure he had got it right.

He held the wood on the back of his hand, and squeezed the nail hard between his fingers. He placed the hammer head on the end of the nail, and breathed in. One hard bang, and the surface would be pierced. He pulled the hammer back and came down with a short jab. It landed dead centre. Instead of skidding, the nail buckled, and the hammer head came down on Eddie's thumb with a crack.

'Shiiiiiiiiiiiiit,' he spat, as the pain exploded in his thumb. He hit the wall with the hammer, and splintered the corner of a brick.

'Bas-tard!'

Sweat prickled on his forehead. He gritted his teeth and sucked in air sharply.

'Fuck, fuck, *fuck*!' he hissed, gingerly unclenching his fist to assess the damage. His thumbnail had split but at least it was still on. He stuck his thumb in his mouth, and looked up. The sky was a dank grey and a fine drizzle was beginning to fall. He decided to jack it in and get some breakfast.

As he picked up his tools and shuffled back across the yard he heard giggling, and looked over his shoulder.

'That's all I need,' Eddie muttered. It was one of the scummy children from next door. He was eight years old, fatherless, and completely out of control; Eddie dreaded to think what he would be like when he grew up. He was one of the reasons Eddie was growing the vine. He planned to surround his yard with trellis, cover it with fast-growing vine, and then thread barbed wire through it. He hoped it would stop them coming over to piss in his yard and steal anything that wasn't bolted down.

'Piss off,' Eddie said, turning back towards his back door.

'I know something you don't,' the kid sang.

Eddie ignored him and shut his eyes. He imagined jabbing the hammer between the child's eyes.

'There's a broken lady in the alley.'

Eddie wondered what he meant.

'She's trying to crawl around,' the kid giggled, 'but she can't.'

Eddie turned to look at him but he was gone. He wondered if it was a ploy to get him out into the alley so they could throw something at him. But he didn't think they were that clever.

He slowly went over to his back gate and started to pull out the bolts. He could see a fresh crack where someone had recently tried to kick it in. The damp wood had expanded so at first the gate wouldn't give. On the third try, he shouldered it open and stepped out cautiously into the alley.

He looked up the hill. All he could see was an array of burnt-out bins and a manky mongrel sniffing at some discarded fast food. There was no one around. He quickly swivelled in the other direction.

It was empty that way too. There was nothing there but a pile of tattered rubbish in the dip in the concrete.

He cursed himself for listening to the stupid kid and started to turn back to his gate. As he moved, something flickered at the edge of his vision. He turned his head sharply and looked down the hill again. The grey drizzle made it difficult to focus on the heap of rubbish. He squinted. He had definitely seen something move down there. He strained and began to make out some definition. He felt a sick empty feeling in his stomach as his subconcious started to make connections. His breath came out short and fast.

He took a step down the slope. He saw another fluttering movement. Something wasn't right down there. An unfocused wave of fear ran through him, priming his senses as his brain started to make sense of the pattern.

Then it sank in.

He suddenly realised what it was that was jutting upwards. It was twisted and limp, and sticking out at an odd angle. But there was no mistaking it now. He felt the breath stick in his throat.

It was an arm. It was an arm, and it was moving.

He tentatively stepped forward, his eyes locked on the twitching shape. As he got closer he made out more; much more. There was a woman on her back among the sodden cardboard and spewing bin-liners; her head was arched back, and her fingers were clawing at the rough concrete surface. His heart started to pound hard.

He moved quickly, kicking a plump sack out of the way, but when he reached her he froze.

He stood over her for a long moment, rooted to the spot, and his first thought – before he could stop it – wasn't about the damage or the pain. It was how young she looked, how vulnerable . . . and how sexy. He didn't want to think it, but he did. She had smooth brown skin, and a mass of long blonde hair straggling on the ground around her. Her piercing blue eyes looked wildly into the air, the whites clear and the pupils invitingly open. A strange, hot feeling swept through him. He couldn't stop himself looking down. Her silver padded jacket and shirt had been ripped open and her leggings dragged down. He recalled it all later: the taut young skin and narrow hips; the all-over tan, no blemishes, no panty line; the narrow-cut fluff of pubic hair. He took it all in a split second. But hated himself for a long time afterwards.

Only then did he see the damage. There were deep ragged tears in her skin where her clothes had been ripped away, and

3

her pelvis jutted up, grazed raw. Her smashed knees were splaying out, grit peppering the skin, and blood caked her thighs. The images burnt themselves into his brain, overlaying what he had just seen.

He realised he didn't know what to do. He felt his stomach clench impotently. She was twitching in front of him as spasms of pain convulsed through her body, shaking so hard it was almost a vibration, and he hadn't a fucking clue what to do.

He bent forward clumsily. And as he did her left eye suddenly appeared to split open. A wave of nausea pulsed through his gut. She blinked and a fragment of membrane caught on her eyelashes. It glinted bright blue, then fell away – and he realised it was just a contact lens that had popped out. He let his breath out slowly and felt his stomach subside. Her exposed iris was a mishmash of brown-grey, and suddenly – that close – he could see she was older than he had thought. Her skin was rough under a thick foundation and her hair was matted, showing dark at the roots. Her breath was thick and rancid; a mixture of cigarettes, vomit and pain.

He felt something flutter against him. He stopped dead as her skin brushed against his, and recoiled as she pulled her hand up. He saw her nails were shattered and broken – dragged back to the quick. He felt himself reeling, his breath deeper in his throat. She feebly started to pull at her shirt, maniacally tugging at the bottom, trying to cover herself up.

And only then did it seem real. The clawing, shaking hand triggered something in his memory. It hit him like an electric shock, and the image of his wife suddenly flooded back to him. How helpless she had looked in hospital just before she died. How her dignity had ebbed away as they had manhandled her around, and daubed at her when she had wet herself. It shook him into action. This was the same; this poor woman, half naked in the middle of this shitty alley, just trying to cover herself up. He bent down to try to help, gagging on the bile in his throat – bile pumped up from his soul, stinging him for what he had seen, and stinging him more for what he had felt.

But all Paula saw was a shape coming for her. Her instinct to survive pumped adrenaline back into her limbs. That bastard – that dirty fucking bastard – had come back for more. She had

4

done everything she could to fight him off – but she'd only had fear to draw on. He'd had hate – a frenzy of seething hate – and she hadn't stood a chance. Now he was back again. She ground her broken teeth, and in her head she wept as she desperately tried to push him away. Pain lanced down her broken arm as it connected with his head.

Eddie jumped back, horrified. She was clawing wildly at him; blindly. Her broken wrists flailed. And he heard a horrible gurgling noise. A noise that came from a small triangular hole punched in her neck.

He bolted back to his house. There was nothing he could do. And he could not stand to look at her any more. He had to call an ambulance.

Paula was dead before he made it to his back door.

# 2

Alex was having a hard time with the woman who owned the house – or what was left of the house – when she heard the news. Stan, the sound engineer, shouted over to her from the van: another body had been found, this time over in Hyson Green. Another prostitute. Alex stopped listening to the woman rambling on in front of her and tried to work out what to do. Her stomach clenched up, and she felt a fizz of excitement. She knew it would happen again. She had known after the first one, but no one had believed her. This proved she was right. At last, something big was happening – and she needed a story like this badly.

She interrupted the woman. 'Excuse me, but I'm going to have to make a call. Can you hang on a minute?'

'I thought you wanted to film my house?'

'Yes, yes I do,' she said reassuringly. 'It's just that I need to make an urgent call. It won't take a minute. Why don't you make yourself a cup of tea.'

'I can't,' the woman said unhappily. 'We don't have a kitchen any more.'

Alex tried to look sympathetic. The woman had a point. She *had* just blown up her house. But Alex didn't have time to placate her. This was not the sort of story she wanted to be remembered for; some poor woman who had left the gas on in the kitchen while she went out shopping, and came back to find a hole in the terrace where her house should be. OK, it was a damn sight better than anything else she had covered in the last year, but opportunity was suddenly knocking elsewhere – big time!

She smiled encouragingly and put her hand lightly on the woman's arm.

'Look, why don't you go over to the van and see Stan,' she said softly. 'He's got a flask. I won't be long.'

'But . . .' the woman started to say.

Alex forced herself to keep smiling and tried to stay calm; she was standing among a rubble of shattered red bricks in a damp, run-down little back street on the wrong side of Nottingham while the story she needed had just dropped out of the sky across town. She had to move quickly.

'I won't be a minute,' she said, starting to turn. She jogged down the cobbled street to the car.

She pressed redial on the mobile, and waited impatiently as the tones slowly unwound in her ear.

'Hi, Harry, it's me . . .'

'No,' he said immediately.

His abruptness threw her slightly.

'Harry, it's me. Alex. I . . .'

'I know. And before you set off, the answer's no!'

'You don't even know what I'm going to say.'

'Yes I do.'

'What?'

'You want to cover the dead whore story . . . Am I right?'

'Well, yes . . . sort of . . . I mean, yes . . .'

'Well, I'm sorry, there's no chance. OK?'

'Harry . . .'

'Alex, we've been through this before. OK? I mean, I admit you were right. Some member of the barmy army is taking out hookers. And you were right that it's going to make a great story. So well done. Have a house point. But there's no way you're going to cover it. So that's that.'

'Come on, Harry. I mean, I deserve it. I . . .'

'Yeah, yeah, yeah . . . Look, don't play the hearts and flowers with me, sweetie. Firstly, it's out of your league, babe. And secondly we're bringing people up from Birmingham. We haven't got the resources. We'll let the big boys cover it, and then we'll recycle it. That's how it works.'

'But Mike gets to play, right?' Alex said miserably.

'Probably. Maybe. I don't know. But I'm sorry, like I say, this is out of your league. Now I've got things to deal with. Just do what you do best.'

'Which is?'

'Empathising with the little people. You know they love you. Now get that story wrapped.'

'Yeah, OK.' She took a deep breath and tried to sound reasonable. 'Look, Harry, can we talk about this?'

'Sure. But when you get back. Now get that one in the can. We need it back here in an hour.'

He cut the line.

She looked at the receiver with disgust. Thanks, Harry. Thanks a lot. She threw the mobile on the passenger seat, and set off to look for the woman.

Alex stalked into the reception area forty-five minutes later. She ran her hand through her short, blonde hair and flicked the oily dampness at a fake pot plant. She felt sticky and filthy all over. They'd had to do five more takes before they had wrapped it. Five more takes in the thick murky drizzle. The woman kept saying things like *Do you think it will need redecorating?* as they stood in the burnt-out shell of her former kitchen. Normally Alex could have seen the funny side – just about – but today it had just made her more agitated. She had left the crew to tidy up, and got out as fast as possible. She had a terrible feeling that things were running away from her.

She punched the lift button, then set off up the stairs without waiting.

She snaked her way through the open-plan space towards Harry's office, catching her hip on a jutting desk along the way.

'Piss,' she spat, as a sharp pain stabbed her hip-bone.

'And you call yourself a lady?' someone piped up jovially in a fake American drawl.

'Leave me alone,' she said, without looking to see who it was. She felt like crying.

Harry's blinds were half shut but she could see his stocky shape behind his desk. She braced herself for the rank cocktail of cigarette smoke and stale sweat that always hung in the air in his office.

She pushed open the door. Harry was on the phone. But Harry was always on the phone, so she went straight in. He tried to ignore her.

'OK, fine. We'll do it anyway,' he said into the receiver, 'then maybe we'll run it later in the week. How's that sound?'

'Good,' he said, after a pause. 'See you.'

He turned around with his finger on his lips. She could see the sweat marks under his arms.

'Before you say anything, Alex, I'm not in the mood. OK?'

She looked exasperated. 'Come on, Harry. You must see my point.'

'No,' he said flatly. 'I don't. Not at all. And you're beginning to get boring. So why don't you tell me something new instead.' He leant back in his chair with his arms behind his head, exposing the full glory of his armpits.

'I know I can do it, Harry. I really can. Can't you give me a break – *just once*?'

Harry rolled his eyes and looked at the ceiling. His neck bulged out of a shirt that was slightly too small for him. He was always flushed but it was getting deeper.

'Look, Alex,' he said, staring back at her. 'There's nothing to talk about. OK? Mike will cover what little there is to cover – *yes*, just like he always does – and that, basically, is that. Business as usual. End of story. Do – you – understand?'

She knew that tone in his voice. It wasn't worth continuing. It would just wind him up to explosion point, and then she would be covering dog shows for the next six months.

'Yeah, I understand,' she said dejectedly. 'Maybe next time, right?'

'That's my girl.' His voice softened back to its normal abrasive tone.

Alex looked at the miserable day through the blinds. The thick grey sky made the multi-storey across the road look even more depressing. The dark stains on the concrete looked as disgusting as Harry's sweat marks. She looked back at Harry. He would give a pep talk now. It was always the same. Harry was nothing if not predictable.

'Look, I know you're frustrated,' he said. 'And I know you want a juicy story. But this one just wasn't a goer, alright? It's nothing personal, babe. You know that.'

She ignored him and looked back at the grey skyline. How

had she ended up stuck here? she thought. This wasn't how it was meant to happen.

Harry breathed in sharply to get her attention.

'Look, Alex, I'll cut the crap. If all you want is a dead body, then you've got a dead body. OK? . . . Now does that make you feel any better?'

She looked at him sceptically. 'What do you mean?'

'I mean it's bargain bucket day today, that's what. Some medic's just been found dead as a dodo in a rehab clinic over in Radford. And since all our other resources are tied up . . . I want you to cover it.'

She rocked back in her chair and tried to work out whether he was being straight with her.

'Are you being serious?'

'Yeah, straight up. You know me.'

'So what do we know?' she asked, trying to sound non-committal.

'The coppers reckon he was working late when some junkies broke in, probably looking for smack or methadone or something. It sounds like pretty juicy stuff. They kicked the shit out of him when he wouldn't open the drug store. Apparently he wasn't looking too sweet when they found him.'

'When did it happen?' she asked, still trying to sound non-committal, but failing.

'Some time last night . . . but don't worry, they only found him a couple of hours ago. There'll still be blood on the walls.' He tapped a cigarette out of a Marlboro soft-pack. 'We'll run it in a couple of days, if it's worth it, when this other story dies down. So how about you move your pretty arse before I change my mind.'

'OK,' she said, starting to rise. She forced herself to smile as sweetly as possible. 'Thanks.'

'Pleasure.' He shrugged, leaning forward for the phone. 'But actually I didn't have any choice. Sir wanted your pretty face on this one.' He shrugged again. 'You never know, honey, maybe your luck's in and he fancies you. Get this one right and he might even promote you to the weather . . .' He smirked. 'Once you've shagged him, that is.'

'Very funny.'

He punched a number, smiling. 'C'mon, Alex. Lighten up. How many times do you get the chance to cover a kosher murder, eh? Who knows, it might even lead somewhere. Now go on, shift your arse.'

And it might not, she thought. But as long as it kept her away from people with strange-shaped marrows and exploding kitchens, things were at least slightly better. She decided to cut her losses.

'OK,' she said, trying to sound sincere, 'I'll do my best.'

'Good girl,' he said, winking.

She smiled back grimly, and quickly left before she said anything else. She had a habit of opening her mouth at times like this, and it never got her anywhere. One day she swore she would be in a position to fire anyone who called her *girl*, *love* or *babe*. One day she would occasionally fax Harry from London, just to tell him who she was interviewing that day, and ask him not to look her up if he was ever in town.

She went and picked up her new schedule, and took it back to her office to see what Harry had got her into.

# 3

Detective Sergeant Grigson slammed the door behind him.

'Is it true, sir?' he asked. His face was flushed, highlighting the deep pockmarks on his cheeks.

Harris looked up from his desk. 'What?'

'They're bringing Hague in as SIO?'

Harris smiled and pushed his chair back. 'Look, this is no longer simply a murder hunt, Dave. We've got a full-scale media event on our hands now. Hague has been brought in at a higher level to co-ordinate. It'll free me up to concentrate on the investigation.'

Grigson sat down and scowled.

'From now on the Senior Investigating Officer role is going to demand a lot of cross-agency co-ordination, handling the media, PR – that sort of thing. That's the kind of thing Hague is good at. I'm just a copper who at heart wants to get out on the streets. So it's fine by me.' He smiled. 'OK?'

'But he's a back-room boy. A jumped-up little Oxbridge shite.'

'And he's also an Assistant Chief Constable.'

'Yes, sir. Sorry.'

'Don't worry ... Anyway, what did forensics come back with?'

Grigson opened the report he'd been carrying and flicked through.

'Three different kinds of semen in the vagina. Two in the rectum. Traces in the stomach and hair. Just a good old country girl at heart.'

'Christ almighty, hadn't she heard of condoms?'

'They also found significant amounts of heroin in her blood, sir. And traces of crack cocaine, marijuana and amphetamines. The veins in her arms were so fucked up she was injecting into her legs and feet, so she probably couldn't care less. And anyway punters'll pay more for unprotected sex. She probably needed the money.'

'HIV?'

'Surprisingly not.'

'Anything that ties back to the other cases?'

Grigson looked across at him and shook his head.

'Nothing.'

'He managed to remove all traces again?'

'Yes, sir.'

Harris placed his fingers together and frowned.

'What the hell are we dealing with here, Dave?'

'I don't know, sir.'

# 4

Alex blinked slowly and glanced at the clock on the dash. It was all hands up – bang on midnight. She groaned silently. If she was lucky she would just about make it home before dropping off.

She turned off the main road into the gloomy Edwardian splendour of Mapperley Park, and drove slowly down the dark boulevard towards her flat. The drizzle had turned to heavy rain which bounced off the bonnet and danced in the headlights, making her eyes smart.

She pulled up on the road outside her flat, and stopped the engine. She sat in the dark with her eyes closed, listening to the rain drumming on the vinyl roof. She wanted to be in bed more than anything else, but she couldn't seem to move.

She had spent most of the morning standing in the drizzle outside the medical centre – the Kallman Institute – waiting for someone to turn up. The building was a characterless modern low-rise on a grubby back road in a particularly dilapidated part of Radford. She noticed that someone had daubed *Child Molesters!* on the wall. It had been painted over but it still showed through.

All round were old half-empty warehouses, some burnt out, and ominous-looking terraces. Damp piles of rubbish matted the drains, and the odd scraggy dog wandered about, jerking madly, and nuzzling through the empty cans of Special Brew and Tennents Super littering the kerb. Groups of youths, with baseball hats high on their shaved heads, occasionally cruised by staring blankly from dodgy BMWs and knackered old saloons.

She had waited with the crew for a couple of hours, but it was pretty obvious the place was shut up for the day. The main door was chained, with police tape pulled taut across the front. They had half-heartedly interviewed a few local residents before they left, but no one had had much to say.

They had wrapped it up with Alex standing solemnly in front of the Institute with her collar turned up against the rain. The camera was adjusted so the streetlights would flare blood red against an ominous dark background.

She put on her best serious face and looked hard at the camera:

'Is this the start of a new wave of drug-related crimes in our city? Will our estates go the same way as those in America? No-go zones after dark, controlled by the crack gangs, and abandoned by the police. Only time will tell, but today we stepped a little closer. This is Alex Brierley, reporting for *Midlands Report East*.'

It would have been a good sign-off if she'd had something decent to put in front of it; but she didn't. It wasn't the start she had been hoping for.

She groped for the door handle, yanked it, and felt the cold, damp air rush into the car. It forced her to move. She snapped the crook-lock over the gear lever and heaved herself out onto the pavement.

She didn't like leaving the car in the open. It was a neat little red Mazda that seemed to invite abuse. She bleeped on the alarm and patted the soft-top as she popped the lock.

'Just don't get stolen, that's all,' she murmured, smiling at the car.

She knew her dear old pals in the local constabulary would just love it if she had to report her car stolen. Their less-than-helpful response earlier confirmed they still hadn't forgotten her.

It was her first – and probably biggest – mistake at the station. She had only been in the job for a couple of weeks when Harry had asked her to cover a case of alleged police corruption. She was surprised – and flattered – that he hadn't given it to someone more experienced. It was only later that she found that no one else would touch it with a bargepole.

The story had been about a rather pathetic, small-time criminal who claimed he'd been stitched up for car theft by the CID. The police had told her there was nothing in it, and had asked her to drop it, but she wouldn't; it was her big chance to prove herself.

She had done a good job at first, interviewing the kid and showing what it was like to be unceremoniously hauled in by the police; how easy it was for what you said to be turned on its head. Her mistake was she had believed him.

It was a big mistake. A big, big, big mistake.

The kid was caught red-handed joy-riding a panda car two days after her piece was run, and the case was dropped like a ton of bricks.

She had done her best to try to patch things up, but it didn't work. They had been politely – but completely – obstructive ever since. She was sure it had contributed to her free fall into the human-interest career dustbin. It was the one place where you never had to come into contact with the police.

She slunk towards the house, hugging her coat around her.

It had taken her all afternoon just to get some bog-standard feedback out of the CID. And then it was only off-the-shelf patter:

Drugs? *Yes.*

Witnesses? *No.*

Suspects? *Hundreds.*

Leads? *No comment.*

She realised they had an excuse for ignoring her on this occasion; but it didn't make her feel any better. It just reminded her of what she was missing. They had three unsolved murders that were suddenly looking very much like a trend. A vicious killer – like nothing else they had come across before – was butchering women on their patch. And now there was an off-the-record rumour that he was *signing* his victims before they died. Stuff like that got out. The tabloids couldn't have invented a better story if they had tried.

She decided to try not to think about it.

She shouldered her way along the alley by the side of the big Edwardian house, being careful not to slide on the crust of pigeon shit that had turned to slime in the rain. The entrance to her flat was at the back. The automatic light had stopped working about a month ago, and the alley was pitch black.

She pulled her coat off, batted some of the greasy moisture

16

onto the floor, then dug into the pocket and pulled out a screwed-up piece of paper. She carefully opened it and managed a smile. A brief highlight in an otherwise shitty day.

She had been tempted to go straight home after the disappointing shoot, but she'd had another idea. The briefing had said that the victim – a fifty-four-year-old psychiatrist called Dr Ian Fisher – had been a consultant at Queens Hospital before taking over as head of the Institute. She decided to go over to Queens to see if she could find someone to comment.

She was on her third cup of nasty vending-machine coffee when two young doctors came striding down the corridor, white coats flapping open, ready to go on shift.

'Hi,' she said, blocking their way before they could disappear through the swing-doors. 'Can you spare a minute?'

They stopped and looked at her warily.

'I'm Alex Brierley from *Midlands Report East*. I wondered if you'd heard about the murder over at the Kallman Institute?'

The nearer of the two was a tall, thin Asian man with a deeply pockmarked face.

'Look . . .' he said sourly. 'I think you need to speak to someone in our public affairs department. Rumour has it that that's what they're for.'

The other man was broader and blonde. 'It'll give them something to do up there,' he said, grinning.

Alex smiled and relaxed slightly.

'Look, you know there's no point in me speaking to some pen-pusher,' she said, with a pained expression. 'You know what they're like. All I want is a bit of background, then I can go home. Simple as that. It'll be off the record.'

She looked at them hopefully.

'OK,' the blonde one said amicably. 'If it means I get to talk to a real live woman for a while, why not?' He smiled broadly again. 'But if it's off the record, then it really must be off the record, alright?'

'No problem,' she said, smiling again; her eyes creased at the edges when it was real.

'Steve Hill,' he said, offering her his hand.

'Pleased to meet you,' she replied, feeling better than she had all day. He shook her hand, holding it for a fraction of a second longer than was necessary. She carefully extracted it, and raised her eyebrow slightly. He had that confident but gawky way about him that young doctors had. Usually it wasn't her thing, but on this occasion she found it quite fetching. He was cute, she thought – he looked like the sort of dashing young doctor who made housewives' hearts flutter in daytime soaps.

He introduced his partner as Raz, which was short for something she didn't quite catch. She was a bit distracted.

She took them over to the vending machine, and bought them both coffee.

'We'll have to keep this brief,' Steve said, looking at his watch.

'Fine,' she replied, pulling out her pad. 'Just tell me what you can about Fisher. Anything's better than nothing.'

'Well,' he said, rubbing the back of his neck, 'he was a pretty controversial figure, that's for sure.' He explained that Fisher had been well known in the psychiatric field for his extreme views – especially when he had been teaching at the hospital. 'He was a firm believer that mental illness was a purely medical problem – physical, maybe even genetic – and should therefore be treated accordingly. He wasn't prepared to compromise, especially when it came to complementary therapies.'

'So he was old-school, you might say?'

Steve glanced at the ceiling and frowned.

'In a way, yeah. I mean, he was anti-therapy, anti-rehab, anti just about anything that didn't involve treatment. But when it came to drugs he was anything but traditional.'

'How do you mean?'

'Look,' Steve said carefully. 'Drugs have their place, OK. But as far as Fisher was concerned they weren't just *a* solution – they were the *only* solution. Which is why he left here and started the Kallman Institute. He set it up as a research centre. It was a sort of personal crusade.'

'So I guess that means there'd be a lot of drugs stored at the Institute?'

Steve nodded. 'And how.'

Raz cleared his throat. 'There's probably more stuff down there than in the whole of this hospital,' he said, lobbing his half-full cup into the bin. 'I did a placement in outreach. It was

18

well known among local users that the Kallman was stuffed full of drugs.'

'Like what?'

'All sorts.' Raz shrugged. 'A lot of people call the place Prozacville, but that's only half of it. Fisher did a lot of work with drug companies, so who knows. He would certainly have had methadone, though, as he did some work with dependants.'

'The place was an obvious target for desperate users,' Steve added. 'I'm surprised it hasn't happened before.' He glanced at his watch. 'Look, I'm afraid we need to go.'

'So who do you think might have done it?' Alex asked quickly.

Steve looked at her and smiled. 'Could have been anybody with a habit. And that's a lot of people. One thing is for sure, though – you won't be short of confessions. I bet there's already about a dozen of Fisher's patients ready to confess to the crime. It goes with the territory.'

He scribbled something on a piece of paper and handed it to her. 'If you've got any more questions, just give me a call, OK?'

'OK,' Alex said, smiling, 'I might just do that.'

She watched the swing-doors flap behind them.

She let her mind wander for a second. They hadn't given her much information – but the important thing was she was up and running. A long-lost feeling had just ignited inside her. It was only a glimmer, a little flicker – but it felt a lot like hope.

Her stomach was light and she felt like dancing back to the station. She had a feeling that things were on the move.

But she was wrong.

She was very wrong.

Three hours later she was right back down there again, sitting hunched in her car in the underground carpark, weeping.

Three hours! She didn't even have the pleasure of sleeping on it. She sat biting her lip, and pinching her skin until it hurt. Harry had taken precisely twenty seconds to dash her enthusiasm when she got back to the station. They were pulling her story. It was like being smacked in the face.

'Life's a bitch,' he said, flatly. 'I'm sorry, but there's just too much going on with the big murder hunt.'

'You can't,' she said hollowly, but Harry didn't seem to hear her.

'It's got a lot bigger than we thought,' he said. 'So if we're going to run anything else it has to be so fluffy it floats. We've got to keep the balance. You know that.'

She murmured something incomprehensible, which didn't matter because Harry wasn't listening. He was talking nineteen to the dozen.

He assured her that when it was over she would be back on the job; but that just made it worse. Harry's assurances were worth about as much as Russian currency on the money markets.

Meanwhile she was back on the human-interest merry-go-round. First stop was a piece on acid rain and ancient monuments, then calling at all stations to nowhere.

She managed to make it to the underground carpark intact before she started to cry. She walked through the dark grey concrete space and felt the tears well up in her eyes. Harry annoyed her just by existing; a scummy, cocky, just-plain-awful Welshman with no social graces – and a ridiculous moustache. His whole manner wound her up. But when he was on a roll – like now – he was soul-destroying.

She sat in the dark in her car for a long time, her tears eating at her make-up, and let her misery swallow her up. And the ugly regret that lurked at the back of her mind rose up. It always came back to haunt her at times like this. Sometimes it felt as if her whole life pivoted on that one decision. And the irony of it was she had made it because she wanted a career.

This!

She had done it for *this*!

She sat in the cold grey space feeling more alone than she had in a long time. Eventually she felt the cold, and she let go of the skin on her wrist and took a deep breath. She could see the finger marks bruised into her pale flesh, and felt the angry rake marks on her thighs.

I've got to get out of here, she thought, turning the ignition. She gunned the engine, and slammed up the exit ramp.

By the time she had parked outside the flat the storm had passed. The drive had burnt off her frustration, and all that was left was a numb, overpowering exhaustion.

20

She went into the living room and turned on the light. The panel on her answer machine showed a big fat double zero.

People had even stopped calling her!

She knew she was just feeling paranoid, but on top of everything else it was too much.

It was five years since she had left London. Five years since she had said she would be back in two. Her plan had been to pick up a couple of years' experience in the provinces, then go back to London, and walk straight into some plummy job at ITN. Simple as that. Meanwhile, all her friends would still be stuck as production assistants, or making fools of themselves on some foreign-language station – and she would be on the fast track.

Good plan!

Except when the two-year contract ran out in Cardiff, things had changed. Franchises had been won and lost, and she had nowhere to go but sideways. She took the contract in Nottingham, waiting for things to pick up. But now another three years had just sort of slipped by, and she was beginning to get desperate.

Most of her friends had done little better – although at least they were still in London – but a couple had started to make it; Alison occasionally cropping up on Sky-syndicated news, and Chris getting credits on the BBC for production.

She looked out of the window. It was pitch black. Then she caught sight of her reflection in the glass. The image was half in shadow, and her eyes were dark holes. She looked like a ghost.

'Oh God!' she murmured, looking at the ceiling. She would be thirty in two months.

She needed to get a grip of herself.

She stepped forward and pulled the blinds down.

She walked slowly around the room, trying to stretch the tension out of her shoulders, the rain drumming rhythmically against the glass in the background. And slowly, she realised she knew what she had to do. She stopped while it sank in, her eyes wide, glinting clear blue.

She had to get that story.

Not for Harry, or the police, or even for the good of mankind.

But for herself. It was the only way she was going to stop herself feeling like a piece of shit. She had to get that story if it killed her. Suddenly her head felt clear, and she realised she had never been surer of anything in her life.

She walked slowly into the kitchen, picked up a bottle of beer from the fridge, and took it into the bathroom. She was going to get out – she was suddenly sure of it. A wave of excitement prickled her skin.

She lay in the bath for forty-five minutes, with the steam warmly saturating the air, and began to feel like a new woman. The alcohol cruised deliciously through her veins.

What she had to do was face the truth. She was not Alex Brierley, ace reporter. She was not the glam-puss TV girl she had always wanted to be – intelligent, cool *and* sexy. She was just still plain old Alexandra Brierley – who had done alright at school, went to an average university, and could look attractive with a bit of effort and the right clothes. Granted, she was less self-conscious about her height – seeing herself as willowy rather than gangly – and had tamed her lank blonde hair with a short cut and peroxide, but she was still the same underneath; still battling to be taken seriously, full of self-doubt, and pushing herself to remain confident.

If she started from this position, then the only way was up.

She wrapped herself in her dressing gown, and went into the living room, resisting the temptation to turn on *Newsnight* and get wound up by some glamorous new reporter.

She shooed Jasper off the sofa; he was another distraction she would have to ignore. He had belonged next door, but the owners had moved out and left him, and he'd just sort of ambled in and made himself at home. Cats were good like that. They could spot a lonely person a mile away; now there was more food for him in the fridge than there was for her. She sank into the sofa and shut her eyes. Jasper jumped up, and she immediately relented, enjoying the warm feeling of him on her lap.

She ran her fingers over her wrist again, then pulled down her sleeve and bit her lip. She stared at the blank screen and tried to keep calm. She could feel the little flame inside her again, and this time she was determined it wouldn't go out.

# 5

Dave jerked his head away from the handset and frowned.

'Jee-sus!' he hissed silently, then put his ear back to the receiver.

Alex grinned; she was huddled in the warmth of the outside broadcast van, sipping sour coffee from Dave's Thermos, listening to the conversation. She could hear Harry's voice booming loud and clear from the mobile.

'You can't shoot a piece on acid rain 'cause it's fucking raining,' he yelled. 'What do you think I am, a fucking moron or what?'

She shut her eyes and stopped herself from agreeing out loud.

'It's just too murky out there, Mr Powell,' Dave said lamely for about the two-hundredth time. He rubbed a hand across his eyes. 'I know, I know, but the cameras won't pick up the surface of the stone. All we'll get is a flat image and no one will know what all the fuss is about. We either need better lighting sent over or we'll have to shoot it another day.'

Alex let her mind wander while Harry bellowed on.

'In that case we'll just have to come back tomorrow, then,' Dave said. 'It's the only option.' He winced as Harry slammed the phone down at the other end.

'Stupid bloody Taff,' he muttered, lobbing the mobile on the seat. He kicked one of the silver camera boxes in frustration.

'Are you OK?' Alex asked, looking up.

'Yeah, I guess,' he said, shaking his head. 'It's just . . . I don't know . . . it's just why does he have to act like such an arsehole all the time?'

23

'Simple,' Alex said, grinning. 'Because he *is* an arsehole, that's why. There's no need for him to act.'

'Yeah,' Dave said, starting to smile. 'I guess you're right.'

'Just try not to let him get to you.'

'And how do you manage that?' Dave asked, pushing open the door.

'You're asking me?' Alex said, raising her hands. 'I'm afraid it's a case of do as I say, not as I do, because he gets to me every time.' She smiled, her eyes creasing at the edges.

'Thanks,' Dave said, shaking his head and laughing. 'If nothing else, it's nice to know I'm not alone.' He jumped out of the van. 'You stay. I'll get the stuff back in the boxes.'

Alex sat quietly in the van. She put her hands behind her head and stretched. She was feeling wonderful – she hadn't slept so well in ages – and had a delicious feeling of anticipation that made her want to go *mmmmm*. She suddenly had a free afternoon, and since the big murder story was pulling in everybody's attention at the station, she knew she wouldn't be missed if she bunked off.

She tapped her teeth with a fingernail. It was now or never, she thought. There was no point in pussyfooting around. It was too good an opportunity to miss.

She jumped up and went to help Dave load up the van.

It was mid-afternoon when they got back to the station and the building was quiet. She slipped into her office, switched her phone over to voicemail, and headed straight back out again.

As she walked through the reception area she glanced at the new interior – it was all neutral colours and blonde expensive-looking wood; part of the station's new corporate identity to show it was up-market and modern. She smiled, swatting a leaf off one of the big ferns – as far as she could see all it really showed was they were now a sad little local news station working out of a dull seventies office block with a very nice reception.

She shook her head and was just about to push open the heavy glass front doors when she noticed Jim nodding behind the front desk. She turned around and sauntered over towards him.

'You look rather cute, Jim,' she said, putting her elbows on the desk. 'Just like a baby.'

'Uh?' Jim said, jerking and opening his eyes. He looked confused for a moment, then smiled as he recognised her. 'What was that?'

Jim was a rarity among the security staff; he was a small, silver-haired man with a nice manner and a subtle sense of humour – a million miles from the bulky younger men who occasionally grunted when she came in.

'I said you look rather cute when you're asleep,' she said, grinning. 'You know, if you were twenty years younger I'd take you with me.'

'Oh, aye?' he said, his watery blue eyes sparkling. 'Well, it's nice to be asked and all that, but I'm afraid you're not my type.' He folded his arms and winked at her. 'Too old.'

'*Jim*!' she said, feigning – or maybe just exaggerating – a look of horror. 'And I thought you were a gentleman.' She dug into her bag for her car keys. 'I'm thirty in a couple of weeks' time, so less of the old, alright?'

'Thirty!' he said, shaking his head. 'You've got nothing to worry about, love. You haven't even started yet!'

'Don't I know it,' she said, shaking her head. She tossed her keys in the air and caught them. 'Anyway . . . I've got to go. See you later, Jim.'

She took the lift down to the underground carpark.

As the doors opened at the bottom a sharp blast of cold air flooded in, stinging her eyes. She shivered and felt a hollow twinge inside her; a throwback to the night before. She stepped out, determined to ignore it.

She drove up the exit ramp, and out onto the main road. The rain had stopped and the clouds that had hung over the city for days had suddenly pulled away, leaving a bright blue, empty sky. It was like driving into another world. A harsh white light was slanting across the city, bringing everything into sharp focus. She screwed up her eyes against the light, and caught a glimpse of herself in her rear-view mirror. The bright light had bleached out her skin and showed up the lines around her eyes and the dark shadows underneath. She touched the side of the mirror, moving it slightly so she couldn't see herself, and concentrated on driving.

The inner-city ring road was unusually quiet. She made most

25

of the lights on green, and tore up the big three-laner out of town. She fumbled in her glove compartment, found some gum, and started chewing happily. She loved an open road ahead.

She parked the car between two boarded-up warehouses around the corner from the Institute. The autumn light was already fading and the sun had dropped behind the buildings, leaving the old red brick black and forlorn. She shivered and prayed that the car would still be there when she got back.

She kicked an empty can as she rounded the corner and instantly regretted it as it clanged across the hard surface. She hurried to the Institute's main door.

The chain and tape had gone, and all that was left of the police presence were the ghostly silver traces of fingerprint powder on the armoured glass. She heaved open the heavy door and went into the reception area.

There was no one behind the Plexiglas at the counter. A red light was flashing silently on the telephone console, and an answering machine busily clicked away by its side.

She drummed her fingers on the counter for a while. All was quiet, and she was pretty certain no one was going to come. She took one last glance over the counter and set off towards the double doors at the end of the corridor.

The building was deadly quiet and her footsteps sounded loud on the tiled floor. She tried to step lightly, putting her heel and toe down at the same time. When she reached the big double doors, she peered through the window. The room on the other side was dark but she could see the silhouettes of tables and low chairs scattered about.

She slowly pushed the doors open and stepped in, a ripple of anticipation running through her.

Her eyes took a few seconds to adjust. She glanced around the room, trying to force her pupils open. She guessed it was a waiting room. The overhead strips were turned off and the only light in the room was a weak, yellow glow oozing from a couple of low-watt night-lights.

'Can I help you?' someone suddenly asked.

Alex jumped, making a small noise in her throat.

She peered through the shadowy space and saw a semicircle of dark shapes sitting directly under the furthest light.

'Hi,' she said, hearing just the slightest waver in her voice. She worked her way through the chairs, making out the shapes of a group of five women sitting close together against the wall. They were slouched in low seats and she could see the bright red glow-worm trail of cigarettes bobbing in the air.

'Hello?' the same voice said, as Alex got close to them.

Alex squinted at the group. The voice came from the woman who was sitting nearest her; she was thin and taller than the rest.

She glanced at the rest of the group. Three of them were wearing overalls and were pulling hard on cigarettes – they looked like they were probably cleaners. The other woman was smaller and squashed in between them.

Alex was about to say something when one of the cleaners suddenly spoke first.

'You're that woman off the telly, ent ya?' she said without much enthusiasm. She had the thick stop-start accent of the inner city, and an extremely long cigarette bounced up and down in her mouth as she spoke. 'The one that used to interview them dogs and that.'

'Er . . .' Alex laughed nervously. It had caught her off balance and she felt the heat rise in her face. 'Yes . . . that was me.'

She laughed again but it sounded false.

It was a period she had tried to forget about, and – thank God – most people seemed to have forgotten about it too. But it had a nasty habit of cropping up in all the wrong places.

It had come straight after her disaster with the police corruption story, when some idiot producer had decided that they were going to run a weekly end-piece on anthropomorphic pets – the kind of little sweethearts that could supposedly sing or tap-dance or some such thing. Up until then she had been on the roster with Mike, sharing out whatever stories came along, but Harry had suddenly decided that *she* was the person to take it on. He didn't give her any choice. He just made a snap decision and that was it.

She had tried to wriggle out of it, but all she had succeeded in doing was winding Harry up to the point of nearly firing her – and from there on her career had gone into a tailspin. She was suddenly the queen of all things furry, and Mike was left to hoover up the hard news without her. And he had been smirking ever since.

She had ended up visiting every dead-beat, out-of-the-way place there was to interview parrots that told jokes and watch dogs that could skateboard. It was as low as you could go. They had pulled the item after six months, and since then she had tried to forget about it and dig her career out of the hole – but she still lived with a lingering fear that the moment when a geriatric shire horse emptied its bowels down her back would crop up on some Christmas worst-moments-of-TV show.

'You're a reporter?' the tall woman asked coldly. Her voice was like an icy slap across the face, and Alex realised she had been standing with an idiot grin on her face.

'Yes, you could say that,' she replied quickly. 'Although sometimes I wonder.' She smiled, but the woman's blank expression didn't change. 'I'm from *Midlands Report East*,' she continued. 'We came over yesterday, but no one was here. I was hoping you might be able to give me some details.'

She paused but the woman didn't say anything.

'I'm Alex Brierley,' she said solemnly, offering her hand.

'Can you give us a couple of minutes?' the woman said, looking at the cleaners and ignoring Alex's outstretched hand.

The three women slowly got up and shuffled off towards the door. It felt as if it was happening in slow motion and seemed to take an age. As the swing-doors finally flapped behind them, Alex heard one of them heaving up phlegm with a rasping, throaty death-rattle.

The thin woman swivelled her eyes back to Alex.

'Anne Dolby,' she said, shaking Alex's hand briefly by the fingers. 'I'm the centre manager.' She turned to her right. 'And this is Jill Squires.'

Alex spun around with her arm outstretched. Her eyes had adjusted to the dim lighting and she could make out Jill more clearly. She was a petite woman with short brown hair, dressed in what Alex thought of as retro-feminist – DMs, baggy trousers and an ethnic-print shirt. Later, Alex would notice that she had the most incredible green eyes. Model's eyes. But for the moment she only noticed one thing. She flinched inside but managed to keep her arm outstretched.

28

Jill had tiny little hands that jutted directly out from her shoulders. They were like the little flippers on a children's boat, and Alex instantly knew what had caused them. *Thalidomide*, she thought, the great-white-hope drug for morning sickness that had messed up a whole load of kids in the sixties. There had been a boy a couple of years ahead of her at school who had been exactly the same. He'd had to put up with being called Billy the Flid – which no doubt contributed to him growing into the kind of bloke who occasionally glassed some stranger in a pub for smiling at him. Alex locked her gaze on Jill and pushed her hand forward.

'Pleased to meet you, Jill.'

Jill smiled quickly, and brushed her fingers across the back of Alex's hand.

'Likewise.'

'So what do you want from us?' Anne asked, gesturing to a chair.

Alex sat down with difficulty. The chair was badly sprung, and she got the sensation that she was going to sink right through. She pulled herself forward and perched on the hard front edge.

'I hoped you might be able to run me through what happened?'

'So the vultures are circling,' Anne said, with a short, mirthless laugh.

'Look, I know this must be a hard time for you,' Alex said carefully. 'And I don't want to intrude. I just want to help get them caught, that's all.'

'Yeah, right.'

'Really.'

Anne shifted in her seat. 'OK, let's get it over with.'

She ran through the events, briskly and clinically, keeping her voice emotionless and looking away as she spoke. She told Alex that the intruders had got in by ramming a car into a side door.

'People have tried to get in before, but we've known all along we'd be a target, so the place is very secure. This lot seemed to know what they were doing, though. They used a Range Rover, for Christ's sake.'

There wasn't much else to know: Ian had been found dead, taped to a chair and beaten beyond recognition; the intruders had

29

tried to get into the drug store but had failed; some prescription pads had been stolen; and that was about it.

'They probably lost their nerve,' Anne said, her lips curling. She moved her hands to her face. 'I'm a liberal woman,' she added, slowly rubbing her eyes. 'But I hope when they catch the bastards they kill them in the process. I really do.' She pushed herself upright in her chair, and pulled a pack of Silk Cut out of her jacket pocket. 'Smoke?'

'No thanks.'

Anne lit her cigarette and exhaled a huge cloud of smoke.

'So do you have any idea who they might be?' Alex asked.

'No,' Anne said flatly.

'What about you, Jill?'

Jill flinched slightly as Alex turned to look at her, and wouldn't catch her eye. 'Er . . . no,' she said, glancing at Anne nervously. 'No. No, I don't.'

'Are you sure?' Alex coaxed, trying to draw her gaze.

'Of course she is,' Anne snapped, her eyes suddenly blazing. 'Or she would have said so, wouldn't she?' She stared hard at Alex, and for a moment Alex had the impression that she might be about to get up and hit her.

'Look, I'm sorry, I didn't mean to be rude, I just . . .' Alex didn't know how to finish the sentence.

Anne looked at her coldly. 'Look, Ms Brierley. When we moved in here the local papers had a field day at our expense. Stories about hordes of drug-crazed lunatics being moved into the community, that kind of thing.' She looked at Alex with distaste. 'Ever since there's been a steady stream of complaints. And the media reporting has always been biased against us. Now I know what you people say is all a load of crap, but . . .' She crossed her arms, a defiant look on her face. 'Mud sticks . . . so if you really do want to help, you'll just leave us alone. OK? You've got what you need.'

Alex nodded. She glanced across at Jill, but she still wouldn't catch her eye. She could feel the static in the air.

She frowned and looked back at Anne. She wasn't going to get anything else. She had done enough interviews to know that.

'OK,' she said levelly. 'Thanks for your time.'

'Yeah.'

Alex fished around in her bag and pulled out a business card. She jotted her home number on the back, feeling her hand tremble slightly, and offered it to Anne.

'If you think of anything else you can get me on this number, OK?'

Anne accepted the card, but shook her head.

'I won't.'

It was dark outside and the air was icy cold. Alex dug her hands into her pockets and walked quickly down the road. She was shivering – but only half from the cold. Anne's anger had got to her. She knew she shouldn't take it personally, but it was a long time since she had been in a confrontational interview and she couldn't help it.

'Piss,' she muttered under her breath. That hadn't gone like she had hoped.

She hugged her coat around her and turned the corner.

The street was poorly lit and bathed in a dull mustard glow from a couple of distant streetlights. She jogged up to her car.

As she was unlocking the door another car cruised slowly by. She glanced up and caught the driver's stare. He was alone and his face was dark, but she saw the whites of his eyes turned towards her. He slowed down slightly, and she looked away and quickly pulled open the door.

She lowered herself into the driver's seat, and watched as the car stopped on the corner ahead of her. A dark figure slowly tore itself away from the shadows, walked to the kerb, and bent down to the passenger window. There was enough light to see that it was a young woman with a mass of blonde hair and a figure-hugging crotch-length dress. As she bent over, she arched her spine and stuck her backside in the air. Five inches of high heels gave her a lot of leverage. She spoke briefly, pulled open the door and got in. The car was gone in seconds.

Alex shuddered and looked around. The road was deserted again. She quickly started the engine. How could she do that? she thought. On her own on a road like this – especially with a killer on the loose.

She pulled the car around in a tight U-turn; suddenly she wanted to get away quickly. She chewed her lip as she accelerated down to the end of the road, ignoring the Institute as she passed it. Then she headed up the hill towards the main road.

The whole area seemed deserted, a dead landscape of boarded-up factories and heavily fortified warehouses. She could see the lights of the cars at the top of the hill.

She forced herself into the heavy traffic on the Alfreton Road, heading back towards the city centre. The road was busy with minicabs ferrying people into town, and along each side – where the kebab shops and Indian restaurants shone brightly – cars were parked badly while people dashed in to pick up takeaways. The traffic was moving slowly, and Alex settled her hand against the wheel.

She took a deep breath and turned over what had happened in her head, trying to look at it from Anne's point of view. She could understand why she might be wary of reporters and that they would all be angry and confused after the murder, but she couldn't make it all add up.

There was something very odd about Anne's anger.

She glanced in the rear-view mirror and chewed her lip. She could see the red tail-lights of the cars streaking out of town flaring in the night.

There had been something else. A familiar feeling hanging in the air that had set off an alarm bell inside her.

She clicked on the indicator and pulled up outside an off-licence, trying to fathom out what it meant. She knew they would be nervous, feeling vulnerable, uncertain about what would happen next.

But the feeling was stronger than that. There had been a raw, animal static crackling in the air like pure undiluted fear.

She shook her head. Maybe she was right . . . but then maybe not. Maybe she was just projecting. Perhaps it was just anger directed at her after all.

She couldn't be sure. She popped the locks and pushed open the armoured door of the off-licence. She could feel her thoughts begin to tangle into a tight feeling behind her eyes where a head-ache was starting.

Her flat was freezing when she got back, and after the ritual shoe removal, she hurried into the kitchen to turn on the heating. Then she opened the wine she had bought, grabbed a large glass, and padded through to the living room. She saw the LED on the answerphone blazing *01* as she groped for the light switch.

She pressed Play and started to pull off her coat.

The machine bleeped, and there was silence. It sounded like a dead recording. She started to move towards the rewind button. Then someone began to speak. The voice was tight and nervous.

'Alex. This is Jill Squires.' The name didn't register at first. 'We met at the Kallman Institute today. Look, I, er . . . I think there's something you need to know.' She paused, and Alex heard her nervously inhale. 'I'm sorry I couldn't tell you earlier but . . . well, I just couldn't, I'm afraid . . . Anyway, I think we should meet. I'll be in the side bar of the Market Porter at six tomorrow. It's at the back of the cattle market. If you're not there by quarter past, I'll assume you're not coming.' She paused. 'Don't try and call me until I've spoken to you, OK? It's very important. And please don't speak to anyone else.'

The machine clicked off.

Alex stared at the machine for a moment, transfixed. She replayed the message. She had interpreted Jill's earlier silence as solidarity with Anne – a passive endorsement of what she had said. But she now knew that she was right about the feeling she had detected. Jill's voice on the machine confirmed it.

She was frightened.

Very frightened.

# 6

The dark outline of a passenger plane cruised low over the motorway ahead of him, its landing lights stabbing into the darkness. The sharp whine of its engines cut into the cab, drowning out the roar of the air through the half-open sunroof. He took one last pull on his cigarette, flicked it through the gap, and wound the sunroof shut.

The plane passed over the car and emerged into the bright, silvery haze of the airport lights on his right. He glanced at it as it disappeared over the top of the embankment, then looked back at the deserted motorway.

Something had caught his eye.

Way ahead, in the canopy of eerie yellow light flooding down from the motorway lights, he could see a figure on the hard shoulder.

He squinted to make it out.

He took his foot off the accelerator, and pulled into the slow lane.

'Well, well, well,' he murmured, as he got closer. It was a woman. She was trying to look confident as she walked away from her car towards the emergency phone, but he knew better.

He could make her out now – a perky little career girl walking away from her big flash car. He smiled – brash as hell on the outside, he thought. But just the same as the rest underneath.

'Where's your daddy now?' he murmured. 'When you need him?'

He locked his attention onto her, assessing the details. It was something he was good at, even at a distance and in the dark. It came from practice. The way she walked said high heels, skirt too tight. Her silhouette showed a jacket tailored into her figure, shoulders padded, waist nipped. In the sodium light the suit looked orange, but he knew how the lights worked. It was red. A tight red suit; *Look at me!* it screamed.

He imagined himself as a bullfighter, standing in the fast lane. The overhead lights flooded the road in a stark white light. Up above was a dark, brooding, blood-red sky. The hard shoulder was packed with people jammed behind a crash barrier and craning their necks to get a better view. They all looked horrified, disgusted with what they were seeing, but they kept on looking. He was using the woman as a cloak, dangling her in front of the oncoming cars as they sped towards him; waving her around, feeling the fine sheer of her stockings tear. When the cars were almost upon him, he pulled her out of the way, and they hurtled past, the crowd roaring.

Then occasionally he started to let her catch on the bumper or thump off a windscreen; blood arcing through the dark sky and splattering wetly on the tarmac in front of them. He sensed the revulsion in their voices, felt the crackle of horror in the air – and heard how they roared even louder.

And they just kept looking.

He contemplated stopping.

He imagined her, pulped in the fast lane like a badger, the red suit shredded and her bare arse stuck in the air. He could hear the whirr of the press cameras as they shot his work. He squeezed his legs together and licked his lips, the thin tip of his tongue flickering across engorged red skin.

But he decided not to stop. Her dark glossy hair and I'm-all-grown-up swagger wasn't right. He knew what he was looking for – and he was running out of time. He needed to stay focused.

He looked up at the dark sky and saw that it was beginning to curdle red as he approached Leicester.

'Hel-lo, Leicester,' he said, smiling. 'Blonde, white and regular, please. To go.' This time he needed someone that somebody really cared about. The real thing. That was the only way they would remember – and never forget.

He cruised the city centre for an hour, hoping to see someone heading home on their own. But people were careful. They travelled in pairs, or made sure they were near groups.

He stopped by the university. Gaggles of confident girls in tight tops and jeans flounced past his car, their arms wrapped around them to keep warm, pushing up their breasts.

Look at me, look at me, look at me!

He shook his head as he watched them clatter by and realised this wasn't the way to do it. He was moving too quickly. He needed seclusion, needed a plan.

He bought a can of Special Brew from a scruffy corner shop, and drove out towards the red-light district with the can wedged between his legs. He sipped the thick warm liquid and started to scan the edges of the road.

He cruised slowly down the main drag, ignoring the girls who stood at the edge of the road, hips slung sideways, trying to catch his stare. Because he knew that for every streetwise girl there was a little tart creeping around in the darkness on her own; girls from shattered homes and abusive care. Girls who had nothing, and thought that no one cared a damn about them. And he knew that no one did care a damn about them – until they were dead.

He rounded the corner and slowed down. A skinny girl was walking slowly in the shadow. He could see the milky whiteness of her thin legs as she tottered on her heels, leaning forward and hugging herself against the cold. And the light from a dim streetlamp caught the blondeness of her hair.

He drove past her and stopped in the dark shadow between two streetlights.

He wound down the passenger window and waited, watching her in his rear-view mirror. She sauntered up to the open window, wiggled her thin hips, then pushed them back and brought her head down.

She was chewing gum, trying to look tough – but he could see that her skin had the softness of a child. She pulled nervously on a cigarette.

'You looking?' she said.

'How much?' he replied, staring straight ahead.

She hitched her microskirt down over her thin thighs.

'Depends on what you want,' she said coyly.

He looked at her, and suddenly felt a wave of pity. She couldn't have been more than fifteen, he thought. Her blonde

36

hair was soft and downy – not the matted peroxide of the older girls. Who was it that brought a kid into the world, he thought, then let her walk the streets when she should still be at school?

'In the car's twenty,' she said, quickly glancing around. 'Oral or hand relief . . . Full sex is twenty-five. And a bit more if you want to mess around.'

He shook his head. Why didn't they care – until it was too late?

'Ten,' he said, staring forward again.

'For what?'

'A blowjob.'

'Oral's twenty.'

He smiled at her slightly indignant tone; they always did that if you made it sound dirty.

She took another shallow pull on her cigarette, then shrugged. 'But I'll do it for fifteen if we don't go far away.'

'I'll give you ten,' he said slowly. 'Now get in the car.'

He popped the lock, looked away and waited – and she pulled the handle and slowly got in. He suddenly felt excited and clenched his legs. Like a lamb to the slaughter, he thought. Filthy and forgotten, but a lamb nonetheless.

He was getting closer.

He drove back on a dark, winding B-road – scanning the blanket of darkness ahead for prowling police cars. Away from the city everything was black apart from the smooth, startled tarmac in the pool of his headlights. He rubbed his ear where she had clawed him, and ran his tongue over his gums. He could still taste the sour, metallic tang of blood. He was always amazed at how hard they fought for a life they didn't seem to want.

He glanced in the mirror to make sure no one was behind. The thumping from the boot had subsided to an occasional weak thud, but he knew it was still enough to give him away if he was pulled up.

He switched the radio on and scanned through the stations, but there was nothing – they had already stopped talking about him. He shook his head sadly; how quickly they forgot. He randomly picked a station playing bland late-night tunes and turned the volume up.

37

He tapped the wheel with his finger and hummed as he drove. Red sky at night, shepherd's delight, he thought, seeing the first tinge of red in the sky ahead. Calm before the storm.

When he reached the edge of the urban sprawl he turned off the main road and cut through the winding estates until he found the school he was looking for.

He stopped the car on the zigzag lines outside the front gates and got out, leaving the engine running.

It was like stepping back in time. The playing fields were dark but the main building was illuminated by the clear, bright night. There were thousands of stars in the sky and the light glinted on the windows. It was just as he remembered it. He could see the silhouettes of trees down one side, and behind them the outlines of houses on the edge of the city; big houses, all shut up and sleeping for the night. Safe houses.

He walked slowly around the car, taking the screwdriver out of his back pocket, and forced open the boot lock.

He stepped forward and looked down tenderly at her. The fumes from the exhaust swirled up around him in the cold air, and reflected the red of the rear lights onto her.

He brushed his fingers on her pale skin and felt her flinch slightly.

'I'm so sorry,' he whispered, running his index finger down her neck and feeling the blood-hardened, ragged edge of the hole punched through the delicate, soft skin. 'I tried . . . I tried, but no one came.'

A large tear suddenly rolled off his cheek and fell onto her skin.

'I . . .'

He looked at her eyes, wide and innocent as a fawn, and a sickening wave of loneliness ran through his body. He winced and felt the empty hole open up inside him and expand like a cancer.

He gripped the edge of the boot, and shut his eyes. Then he slowly pulled back his hand, bunched his fist and drove it down into the space.

'It wasn't my fault,' he whimpered as his fist connected. He opened his eyes and looked at her, feeling his knuckles smart.

'It wasn't my fault!'

38

Then he slammed his fist down again and again, throwing all his weight into it, tears streaming from his smarting eyes while the car lurched on its suspension.

He stopped suddenly when his shoulder cramped up and pain raced down his arm. He stepped back slightly, rubbing his neck. A thick mass of confusion had knotted up in his head and throbbed behind his eyes.

It was . . . it was . . . *their* fault, he thought, his breath coming out in short painful pants. Not hers, not his. Them! His mouth was dry and he felt his heart pounding. He quickly shut the boot and looked around.

He felt the cold sweat on his back, the searing pain in his arm, and slowly his mind began to clear. He shivered. There wasn't long left, he thought, looking up at the full white moon.

He smiled crookedly. This time they wouldn't forget him.

# 7

Alex jammed her foot on the brake pedal and felt her body lurch forward; the silver Merc on her right had jumped ahead and cut her up just as she was about the switch lanes.

'Thanks a lot!' she muttered, shaking the gear lever into neutral and staring across at the driver.

She took a deep breath and looked at her watch. Ten to six. If she didn't move soon she would miss Jill. She drummed her fingers on the wheel and tried to stay calm. The evening traffic was far heavier than usual because of the murder – the story had hit the bulletins at lunch-time and the city centre was swamped with husbands and fathers scurrying anxiously in to pick up women who would normally take the train or bus.

She looked at the drivers in the other cars. They were nearly all alone, sitting grimly immersed in their thoughts. She saw a woman smoking anxiously, her fingers drumming on the wheel like her own. What was going on? she thought. She was amazed that he had struck again so quickly. It wasn't meant to happen like this. And it was as if everyone had suddenly realised that something was different. He had broken the rules. But why? Why so quickly? She couldn't work out what it meant.

They had found the girl some time in the morning, and since then there had been very little information. Just an endless turnover of speculation; so far all the police had confirmed was that she was another prostitute and that she had been mutilated in a similar way to the others. That was all. But a pulse of fear had rippled through the city – just as in a wildlife documentary when suddenly all the chimps start shrieking for no obvious reason.

The police had promised a press conference at four o'clock but had subsequently postponed it. She knew that meant something was different – something new – and she was dying to know what it was. If only she had been allowed to work on it, she thought, biting her lip in frustration.

She jammed the gear lever into first as the traffic sluggishly began to move.

There was something different about the story. She could feel it – but she had her own story to worry about. She needed to concentrate on that. She jerked the car into the outside lane and focused on getting to the pub before Jill left.

She followed the stream of traffic away from the city centre, turning off the main road as it dog-legged around the back of Notts County's small box-like stadium, and drove into the market through the main gates. She looked in her rear-view mirror. She could see the stream of bright lights at the end of the road. Everyone was driving home. *Everyone.* It was like an exodus from some stricken city.

The market was already dark and deserted. She drove slowly past a couple of closed-up auction sheds and the black skeletal outlines of the cattle pens; there were only a few flickering lights on the road and the low market buildings loomed darkly around her.

The Market Porter sat away at the back of the huge carpark, dwarfed by the grey looming bulk of the refuse incineration plant across the wasteland behind it. It was a tatty low redbrick building that had once been part of the railway when the line had come right up to the market. Now it sat stranded and forgotten on its own.

She parked outside. There were a few other cars – mainly beaten-up old saloons – and a couple of battered vans.

She snapped the crook-lock over the wheel and got out. A sharp tang of rotting vegetables hung in the air. She looked at her watch – it was just after six. She walked quickly towards the front door, trying to breathe through her mouth.

She pushed open the door to the main bar and went in. A musty smell hit her – and she knew immediately she had made a mistake. The place was a nicotine-stained dive – all shades of brown and sickly yellow – and was half full of beer-bellied men

41

with tattoos and greasy skin. The atmosphere was stagnant and frustrated; no music, no women, and certainly no fun. But a charge ran through the air as flesh twisted, bodies shifted position, and she was assaulted by two dozen pairs of eyes.

'Who called the stripper?' someone shouted.

A dull, humourless laugh filled the space.

'Can I help you, love?' a voice grated on her left. She glanced round and met the piggy stare of a large man in a Nottingham Forest football shirt; the shiny material was taut and glistening across his heavy stomach, warping the Labatt's logo in the centre. He shifted his bulk and let his eyes run down her body.

'You looking for somebody?'

Her stomach twinged, but she resisted the urge to bolt. She looked blankly around as if the place were empty, then she twisted on her heels and went back through the door, trying not to hurry.

As the door shut behind her, the ghost of a wolfwhistle and another ripple of dead laughter followed her. She shuddered, took a deep breath, and gingerly opened the door into the side bar.

It was a small, dimly lit space with high-backed booths and ancient wallpaper – and at first glance she thought there was no one there. The bar staff were busy servicing the other bar, and all the tables were empty. But when she scanned around the room, she saw Jill sitting against the wall in a dark booth.

Alex stalked across the sticky carpet and slid in opposite her.

'Sorry I'm late,' she said, feeling her hands shaking slightly. She glanced at the empty bar. 'Can I get you a drink?'

'Sure, yeah. Half of lager please . . . with a straw.'

Alex walked over to the bar and craned her head over the counter. She could see into the other room; a thin woman in wrinkled leggings and dodgy red slingbacks was slowly pulling a pint of soapy-looking bitter. Alex dropped her head and tried to coax her to look her way.

Jill was staring at the table when she returned.

'So, what's a nice girl like you doing in a place like this?' Alex asked brightly as she placed the drinks on the table.

'I wanted somewhere where no one would recognise us,' Jill said, looking up with a tight smile.

42

'You mean you don't know any of those boys through there?' Alex grinned, nodding at the door.

Jill managed another tight-lipped smile, then stared at her for a moment without blinking. 'Look,' she said, 'before I tell you anything I need to know I can trust you, OK?' Her eyes glinted green as she spoke. 'Can I?'

Alex stopped smiling and nodded slowly. 'Of course.'

'Stupid question.'

Alex crossed her arms and leant on the table. 'Look, all I can do is give you my word. I mean it, though.'

'OK,' Jill said levelly. She bit her lip, and glanced at the door. 'I don't think Fisher's death was an accident.'

'Really?' Alex said, feeling herself tense.

'And I don't think they were after drugs either. I think they just wanted to make it look that way.'

'What makes you think that?'

Jill took a pull on the straw. 'Because when I checked Ian's office before the scene-of-crime people arrived I noticed that someone had been through one of his filing cabinets, and some stuff had gone.'

'Couldn't they have been looking for prescription pads or something?'

Jill shook her head.

'No, they were too neat. Too organised. It's like they knew what they were looking for. But anyway, that's not all. I went back into his office later. He had this portable PC that he never used to let out of his sight, and I have to confess I was curious, and I couldn't see the harm in having a quick look. But when I switched it on it was blank. There was nothing there at all.'

Alex furrowed her brow. 'So what? I mean ... maybe he didn't use it for anything important.'

'Maybe he didn't,' said Jill, 'but I use a PC a lot because I find it difficult to write. What I mean is, it was *completely* blank. No files, no software, no anything. No one carries a computer around with them that has nothing on it. Without software it's useless. It had been wiped.'

'So you think whoever broke in wiped the PC?'

'Yeah.'

Alex ran her tongue over her top lip as she thought. 'So what were they after, then?'

'Well, that's the million-dollar question. But there's one more thing. Something that makes me think it wasn't a coincidence they decided to break in now. Y'see, I'm responsible for the drugs we get in for clinical trials. So I know exactly what's in the building, what it's for, where it's from, blah blah blah. Recently I came across some supplies in our store that shouldn't have been there. They hadn't been booked in, and they were unmarked, which is very bizarre. When I asked Ian about them he denied that they existed, and when I went back to check, they'd gone.'

Alex shook her head in confusion.

'Look, to cut a long story short,' Jill said, fixing her eyes on Alex, 'what I'm saying is that I think that Fisher was running a trial on the side for someone. In many ways that wouldn't surprise me because he didn't like the constraints of regulations. He was like that. But if it was true, he would have been putting his whole career on the line. So it must have been something pretty special.'

'Right,' Alex said quietly. 'I see. Like what?'

'God knows. But it must have been something very, *very* special to take such a risk.'

'Wow,' Alex said, as it sank in. 'Are you sure there isn't a more obvious answer?'

'No. No, I'm not sure. I mean, it might just be a coincidence that someone breaks in, steals some files, and Fisher gets beaten to a pulp. But I saw what he looked like afterwards. He was tied up carefully and beaten. For a long time. Now I don't exactly know what Fisher had got into, but I'm pretty sure it's why he's dead.'

'So what did the police say?' Alex asked carefully.

'About what?'

The bar door suddenly crashed open and they both jumped. An old man in a donkey jacket and flat cap shuffled over to the bar. Alex lowered her voice.

'You have told the police?'

'Yes . . . yes, of course I did. Or at least I started to but . . . but they didn't really listen, to be honest. So I stopped.' She looked at Alex defiantly.

44

'Why?'

'Because they had decided that what Anne had to say was the only thing that could have happened, that's why.'

'What? She told a different story?'

'Yes. I mean, I don't think she's doing it deliberately. She's just very loyal to Ian so she saw what she wanted to see. And at first glance it did look like they said. Everybody assumed they were there to steal drugs. It's an obvious answer.'

'So why didn't you just tell them what you told me?'

Jill pushed herself back against the booth. 'Come on, Alex. I saw the way you hesitated when you met me.'

Alex shifted uncomfortably on her seat.

'Don't worry,' Jill said soothingly. 'Everybody does it, and you did your best – but it's a common reaction. They just saw me as some neurotic little cripple with a stupid story. They didn't want to know . . . so I thought fuck 'em.'

'Well, it's good to know it's not just me they mess about,' Alex said, smiling. She glanced around. The old man at the bar was staring vacantly at a *Sunday Sport* calendar behind the counter; he looked as if his mind was on other things. 'So what do you want from me?'

'I need some help. So I want to trade.'

'Go on.'

Jill ran through her plans. She kept her voice low and Alex leant forward on her elbows and listened intently. Jill had decided that when she got the opportunity she was going to search through Fisher's personal files in his office; she was sure there would be something there.

'The thing is, if I find something I don't want to hang onto it. I don't scare easily, but this has got me rattled. So whatever *it* is, I want you to look after it. As long as no one knows we know each other it will be fine. And then . . . when we're done, you'll have your story.' She looked earnestly at Alex. 'So what do you reckon?'

'OK,' Alex said tentatively. She picked up a beer mat and ran her fingernail around the edge. 'What I don't understand is why you want to stick your neck out.'

'Simple,' Jill said, nodding down at her body. 'The reason I'm like this is because a drug wasn't tested properly. That's why I got into this game. To try and make sure it never happens again. It might sound melodramatic, but it gives me something to aim for. It's why I work with people like Fisher. I mean, there are plenty of nicer places I could be, but it's people like him who do the damage.' She paused and slowly let her breath out. 'To be honest, I can't say I'm sorry he's dead. If he was fucking people around with some untested drug then he deserves it, but – if he was – he'll just be the tip of the iceberg. There'll be a big organisation behind him. It's them I want to find.'

Alex twisted the beer mat, breaking it in half. 'OK, it's a deal,' she said after a pause.

'Good,' Jill said, finishing off her drink. 'I'll give you a call in a couple of days when I know more.'

'So where do you live?' Alex asked as they got up.

'Over by the university,' Jill said vaguely.

'Can I give you a lift?'

'Thanks, but I think I'll take a taxi. I want to be very careful until I know who we're dealing with.'

They pushed open the door and went out silently.

Jill stopped and looked at her. The night was cold and her breath fogged as she spoke. 'Thanks, Alex,' she said seriously.

'No problem. You're going to help me make my fortune.'

Alex watched as Jill walked across the deserted carpark towards the main gates, gradually becoming yellow as she headed towards the faraway lights. Kebab wrappers blew across the rough concrete behind her like tumbleweed in a western. Out of the warmth of the pub she looked small and vulnerable.

'Take care,' Alex shouted after her, but she wasn't sure if she heard.

# 8

Mike let his hand rest on Alex's shoulder. He put his thumb against the material of her jacket and rubbed slightly. She stiffened and turned towards him slowly.

'Get – your – fucking – hand – off me,' she said icily.

He let his hand linger slightly then pulled it away, stroking his fingers across her shoulder.

'I just wondered if you had finished proofing my script yet, that's all,' he said, giving her his best trademark twinkly smile. 'Harry said you'd been kind enough to do it for me.'

She swivelled around in her chair.

'Listen, Mike, you've had a lucky break, that's all,' she said, staring straight at him. 'So enjoy it while you can.' She picked up a stack of paper and handed it to him.

'You've finished it, then?' he said smirking.

'Finished rewriting it, if that's what you mean. It was a piece of shit, Mike, and you know it.'

He gave her the twinkly smile again. She found it intensely irritating, but she knew it was his big selling point. He had pale skin, thick dark hair and the kind of washed-out Irish eyes some women seemed to die for – the smile topped it off and he milked it for all it was worth.

He put his head on one side. 'I remember my mother said that one day I'd fall for a pretty girl with big blue eyes,' he said, with a mock sigh. 'And you know, when I first met you, Ali, I thought you might just be the one.' He raised his eyebrows. 'Until you opened your mouth, that was.'

She knew he called her Ali to wind her up. She had made the

mistake of getting drunk with Gena once, just after her relationship with Rob had finally ended, and had finished up telling her a lot of personal things – the Ali thing being one of them. She had known it had been a bad idea the next day when she woke with a stinking hangover – because Gena, nice as she was, was a bit of a motormouth. But she had realised it was a major error a couple of weeks later when she found out that Gena had started seeing Mike.

'At least when I open my mouth I don't let Harry put his dick in it,' Alex said sweetly.

'That's not what I heard.'

'You boys and your sad little dreams,' she said, turning back to her desk again. 'Anyway, listen, Mike, I'd just love to sit around chatting with you all afternoon, but you know how it is.'

She was just about to pick up her phone when it rang.

'Bye-bye,' she said sweetly, waving with her fingers as she picked up the receiver.

'I've got Jill Squires on the line for you,' the receptionist said in her ear. 'Shall I put her through?'

'Sure, yes,' she said, glancing over her shoulder to make sure Mike had gone. 'Put her through.' She felt her stomach flutter. At last, she thought. It had been three days since she had met Jill. Three of the longest days of her life.

The big murder story had gone ballistic after the police had released the full details of the killing, and she had been running around like a blue-arsed fly ever since. The profile of the latest victim had changed everything, and they were suddenly looking at one of those once-in-a-lifetime stories. Harry had pulled everybody in to help out while they weathered the initial media blitzkrieg. As far as Alex was concerned, it was worse than *not* working on the story. It was like badly wanting to be invited to a party, then ending up serving behind the bar while everybody else had a good time.

The reason things had suddenly changed was that the victim had only been thirteen years old. She was fresh into care, having been dumped by her foster parents, and had only been on the game for a couple of months. This time, instead of a tarty mugshot of a miserable girl who had just been arrested, the police released a family snap showing a cute, happy kid on a bright summer's day. It changed the whole angle of the story. Suddenly she wasn't just a whore – she looked like she could be somebody's daughter; *anybody's* daughter.

Alex had felt sick as the new story unwound. She had seen it too many times before; the way the media could only deal with absolutes in a crisis – black and white, good and bad. She had listened to Mike on the out-takes as he gravely described the girl – Tina, a bright thirteen-year-old whose parents had abandoned her, forcing her onto the street – and she had wondered when you crossed the line from being completely blameless to responsible for what happened to you. Where was the boundary – and how did you know?

'Hi . . . Alex?' she heard Jill say in her ear.

'Jill!' she said, shaking her head, and pushing the receiver closer to her mouth. 'Thank goodness. How are you?'

'OK. You?'

'Yeah, bearing up, I suppose. Anyway, listen, the suspense has been killing me. What's happening?'

'Look, I'll have to keep this brief 'cause I'm still at work. But the good news is I've found a couple of things that look pretty interesting.'

'Really?' Alex said quickly. 'What?'

'I'm afraid it'll take a bit of time to explain, and there're people about at the moment, so it'll have to wait. I just thought I'd ring to tell you I'm sticking them in the post tonight.'

'OK, fine. But can't you give me a clue?'

'Not now, but I'll put a note in with them so you'll know what's what.' She lowered her voice. 'Look, I need to go, but I've got some more good news. I've just got hold of the keys to Fisher's main filing cabinet.' She paused then lowered her voice further. 'If there's anything crucial to be had I reckon it's going to be in there.'

'How'd you manage that?'

'I cannot reveal my sources,' Jill said, badly feigning an eastern European accent. 'But suffice to say, she's a cleaner and she found it down the side of his chair. God knows why she thought it might be mine.'

'Brilliant,' Alex said. 'But be careful, won't you.'

'I'll be OK,' Jill chuckled. 'I'm good at being invisible. You get good at it when people stare at you all the time. Anyhow, don't worry, if there's anything useful in there I'll just copy it and send it straight over to you. Then we can look at it all later.'

Alex glanced around. The office was all but empty. Most people had gone down to watch the new reports as they came hot off the feeds.

'Look, Jill, if it's going to be a big package, send it to me here at the station. I'm never in when the post arrives at home, so if it won't go through the door they'll take it back to the sorting office.'

'Fine. What's your address?'

Alex spelt out her address slowly while Jill wrote it down.

'And there's one more thing,' Alex said, when she had given Jill the details. 'Mark it Private and Confidential. There's some pretty nosy people round here. It's the only way to keep them out.'

'No problem. Look, I've got to go. I'm going to work late tonight, then have a poke around in Fisher's office when everybody's gone. I'll give you a call tomorrow. OK?'

'OK,' said Alex. 'Good luck.'

She sat at her desk for a couple of minutes after the call, and looked out of the window. The days were getting shorter and the light in the evenings was changing as the sun dropped more quickly from the sky.

She got up and walked over to the window. She was on the fifth floor and she could see right out across the urban sprawl. The sky was still slightly blue, but the wispy white clouds had turned thick and dark, and hung ominously over the city. The sun had dropped out of sight, leaving the faintest of red tinges on the horizon. Red sky at night was supposed to be good news, she thought, but it felt like the heavens were about to open.

She put her face right up against the glass to cut out the reflection from the strip lights. She could see right out to the power station beyond the city limits – the steam from the cooling towers boiled into the sky like black smoke from a massive witch's cauldron, swirling into the blanket of clouds above. And she suddenly wondered where the killer was at that moment. The face of the dead girl lit up in her mind and she felt a stab of sorrow inside her. He was out there somewhere, she thought. A real person. It was easy to forget that sometimes. The profile of the new victim had changed the perception of him – letting him step out of the dark shadows of *somewhere else* and into a place where everyone was at risk. But he was still just a faceless monster; a shapeless source of evil lurking in the dark.

She ran her finger across the cold glass.

She could feel an empty space at the bottom of her stomach. A gut feeling that she – and everybody else – was going about it all wrong. What were they all trying to achieve? The media had taken up the story with a vengeance, dredging up every expert they could find. *Newsnight* had run a satellite interview with a professor of criminal psychology at UCLA who had outlined the murderer's profile. He had linked the killer's behaviour with a similar story in the States where the murderer had clocked up seventeen victims and was still at large. It was sexy stuff, but Alex knew that the killer actually bore more resemblance to the Yorkshire Ripper than the random patterns of the American psychopath. But she also knew that an all-American serial killer was far more fashionable. Another step away from reality, she thought.

She swept her gaze over the outline of the city as it flattened out into the suburbs. There were thousands of little houses sprawling right out to the motorway. Where did he live? she thought. What was he doing? Was he lurking on the streets at that very moment or just watching TV like everyone else?

She wanted to know.

She shivered. October always made her morbid. It was a time when things began to change, when the end of another year suddenly loomed up ahead. And it was the time of year when things tended to happen to her – good and bad. So she was used to experiencing a nagging feeling of anticipation.

But this year felt different.

The usual tightness in her stomach and the vague feeling that something wasn't quite right had gone. It had been replaced with something far more profound. It felt as if a fault line – one that had always been there – was opening up in her life, slowly ripping away the grey web of frustration that sat on the surface and exposing an angry, swirling mess below. And as the ragged gash cut through the layers of confusion that snared her in her life,

51

she was beginning to see things more clearly – and everything she had thought she knew seemed to be flipping over.

As she looked out over the city, feeling her way across the dark buildings and into the maze of streets below, she realised that what was really disturbing about the string of murders wasn't that someone had suddenly started killing people. It was why more people didn't go out and do it. All those people riddled with the disappointment frustration of lives they didn't want. What stopped them letting loose?

And suddenly – with a cool but dizzying clarity – she understood what the knotted-up feeling was that had been with her all her life, slowly growing inside her as she got older. She had always thought it was an emptiness – something missing – and had spent years trying to fill it; trying but failing to satisfy something she didn't understand. But now she knew it wasn't a gap at all. It was something in the way. And she realised that what she had been feeling was basically quite simple.

It was fear.

An anxious, searing buzz that ran through her, ringing every emotional alarm bell she had.

She looked out over the city as the sky turned black and wondered what it was that she was so scared of.

# 9

'You can go through, Detective Inspector Harris,' Jane said as the intercom buzzed.

'Thanks,' Harris said, getting up. He pushed open his old office door and walked in.

'DI Harris,' Hague said, standing up and shaking his hand. 'Thanks for coming.'

'It's a pleasure, sir.'

'So,' Hague said briskly. 'I'm a bit short of time, so let's get straight to it. Have you had a chance to read the psychological profile yet?'

'Yes, sir.'

'Good. What did you think?'

'It's very interesting.'

'It is, isn't it. I think it gives us a clear steer on where we need to be focusing resources.'

'But I'm not sure I agree about the neck wound, though, sir.'

'How do you mean?'

'I don't think the attacker's motives are sexual.'

A smile flickered across Hague's mouth.

'I think you'll find that's what Professor Miller thinks too. What he said is that the neck injuries are an extension of the wish to penetrate the body. All of the women have been assaulted vaginally, anally and orally. But the point is these are violent acts. Not sexual. The puncturing of the soft tissue of the neck is a further expression of that desire to violate.'

'I understand that, sir. What I am saying is I don't think this is the case here. I think the punctures to the neck are something

53

completely different. Something more literal. There's also a chance he may not actually be raping the women at all. There's no forensic evidence.'

'Don't you think the reason there is no forensic evidence might just have something to do with the fact that he is cleaning up his victims when he's finished?'

'Yes, sir. But I think he's doing just that. Cleaning them. I don't think he's trying to cover his tracks. He's just too . . .'

'Yes?'

'I don't know. Delicate, I suppose.'

'Delicate?' Hague laughed. 'You call butchering a tart in a back alley delicate? Come on.'

'I think there's something in it, sir.'

Hague looked at him intently. 'Listen, Harris. I'll be honest. I didn't bring you here to debate psychology. I'm interested in tactics. Our job is to act, and this report gives us a clear steer. We know we're dealing with a creature of habit, and we know what underpins those habits. He will have covered the same ground many times. So someone else must have seen him. What *we* need to be is proactive. I want to find a tart who's seen him. Someone must have come across him.'

'We've pretty much exhausted that route, sir.'

'Well, try again.'

# 10

A faint trace of grey light leaked through the crack in the curtains, taking the edge off the darkness in the room. Alex lay on the sofa, the light from the TV flickering on her skin, and watched Mike's mouth moving silently. She had turned the sound right down because she really didn't want to hear his cloying Oirish babble so early in the morning. But she did want to see how it all hung together; see how convincing it was.

She had stayed late at the station the night before and watched as they had recorded short takes of Mike earnestly nodding and frowning in the studio, then spliced them in with the interview he had done earlier with a criminologist from the university. She had only seen a rough version of the completed item, but although it lacked some of the showbiz glamour of the media-friendly Californian academics, it sounded pretty good. The authoritative voice of a British academic made it seem all the more real. The interview was going to run nationwide on breakfast TV, which was a real coup for Mike, and she had felt the familiar wave of frustration engulf her again.

Now, as she watched the item silently go out live, she realised what a joke the whole thing was. Mike's nods and frowns were so convincing they were excruciating. But it was fake. All they were really doing was pretending, talking the talk. Meanwhile reality went on elsewhere.

She clicked the set off with the remote and the white light died, leaving the room in darkness. She dragged herself up, pulling her dressing gown around her, and pinched the skin on her forehead. She hadn't dared open the curtains yet. She had drunk a whole bottle of heavy red wine when she had got home, and a dull pressure was throbbing behind her eyes.

She pulled open the curtains, squinting against the thin morning light, and looked at her watch. It was over eighty hours since Jill had called her at the station, and since then she hadn't heard a thing.

She shook her head. She had managed to keep her mind off Jill while she had been run off her feet at the station. But all along a nagging feeling had lurked somewhere deep down, and when she got back to her flat after watching Mike's interview there was no escaping it. There were no messages on the machine, no packages, no nothing.

'Where are you, Jill?' she muttered as she went through to the kitchen.

As she filled the kettle she caught sight of her reflection in the kitchen window. She looked like an extra from *The Evil Dead*, she thought, as she stared at the ghostly image. She slammed the kettle onto the hob. What the fuck are you up to, Jill? she thought. She had expected better.

She sat in the cold front room, idly stroking Jasper under the chin, and worked out what to do. And as the plan unwound in her head she began to feel better – in control again.

'OK, Jasp,' she said, running her hand down his back. He nuzzled up to her hand with his eyes closed. 'If I lose the plot again I want you to remind me, OK?'

She gripped the hot cup and stretched, blowing condensed breath out into the cold air.

She looked at Jasper and ruffled his fur again. 'You've known all along, haven't you?' she said in a baby voice. 'You've just got to look after number one.'


She waited until the office was empty at lunch-time, then punched the number of the Institute on her phone.

She silently whispered the name *Sheila Cole* to herself while she waited for the line to connect; it was the name of someone she had been at school with. She knew if she used a real name as cover it would make it easier to pull off.

'Kallman Institute,' someone said after a click.

'Hello. Could you put me through to Jill Squires, please?' Alex asked politely.

There was a pause.

'Why do you want to speak to her?'

Alex made sure she sounded confident. 'We were meant to meet for lunch today, but she hasn't shown up. I just wondered if she was still there?'

'No. No, she's not, er . . . could you hang on a minute?'

There was the sound of muffled voices on the other end of the line. Alex looked out of the office window and waited.

'Who am I speaking to?' a voice suddenly said.

Alex jerked her gaze away from the window. She felt static run across her skin as something in her head fired off a warning.

She knew that tone.

Later, she realised she had already known what was about to happen. Or felt it anyway. It was a premonition, like the strange silence people describe before a bomb goes off, and a cold, clammy fear spread out slowly across her skin.

'Sheila Cole,' she repeated. Her voice sounded hollow. The name suddenly rang false. She swallowed hard and felt her gut contract.

'And who are you?'

'I'm a friend of Jill's.'

There was a silence. 'I see. Listen, Miss Cole, this is DS Taylor speaking. I'm from the CID. I'm afraid there has been an incident involving Ms Squires. Are you not aware of what has happened?'

'No. No. I'm afraid . . . what incident?'

'Would it be possible for you to come down to the station?'

Her knuckles were hard and cold as she gripped the phone, and she felt exposed sitting in the open-plan office.

'Er, yes, yes . . . No . . . Look, I need to know what's going on first.' She felt a nervous flutter in her stomach.

There was a slight pause.

'I'm sorry . . . but I have to inform you that Ms Squires is dead.'

'What?' Her mind struggled to grab the words as they washed over her. 'Are you . . . are you sure? When?'

'Two days ago.'

Suddenly the room seemed to be full of bright light. She put her elbows on the desk and squinted. 'That can't be right,' she said, almost to herself.

'I'm sorry.'

'But how? How ... where did it happen?' She heard herself speaking somewhere in the background, but her head was suddenly full of noise.

'When can you be at the station, Miss Cole?' the voice asked flatly.

Alex slowly put the receiver down, trying to control her breathing, but when she let go of the handset her hand began to shake.

She stared at the telephone for a long time. It couldn't be true. It had to be a sick joke. But then she had heard it from a policewoman. There was no mistaking that delivery.

Jill was dead?

She couldn't be, but ...

She gripped the desktop as the full force of it hit her. The second wave of shock – as understanding turned to realisation – hit her like a punch in the stomach. The tremble in Jill's voice and her tight, nervous smile had been real enough, but Alex hadn't felt the fear herself. Now she knew how Jill must have been feeling. Someone you knew – someone who was real, live, flesh and blood – was suddenly dead. And she didn't know why. She tried to control her rising panic.

She heard the lift engine whine into life and suddenly remembered she was in the office. She knew she wouldn't be able to face anyone if they came in.

She had to get out.

She stood up, catching her hip heavily on her desk, and realised she couldn't seem to breathe in; the air was stuck in her throat. She knew she was panicking. She had to stay calm. She put one hand on the wall, and closed her eyes for a second.

Then she was out, and on the back stairs, her feet hammering on the hard concrete steps.

She pushed through the fire doors at the bottom and into the reception area. It was busy – there seemed to be people everywhere. She focused on the main doors ahead and strode through the lobby, keeping her eyes locked on the street outside.

58

She heard someone call her name but ignored them, almost falling through the revolving door and out onto the street. The light outside seemed far too bright. She screwed her eyes up but the sharp white light still stabbed into her retinas. She put her hand over her eyes to shade them. All she knew was she had to get to her car, which was parked up on a meter across the road, and get away.

She stumbled across the pavement, her eyes watering in the cold air, and put one foot onto the road without thinking. A car blared its horn and the side of a bus blurred across the front of her face. She stepped back, shook her head, and tried to concentrate. She could feel her heart pounding.

She jogged unsteadily down to the pedestrian crossing and punched the button. It felt like a dream, nothing around her seemed real. She was breathing short and fast, and the cold, gritty air felt raw on the back of her throat. She moved from foot to foot while she waited, feeling the cold sweat in the small of her back, and the traffic noise fizzing in her ears.

Her mind was a muddle of thoughts all ricocheting around at the same time.

The initial shock was beginning to wear off, and she began to shiver violently as the adrenaline subsided. The reality – the admission that it really *was* true – had sunk through her like nitric acid.

Jill – was – dead!

She crossed the road, feeling the presence of the traffic straining to move as the green man blinked, but didn't look around. Her gaze was fixed on the little newsagent's on the other side. She needed something to hang on to.

She went in and bought a packet of Silk Cut, dragging the Cellophane off and clawing out a cigarette, while the shopkeeper got her change. She lit it in the doorway, pulling deeply, and blowing the smoke out towards the road. The nicotine hit her instantly and her head swam. She felt slightly sick, but took another pull and felt her body sluggishly begin to relax.

She knew she had to get a grip on herself.

She glanced around and saw the small Asian shopkeeper looking at her warily. She forced herself to smile, then looked back out onto the road.

She took two more deep pulls, then flicked the cigarette into the gutter. She had to keep going, she couldn't stop to think. Otherwise she would lose it. She needed to ask some questions.

She went over to her car. Her mind was numb as she drove across town, and she kept missing when she changed gear.

She parked the car on the double yellow lines outside the Institute's front door and went in, ignoring the receptionist.

Anne's office was big and shambling; full of bookshelves packed with textbooks and neatly stacked piles of paper.

'I thought I told you I had nothing else to say to you,' Anne said calmly, watching Alex as she sat down.

'You did. But now someone else is dead.'

Anne leant back in her chair. 'Ah . . . right, I see. So the vultures are back?' she said, smiling coldly. 'Who told you?'

'We get a report from the police,' Alex lied.

Anne rocked forward, raising her eyebrows. 'So you'll know what happened, then?' She shifted in her chair and stared at Alex, looking bemused.

'It only logs the event,' Alex said, 'and I haven't had a chance to look into it yet. I came straight here.'

Anne smiled coldly and shook her head. 'So I was right, then, wasn't I? You are just like the rest: jumping to conclusions, before you have the facts. I suppose you've decided that two deaths in ten days has to prove something is amiss. That's why you're here, right?'

She raised her chin, and waited for Alex to reply.

'Yes,' Alex said warily. 'Of course, two murders in a week. What do you expect?'

'Who said anything about murder?' Anne said sharply. She leant forward and stared at Alex.

'What?'

'You haven't a clue, have you?' Anne said levelly. 'You've just come blundering in before you know what on earth is going on. Well, I'll tell you. Ian Fisher was murdered, yes. But not Jill.'

'What do you mean?' Alex asked. 'I mean, I . . .' She stopped herself from saying she had heard it when she rang up.

'Jill killed herself,' Anne said bluntly, watching for the news to sink in. 'Suicide.'

'What?' Alex blurted. Her mind started to spin again. 'Are you sure?' She couldn't work out what was going on.

'They found her locked in her car in her garage with a hose-pipe attached to the exhaust. So yes, I'm pretty sure,' Anne said flatly. 'There was a note as well.'

'Why?' was all Alex could say. She hadn't really worked out what she was going to say when she arrived, and the news caught her completely off balance.

'We don't know yet. I mean, Jill had taken Ian's death badly, just like the rest of us. So maybe that contributed. I don't know. But as you know she was physically challenged as well, so maybe it all just got too much.'

Alex sat and stared at her – none of it made any sense.

'She had a car?'

'Yes,' Anne said sharply. 'Converted. Look . . .'

'And the note was in her writing?' Alex asked, her voice sounding hollow.

'No,' Anne replied icily. 'But before you jump to any idiotic conclusions, you should know that Jill didn't write. She used a computer. It was on a print-out.' She leant back and moved some papers on her desk. 'Now I hope that's all you wanted to know because I have things to do. So why don't you just leave us alone, and let us grieve?'

When Alex didn't move she added, 'I want you to go now.'

Alex tried to work out what on earth was going on; Anne was lying, she had to be. Fisher's death was the last thing that would cause Jill to commit suicide; she was more likely to have thrown a party. But then Alex wasn't meant to know that.

She fixed a blank expression on her face, and tried to untangle her thoughts. She nodded slowly, then got up and put out her hand.

'You're right,' Alex said, 'I jumped to conclusions. I'm sorry. I'll take your advice and let it go.'

Anne shook her hand with a brief flick of the wrist, nodding that she acknowledged the apology.

'Good,' she said curtly, glancing towards the door.

Alex pulled the door of her flat shut behind her and leant heavily on the wall. She fumbled in her pockets, yanked out the cigarettes, and lit one with a shaking hand. She exhaled a huge cloud of smoke and closed her eyes. She slowly worked her shoes off with her toes, and kicked them aside while she tried to calm herself down.

She felt exhausted, completely out of energy. The anticipation of the last week had bottled it up inside her, but she had burnt it all off in the last couple of hours. Her limbs felt heavy.

She bent over stiffly and started automatically to shuffle through the junk mail and fliers behind the door. She was just about to straighten up and head down to the kitchen when she saw the corner of a big brown envelope sticking out at the bottom of the pile.

She took a sharp, deep breath. She already knew who it was from. Her body kick-started as fresh adrenaline seeped into her blood.

She bent over and scooped it up. It was a big, thick Jiffy bag. The label was printed on a cheap printer; she could see the dots that made up the letters.

As she turned it over, she remembered that she had picked up the mail that morning. It had come early. Two bills and a bank statement. All the other stuff on the floor had been pushed through later by pizza delivery companies and local taxi services. Then she realised what must have happened. The postmark was four days old. It must have been delivered to the front door of the house, and one of her neighbours had only just got around to dropping it off.

She tore it open.

There was a sheet of typed A4 with a crinkly piece of fax paper clipped to the back.

The letter was printed in the same rough typeface as the label:

*Dear Alex,*
*Sorry for the delay. As I said on the phone, people are a*
*bit jumpy down here at the moment. Anyway, enclosed is*
*my first haul. Please keep it in a safe place. You can keep*
*the paper wherever you like but you need to store the*
*blister pack at room temperature.*

*I found the pack when I did an audit of our clinical trials supplies. They're not registered in our protocol and there was only a small unmarked box of them at the back of the pharmacy. It also doesn't have a telephone number on which is very unusual as companies have to supply a number to call in case someone experiences side effects. If you hang on to it, when we know more about what is going on we can have them analysed. That's how we can nail them.*

*The fax audit page I have enclosed was my big breakthrough. I printed it off Ian's private fax machine in his office. It didn't make sense at first but I looked the name Numen up. They are a biotech firm near Cambridge, and biotechnology is exactly the sort of area Ian would have been keen to get involved with – sexy would have been his word. Anyway, I'll give them a call and see what they have to say.*

*I'll speak to you soon. Take care.*
*Jill.*

She dug her hand into the bag and pulled out the blister pack. It looked just like a pack of tablets you might get from the chemist.

She looked at the fax sheet. It was a list of telephone numbers, with the dates and the times the messages were sent. Against each was the acknowledgement code sent from the receiving machine. Alex had seen them before. Harry occasionally walked around the offices waving them when the telephone bill was particularly high. Jill had highlighted three lines with a dayglo pen. All three were the same number. The acknowledgement code against each of them said NUMEN MED SCI.

Underneath someone had scrawled in big uncertain letters: NUMEN BIOTECHNOLOGY, CAMBS!!!

'Oh, God,' Alex said slowly, shutting her eyes. The big childish letters must have been Jill's handwriting.

She slumped backwards and sank down against the wall. Her coat bunched up around her. She heard a sharp rap as a tear splattered onto the envelope in front of her. Then another. She looked at the dark patches expanding on the brown paper as the liquid was absorbed.

'There's no point in crying, sweetheart,' she murmured, snorting and swallowing. She wiped the moisture from the bottom of her eyes.

She felt something hot at the end of her hand, and realised the cigarette was burning down. She took one last drag, gagging slightly on the dry, hot smoke, and ground the butt out on the doormat.

'You got yourself into this mess, now you've got to get yourself out.'

# 11

Alex rubbed her hand slowly across her face while the vending machine splattered liquid into a plastic cup. Her skin felt rough and greasy, and little crystals of sleep were encrusted in the corners of her eyes. She scratched a piece of dead skin off her nose and examined it on her nail.

'Christ,' she muttered. She felt terrible.

She hadn't eaten anything before she set off – in fact she hadn't eaten anything solid for about eighteen hours – and she could feel her stomach gurgling caustically. Her whole body felt stiff and out of shape, as if it hadn't worked out that she was actually awake.

She needed to kick-start herself into action, she thought, glancing furtively up and down the corridor. It was Saturday morning and it wasn't even eight o'clock so she was probably safe. She dug into her pocket and pulled out her cigarettes.

She leant against the wall and tentatively sipped the hot yellow liquid. It was meant to be coffee, but after one sip she realised it wasn't – as far as she could tell it was the diluted contents of someone's stomach raised to just below boiling point. She lobbed the bulging cup into the bin, and lit a cigarette. She took a couple of long pulls and began to feel better.

She closed her eyes and let her breath out slowly, feeling the warm smoke run up her face. It felt odd being in the station so early – it was a get-in-late-stay-late kind of culture. She wasn't used to it being so empty. The whole place felt sterile and lifeless, as if the rest of the world was getting on with life somewhere else. It made her nervous. She felt a bit like a kid smoking surreptitiously behind the bike sheds, waiting for the inevitable moment when some psychotic PE teacher wandered by – which made her think of Harry. She couldn't remember a time when she had been in the station and he wasn't there.

She went over to the bin and dropped her cigarette into her discarded coffee cup, hearing the dog-end hiss as the tip was extinguished by the remains of the liquid. She didn't have time to waste. The early morning shift would be coming on soon. She set off towards the computer room.

The room was empty when she got there. It was a brightly lit, air-conditioned space, decked out in the usual crushingly dull greys and washed-out browns that corporate computer companies seemed to love. It hummed with the noise of a dozen PCs and had a self-contained air, as if the machines were quite happy doing whatever they were doing without any need for human input. It always made her think of HAL in *2001* when she ventured in there; as if someone was watching you even when you were on your own. She glanced around anxiously, wondering which was the best machine to use. Just as she was about to plump on a sleek, new-looking box in the corner with a particularly big screen, she heard something banging behind the row of machines.

'Hello?' she shouted over the whirr of the fans.

A head popped up from behind one of the benches, making her jump and murmur in surprise. She hadn't been expecting anybody to be there. She felt a twinge of anger inside her, and was about to say something when she realised who it was. It was Forester, the station's computer expert. She couldn't help but smile. It was impossible to get cross with Forester. He was just too . . . well, nerdy was the best word, but in a sweet, innocent sort of way. She felt the edges of her eyes crinkle as she looked at him. His tie was pushed into his top pocket. He had told her once it stopped it getting caught on the circuit boards when he was working inside a computer, but it was always like that. When he stood up he looked like an etiolated version of Brains in *Thunderbirds*.

'Hi, Alex,' he said, waving awkwardly. 'Just sorting out the network.'

'Good,' Alex said, nodding, unsure whether it was good or

not. 'Anyway, how are you, Forester? I haven't seen you for a while.'

'Oh, er . . . y'know, fine,' he said vaguely, looking uncomfortable.

She knew he was much happier talking about machines than himself, so she decided to change tack.

'Is it OK for me to do a search?' she said hopefully.

He frowned, and looked troubled.

'Inside or outside the firewall?'

He tended to talk like this, and she never knew what to say next.

'Not sure. I think it's that one over there,' she pointed out helpfully.

'Ah, yes, thought so.' He paused, and stroked his chin. 'Look, I think it should be OK. Ever since I upgraded the network I've been having a bit of a problem with protocol violations. I thought I was on top of it, but the server just stack-dumped a couple of minutes ago.'

'Er, great.' She frowned. 'Does that mean I can use it?'

'Think so,' he said, nodding solemnly, 'but don't be surprised if it goes down on you.'

She raised her eyebrows and grinned.

'I'll be very surprised if it goes down on me, Forester. But if it's any good it'll save putting up with stubble rash – which has to be a bonus.'

He looked at her blankly, then blushed. 'Oh, yes. I see,' he said, ducking back behind the bench.

She heard his muffled voice from under the desk. 'If you have any problems I'll be down here.'

She went over to the PC and sat down. She caught sight of the dark outline of her head and shoulders in the lifeless screen, and the smile died on her lips. It reminded her of the jumble of dreams she'd had the night before; a high-gloss Technicolor montage of images of Jill – some genuine, some made up, but all equally vivid. She could remember every detail of the reconstruction of Jill's death that her imagination had pieced together as if she had actually been there. The milky white of her neck as her head rolled back, and the murky green of her eyes as the carbon monoxide extinguished the last light of life, were just as

67

vivid as the glittery images from the pub.

She flicked on the PC and shook her head as the screen fizzed into life. Her head was a mess of thoughts and a tight corset of guilt was wrapped round her body.

She clicked the mouse impatiently as the machine ground slowly into action, flashing up a series of incomprehensible messages along the way.

She hoped that Forester stayed out of the way. It usually took her a while to fathom out how to use the system, but she knew that if she was left on her own she would work it out eventually. But Forester had a habit of wanting to get involved. He was incredibly well meaning, but he usually left her more confused than when she had started out. Last time it had happened he had rabbited away in some weird and impenetrable technospeak for so long that by the end of it she wasn't sure what her name was any more. It was a lot easier with him out of the way.

She heard his voice from behind the desk, and was about to think of a polite way of saying *Please, please, please don't try and help me!* when she realised he was speaking to someone else. She could see a phone line pulled taut across the edge of the bench.

'Look,' he said, sounding frustrated, 'I've tried that and it still doesn't work. What should I do now?' There was a pause, and then the pitch of his voice rose. 'How should I know? *You're* supposed to be the experts.'

Alex pursed her lips. It sounded as if he was speaking to someone whose plain English skills were on a similar level to his own. It would keep him busy for hours.

It took her a couple of minutes to work out the menu system, but once she had got the hang of it, it was pretty simple. She drilled through the screens until she found the one she wanted. It was a system for looking up company names.

She typed in NUMEN when it prompted her for a keyword.

The screen went blank, then threw back a single line:

*NO REFERENCES FOUND.*

She bit her lip.

She worked her way back out, and went into the station's

68

periodicals system – if Numen had been mentioned in a listed periodical it would tell her there.

The screen filled up with a list of magazine titles. She quickly scanned down the names. Most of them were trade press, obscure pharmaceutical industry publications, but a couple were from the *Financial Times*.

'Bingo,' she mouthed; they would have those on fiche – the others she would have to get from the library.

She printed out the list and set off for the microfibre room. She flipped on the strip lights and headed over to the long rows of filing cabinets.

The first couple of articles merely name-checked Numen, but the last one was a longer news feature, written six months earlier. It covered the takeover of Numen by Kogai Chemical, a Japanese industrial conglomerate. Kogai had paid well over the odds which, the article speculated, meant Numen must have something pretty special in the pipeline. Numen's area of expertise was Central Nervous System drugs – so it was probably an antidepressant or anti-psychotic.

'Right up your alley, Dr Fisher,' she murmured.

She went back up to the computer room and typed KOGAI CHEM into the commercial database. This time the cursor flashed for a second then threw a couple of lines of text onto the screen:

*Kogai Chemical. The chemical and pharmaceutical
division of Kogai Heavy Industries, Osaka, Jpn. Currently
ranked nine on the Nikkei.*

She printed out the information, and took it back to her office.

Ted Connor was in his office at the end of the open-plan space when she got there. He had opened his blinds to let in the light, and she could see him pulling the lid off a Styrofoam cup; the deli across the road must have opened up, which was good news – she could still taste the sour vending-machine coffee from earlier. He waved from behind the plate-glass window when he saw her. She smiled and waved back, then sat down at her desk. She wanted to get out before anyone else arrived.

She rang the library, but none of the trade magazines were

available off the shelf. She placed an order, then stared blankly out of the window, wondering what to do next.

'Damn,' she muttered; her next step was to get in touch with Numen – and that meant waiting until Monday.

She focused on the skyline. Outside it was a cold bright blue day. The wind had picked up overnight and clouds scudded across the sky as if in a speeded-up film. There was a whole weekend to kill before then.

She picked up the phone and punched Amy's number; she had been meaning to call her for weeks. Amy had been a temp at the station for a while, and was the sort of person you only saw if you were prepared to get drunk. Very drunk. And that was exactly what she needed to do. She needed a distraction or she would go mad.

Amy sounded breathless when she answered.

'I'd just locked the front door when the phone began to ring,' she explained in between breaths. 'I'm just on my way to the station to catch a train.'

'Oh, I see . . . it's just that I was wondering if maybe you were free for a drink later?'

'Sorry,' Amy said. 'I'm off to see my baby brother in Manchester. He's just started some god-awful engineering course, and I said I'd go and see him. But it should be a blast. Cheap booze and a ratio of about ten men to every woman. I'm going to show them how it's done.'

'Oh,' Alex said flatly.

'Why don't you come along?'

'Er, no. Thanks, though.'

'You're such a party-pooper, Alex.'

'I need to stay in town. How about when you get back?'

'Yeah, definitely. I'll call you, OK? I haven't seen you in ages. Listen, I need to dash.'

Alex put the phone down.

She folded the print-outs and put them into her bag. Mario laid on newspapers at the deli. She could kill a couple of hours there while she read about what else was happening in the world over a coffee.

Other than that it looked like a night in with a bottle of wine

70

and Jasper again. She got up and pulled on her coat. One more night in on her own wouldn't kill her.

# 12

He sidled up to the girl at the pedestrian crossing, a wave of anticipation knotting up inside him. He had followed her all the way from the city square, watching her totter unevenly, the tight black fabric of her flared hipsters clinging to her plump high-slung arse.

'You been in town?' he asked idly as they waited for the green man.

She glanced at him briefly, a faint expression of disgust flitting across her face, then looked the other way.

'Busy, isn't it?' he continued, stepping slightly closer to her. 'I haven't seen this many people on a Saturday for a long time.'

She flicked her hair and turned her head as far away from him as she could.

He looked down at her fake crocodile-skin boots.

'You a student, then?' he said, trying to sound as friendly as possible.

She stuck her hand out, trying to attract the attention of a taxi.

'I said, are you a student?' he repeated slowly, feeling the anger begin to burn behind his eyes.

She swivelled her head around, her eyes flashing a mixture of anger and fear.

'Why don't you fuck off and bother someone else?' she spat.

He bunched his fist, feeling the skin stretch across his knuckles.

'You what?'

'I said fuck off,' she repeated more confidently as she heard the rattle of a diesel engine behind her.

He looked at her coldly as the cab pulled up to the kerb behind her. He wanted to punch her in the face there and then.

'You've just been very lucky,' he said quietly, as she stepped into the road.

She turned towards him.

'Yeah, right,' she sneered, then ducked into the cab. 'Loser!'

He turned around and walked slowly down the underpass leading back to the town centre. He hadn't felt so completely alone for a long time; no one cared that he existed. He had spent two hours walking around the city, smiling at passers-by, trying to join in, but no one would have any of it.

The bastards!

They had the audacity to call him sick. He had seen it all in the last couple of hours: a girl being shagged on the bonnet of a car behind Ritzy's; boys walking bare-chested in the freezing night, spoiling for a fight; people howling, people shouting, people wrecking anything they could find – all in the name of fun; a sweet young girl rubbing her vomit-stained fingers against her ruched silk dress as she sat glazed-eyed against her boyfriend. If you wanted Sodom and Gomorrah you had to look no further. It disgusted him.

He walked slowly through the closed-up shopping centre, and out onto the paved area towards the square.

He watched as a group of men pretended to throw a girl into the fountain in the square. Her shrieks pierced the night, a fake shrill of alarm with a deeper undertone of sex. He turned around wearily and started back towards the university where his car was parked.

As he walked up the hill away from the square he had to weave through crowds that had flooded out of the pubs and clubs and were busy jostling for buses back to the suburbs. Even though it was nearly freezing, there was not a coat in sight. Orange legs protruded from crutch-length one-pieces, the material so tight you could spot an appendix scar. And more orange flesh bulged on exposed forearms, and dipping necklines. There was acres of it. All the same glowing radioactive colour. The colour northern European skin goes when it's baked raw under a UV lamp.

Groups of men cut through the crowd, uniform in white shirts fresh from the packet, their hands dug into their pockets to pull the material tight across their buttocks.

He walked with his head down, feeling overdressed, like an old person on a summer's day.

As he reached the top of the hill he suddenly became aware that someone was in his way, and whichever way he moved, they seemed to stay in the way. He looked up and was confronted by a girl, hands on her hips, staring straight at him.

When she realised she had his attention she glanced over her shoulder to her friends, and they giggled.

'What you looking at?' she challenged.

'Pardon?'

'I said, what were you looking at?'

He felt the blood rush to his face. 'Nothing.'

'You were looking at my tits, weren't you, you dirty bastard?'

Her face hardened, and she sucked in air, stretching the Lycra across her breasts. 'Well?'

He looked around, unsure what to say.

'No,' he said, glancing at her then dropping his eyes. They briefly caught on her white stilettos.

He looked up at her, but she was looking over her shoulder again. One of her friends dropped her head and snorted.

He didn't know what to do.

'Why not?' the girl said, turning suddenly. Her face showed mock dismay. 'You a puff or something?' She winked at him and chuckled, a broad grin breaking out on her face, and her friends howled with laughter.

The noise swirled around his head. He couldn't think of anything to say. In a few hours he knew he would think of something. But now he just stood looking blank and stupid as the group clattered off towards the bus stop.

He felt exposed in the crowd, as if their whoops had spotlit him – the only man with pale blotchy skin, the only man on his own – but when he looked around no one seemed to have noticed. They were all intent on hitting the taxi ranks and buses, already worrying about explaining love bites and vomit stains to their parents.

He wandered slowly through the empty streets – occasionally seeing a gaggle of noisy students staggering back towards the halls of residence – and meandered up towards the cemetery. The moon lit up the sky, casting a milky light across the pavement.

He pulled himself up and wriggled through the gap in the railings, dropping silently down into the damp long grass on the other side.

It was like entering another world.

He walked up the hill looking at the silhouettes of the headstones picked out in the bright creamy light. A light mist hovered above the grass.

He stopped at the top of the hill just behind the main gates, and sat on top of a flat grave. His skin felt cold and fresh in the crisp, sharp air.

Behind him he could hear yells and screams floating up from the pubs on Canning Circus as they emptied out.

He looked up at the moon – and wondered where it had all gone wrong.

# 13

Alex held the handset against her ear with her shoulder while she leafed through the pages of her Filofax. She felt sick and her hands were shaking slightly – this was the moment she had been waiting for all weekend. She repeated the numbers as she punched them. It took her two attempts to get it right. The phone rang twice, then she heard it click over to an answerphone. It was still on night service.

'Come on!' she muttered, looking at her watch; it was ten to nine already.

She put the receiver down, and drummed her nails on the desk. She was due at the scheduling meeting with Harry in ten minutes – but then things rarely started bang on time first thing on Monday morning. She decided to hang on until nine, then call again.

It was a sharp, bright autumn morning outside, and light slanted into the office through the half-closed blinds. She squinted and felt her skin wrinkle dryly.

She leant stiffly over and rummaged in her drawer. Her head felt as if it was about to implode. She fished out a bottle of Nurofen, and washed a couple of tablets down with the remainder of the cold coffee from the deli.

She hit redial bang on the hour.

'Numen Biotechnology,' a woman answered.

'Oh, hi,' Alex said brightly. 'Can you put me through to your Med Sci people, please?'

'I'm sorry?'

'Erm, I want to speak to someone who is responsible for Med Sci.'

'I'm sorry, but we don't actually have a department by that name. Are you sure you've got the right number? This is Numen Biotechnology.'

'Yes, that's right ... OK ... Look, I've been sent this fax from Numen and it says Med Sci at the top. That's who I want to contact. Do you know who it might be from?'

There was a slight pause.

'Ah, right. I see. Yes. That probably means Medical Sciences. Who do you want to speak to?'

'I'm not sure.'

'I'll put you through to their reception, then. Hold the line, please.'

After a brief pause another woman came on.

'Medical Sciences. Can I help you?'

'Yes,' Alex answered confidently. 'I'd like to speak to some-one responsible for clinical trials.'

'You'll have to be a bit more specific. We run a lot of different trials. What programme is it from?'

'It's one you're running at the Kallman Institute. I'm afraid that's all I know.'

'I see. I'll just try to find out who's responsible for that one. Who shall I say is calling?'

'Alex Brierley.'

'From?'

'From *Midlands Report East*.'

'Midlands Report what? Is that a company?'

'No. It's a news programme.'

'You're a reporter?' the woman asked warily.

'Yes. That's right.'

'I'll put you through to the programme manager, then.'

'Who is ...?'

But she was on hold. Tinny chamber music strained in the background.

She hummed vaguely along with the tune and fiddled with the edge of her desk. The music was beginning its second cycle when the line clicked.

'I'm sorry, he's not here at the moment. I'll have to get him to call you back. What number are you on?'

'Look, is there anyone else I can speak to? I'm a bit short of time.'

'No, I'm afraid not.'

Alex knew she was being stonewalled – but then she had expected to be. She was just making sure they took the bait.

'Your number, Miss Brierley?'

She reeled off her number.

'He'll get back to you as soon as he can.'

'Who's he?' Alex said, aware that the lightness was leaving her voice. Her frustration was beginning to get the better of her. She took a silent deep breath.

'Pardon?'

'I just wondered who the he was who's going to call.'

'He'll call you as soon as he can. Goodbye, Miss Brierley.'

Alex let the receiver drop out of her hand. It bounced on the desk with a hard thunk.

She took a deep breath and sat down. She ran her fingers over her face then through her hair. The frustration of sitting around all weekend was balled up inside her. She closed her eyes and rubbed her forehead.

When she glanced up at the clock it was a quarter past nine. She quickly switched her phone over to voicemail, grabbed her workbook, and headed for the lift.

Harry was already talking when she got there. She slipped in and sat at the back.

'Afternoon, Alex,' he said without looking at her.

'Sorry I'm late, Harry. I was powdering my nose,' she explained sweetly.

'As long as that was all you were powdering, sweetheart.'

He lifted his eyebrows at the boys in the front row, and they snorted with laughter.

Alex rolled her eyes, then saw Gena looking over at her; she was shaking her head slowly and frowning. Alex smiled and nodded, raising her eyebrows to acknowledge her support.

She frowned as Gena turned away and felt a little stab of sadness.

She used to be good friends with Gena – but things hadn't been the same since she had starting seeing Mike. Alex had known what Mike was like then, and he hadn't changed since – even now, when he and Gena were technically engaged, she knew he was still putting it about among the temps and student placements. But she also knew that Gena wouldn't want to hear it from her. She shook her head, turned back to the front and tried to concentrate.

Harry had drawn some complicated diagrams on the white board.

'OK, folks,' he said, rapping his knuckles on the desk. 'The big cheeses have been pretty damned pleased with the coverage so far. So well done. We've had *three* major items networked from our very own cameras this week, which is a record.' He nodded at the front row. 'And Mikey-boy here's turning into a bit of a household name. He'll have the wifies sending their knickers in soon.'

'There's already a bagful in reception,' someone said at the front.

'So that's what the smell was in the lift,' someone else shouted. 'I thought it was fish.' The front row boomed in support.

'Enough!' Harry commanded, raising his hand. 'They want us to put the big murder story on the back burner for a couple of days.'

There was a groan at the front.

'Don't worry. It's only for a couple of days. There's not a lot of new stuff coming in on it at the moment, but they're convinced something's going to happen soon. And I think we'd all agree with that. So I want Mike and his team to keep at it, maybe spend some time trying to get the families to talk. That should be good for a laugh if nothing else.

'But for the rest of you, it's business as usual. There's been a lot of shit going on recently, so we need to keep the sweeteners running. They've been drying up lately. Remember, the punters are having their tea, for Christ's sake. We don't want them throwing up. So make sure those end bits make them smile.'

He ran down the week's schedules. Alex's first job was to interview a local jockey who had just been signed to a rich Arab sheikh's stable in Dubai. It wasn't as bad as she had been expecting. She had done far worse. She jotted down the rest of her schedule and got up to leave.

Mike cruised up to her.

'How's it going, Goldilocks?' he smarmed. 'Want to come and taste my porridge?'

'Get lost,' she replied, without looking at him.

'Time of the month?'

'At least I have a time of the month,' she said, swivelling around. 'Wait till your voice breaks, sunshine. Then you might actually grow some balls.'

'Tetchy,' he said, moving closer to her. 'You're not looking forward to the jockey? If you're lucky he might even give you a ride.' He moved his mouth close to her ear. 'I bet he could give you head while he's still standing up.'

'You're only jealous, Shamus,' she cooed innocently. 'You having another of your little-boy fantasies?'

She heard him catch his breath. 'Raw nerve?' she smirked, and stepped around him. 'What's wrong, eh? One of the little girlies turn you down?'

He caught her arm.

'You watch your mouth, you stuck-up bitch.'

She jerked her arm away from him.

'Go and sit on your mike, Mike,' she said, smoothing the arm of her jacket and smiling sweetly. 'It's the only friend you've got.'

She watched him stalk off and wondered what he would be like when his star began to descend – she hoped it would be very soon, and that she wasn't still around to see it.

Normally she would have joined the ruck arguing with Harry about the schedules, but this time she left them to it. She went back up to her desk.

There was a message waiting for her on her voicemail:

'Miss Brierley. This is Dr Edward Shaw, Director of Medical Affairs at Numen Biotechnology. I believe you wanted to speak to someone about our clinical trials programme. I'll be at my desk for most of today, so feel free to call me whenever you want.'

She saved the message, and looked around. The office was still empty.

She punched Numen's number.

'Dr Shaw is in a meeting at the moment,' his secretary explained. 'Who is it calling?'

'Alex Brierley.'

'Oh, I see,' the woman said briskly. 'I'll see if I can page him.'

There was a slight pause, then a loud, confident voice spoke.

'Ah, Miss Brierley. Ted Shaw here. How can I help you?'

'I'm covering the murder of Ian Fisher at the Kallman Institute in Nottingham. And I just wondered if you had anything to say about it.'

'Oh, I see . . . Well, I was obviously deeply saddened to read about Dr Fisher's death – but why are you asking me?'

'I believe you were running a clinical trial with Dr Fisher at the time?'

'No. No, I'm afraid that isn't correct. What made you come to that conclusion?'

'Because Dr Fisher was in regular contact with you.'

There was a pause.

'I'm sure he was,' Shaw said calmly. 'And I'm sure there is a rational explanation. But I'll need to check the details before I can fully appraise you.'

Alex heard a noise behind her. She glanced around. The lift doors were opening – people were coming back from the meeting.

'Look, would it be possible for us to meet to talk about this, Dr Shaw?'

'I'm afraid I'm quite tied up at the moment, but I can arrange for someone else to give you some time. I mean, it's obviously in both our interests to make sure we set the record straight, wouldn't you agree?'

'Certainly.'

'Splendid. I'll get someone to call you.'

Alex put the receiver down and drummed her fingers on the desk. She bit her nail then snatched the handset up again and called down to reception, telling them to hold all her calls unless it was from Numen.

Ted Connor walked past and waved. The office was beginning to fill up.

She waved back and cradled the receiver on her shoulder. It was time to do some work. She called the stable where the jockey worked and arranged a provisional time to shoot.

It was late afternoon when she heard the bleep in her ear. She briskly told the PR she was speaking to that she'd call her back, and switched to the incoming call.

81

'Ms Brierley?' a cultured male voice enquired.

'Yes?'

'My name is Jack O'Neill.' The voice was smooth and controlled. 'I'm a legal adviser to Numen Biotechnology. I believe you are interested in meeting to clarifying Numen's position vis-à-vis Dr Ian Fisher.'

'Yes. I am interested to know why he contacted Numen just before he died.'

'I see,' O'Neill said calmly. 'Well, I'm afraid it's nothing sinister, but I am more than happy to meet. What about Friday? I'm afraid I'm busy until then.'

'OK.'

'Where are you based?'

'Nottingham.'

'Fine. Let's meet at Toddington Services on the M1. That's about halfway between us.'

'What's wrong with coming to Numen?'

'I'm afraid they don't permit unauthorised personnel on their site. It is very high-security. And anyway, I'd prefer to keep this informal. A neutral environment would seem more appropriate.'

'OK. Whatever.'

She jotted down the time in her diary.

'One more thing. I would ask you not to jump to any conclusions until we've discussed this.'

'Why's that?'

'Because you are a reporter, Ms Brierley. And I wouldn't want Numen to be unfairly represented. I'm sure you can see my point.'

When she had put the phone down, a fizz of excitement raced through her. Things were beginning to move. She wasn't sure what had made her so certain – something they had said, a tone in their voice, or just a gut feeling – but she *knew* she was on the right track.

Her senses had locked onto the faintest trace of something under the surface, like a strung-out junkie tasting the bitter taste of opiate on burnt-out foil.

She leant back in her chair and looked at the darkening sky. She shivered, suddenly aware of a hollow feeling inside her, a strange sense of aniticpation that told her that she needed to move quickly. She stared at the thin crescent of the moon hanging prematurely in the autumn sky, and tried to ignore the feeling that had rushed back at her again – that something awful was about to happen.

That something was about to die.

# 14

The service station carpark was awash with people. Alex wove her car slowly through the crowd – resisting the urge to rev the engine and plough over the bulky Nike-clad youths who slouched in front of her, scowling.

As she scanned the rows of cars for an empty space a big black BMW suddenly reversed out in front of her. She jammed on the brake, feeling her seat belt bite into her shoulder. The car stopped abruptly halfway out of the space; the reverse lights flashed on again, then off. She glanced at the dashboard clock.

'Come on', she muttered. She was already ten minutes late.

The reverse lights flickered again but the car didn't move.

'For God's sake,' she exclaimed, shaking the gear lever into neutral; there wasn't enough space to get around him.

She gripped the wheel hard. The big Seven Series was a rich shining black with tinted windows. She couldn't see in. A little man in a big car, she guessed. The worst kind – hiding behind the blacked-out exterior.

The car jolted a foot forward then stopped again, leaving a slight gap behind it. That was all she needed. She jammed the gear lever into first and lurched through the gap.

She swung the Mazda into a vacant space at the end of the row, and kicked off her shoes while she opened the door.

She pulled her high heels out from under the seat and dropped them out onto the tarmac. As she wiggled her toes into the tight leather, she could see the groups of people slouching back to their cars at the edge of her vision. These were *her* people, she thought grimly, looking up as a chunky youth exposed the pasty flab of his lower back while he bent over to tie up his Reeboks – the dazed and confused whose need for instant consumption underpinned her whole career.

She shut her eyes, trying to blot out the image of the youth's half-exposed backside. She had to concentrate on what she was doing. O'Neill would be waiting for her inside. She needed him to tell her something she didn't already know – and since he was a lawyer, the odds were already stacked against her. Lawyers existed to tell you nothing and charge you for the privilege.

She stepped out of the car, cupped her hands over a B&H and pulled on the flame from her lighter. She was nervous. If she blew this she had nowhere else to go.

She smoothed her skirt down over her thighs. She was wearing her best suit; a pale blue Nicole Farhi number. She hoped it made her look the part – elegant, confident, enigmatic – but the most important thing was it made her *feel* the part. She was ready for them – or as ready as she ever would be. She set off towards the main entrance.

She stopped outside the restaurant and took one last pull on the B&H. The filter was smeared with her lipstick and stuck to her fingers. She blew the smoke into the air and flicked the butt into a large fake fern. She dabbed at her lips with her finger, and pushed her shoulders back.

'Come on, Al,' she muttered. 'You've practised this often enough.'

It was all about confidence. She had spent half her adolescence telling herself that. But at times like this she just wanted to roll her shoulders forward and try to disappear. Five ten felt way too tall.

She took a deep breath and strode into the restaurant, scanning the tables without moving her head. There were men in grey suits at every other table, but she spotted O'Neill and his colleague immediately. They stood out – dark Savile Row wool, white shirts, subtle but expensive silk ties. Mentally, she rolled her eyes – these were big fish. But she kept the same expressionless look on her face.

She approached the table, setting her lips into the faintest of smiles, and slowly switching her gaze between them. She had good eyes; a washed-out pale blue. They were the only feature she really liked. And she knew how to use them to good effect.

'Mr O'Neill?' she asked. She glanced at both of them. The taller of the two rose and put out his hand.

'Call me Jack,' he said, smiling.

'Alex,' she replied, nodding her head.

'And this is Charles Cunningham.'

Alex shook both their hands. They were firm and confident. People who learnt to shake hands before they could walk. They looked like something out of a Hugo Boss advert. All dark hair, chiselled features and designer smiles. The only thing missing was an elegant model draping her arm over their shoulders.

'Take a seat,' Jack offered, waving to the other side of the table. 'Can I get you a coffee?'

Alex nodded.

Charles silently got up, and set off towards the counter.

'Nice,' Alex said, glancing at Charles. 'Is he house-trained?'

'I think so,' Jack smiled.

She knew it was the kind of smile he'd only use when alone with a woman – a politician's smile – but she smiled back sweetly.

'So did you find it alright?' he asked, leaning back in his chair.

'Yes thanks, no problem.'

'Excellent.' He glanced at his watch, then stared at her for a moment as if he were weighing her up. It was meant to unsettle her, she thought. But she was used to it. It was no worse than having a camera pointed at her.

'Tell me, Alex,' he said suddenly. 'What's this story of yours all about? Give me some background.'

She held his gaze, then casually glanced around the room.

'Well, it's about a break-in at a health centre. Some unexplained drugs, and a dead doctor.' She looked back at him gravely. 'Oh yes, and a little old company called Numen Biotechnology. Are you sitting comfortably?'

'Go on,' he said, placing his hands carefully on the table.

She briefly outlined what had happened. He nodded his head as she spoke, keeping an attentive but impassive expression on his face. She watched carefully as she told him about the fax. If he knew something he was keeping it well hidden, she thought. But then that was his business.

'It's a strange old world we live in,' he said when she had finished. 'I don't know what makes these people tick.'

He turned around as Charles arrived. 'Thank you, Charles,' he said, taking a cup.

'Sugar?' He gestured to Alex.

'No thanks . . . What people?'

'Junkies,' he said seriously, stirring his black coffee for effect. 'Just can't see it myself.'

'Like I said, Jack, I don't think this has anything to do with junkies. I think it was something more serious.'

'Yes, yes, you said,' he responded, raising his eyebrow. 'Anyway, fascinating as all this is, my main interest is that you don't accidentally get Numen mixed up in your story. That wouldn't help anybody. I believe you wanted to know why Dr Fisher was in contact with us.'

'Yes.'

'Fine,' he said, holding her stare. He gestured to his side. 'Charles.'

Charles pulled some papers out of his briefcase. He put them on the table, and pushed them towards her.

'Every year the CPDD run a conference on global CNS drug developments . . .'

Alex raised her eyebrows enquiringly.

'The Council for Psychiatric Drug Development. Ian Fisher was a regular guest. He was a very good keynote speaker, so he was greatly in demand. This year he was going as Numen's guest. It is – or *was* – a considerable coup for Numen. Guests of Dr Fisher's calibre usually go with the big boys. That's what we were in contact about. Nothing else.'

She looked at the papers; they were copies of faxes.

'So Numen pay for Fisher to go all the way to Marseilles. What do you get out of it?'

'It's good PR. It gives them a forum in which to explain what they are thinking of developing. Ian Fisher's views would be very valuable. As an opinion leader it is important he endorses whatever they are working on.'

'And what are they working on?'

He stopped and smiled.

'I'm afraid I can't tell you that.'

87

Alex cocked her head as if it didn't matter. 'So how come Fisher and Co. get to know?'

'They sign a non-disclosure contract, and we give them pre-release information. It ensures they are aware of new products that are going to hit the market that could benefit their patients.'

'Sounds to me like you buy them.'

'That's a little naïve, if you don't mind me saying,' Jack said, forcing a grin, but struggling to keep his voice pleasant. 'It's called marketing, Alex. It's the way all industries work. The pharmaceutical industry is no different to any other.'

He obviously couldn't keep the charm going for long, she thought. He was used to getting what he wanted.

'Numen pay for him to attend, so they can canvas his opinion. It's very symbiotic. As a doctor he has to keep abreast of new developments. That's what the conference is for.'

Alex shook her head. 'And that's it?'

'Yes,' O'Neill said, leaning forward. He had his best smile on again. 'I'm glad you understand.'

She shrugged, deciding to change tack. 'So how come you don't work for Numen, Jack?'

He looked at her hard for a second.

'Numen are only a small company. I act as their representative when they need me, A corporate troubleshooter, you might say. That's why I'm here.'

'Don't Kogai have their own lawyer?' she asked quickly, studying him carefully to see if the name had any effect. His face was impassive – a poker face – but she noticed a faint nervous ripple run across the thin skin under his left eye.

'Kogai wholly own Numen,' he replied slowly, then paused, weighing her up. 'But I imagine you know that – it's in the public domain. They bought them for their R&D ability. It's an area the Japanese have been traditionally weak in. So they are allowing Numen to steer their own course.'

'And Kogai don't mind them lavishing money on freebies?'

'Small change, Alex, I assure you.'

She stared at him as he stretched his fingers and examined his nails. She didn't want to believe him, but he had made a pretty convincing case.

Jack looked up again and smiled. 'As you can imagine, Dr

Shaw was keen that you were fully up to speed with the facts, Alex. Can I tell him you are now clear about Numen's relationship with Dr Fisher?'

Alex rolled her tongue across her gums, then nodded slowly.

'Uh-huh.'

'Therefore I can assume that your interest in Numen is now over.'

'Maybe, Jack. Maybe,' Alex replied coyly. She knew she wasn't going to get anything else from him. But she wasn't going to roll over for him.

She tensed the muscles in her thighs, ready to stand.

'What do you mean maybe?'

She relaxed into the chair again.

'Look, Jack, I hear what you're saying. And it all seems to make sense to me at the moment. So you can rest assured that I won't go jumping to conclusions about Numen. How's that sound?'

'Fine,' he conceded, smiling thinly. 'But you haven't answered my question.'

His eyes flashed darkly, and the skin under his left eye trembled slightly. His voice had lost the gloss again.

'From what you've said, Dr Shaw needn't worry. If it's true, then that is the end of it.'

'It is true. Take my word for it.'

'Then fine, Numen are history as far as I'm concerned. And they'll stay that way until I have another reason to think so.'

She started to get up.

Jack looked at her coldly. He placed both his palms down on the table.

'Look, let's cut the crap, shall we, Alex. I'll get straight to it. I don't care what fantasy you concoct. You have a job to do. I can see that. As long as it doesn't include Numen Biotechnology I don't care. But if you make a wrong assumption, and jump to the wrong conclusions, then suddenly I'm very concerned. If you in any way incorrectly link Numen to the case then we will act with extreme prejudice. Do you understand?'

Alex put her hands on the table and leaned towards him.

'I always get wary when people try to force my hand, Jack. It usually means they've got something to hide. I hope this isn't the case. Then dear old Dr Shaw can sleep easy and I won't have to meet you again. But if there is anything else, then I'll find it. OK?'

He stared at her levelly but didn't speak. He had green eyes. The same colour as Jill's.

She tilted her head sideways. 'Thanks for your time, Mr O'Neill,' she said, curling the corner of her lip slightly. 'It was a pleasure.' She nodded in Charles's direction. 'Mr Cunningham.'

She strode across the restaurant. A group of businessmen turned to look at her. She ignored them and walked out; her legs felt shaky.

She was halfway back to her car when something made her look back. She wasn't sure what – it was just a feeling that someone was watching her. She stared back across the huge car-park, squinting against the harsh white light.

She put her hand up to shield her eyes, but all she could see was the gauzy outlines of the rows of cars and the graduated haze of light falling across the wide open space.

She was about to turn back when the sheet of light caught something – a sudden sharp flash. She shielded her eyes with both hands, squinting hard to focus.

There was a lone figure way out on the far side of the apron of tarmac; a hazy outline with something glinting near their face. The overbearing light had reduced it to a bleached-out shape, and all she could tell was that it was male. But she sensed he was looking straight at her.

She squinted harder, almost closing her eyes. She felt the muscles around her eyes strain and start to flutter. Her field of vision flickered – flattening the image to a grainy black and white – but she could see more definition in the figure. He was tall, slim, and probably wearing a suit; it could have been Charles, but she wasn't sure. But she could see he was holding something to his face, pointing it straight at her.

'What?' she muttered, suddenly realising what it was. It was a long-lensed camera.

He was taking her picture!

He must know she had seen him, she thought. But he made no effort to move. What was he up to?

As she started to step forward a large car cruised across the shimmering tarmac and pulled up by his side.

He casually lowered the camera, stared at her, then raised it one last time, before slipping into the dark shape.

The car circled slowly and moved towards the exit. It was a big, shining executive model; a Mercedes or Lexus – or maybe a top-end BMW. Whatever it was, it was obvious they wanted her to see them.

She tried to work out what it meant.

'What are you up to, Jackie-boy?' she murmured, as she watched the car disappear up the slip road. Why did they want her photograph?

It made her uneasy. As if something had crawled inside her. But she didn't know what.

# 15

He cruised slowly up Mapperley Road, past the big Gothic houses at the bottom of the hill. Up ahead a young mother was unloading a child from a baby seat in a VW Golf. He slowed down, glancing at her as he passed. Behind her a huge Victorian house glowed opulently and the front door opened as her husband came out to bring in more Sainsbury's bags.

It always surprised him how quickly things changed as you climbed the hill.

There was a point somewhere towards the top when you passed an unmarked line. He was never quite sure where it was. But somewhere, as the safe middle-class area ran towards the grinding poverty of St Anne's, things changed.

He saw the first couple of girls as he rounded the bend at the top of the hill; two scraggy, nervous-looking teenagers huddled by the postbox on the corner. They were both thin and scantily dressed, gripping their cans of Special Brew as if they might be a source of heat. He slowed down and turned up the dark street. They both walked towards the kerb, thinking he was going to stop, but he didn't. He headed into the maze of back streets, scanning the dark pavements.

He knew who he was looking for.

There were a lot of girls out; they stared back with a twitch of the hips as he squinted at them in the shadows, or walked slowly, arms crossed, backsides on show in tight jeans and high heels.

He looped around three times looking for her, but she was nowhere to be seen.

Then, as he cruised back down the big wide boulevard that sank into Mapperley Park, he saw her. She was walking in the shadows, a slow, casual walk through the piles of leaves from the huge oak tree that flanked the road.

He slowed down.

She glanced over her shoulder as she heard him cruise up behind her. She was wearing skin-tight trousers and an orange padded jacket, and chewed gum like the other girls. But she had a different air about her. A dignity in the way she walked, in the way she carried herself. She turned back around and kept walking.

He gave the accelerator a jab and passed her by, then pulled up by the kerb ahead of her. He watched her in the wing mirror as the electric window purred open.

She sauntered casually up to the open window.

'You busy?' he asked.

She glanced up and down the road.

'Not especially,' she said with a shrug. 'It's slow tonight and I was just thinking of jacking it in.'

'Can I have some of your time, then?'

She smiled. 'If you'll give me a lift home afterwards. It'll save me the cab fare.'

'OK.'

She glanced quickly around again, and pulled the door open.

He drove carefully down the stony track, leaving the houses behind, stopping at the end where the ground abruptly fell away. Out in the front the city twinkled and flashed, like a warped Technicolor reflection of the sky.

She unclicked her seat belt and wriggled out of her jacket, then twisted around to look at him.

'It's good to get out of the cold,' she said, running her fingers through her hair.

Harris looked at her in the dark. She was quite a big woman with blunt features, and the last few years had hardened her face – but there was something about her; a calm, a self-assurance. Like she knew she mattered. She was the sort of woman you wanted to lean over and touch. Just run your finger softly across her cheek.

'I haven't seen you about for a while, Emma,' he said.

'I got another pub job, so I haven't needed to so much.'

'I thought it might be because of the murders.'

'Nah,' she said off-handedly. 'I know how to keep out of trouble.' She stretched, yawning as she arched her spine. 'So what can I do for you, Detective Inspector?'

'Give me some advice.'

She half turned, and squinted at him. 'Are you serious?'

'Yes.' He pushed his seat back slightly and stretched his legs. 'What would stop you getting into a car with someone? What is it about them?'

She looked out of the window. 'You just know,' she said after a long pause.

'But there must be something about them?'

'Yeah. But it's not about what they are. It's what they aren't. Most punters are basically the same. They might be feeling lonely, or unhappy, or just out for the excitement, the thrill of cruising around. But they all act pretty much the same. It's when they don't that you know something's wrong.'

'So have you any idea who we should be looking for?'

'Someone who's got other reasons. Someone who doesn't fit in.'

'Like what?'

She looked around at him. 'That's your job, Detective Inspector. To pick up the ones I turn away.'

'So have your instincts ever let you down?'

She shrugged. 'Not really. There was a time a couple of years ago when I'd just started and this guy said he wanted to smack me. He offered me a lot of money and I needed it. But I knew his sort. Uptight public school boy, probably a lawyer or something. He was a lot rougher than I expected, though. Broke my wrist. That surprised me. But only because of the severity. Not what he did.'

'You could have told us.'

'Why should I? He paid.'

They sat in silence, both looking at the city.

'So how are your kids?' Harris said eventually.

'OK.' She glanced across at him, then turned back and looked out of the window. 'It's taken them a while to settle. But things are better now.'

'I'm glad.' He let his eyes wander across the web of street-lights down below. 'Seeing anyone?'

She looked at him and smiled. 'The last thing I want is another man in my life, Detective Inspector. I've got the two boys. They're all I need at the moment.'

He turned the key and the engine purred into life.

'I'll take you home.'

'Thanks.'

# 16

Alex stopped outside her flat, and switched off the engine. She stretched her head back against the rest and shut her eyes; the muscles in her neck felt like knotted steel.

She took a deep breath and heaved herself out of the car, wiggling her shoulders to try to loosen them up, while she fumbled with the lock. It had started to rain again, and the fine drizzle that permeated the air coated her skin with a greasy, cloying film.

She walked towards the house with her head down. The light was fading fast and the streetlights had just come on. They flickered uncertainly, a low, brooding red glowing at the edge of her vision. It was as if the damp from the thick drizzle had saturated them, stopping them fully catching alight.

She glanced up at the house. It looked dark and empty, and suddenly she felt very alone. It was as if having her picture taken had robbed her of something. She knew it was ridiculous; like some primitive tribesman who thought the camera took away their soul. But being caught out in the open had made her feel exposed. It was as if the long lens had pushed itself inside her.

She shuddered and walked quickly towards her flat.

'Oh God,' she murmured at nothing in particular, as the door slammed behind her.

Her thoughts were all jumbled up again. Every instinct she had told her O'Neill and his cronies were covering something up. They wouldn't give a damn about her otherwise. But she couldn't piece it together. Something at the back of her mind kept nagging at her, but it wouldn't surface. All she was left with was an uneasy feeling that something had changed. That suddenly, instead of pushing her way up a hill, she was sliding down a slope – fast. And she could no longer stop herself, even if she wanted to.

The flat was icy cold; a sharp, dead chill. She kept her coat on while she sifted through the mail. There were three envelopes strewn behind the door. But none of them was from Jill. She had still been half hoping that something would arrive, but now she knew it was too late. Jill had not been able to send anything else before she was killed.

She walked slowly into the kitchen. There was a single message flashing on the machine. She pressed Play, and leaned against the worktop.

'Hey, Ali, it's Amy. I'm just back from Manchester. I'll tell you all about it when I see you, OK? Give me a call when you're back.'

Alex screwed up her face. Ali again. Twice in a couple of days. It was a name that didn't fit any more – a name that belonged in the past – but it triggered something inside her. She felt her head swim slightly.

She looked around her kitchen at the debris of her life; bits and pieces of food, tapes strewn on the table. The flat had become a shell around her. Somewhere she had made her own. Somewhere she felt safe. But something had changed that now – O'Neill, the figure with the camera, and now that name again.

Why did she feel it now? she thought. When she had spent so long making sure she could look after herself, slowly shoring up the weak spots, until she felt emotionally self-contained. It was nearly three years since Rob had broken up with her. Three years since he had driven up from Cardiff and told her that he had met someone else – some little tart at the station there – and that he wanted out. But suddenly it felt like only yesterday.

She rubbed the slight bulge of her lower stomach, feeling the empty space inside her. She knew that he'd been right; she *had* only been thinking of herself when she had left Cardiff. But why was it that men always had to find another woman before they had the courage to get out? Why did they just grab at the nearest thing available? It was just so pathetically lazy. And just when she had *really* needed him.

She felt her lips peel away from each other as the dry skin parted, and her eyelashes twitch leavily, weighed down by tears like leaves in a rainstorm.

Three years had gone by since then – and it was nearly a year since she had slept with anyone. And suddenly she realised it wasn't Rob she missed. Just someone. Someone to be there with her. Someone to hold her. Just someone.

She shook her head.

'Come on, Al,' she murmured, forcing herself to laugh. 'You can do better than this. This is what the bastards wanted.'

She groped for the phone.

Amy answered on the second ring.

'Alex!' she shouted. 'Where have you been?'

Alex recoiled at the volume.

'Working,' she answered croakily, holding the phone away from her ear.

'Is that all? Don't you have a life?'

'Not at the moment, no.'

'You're turning into a sad old lady, you know that? Anyway, listen, the good news is I'm out on the razz tonight. Why don't you come along and get pissed? It'll do you good.'

'Don't you ever stop?' Alex asked, rubbing her face. She stretched over for her cigarettes.

'What for? You've got to stay one step ahead of the game, sweetheart. Take my word for it. I've had a hangover chasing me all week. Are you on?'

Alex felt herself start to smile.

'Go on, then, you're on. As long as you're sure you don't mind dragging an old crone around.'

'Nah. I can always say you're my mother.'

'Just try it.'

'Maybe I will. I'll have to take you to a grab-a-granny night somewhere.'

'That's fighting talk,' Alex said, an unlit cigarette bobbing up and down in the corner of her mouth. She flicked her lighter and lit it. 'I can see I'm going to have to show you what's what,' she said gravely, exhaling the smoke.

She hung up and smiled, feeling slightly better. It was the weekend, she thought. She just needed to get out and forget all about O'Neill, and the Institute, and everything else. Then she would be alright.

It was a good idea.

But wrong.

# 17

The gunmetal-grey Jensen dropped down into the underpass, the big V8 engine surging as the gears changed. Ted Shaw's voice disappeared in a hiss of static.

Jack glanced in the rear-view mirror – the roads through the City were quiet; everyone was either in the pub or had scuttled home early for the weekend. He caught a glimpse of the BT tower blinking on the skyline way over in the West End, and wished he was over there – that his week was over. But it wasn't, he knew that; it was only just beginning.

The silence in the car was unnerving. He didn't like admitting he had failed to get a result. In fact he hated it. And Ted Shaw was not about to let him off lightly. Cellnet had been quite capable of conveying the malice in his voice. He waited grimly for Shaw's acidic voice to come back on.

A sickly yellow light filled the car as the overhead lights in the underpass changed. He switched the phone over to loud-speaker, and put the handset down. He gunned the car up the exit ramp, and waited for the connection to relink.

'Ted, are you still there?'

The line crackled.

'Yes. What happened?'

'We lost the connection. What were you saying?'

'That I don't give a toss about the preamble, or excuses, or any of that shit. The bottom line is did you convince her? That's all I am interested in . . . So did you?'

'I think so. She seemed to take it on board. Yes.'

'So that's the end of it?'

'It should be, yes.'

'Should be? What do you mean, should? Come on, Jack, that's not good enough. I don't like what I'm hearing. I need to know for a fact that we're clear. Did you ask her outright?'

'Yes.'

'And?'

'And I think she took it. I mean, she's a real smartarse, Ted – you know the sort – but she implied she was convinced. She just wouldn't commit verbally.' He hated to hear himself say that. He floored the accelerator. 'I'm pretty certain it'll be OK.'

The line buzzed as he passed some unseen power supply.

'That's bullshit and you know it. There's no point in getting it in her mouth if you can't make her swallow. Otherwise she'll spit it back in your face when you're least expecting it. So, I think it's safest to assume she'll keep digging. And that's not what I needed to hear. We can't afford this at the moment.'

The speaker crackled and went silent.

'Are you still there?' Jack asked, pulling the car out around a slow-moving delivery van.

'Yes, I'm here. I was just running through the options . . . I'm very disappointed you didn't get a result, Jack. It's what I pay you for.'

'Sorry, but . . .'

'Shut up. Apologies won't get us anywhere. We need this sorted out fast. And it looks like we only have one option left. So no more pussyfooting around. It's time to take route one. Make it happen, Jack, and don't balls it up this time.'

Jack rolled his eyes. 'Come on. That's sticking our neck out. There must be another way.'

'Look,' the voice said icily, 'we're bending over with our bare arse stuck in the air at the moment. And it's not you who's about to be shafted. I can't afford to take any risks. The stakes are far too high. So do what it takes. And do it soon. I need some firm assurances . . . And whatever else you do, do not fuck it up again. All right?'

'What about . . .?' Jack started to say, but the line went dead.

He pumped the pedal again, and hammered through the lights. They had been red for over a second, and a taxi jolted to a halt as he shot through the junction.

'Bitch,' he spat, hitting the wheel with the ball of his hand. A haze of saliva rained across the steering column. His face was completely washed out in the sodium glare. The overheads flashed off his eyes. His irises looked completely black.

Nobody made him look like a fool. Nobody. Ted Shaw could go and fuck himself for all he cared. But he had his professional pride to think about.

He picked up the handset, and dialled another number.

# 18

Alex turned sideways and looked at herself in the mirror on her wardrobe. She pinched her battered 501s together at the front to see how they looked.

Not bad, she thought, smiling. Not bad at all; they went well with her old biker boots. She knew she had to dress down for Amy as she didn't want to look completely out of place among her artily crusty friends.

Jasper padded up and rubbed himself against her leg.

'What do you reckon, Jasp?' she said, lowering her hip and sticking her backside out. 'Do I look the part or what?'

She dug around in the cupboard, and pulled out a chunky black belt, hooking it through the loops in her jeans and pulling it tight. The old denim was soft against the back of her legs, making her skin prickle lushly with anticipation. She hitched up the Levis and jutted her hip out in front of the mirror. They looked good. Her stomach was beginning to buzz.

She was surprised by how much she needed to get out.

She ran her fingers down the front of the soft denim – pushing her nail between the studs of the fly. She could feel the damp warmth of her body pulsing through the thin cotton of her knickers. She rolled her shoulders and closed her eyes, feeling the lush heat of desire wash through her body.

It was a long time since she had felt it so sweetly. Uusually it came as a sudden surge some time in the dead of night, when frustration held her tense and awake. But she could deal with that on her own, deftly stimulating herself until the lust exploded away as fast as it had arrived.

But this was different. It was the slow burn of desire. The rose-coloured warmth that craved someone else. Someone special.

It was a long time since she had felt it so strongly – since she had wanted to be fucked so badly.

She dragged her nails slowly upward then pulled them away. The chance of meeting anyone half decent among Amy's motley crew was pretty slim. But it still felt nice; it made her feel whole and attractive – a fully fledged woman.

She stepped up to the mirror, pouted her lips, and smeared them a deep, rich red. It would leave a satisfying stain on her cigarette filter. She dropped the lipstick into her bag, and looked at herself again in the mirror, deciding to keep the dark red silk shirt unbuttoned over her Lycra body. Then she went to work on her eyes.

When she had finished she was pleased with the result. She dabbed some Escape behind her ear, then wiped the rest down the front of her jeans.

It was time to party!

She looked at her watch. She had ten minutes before she had to leave for the bus; just enough time for a swig of J&B and a cigarette to calm her nerves.

The taxi dropped her back outside the house at just after three. The clock on the church nearby was slow and was still ringing up the last note. It was the latest she had been back in months.

She giggled as she tried to fish some change out of her pocket. The cabby was itching to get back into town for a last fare, and she managed to drop a pound coin on the floor before she finally paid him.

'Ni-ight,' she said amiably as she slammed the door.

She rocked unsteadily on the kerb as the cab pulled away, and wondered where her keys were. She dug into her pockets – but they weren't there, and for some reason it all seemed very funny.

'Oh dear,' she giggled, putting her head on one side.

She stood on the path uncertainly and wondered what to do. Then, as the cold air cleared her head slightly, she realised what the lump that had been sticking in her backside all evening was. Her keys were in her back pocket.

'Go-oood,' she said, patting them with her hand. It was time for bed.

She had been mildly interested in one of Amy's friends. He had come on to her all night, and had been nice-looking – without a nose-ring in sight. And he had been able to string whole paragraphs together that weren't about himself – which was quite rare in the men she came across. She had enjoyed the constant attention. But now she was near clean sheets and sleep, she knew she had made a good call. She was looking forward to the warmth of her bed – on her own.

The big dark house sat between her and the door to her flat. She wrapped her arms across her chest and walked briskly through the gate.

Around the back a dark shape moved, shying into the dark, away from the noise of her feet.

She carefully stepped into the pitch-black side alley, and cursed silently as her heel skidded, knowing the rancid green goo would get wedged in the tread on her boots. That was something to look forward to in the morning, she thought. She moved over to the edge, walking uncertainly against the wall, and whistling quietly through her teeth.

She stopped halfway down the alley and lifted her sole, but it was too dark to see the damage. She was just about to set off again when something scraped against the concrete at the end of the alley.

She froze – the smile gone from her face – and raised her head, straining her eyes to make out what it was. But it was too dark. All she could see was the oily darkness, and the faint outline of the corner of the house.

She held her breath, trying to make out something else, but it was silent again. All she could hear was the thud of her quickening heart. The cold air wrapped itself around her. She let the air out of her lungs slowly, wisps of white vapour curling from her mouth.

A cat, she thought. It had to be a cat. There were hundreds around here. Maybe it was Jasper, even – although he was too bright to be out on such a cold night. She slowly stepped forward, her boots sounding loud on the rough surface.

She tried to concentrate on the space at the end of the alley as she approached it. She could make out the sharp black edge of the house and a deep blue darkness behind. There was nobody there, she thought. It definitely must have been one of Jasper's buddies coming round to play. She felt her stomach muscles start to unknot.

She stepped tentatively around the corner. There was slightly more light there, and she could see the outline of the door. She put her hand around her back to get the keys out of her pocket.

She was about the pull them out when the feeling hit her.

She felt a damp, cold finger of terror run slowly down her back, her skin bristling and pulling back from its icy touch.

Suddenly time seemed to slow down as something went off in her head; a vague but agitated warning signal that told her – with absolute clarity – that she was in danger. She felt her head spin, fighting the conflicting urges to run and stay as still as possible – she instinctively opted for the second, not knowing which way to go.

She felt the cold metal of her keys and pulled her hand slowly from her pocket, hardly daring to breathe. The rest of her body was completely still.

As the keys came out of her pocket, her hand twitched slightly, and suddenly they were gone, falling away and clattering to the floor. The metallic tinkling reverberated back off the concrete and brick, shattering the silence like breaking glass.

She didn't move to pick them up. She scanned the dark space out of the corner of her eyes, but she couldn't see anything.

But she knew. She could feel the presence – *his* presence.

A dog barked miles away, but everything else was silent.

Then suddenly her breath came through her nose in a nervous snort as she made him out; a dark shape at the edge of her vision. He was close – much closer than she had expected – almost standing by her side.

Her mouth dropped open and she heard her breath come out in a hoarse croak. She tried to move, but nothing seemed to happen.

'All right, darling?' said a male voice slowly, a laconic sneer snaking under the calm surface. She felt the static bristle across the hair on her neck – the hand of the Devil caressing her skin.

'Who . . .?' she started to ask, but the rest of the sentence snagged in her throat.

She managed to turn her head stiffly.

All she could see was his outline – a dark empty space soaking up the light like a black hole. But she could tell he was big.

'What do you want?' she heard herself croak weakly. Her bones had seized together, locked fast in panic. But her muscles twitched in a spasm of uncontrollable fear; she felt a crippling wave of panic engulf her. She knew he was going to hurt her.

He stepped forward, and the little light there was disappeared behind his bulk.

'What the fuck do you think?' he said mockingly. She could smell the rancid stench of stale beer on his breath.

'Oh, sweet Jesus,' she whispered, backing away. She felt the ice-cold bricks against her palms.

'He ain't here, sweetheart. It's just you and me . . . if you know what I mean.'

She wanted to scream but her voice was lost way, way down in her throat, and the saliva in her mouth had turned into a thick, sticky glue. She moved back against the wall, the muscles in her groin tightening. She had often imagined what she would do at a moment like this. It had all seemed so obvious. But now it was happening she was transfixed. Sheer terror made it impossible to do anything.

She pushed up against the bricks – and she knew there was no way out.

He moved slowly at first. He ran his hand up the smooth skin of her neck, caressing her jaw, then pushing her up against the wall. His breath came out short and hard as he touched her, snorting through his nose. She felt sick, a red-hot uncontrollable churning in her guts, and her body recoiled, pulling back from his touch.

She felt his other hand move against her chest – a slow, cold pressure like a huge slug sliding across her skin – and she twitched; a reflex spasm against his clutching hand. He pushed her hard against the wall, and she felt his fingers dig into her neck and the soft flesh of her breast.

Then he snapped; a flurry of movement, and the charge of animal lust crackling in the darkness. He moved so fast she didn't

107

know what was happening. He pulled her forward then slammed her back against the wall, hammering the air out of her lungs. She saw white lights as her skull hit the brick, and felt her lungs contract.

Then she felt something tugging at her belt. A frenzied yanking, ripping at the leather. The ridge of her jeans cut up into her crotch, and she started to panic; a thin noise came from deep down in her throat and a cold dead feeling ran up her body. He was trying to drag her jeans down.

And he was laughing; a cruel, mocking, soulless noise. She tried to keep her knees together but he jammed his leg in between them.

She managed to raise her hand. It was only a flutter, a reflex action, but it connected with something, sticking slightly as her nail dug into his skin.

'Bitch,' he spat, slamming her back against the bricks again.

He dragged her forward. Her legs started to buckle, but he held her up.

'OK, that's enough,' another voice said calmly.

She twisted her head to see where it came from, but she couldn't see anything. All she could make out was swirling darkness. She let her head fall forward; it felt heavy, far too heavy for her neck. She felt like a rag doll, hanging limply, waiting for the cruel twist of childish hands.

She was on the edge of consciousness and she wasn't sure what was happening any more.

'Now, Alex,' the new voice continued. She raised her head; hearing her name gave her something to hang on to. She blinked and swallowed, and tried to support her weight on her legs. 'What I want you to do is think hard about what would have happened if I hadn't been here. Think very hard indeed. Then listen carefully to what I have to say.'

Then a fist hammered into her face. She felt a searing pain behind her eyes. Her nose was blocked, and her legs collapsed underneath her.

She came round on the ground and felt something pressing down hard on her neck. She didn't know what had happened for a second. She was finding it difficult to breathe. Her head felt as if it were on fire, but the rest of her body was freezing, the little

108

heat there was soaking away into the icy concrete. Then it came back to her. Another wave of panic pulsed through her, and she tried to struggle.

'Stay still, you stupid bitch,' the first voice said coldly. 'Or I'll fuck you in the mouth, up the arse – where I want. You hear me?'

She froze, feeling the pressure increase on her throat. He was standing above her with his boot pressed down on her neck. Cold dead fear sapped the energy from her limbs.

Then the other voice came from the side. He was squatting down beside her.

'I must apologise for my colleague, Ms Brierley. He has no manners. But – at this juncture – it's probably worth remembering that if there has to be a next time, he'll be on his own. I suggest you keep that firmly in your mind.'

Her eyes wouldn't focus, but she could see a dark leg towering above her, and the vague outline of a body.

'Now pay attention,' the second voice continued. 'I want you to listen. And listen well. Because this is your one big chance to save your pretty face.'

She tried to twist her head so she could breathe better, but the boot pushed down harder, causing her to gag.

'So,' he continued softly, 'since I want you to take this very seriously, and since we're not prepared to play games any more, I want you to remember how it feels.'

The pressure on her neck relaxed. She heaved air into her lungs, and was starting to twist over when the boot slammed into her side. It was like being stabbed – a massive white-hot pain. Her ribs buckled and sprang back. She screamed in her head, but nothing would come out of her mouth.

He kicked her again – this time harder.

Her body snapped, a whiplash of pure, excruciating pain streaking through her bones as the steel toecap came down full force.

Then the boot was back on her neck. Her head pleaded for oxygen but there was none there, and suddenly she was sure she was going to die.

'So, about this business with the Kallman Institute, Alex. This is what I want you to do. I want you to tell me you're looking for something that isn't there. And I want you to tell me you'll leave well alone from now on. OK? It's as simple as that.'

Alex could feel the blood pressure behind her eyes; a thick, bulging pressure that bent her vision.

'And I want to hear it from your pretty lips.' He leant closer.

She tried to concentrate but she couldn't make her mouth work.

'Make me believe you,' he whispered.

Her voice cracked in her throat, but no words came out.

'Again,' the voice said louder, sounding bored.

This time the toe of the boot sank right between her ribs, and she convulsed with one sharp, sickening snap of her spine. Bile gurgled up in her throat, and ate into the thin skin at the back of her mouth.

'OK,' she managed to say thickly. Her nails scraped across the rough concrete.

Her hip jolted as the boot jabbed at her knee, splaying her legs apart.

'OK what?'

'OK. Whatever . . . whatever you want.'

'You'll forget that the Kallman Institute even exists. That's what I want. Will you tell me you'll do that for me?'

'Ye-es,' she said, choking.

'Good . . . I'm glad to hear it. Now that wasn't too hard, was it?'

She gagged as vomit rose in her throat, held back by the constriction on her neck.

'That's enough,' he commanded quietly, and the pressure was lifted.

'This is your one and only chance, Alex. Leave well alone and you'll be OK. Do anything – *anything* – that connects you to Kallman again, and you'll wish you hadn't been born.'

She heard them step around her, gravel grating under their feet.

'Think about it.'

She realised they were going. A pathetic feeling of relief swamped her, and she almost wanted to thank them. She rolled stiffly onto her side, and could see them moving in the dark.

Her eyes were full of water. She tried to focus, grit scraping painfully against her retinas as she blinked.

Suddenly the whole place was flooded in bright light. The harsh glare pierced her pupils, stabbing at her optic nerve. She put her hand up to protect her eyes. She wasn't sure what was happening. Then she realised that they must have triggered the infrared light in the garden next door – it happened if you got too near the fence.

The first figure had disappeared into the alley, but as she looked up she saw the other. She took in every feature of his face under the thousand-watt lamp.

He saw her, and stepped forward. She closed her eyes and prayed, waiting for the impact.

When he spoke it was the first voice she had heard.

'If you do anything stupid, bitch, I'll come for you. You fucking hear that? Now keep that in your head and go and look at your car. Then think about your face. All right?' Anger twisted his face. 'All right?'

'Yes,' she heard herself croak; her lips felt bone dry as she spoke. Then her vision suddenly jumped like a faulty TV, and she felt her head spin.

'One false move and I'll have you on a fucking meat rack.'

She shut her eyes, sure he would kick her again. There was nothing she could do. She couldn't even tense her muscles against the assault. But nothing happened, and when she opened her eyes it was dark and he had gone.

She tried to turn over, but her ribs wouldn't let her. The pain was excruciating; it felt as if a knife were slicing into her when she tried to move. She clawed at the floor, her eyes panning dully across the sky, and passed out.

When she came around, she was freezing – colder than she had ever been before – and it took her a long time to move. She groped for her keys, found them, and crawled slowly to her front door.

She pulled herself up and dragged herself down the hall, gagging on the acidic vomit at the back of her throat. She walked unsteadily into the bathroom and looked at herself in the mirror; there was pigeon shit in her hair, and the side of her face was red and raw. Then she threw up in the basin, a thick, biley vomit

111

hanging from her mouth. She wiped it away with the back of her hand, and spat the blood-flecked dregs into the sink.

She was so scared she couldn't stop shaking.

She hugged herself tightly, but it didn't make any difference. She needed to be somewhere safe.

She stumbled into the kitchen, picked up the phone and punched Amy's number.

'It's four thirty, Alex. What's going on?' Amy drawled sleepily.

'I've just been beaten up,' Alex said, her voice cracking. She started to cry. Big sobs rattled in her throat, and made short stabs of pain shoot through her abdomen. 'Please come and get me.'

Alex stared blankly at the dark patch on the side of her Mazda, while Amy unlocked the passenger door of her battered old Metro. The acid still fizzed at the edges, and the front tyre shone glossily where the paint stripper had flowed down it. She could smell burning rubber and imagined the acid digging into her face. She could almost feel it on her skin.

'Come on, chicken,' Amy said softly, as she gently steered Alex towards her car. 'Let's get you out of here.'

Amy drove quickly through the empty back streets, concentrating silently on the road until she pulled into a tight space a little way down from her house; she lived in a ramshackle terrace deep in the heart of student-land, and the road was cluttered with dilapidated cars and posh little rich-kid hatchbacks. She jerked on the handbrake, then turned and gently put her hand under Alex's chin. Alex's left eye was beginning to close as the swelling turned black.

'Bastard,' Amy murmured. 'Who did it, Alex? Why did they do this to you?'

Alex put her hands over her face and shook her head.

Amy's voice rose slightly. 'Come on, Alex. Was it an old boyfriend or something?'

'Not now,' Alex said, avoiding her gaze. 'Maybe later.'

'OK,' Amy said, smiling. 'Whenever.' She bent down to meet Alex's eyes. 'Is it always this exciting when you go out?'

Alex managed to smile. 'That was a dull night. You want to see it when I'm on a roll.' She shut her eyes and felt the muscles

112

in her neck go slack; she was suddenly overwhelmed with exhaustion. The adrenaline had left her, leaving her limbs heavy and tired.

'I think I need to sleep,' she said, hardly moving her mouth.

'Come on,' Amy said, jerking open the door. 'Let's get you in.'

Alex lay in the dark for a long time, the room spinning around her, and slowly drifted into a restless half-sleep, caught somewhere in the hinterland between conscious and unconscious; the delta state, when the mind runs wild on its own. Her eyelids flickered as a montage of vivid images started to unwind in her head.

Suddenly she was in a bright, white space where light swamped everything, bleaching out the background and stabbing at her eyes. Laughter echoed around, booming like the sounds in a swimming pool, and she could see the vague, hazy outlines of people moving in front of her. Then someone pushed her hard in the back and she fell forward, her hands and knees ripping as she landed on all fours. She could feel something around her neck, someone behind her, but she couldn't see who it was.

She heard a mirthless laughter in front of her and looked up. And there – every feature sharply focused in the white, white glare – was Jack O'Neill sitting at a table. Or something that looked like him. It was a sneering caricature of O'Neill, half-person, half-jackal, the lips pulled back, exposing long, sharp teeth and bright red gums.

As he got up and walked towards her, someone grabbed her from behind, pulling her up on her knees. O'Neill smiled slightly as he stepped in front of her. His skin was bone white and his gaze bore into her, staring right into her soul.

He stopped and let his eyes run down her body, then touched the bulging skin of her belly and shook his head. She flinched, feeling something stir inside. Then his mouth started to move soundlessly, repeating the same phrase, over and over; he was slapping her hard across the face as he enunciated each word.

She woke with a start, and glanced around in panic until she realised she had been asleep. The words were still looping in her mind.

113

'Oh God,' she said, gritting her teeth as a pulse of dull pain throbbed through her body. She had never been so scared in her life. She just wanted to crawl away and hide. But she knew she couldn't. Those words were there in her head.

You – can – run – but – you – can't – hide.

She didn't want to shut her eyes again because she knew she would see O'Neill's glossy black pupils staring back.

Maybe this was her payback? she thought, staring into space. What goes around, comes around.

Eventually she fell into a fitful, uneasy sleep. The face that she had seen in the light outside her flat kept coming back to haunt her. And in her dreams he was on his own.

# 19

He carefully pulled his legs out from under the steering wheel and swung them up onto the passenger seat. He still had a while to wait; the first cars had only just begun to arrive. He leant forward and wiped the condensation off the windscreen with his sleeve, rubbing the glass carefully, then leaning back again. It gave him a clear view of the entrance to the swimming pool.

The carpark was shrouded in a grainy, grey half-light – it was still too early for the overhead floods. He watched the huge brake lights of a big Audi flare as it jerked to a halt in a parking space by the door.

He watched closely as a man pulled himself out of the car and glanced anxiously at his watch. A dad, he thought, smiling as the man tried in vain to set his car alarm with the remote. A very rare species – he probably had a wife who couldn't drive, wouldn't drive, or was just too tranked-up to make the journey. Or maybe he was one of those blokes who insisted on making the run even though he didn't have the time. He grinned and watched the figure stride across the carpark, trying to pull his jacket on and jab at a mobile phone at the same time. First call before breakfast, he thought. That was a bad habit. A forty-calls-a-day man.

He looked at his watch – 6.55 am – five minutes before the training session ended. He twisted around and cranked the window open slightly. The car was a rusty old D-reg Volvo estate; and old smoker that blended perfectly with the jaunty hatchbacks and cronky second cars that came to pick the kids up, whisking them back home before school – but he missed the luxury of electrics and a decent stereo. He dug into his tracksuit pocket, pulled out a packet of JPS and lit one, blowing the smoke over his shoulder towards the gap in the window.

He felt the tingling again, and squeezed his legs together. This was the bit he enjoyed. Watching the kids thin out until only one was left.

He leant back against the door and watched as the cars started to cruise past, each one trying to park as close to the entrance as possible.

Suzanne took the turn off the main road too fast, hanging on grimly to the wheel as the car lurched up the sliproad towards the pool.

'Bugger, bugger, bugger,' she mouthed silently. This was the third time she had been late in a fortnight. It was almost as if David was doing it deliberately – lingering over his breakfast so she would only just make it in time. It was ironic – all those times she had banged on about him not talking to her, and nothing, and now suddenly he got all chatty.

She bounced over the last sleeping policeman, pulling a face as she heard the exhaust pipe scrape the ground. She could feel the sweat beading out in her bristly armpits. She hadn't bothered to shave them the night before, which was a first.

Maybe things were cooling off.

She looked anxiously at the carpark. It was all but empty – but there were two cars left; a big estate car and a dark saloon parked way over in the corner.

She felt the edges of her mouth rise.

He was still there, she thought. And she was pleased – so maybe not!

She pulled the car around in a tight curve, and parked right by the front door.

She got out quickly, keeping her back to the carpark, and locked the door. Then, with a quick glance over her shoulder, she walked briskly towards the pool entrance.

'Oh, hi, Ella, sweetheart,' she said as she rushed into the lobby. 'I'm so sorry I'm late.'

She pulled her gloves off and yanked the handbag out from under her arm as the little girl turned from the noticeboard. She

116

was the last one there, Suzanne realised – that was twice now that she had been the last one left on her own. This is getting out of hand, she thought unhappily – but she kept the big smile on her face. 'Listen, honey,' she said, rummaging in her bag, 'can you just wait here a little big longer? I've just got to talk to somebody.'

She pulled out a lipstick and a little mirror and quickly smeared her bottom lip.

'But Mum-my, I need to get to school early today.'

Suzanne sucked in her bottom lip, then pressed both lips together to spread the lipstick out evenly.

'It won't take a sec, sweetie, OK?' she said, rubbing some stray red off her skin.

'But I don't want to wait around,' Ella said, twisting her hands behind her back.

Suzanne looked at her sadly; she had her own fair complexion and soft blonde hair, but the twitchy mannerisms and whine were all David's. She stroked her hand down the side of her face.

'I won't be long, sweetie, honest. Now you wait here.'

'OK,' Ella said sulkily. 'Can I have a hot chocolate while I wait?'

'Sure,' Suzanne conceded, digging into her bag for her purse. She pulled out a pound coin and gave it to her. 'There you go. Get some crisps as well.'

'Can I have an Aero as well?'

'Sure, sure, of course. Whatever you want. I mean, you've earned it, haven't you?'

Ella smiled, exposing the space where her front baby teeth had just fallen out. 'Thanks, Mum.'

Suzanne watched as she set off towards the vending machine. A pang of guilt clutched her gut. 'Stay here, honey,' she shouted after her. 'Until Mummy comes back.' Then she turned, pushed open the doors and went back out into the carpark.

Outside the light was improving rapidly. She glanced briefly at the shabby Volvo in the middle of the carpark, then turned and walked quickly towards the Mondeo parked in the dark space in the corner by the trees.

As she turned her back on the swimming pool the door of the Volvo swung open behind her.

He watched her walk awkwardly across the tarmac, her back straight and her head held high. It had become a bit of a ritual; normally she was there half an hour earlier, but she was getting later. He knew she wouldn't look back. She never did.

He watched as she pulled open the passenger door, and with a flick of the hair and twitch of the hips she was gone, disappearing into the darkness of the car – shrouded by the overhanging branches from the big evergreens.

Slipping off the path of life and into the darkness, he thought, smiling grimly.

He dug his hands into his pockets and set off towards the pool.

She was standing by the vending machine when he got in. He unzipped his tracksuit top and walked towards her, the stopwatch around his neck swinging slightly as he moved.

'You having problems, love?' he asked casually, as he walked behind her towards the noticeboard.

She turned her head, looking at him over her shoulder.

'It doesn't seem to be working.'

'Oh, not again!' he tutted. He turned back around and ambled up to her. 'Let's have a look.'

He glanced down at her. She had big blue eyes, a little turned-up nose and a smattering of freckles. She was so perfect – so close to how he remembered that he had to remind himself where he was, and stop himself from reaching out to hold her.

'Now then.' He squinted at the machine. 'What did you select?'

'Hot chocolate.'

'Ah well, that's it, then,' he said, squatting down and holding her arm. 'See that little orange light there?' He pointed at the machine.

'Yes.'

'That means it's run out. Now is there anything else you would like?'

'What about a frothy coffee?'

He squinted up at the machine again.

'Yep, that looks OK ... frothy coffee it is, then,' he said brightly, getting up.

'With extra sugar.'

'For you, princess,' he laughed, 'whatever you want.'

He pressed the button and stepped back to her side as the cup fell and the machine began to whirr.

'No!' Suzanne protested, taking his hand off her leg.

'Why not?'

'Because this is getting sordid.'

He twisted in his seat and looked at her, a sad expression suddenly filling his face. Normally she loved the way he showed his emotions so easily, but today it just annoyed her.

'So you don't enjoy it any more?' he asked quietly.

'That's not what I said.'

'Well, what, then?'

'Look,' she said, turning to him, her eyes flashing, 'I'm thirty-eight years old and I'm married. *You're* married, for Christ's sake. And we're shagging each other in a carpark. We're not kids any more.'

He looked down and blinked.

'Come on, Chris . . .' she said in exasperation.

'I don't know,' he said unhappily. 'I just want to be with you, that's all, but . . .'

'But what?'

'But I don't know what.'

She looked at him for a long moment, then put out her hand.

'We need to talk about this,' she said tenderly.

'I know,' he agreed, looking up.

'But not now. Not here.'

Ella sat on the bottom step, blowing the steam off her cup. She looked so small, he thought, sitting there on her own. And so fragile. He wanted to put his arm around her tightly, and look after, care for her – make sure she was safe. He suddenly felt dizzy, the familiar spinning as his mind searched for something that wasn't there any more. He closed his eyes tightly, and tried to stop it. Sometimes he felt like a space traveller lost way out in space, knowing that the planet he had left behind had been destroyed – a huge wrecked void inside him where all the connections to his friends and family had been torn out. He felt as if he were drifting alone, moving away from where he was meant to be, but knowing there was nothing back there to return to. He

119

opened his eyes and looked at her again.

You little bitch, he thought, as he watched her play with her hair. You stupid little bitch. Why couldn't you look after yourself?

He turned stiffly and peered through the armoured glass door, squinting at the car over by the trees.

'Listen, love, I've got to go,' he said, walking back slowly with a concerned expression on his face. 'What's your mummy look like?'

'She's sort of big, with white hair.'

'White hair?'

'Like mine.'

'Ah, blonde, you mean?'

'Yes, blonde, that's it.'

'And was she wearing jeans and a big blue jumper?'

'Yes. Do you know her?'

'No.' He looked at his watch. 'It's just that I think I saw her driving off with someone when I came in, that's all.' He zipped up his tracksuit top. 'Anyway . . .' he started to say, then stopped as he saw the look of dismay of her face. 'What's wrong?'

'She can't have gone.'

He stepped up to her and squatted down, putting his hand on her shoulder. 'It's OK, love. I'm sure she'll be back.'

She stared at her feet and tears welled up in her eyes.

He glanced at his watch again.

'I've got to go now, love, but maybe . . .' He glanced over at the door as if he were thinking. 'Look why don't I give you a lift?'

She looked up at him quickly, an expression of confusion flitting across her face. 'I'm not meant to take lifts.'

'Yeah, you're right,' he said, getting up. 'I'll be off, then. Take care.'

He started to stride towards the door.

'Bye . . .' she said uncertainly.

He stopped with his back to her and smiled. *Gotcha*, he thought – that thin, sad tone in her voice said it all. He dug his hand into his pocket, and slowly fingered the coil of fuse wire with his index finger. It felt cold and sharp; thin, gritty metal that wouldn't give.

'Gotcha!' he murmured, then adjusted his expression and turned back to her.

'I'll tell you what,' he suggested, as if the idea had just come to him. 'Why don't we stick a note on the front door?'

'Well . . .' She twisted her hands behind her back and bit her lip.

He walked back to her, smiling.

'OK,' she agreed slowly.

'Great.' He put out his hand to help her up. 'Come on, then.'

He was just about to turn when he saw her staring at the door, her eyes suddenly bright and wide.

'There she is,' she said, pointing.

He glanced over his shoulder. He could see the shape of a woman outside, cut in half by the metal strip down the middle of the door. She was rummaging in her bag while she patted her hair down with her hand.

He knew why, he thought, straining to stop his lips curling. He squeezed the coil in his pocket and felt the thin wire bite into his palm.

'Go and let her in, love.' His voice wavered.

Ella scuttled towards the door.

'Hi, Mummy,' she said as Suzanne pulled the door open. 'We thought you'd gone.'

'Who's we?' Suzanne asked, still looking in her bag. She put her hand in, pulled out her lipstick, and awkwardly smeared her lips while she clamped the bag under her arm.

'Me and . . .' Ella looked over her shoulder – but no one was there. 'There was a man.'

'Where?' Suzanne asked, glancing up quickly.

'He was here,' Ella whispered, sounding confused. 'But now he's . . . gone.'

Suzanne slowly dropped the lipstick and mirror back into her bag and looked around. The lobby was warm and damp from the pool water, but suddenly she felt cold.

'Come on.' She felt for Ella's hand, her eyes darting around the lobby. A cold, dirty sweat prickled her skin – and she suddenly felt soiled by Chris's touch.

She pulled open the door and dragged Ella out. She had a strange feeling like vertigo – as if she had just stepped very close

121

to the edge of a huge drop without actually knowing it.

'Come on. We need to go,' she said, her voice shaking as she spoke.

Outside the sun had spread a thin light across the tarmac – and both cars had gone.

She hugged Ella close to her side, pulling her quickly towards her car.

# 20

Alex felt the wind drag at her hair as she looked down on the wide open space – a huge, blank wilderness that melted away into a blanket of milky-white sky. She felt the air buffet her, but nothing else – nothing holding her, nothing solid under her feet.

She watched helplessly as way, way down below her, the dark figure passed behind the little girl. She felt her mouth moving, her lungs straining as she shouted – telling her to run, to come towards her – but the words were torn away from her mouth and sent cascading across the sky.

The girl suddenly looked up at Alex and smiled, the wind slapping her blonde hair across her face and the light sparkling on her pale blue eyes. Behind her the dark creature slowed and turned its head, stalking painfully on all fours – it was almost a man, but the back was broken, hunched up at the neck, and the lips were pulled back away from the gums.

'Noooooooo!' Alex cried, her voice suddenly dull and flat in her head.

Then the sky started to darken, curdling from cream through yellow to a thick, fleshy pink. The creature looked up at her, arrogantly meeting her gaze, taunting her to do something.

But the wind held her there, a spectator, unable to get down.

The sky darkened further, sending a shadow racing across the empty plain.

He switched his gaze to the girl and smiled.

'No,' she heard herself whimper.

'Alex,' someone said softly.

Then – with the small girl still unaware, still staring wide-eyed into the sky – the beast turned away, and started to lumber slowly off into the darkness.

'Alex!' the voice said more urgently.

'Thank you,' Alex murmured as the creature disappeared into the darkness. She had another chance!

The image began to fade as she was pulled higher, dragged away into the sky.

'I'm sorry,' Alex whispered as she strained to see the girl, a tiny fleck in the wilderness. Suddenly alone under the blood red sky.

'It's OK,' Amy said, gently shaking her shoulder.

'What?' Alex muttered uncertainly, trying to open her eyes.

'It's OK.' Amy sat down on the edge of the bed. 'It's me. Amy.'

Alex moaned and tried to bury her head in the pillow.

'Come on,' Amy whispered, touching her shoulder again. 'Look at me.'

'No.' She squeezed her eyes shut against the light.

'Come on, let's have a look, sweetheart. The sheets are covered in blood.'

'I'll be OK.' Alex rubbed her eyes with her knuckles, then opened the left one.

'Yeah, right,' Amy said, stroking her hair. 'There can't be that much left inside you.'

Alex pulled her hand away from her face and opened her other eye. She wasn't quite sure where she was. Her mind struggled to tease the memory of the night before out from the blur of dreams.

'Good grief, Alex. You look like the living dead. I'm taking you to hospital.'

'No,' Alex murmured, putting her hand up to shield her eyes.

'*Alex!*'

'I'll be alright. I just need to rest.'

'You need to see a doctor.'

'Look, I'll be alright,' Alex said, trying to push herself up on her elbows. 'Honestly. It probably looks worse than it really is. I just need to rest.'

'OK,' Amy conceded, raising her hands. 'OK. Whatever you

say. It's your body at the end of the day. But if you die in here I'm not going to move you.'

Alex managed to smile.

She looked up at the window – a thin grey light seeped in through the nets.

'What time is it?'

'Four o'clock,' Amy said. 'In the afternoon,' she added when she saw Alex's look of confusion.

'How long have I been asleep?' Alex asked, sinking down into the bed again.

'About twelve hours.'

She shut her eyes, suddenly overwhelmed by exhaustion again.

'I think . . .' she said, shutting her eyes. 'I think I just need to sleep, that's all.'

She felt the bed bounce as Amy got up.

'OK, I'll come back later.'

Alex heard her softly walk across the room and pull the curtains shut. The inside of her eyelids darkened, and she let herself go, gratefully falling into a deep, dreamless sleep.

# 21

Hague adjusted the air-conditioning dial on the wall, then walked quickly around the conference-room table. 'I'm sorry I'm late, Harris,' he said briskly as he placed his briefcase on the floor. He pulled out a chair. 'You wanted to see me?'

'Yes, sir.'

'What can I do for you?'

'I think we might be off the mark, sir.'

'Really? What makes you say that?'

'I don't think this is about prostitutes, sir. None of the girls on the streets we've spoken to have reported anyone unusual. Just regular punters, nothing else.'

'Come on!' Hague laughed. 'These are tarts we're talking about here. Not Tesco's. There is no such thing as business as usual.'

'There's something else as well. We had a report a couple of days ago about a possible aborted abduction at a swimming pool. It was very close to a school, sir, and that was where he abandoned his last victim. I think they might be connected.'

'Go on.'

'It was a little girl, sir. Nine years old. Blonde.'

'What?'

'She was blonde, sir. All the victims have been blonde, similar physical characteristics, and young – or at least they appeared to be young. I think it's worth chasing up.'

'Do you have anything concrete to base this on?'

'Well, so far the mother's been quite evasive. Her story doesn't add up. I'd like to bring her in and push her a bit.'

'You're talking about bringing in innocent members of the public when we've got the full glare of the media on us? For what? The vaguest of hunches. There's nothing connecting this. This is just a normal little girl, for Christ's sake.'

'I think it's worth the risk, sir.'

'Well, I don't, Harris. I think they'd skin us. If we chased every paranoid mother's lead up we'd have every middle-class woman in the city in here.'

'Look, sir, I honestly think there's something there. I can feel it. I think we're wrong to assume he'll stick with prostitutes.'

'All four of his victims have been tarts. Granted, all blonde and young. But that's no surprise. Are you telling me that's coincidence?'

'No, sir. But prostitutes are an obvious starting point. They're vulnerable. I think he's working up to something.'

'Look, Harris,' Hague said, frowning. 'This is all very interesting. But it's supposition. And what I'm interested in is facts. This is a modern, sophisticated case, so we need to use modern, sophisticated techniques. Tried and tested. Evidence-based. Not gut feeling and hunches. Professor Miller is one of the best criminal psychologists in the land, so I think we can be assured he knows what he's talking about, OK? So I think it would be better if you used your creative thinking to work out how best to approach your own tasks. We've had clearance to start chasing up the drivers of the cars we've picked up on the CCTV on Mapperley Road. So I want you on it as soon as possible. OK?'

'Yes, sir.'

# 22

Alex shook two of the big red painkillers into her hand and looked at them. She was only meant to take one at a time, but she had been downing them in twos ever since Amy had brought them back with her from work. She was pretty sure they weren't doing her liver or kidneys any good. But then they had reduced the pain to a dull ache.

Two more aren't going to make any difference, she thought, as she lobbed them in her mouth.

She swallowed them with a mouthful of lukewarm coffee and went over to the bay window, kicking a discarded kebab wrapper out of the way – she was beginning to run out of ideas on how to entertain herself.

The doctor had told her to rest for at least a week, which had seemed like a great idea at the time, but now she'd been cooped up in the house for three days she was beginning to climb the walls.

She watched as a cat stalked carefully along the top of the wall across the road. This is getting me nowhere, she thought. She lit a cigarette, blew a cloud of smoke towards the ceiling, and went over to the big gilt-edged mirror hanging over the fireplace.

She looked at her bruised face in the blotchy glass. The angry swelling under her eyes had subsided to deep black.

That would go, she thought, as would the raw abrasion down the side of her face. But the rest – the fine strands of crow's-feet around her eyes and the little tucks by her mouth – were there to stay. She smiled. She was getting to the point where the pattern of her life would soon be mapped out on her face for everyone to see; happiness, sadness, the pain and the disappointment – it would all be there.

'It's up to you, Al,' she murmured, staring back at herself. 'There's no point in hiding.'

She emerged through the front door just after noon. She pulled Amy's fake fur coat around her, and hitched the sunglasses up on her face; they were black with thick plastic rims, a bit like the ones Jackie O used to wear. Just what she needed to cover up the mess around her eyes.

As she stepped through the gate, a buzz of anticipation – a little warning shot from her memory – made her stomach twinge; suddenly the world seemed very big.

'You'll be alright,' she muttered, digging her hands into the pockets of her coat.

She kept her head up and slowly walked to the bus stop. It seemed to take forever. The traffic noise boomed in her head, and the bright light cut into the corners of her pupils from the sides of the glasses.

She tried to ignore the feeling of sickness in her stomach as the bus slowly pulled up by the city square.

They had rattled her, she thought, stroking her fingers down her face without knowing it. In fact they had scared the living daylights out of her. But the more she thought about it, the more she realised that she had no option but to find out what Numen were trying to hide. Sure, if she stayed on the case and they found her, then acid in the face was the least of her worries. But the thing was, if she went to the police, or anything came out about Numen, then they might just do it anyway; just in case she had been involved or maybe just for the hell of it. She would never know. O'Neill had made a major error by choosing such complete headcases. It had put her in a position where she couldn't back down – because quite simply she had to get them, before they got her. She shuddered when she thought about it. She had felt the pleasure crackle in the air as she was slammed up against the wall, and the reek of violent sexual anger as he pushed up against her. She could still smell it inside her head – his scent was on her, the smell of unfinished business, marking her out for later.

She walked slowly across the square, trying not to glance over her shoulder. It was packed with people enjoying the bright, cool weather. Kids chased the pigeons across the slabs and the light wind blew a haze of water off the fountains into the air. She held her head up stiffly and walked slowly, but surely, towards the library.

She picked up the magazines she had ordered from the counter on the second floor, and took them to a desk hidden at the end of a row of shelves. They were all technical-looking trade magazines, full of earnest-looking articles with abstracts and footnotes.

She sat down and tried to concentrate on the densely typed text. The first two articles were long and extremely technical. She skim-read them, ignoring the more absurd words. She didn't understand a lot of the jargon, but she got the gist; Numen specialised in antidepressants and antipsychotic drugs, and from what she could understand they were working at the cutting edge of the field – although what that meant exactly was beyond her O-level biology vocabulary.

As she worked her way slowly down the pile her brain started to recognise the patterns of the words – tricycle, phenothiazine, psychotropic – working out roughly what they meant from their context.

She stopped halfway down the pile and rubbed her eyes. It was all useful background but it didn't really help. She absent-mindedly flicked through the rest of the pile, and was just about to pick them up and take them back to the desk when her thumb came to rest on a single glossy sheet.

She pulled it out.

It was an analysis extracted from *Pharmaceutical Business Review* – and it was written in something that came pretty close to normal English. She sat up in her chair, and read it carefully. It profiled the Kogai takeover, estimating that they had paid over five times the market value for Numen which – even though Numen was small, and therefore relatively cheap – was a lot to pay. The article speculated on a number of possible reasons why Kogai might have wanted Numen so badly, but came to the conclusion that the only logical answer was that Numen must have a product in development with a massive market potential. If they had, though, what was unusual was that they had kept it very secret; there had been no signs that something was in development. Normal practice was to prime the market with papers and 'intellectual seeding'. But nothing had come from Numen so far. The article ended with the speculative conclusion that since Numen were a biotechnology company, they might well have hit on something completely new – like some of the radical cancer and HIV treatments showing promise at other biotech outfits – but as to what, they weren't really sure yet; it was a *watch this space, buy our next review* kind of ending.

Alex read it three times, trying to understand what it meant. In buying the company outright, Kogai had acquired global rights to the new product. If it existed, that was. And that was a big if. But it did seem the only logical answer to such an over-the-top bid. If Numen had some wonder drug up their sleeve, and there was a worldwide market, Kogai's strength in chemical production would mean that they could meet demands in months. If the market was anywhere near as big as for other blockbuster drugs she had read about, they were talking billions rather than millions of pounds – even a modest seller would pay them back for their investment within a couple of years. So why were they so worried about a tiny operation like the Kallman Institute?

She stacked the magazines in a neat pile, and rocked on the back of her chair. Numen working on something radical was exactly the kind of thing Fisher would have had wet dreams about. It fitted. There was so much smoke she was choking; what she couldn't see was the fire. What she needed now was some hard evidence. She drummed her fingers on the desk, running her tongue across her lips while she thought; since she was less than willing to go back to the Institute, there was only one other place she could think to look.

And it wasn't somewhere she wanted to go.

She took the articles over to the photocopier, and copied the sections that might be useful. When she had finished she returned the magazines to the counter, and asked where she could find the telephone directories.

The autumn sun was dipping coldly towards the rooftops by the time she left the library, throwing grainy white light across the flagstones. The last bright rays caught the clock face high up on the tower of the domed town hall. She walked quickly to the bus stop, glad that the bright daylight was subsiding, but not looking forward to the dark.

The butterflies were beginning to swarm in her stomach. She knew what she had to do – and that if she thought about it for too long she would bottle out.

It was now or never.

# 23

Alex stopped dead as the bough of a tree creaked above her in the darkness. The air around her felt strange – completely still on the ground, but windy high above, with wisps of dark cloud scudding across the star-peppered sky.

She looked into the pitch-black mouth of the drive. The scree of pebbles nearest the entrance seemed to glow slightly, but as she glanced towards the house the bone-white carpet of tiny fragments was swallowed up into the darkness, gradually swamped under a thick yellow matting of rotting leaves.

Jill's house was at the end of a quiet, gloomy cul-de-sac. It was a small postwar bungalow set back in an overgrown garden surrounded by a high evergreen hedge.

Alex knew that if she hung around for too long some curtain-twitching neighbour would spot her. She swallowed hard, and stepped onto the damp gravel; it crunched loudly under her boots as she was sucked up into the shadows.

She walked carefully down the narrow alley between the house and the garage, and slipped into the darkness around the back where the high hedge totally secluded the house.

She glanced at the pale outline of the door frame. She hadn't been sure how she would get in; she had a number of hefty-looking pieces of hardware from Amy's cellar in the duffel bag cutting into her shoulder. But as her eyes adjusted to the darkness, she realised that her entry problem had already been solved.

She felt her legs suddenly go weak.

The good news was that she wouldn't have to force her way in. The bad news – the very, *very* bad news – was that someone had already done it for her. Someone had smashed the lock and kicked the door off its hinges, the buckled panels and sheared screws showing the force that had been used.

The scream of a distant car engine cut sharply into the icy stillness and made her jump. She glanced nervously around the garden.

As she turned back, the light caught on the silvery mesh of a large spider's web woven between the door and the splintered jamb. She felt the tightness in her chest give. There was at least two days' work there, she thought – even for a hyperactive spider.

She took a deep breath and slowly stepped into the house.

She pulled a torch out of the bag, swallowed hard, and clicked it on. The light reflected brightly off shattered plastic and metal. She was in the kitchen. Or what was left of the kitchen. The floor was covered with a rubble of cutlery and trampled food. She stepped carefully over an upturned box, and went through to the hall.

She moved slowly from room to room. The scene was repeated throughout the house. Every room looked as if a hurricane had swept through. They had even emptied the boxes of tampons in the bathroom, strewing them across the floor and into the hall.

There were bits of paper everywhere, but she didn't stop to read them. She was pretty sure they would have found anything worth finding.

As she half-heartedly flicked the beam around the last room, the light panned across grey metal. She slowly moved the beam back, and held it steady.

'Well, well,' she murmured. 'What have we here?'

It was a computer; a big, old-looking PC. It seemed it had been pushed to the side of the desk, maybe so the intruders could see if there way anything underneath it.

That's what comes of employing meatheads, Jack, she thought, smiling. They probably thought it was a paperweight.

She slithered her fingers under the machine and lifted it slightly, feeling her ribs twinge. It was heavy. Far too heavy to lug home.

She chewed her lip. There was only one thing for it. She felt around the edge and clicked it on.

She waited impatiently while the machine started up. The whirr of the fan and the frantic judder of the disk made her nervous. It was not particularly loud – it would have been drowned in her office – but against the backdrop of silence it sounded as harsh as a jet engine. And it stopped her hearing other things, and even if that other thing was silence, she was still happier hearing it.

She pulled up a foldaway chair and sat down as the screen flickered into life. It was indeed an old machine and the menu system was similar to the one on her machine at the station. She clicked on *File Find* with the mouse.

It took her a while to find anything. Jill had a very disorganised system. There were hundreds of files, and none of them had names that were at all helpful.

She worked through the directories until she found two files stashed away deep down in the sub-directory structure; they had been created the week before Jill's death.

She held her breath.

'Bingo,' she muttered as it came up on the screen; it was an inventory of the Institute's stores. Each line detailed the various drugs they were storing, which company they were from, and who was responsible for their storage. At the bottom was a single line flagged *Untitled*. There was no company listed against it, and it was the only entry with Fisher's name against it. Jill had red-lined it with a simple note to herself:

'Not indexed. Check.'

The second file was structured like a diary. Jill had entered everything she had done at the Institute on a day-to-day basis. Alex scanned through the file, noting that Jill had decided to contact Numen two days before she was killed. The other entries were things she already knew: their meeting, finding the blister pack, the fax, and sending the package. She scanned down the page, carefully reading each entry. She tried to put herself in Jill's position to work out what she was thinking. Her breath came out in short, wispy clouds, but she didn't feel the cold – she was too wrapped up to notice. The last line caught her eye:

'Must get hold of Ian's portable. That's where the trial data is! Should be able to undelete them!'

Alex sat up, turning the words over in her mind. She was so

135

wrapped up in the sentence she was oblivious to everything else: the stiff cold in her fingers, the wrecked house around her, and the barely audible rumble of male voices leaking through the door.

If she had been listening she would have known they were in the house.

But she wasn't; they were just part of the background noise.

She shook her head and frowned; she really didn't understand what Jill meant. Maybe she was too tired. As her mind let go of the problem she suddenly became aware of her surroundings and glanced around the room, realising how cold she was. She shivered and stiffly flexed her fingers. She needed to print the documents out and get them home – then she could think about them over a glass of wine in the warmth.

She fumbled for the switch on the little Olivetti printer and turned it on. It jolted a couple of times, and the Ready light came on.

She closed down the file, and clicked on print. Nothing happened. She looked at the printer then back at the screen:

'1 Document Deleted.'

'Piss!' she hissed. She knew exactly what she had done. It wasn't the first time. She had clicked on the wrong bar on the menu, and then confirmed without reading it, deleting the whole file.

'Oh God,' she muttered. Why didn't she learn?

She rocked back in the chair, feeling it give slightly under her weight. At least there wasn't much to remember, she thought. She would ask Forester what undelete meant. It was the sort of word he would use.

She snapped the PC off and stood up, stretching her arms to try to release the tension in her shoulders.

As the noise of the fan receded, the breath froze in her throat.

She heard a noise.

A cold static flickered across her skin. She heard the muffled voices. Male voices. Not right outside, but close. In-the-house close. She fought to control the sudden wave of panic that surged through her. There were only two kinds of people, she told herself; the quick and the dead. And if she thought like a victim she was dead.

She looked around the room. There was only one place to hide, and that was so obvious it was ridiculous. But she had no choice. She dropped to her knees and rolled under the bed.

She lay on the hard wood floor and struggled to control her breathing. Her heart was pounding against her ribs, and her bruised side was sore against the boards.

She tried to think if she had left telltale signs; the computer was off, and she was clutching her duffel bag like a baby, so there should be nothing to alert them to the fact she was there. She just had to keep calm.

She heard a bang and a raised voice. It felt close, but the words were a blur. They were about to come in.

Then – with an icy-cold feeling of terror – she remembered the printer. She felt her eyes bulge.

She hadn't turned the printer off. The little red light would be blinking at them, and they would know someone had been in there.

She craned her head and looked at the door. It was half open. Someone was shuffling around outside, but she couldn't see them.

She turned her head and looked across the floor to the desk. There was a single socket under it with a multi-block attached. If she could switch the socket off, it would kill the light. She stretched towards it. Pain shot down her side.

'In here,' the voice shouted.

'What?' another voice said, slightly further away.

Her fingers touched the plastic. Then the first voice spoke again – and it was inside the room. She stopped moving.

'It must be in here.'

'It's down the other end,' a second voice said outside. 'I remember seeing it.'

'OK. You're the boss,' the first voice said, subsiding as its owner left the room.

Her fingers brushed the surface of the plastic. For a second they wouldn't do anything. Then they flexed, and the switch clicked off. She drew back under the bed; shrinking back quickly like a crab into a shell. Her heart was pounding again, and her bladder was twitching as if she had really bad cystitis.

They came back into the room less than twenty seconds after

she had pulled back under the bed. A torch bobbed around, and feet moved close to her head. She tried to make herself as small as possible.

'Well, well. What have we got here?' the first voice shouted. She shut her eyes.

It seemed like an age before anyone spoke.

'I told you it was here.'

They both moved around to the same side of the bed.

'Is that it?' the first voice said. 'What the fuck does he want with this pile of shit?'

'How should I know? He just does, right? So let's get it out of here.'

She heard them drag the computer off the desk.

'For fuck's sake!'

She strained to see what was happening out of the corner of her eyes. They hadn't unplugged the power cable. She could see the wire pulled taut from the socket. For a long, terrible moment she thought that one of them was going to drop to his knees and remove the plug.

But it didn't happen. They clumsily yanked the cord free, and heaved it out of the room with the cable dragging behind them. She heard one of them shout in the hallway as he tripped on it.

'Cunt!' he hollered, which was followed by a loud thump that sounded as if he had kicked the wall – hard. Her ribs prickled.

Then they were gone.

She waited under the bed for a long time. The air around her felt freezing, and the sweat on her skin cooled quickly and congealed. She waited until she was sure they had gone. And then she waited some more. Her breathing was barely audible, and her body was ice cold. When she eventually moved, her arm had gone to sleep.

She rolled awkwardly out from under the bed and painfully pulled herself up, coaxing the blood back into her limbs. She was half frozen to death.

But more importantly she was half still alive.

She tiptoed slowly down the corridor. The beam of her torch bobbed up and down madly as her hands shook, and shadows danced everywhere; she was sure they were gone, but the ghosts on the walls remained to haunt her.

138

She stepped out into the night and stopped. Still she heard nothing. Then, with a quick glance back at the shattered door, she slipped down the alley and out into the street, heading back to the main road.

As she waited at the bus stop, a car cruised by slowly. The leer from the passenger was nothing unusual. They were just a couple of puffed-up teenage boys out in Daddy's car. Normally she would have looked straight through them. Or on a good day maybe given them the finger. But this time she looked away, jumping slightly as they blared the horn and skidded away with a flick of the back end.

She couldn't be too sure.

She looked up the road, and waited for the bus. Cars streaked by, heading out of town. That had been too close for comfort, she thought. Far too close. But Jill had told her what to do. She had to get hold of Fisher's portable.

Thanks, Jill, she thought, looking up at the sky. I guess the rest is up to me.

And that meant going back to the Institute.

Her nostrils flared at the cold exhaust fumes hanging in the air. The cocktail of burnt petrol and diesel made her think. It made her think about the acid oozing down the tyre of her car. It made her remember the way nitric acid ate into the desk at school, and how the brown curling smoke stuck in your throat. And it made her wonder what it smelt like when it stripped the skin off your face.

# 24

Amy stood in her way.

'Look, Ali, honey, it's Friday, for Christ's sake, and you're going home tomorrow. I mean, you've got to get back out there some time so it might as well be tonight. Then you can return to your little flat, go back to whatever you do, and I'll leave you alone.'

Alex wasn't so sure.

'And I can have my clothes back,' Amy added, nodding at her. She was wearing one of Amy's waistcoats over a T-shirt, with her trusty old 501s.

Alex sat down on the bed, and swung her feet up onto a chair. 'You've been a good influence,' she mused, looking at her battered boots. 'I might even start wearing these to work.'

'Don't change the subject,' Amy scolded. 'Come on, tell me, what's your problem?'

Alex sighed. She was still bruised, and her ribs twinged occasionally, but that wasn't really it. In fact she couldn't wait to get out of the house. All she had done was pace around since she came back from Jill's, as there was absolutely nothing she could do until she could speak to Forester. She decided to come clean.

'It'd be OK if it wasn't for this bloody eye. I look like a battered wife.'

'You are!'

'Well, yes. Sort of. But I hate the way everyone keeps giving me pitying looks. The last thing I want is everyone treating me like a victim. It's not what I need at the moment!'

'Is that all?' Amy said, wide-eyed. 'Your eye!'

Alex was about to protest, but Amy was on a roll.

'If that's all you're worried about, honey, then let Aunty Amy at you. I can sort it.'

'But look at the state of it.'

'Trust me, Alex,' Amy said, pretending to be serious. 'I've seen worse. I have some very ugly friends. Now come here. I can make you look brand new. In fact, I can make you better than that. It'll make the real Alex Brierley – the dull old boring one – really jealous.'

'What do you mean?'

'Trust me and I'll show you.'

'OK,' Alex agreed, shrugging and raising her hands in surrender. 'Why not? Do your worst.'

'I look like I've been dead for a month,' Alex moaned, as she stared into the mirror ten minutes later.

'Rubbish,' Amy said indignantly. 'It's your hair. You're just not a natural blonde. It makes you look washed out.'

'I am!'

'Well, not this shade of blonde you're not.' Amy pulled at a clump of hair. 'You only get this with Domestos.'

'Go near my hair and you're dead.'

'Don't worry, kitten,' Amy cooed, stroking her finger across the fine hairs on her neck. 'I'm not going to mess with your golden locks.' She put her thumb on Alex's neck for a second and went quiet.

'I know,' she said slowly.

She bounced across the room and started rummaging about in one of her trunks.

'Here you go,' she said, as she turned back.

Alex half turned then ducked as she saw something remarkably like a long-haired cat flying through the air.

'What is it?' she cried, as it landed on the back of her head.

Amy stepped forward, and started to straighten it on her head. It was a wig.

'It's very yo-ou,' she giggled.

'Give me a break,' Alex protested.

'But it is one of my best,' Amy said defensively.

141

'Yeah. Right.'

'Trust me. It'll look really good.'

'But it's a wig. I can't go out in a wig!'

'You're such a bore at times,' Amy said, going to work. 'Now hold still.'

Alex looked at the reflection of the strange woman in the mirror half an hour later, and reluctantly had to agree.

'Good grief,' she muttered. She wasn't sure she would always want to look like this, but it was quite impressive. And there wasn't a bruise in sight.

'All right, alright, alright. You win,' she conceded. 'Let's go.'


The queue shuffled forward as a group of unhappy-looking male students was turned away.

'Fuck you,' one of them muttered as he walked off – but not loud enough for the bouncer to hear.

The queue settled into silence again as the door closed.

Alex stamped her feet on the ground to keep warm, and watched as two girls in skin-tight one-pieces clattered by. The city square was awash with people coming and going between the pubs and clubs.

'How do they do that?' she asked, shaking her head as they sauntered past.

'What?' Amy asked, diverting her attention from the door.

'How come they manage to walk around all but naked without their nipples standing on end?' she said, nodding after the two girls. 'I just don't get it. Mine would be like traffic cones if I was wearing that.'

Amy glanced after them. 'They probably Sellotape them down,' she replied, shrugging. 'Anyway, listen, I need to concentrate on getting us into this place,' she added solemnly, then opened her eyes wide and smirked. 'They don't let any old riff-raff in, you know, which is going to be a problem with you in tow, honey. Despite my best efforts.'

She smiled at Alex, carefully checking that she knew it was a joke, then turned back around to see what was happening at the door.

'OK,' Alex said, stifling a yawn. She was beginning to feel tired. The pubs were just emptying out, and the queues for the club ran right down the row of the shops and around the corner of the fake Irish pub on the corner. They had already been there twenty minutes.

When the queue finally lurched forward again Amy made sure she ended up next to the huge doorman who seemed to be chief decision-maker. When he looked around she tugged at the bottom of her short shirt, put on her best girlie voice and started talking to him. Alex hung back, knowing that if she joined in she would probably say something sarcastic, and that would be the end of it.

Instead she scanned the other two doormen – letting her eyes cruise disinterestedly over them. They were the usual model; big, violent-looking and . . .

She let her breath out slowly as the shorter of the two looked at her.

His eyes only rested on her for a split second – but it was enough. She felt her stomach lurch.

She knew who he was.

He looked away, panning his eyes over the rest of the queue, and saying something out of the corner of his mouth to his colleague as a group of girls with big hair tottered by. They both laughed.

He had just glanced at her, she thought. That was all. Nothing special.

And he hadn't recognised her.

You're OK, she thought. Just stay cool. Amy had done a good job.

She turned away, looking at him out of the corner of her eye. That face, she thought, unable to suppress a slight shudder. That face was cut deep into her mind. It was the face she had seen when the floodlight flashed on. The face of the man who had kicked her so badly she had thrown up blood – the man whose lust had chewed at her soul. She fought to remain calm – at least on the outside.

'We're in!' Amy said, glancing excitedly over her shoulder.

'Good,' Alex muttered, her voice sounding hoarse and dry.

It seemed to take an age before they moved. Alex watched him – a pockmarked nightmare at the edge of her vision. He was less than three feet away from her. She could almost feel his

143

breath on her skin again. It was the ultimate test of Amy's work. Every time his gaze scanned across her, she felt like an escaped convict caught in the spotlight.

'Come on, you slag,' Amy said, grabbing her and yanking her through the door. Alex silently thanked her for not using her name.

'Are you alright?' Amy asked, when they got in. She pulled Alex towards her and scanned her face with concern.

'Yeah, I'll be fine.'

Amy let go of her hand. 'You sure?'

'Don't worry.' Alex forced herself to smile.

Amy took her hand again and slipped something into her palm. 'Here you go, sweetie. Take this. It'll make you feel a lot better.'

'What is it?' Alex squinted at the little white tablet. It had a rough surface with a crude imprint that looked vaguely like a bird.

'What do you think?' Amy asked, shaking her head pityingly and taking her coat. 'Now either put it in your mouth or your pocket, but for Christ's sake stop waving it around.'

'Oh, I see . . . right.' Alex looked at her dumbly. 'I, er . . .'

'Go on, be a devil,' Amy said, smiling like a Cheshire cat as she set off towards the cloakrooms.

'Why not?' Alex shrugged.

She chewed her tongue until she had enough spit to swallow, then put the little tablet in her mouth and gulped it down.

In for a penny, she thought, sauntering over to the cigarette machine and carefully slotting in some coins. She selected a full-strength Marlboro.

She lit one and shut her eyes as she exhaled deeply.

'Are you testing me or something?' she muttered, glancing at the ceiling. 'If so, it had better be bloody good up there.'

# 25

He walked slowly across the playing field, almost tiptoeing, feeling the dampness from the springy grass sinking through his trainers. It was pitch black but he felt exposed in the wide open space. He glanced nervously over his shoulder. He could still make out the top of the main school block, a black rectangle jutting into inky sky, but the rest of the buildings had already sunk back into the night. He swivelled his head back around, panning his gaze across the darkness in front of him. He knew that vast field fell away down an incline. At the bottom was a battered chain-mesh fence with a little path squashed in by a thick evergreen hedge.

He strained to see into the darkness. He couldn't make out anything in the foreground. But in the distance he could see a smear of red in the sky – behind where the hedge would be, and over the unseen sprawl of suburbs, the glow of the city light reflected off the dark blanket of cloud.

He watched the light dance as the clouds moved. It was like the reflections of a fire below.

He felt his lips curl as he thought about what would be happening down there. Another weekend. The first night of the festival of nothing. The pointless cycle of waste and excess.

He suddenly felt sullied. Having to walk among them, feeling their contemptuous gaze, polluted by their filth.

He didn't have to be down there to know what was happening. He'd seen enough to know what it was like.

That glow in the dark. The reflection of the fire. Down there – legitimised by a corrupt and dying society – dancing like pagans in the night.

Drunk.

Debauched.

Running like dogs through the streets.

Those that pass their filthy seed, who have no purpose, who bask in the reflection of a fake world; false idols, TV, the liars who leach, who hide behind the phoney façades of the hypocritical organisations they represent.

He hated the filthiness of it all, the stupidity of them all.

They knew nothing. They didn't deserve their lives. They didn't deserve to walk this earth when others far better had theirs taken away.

He threw his head back as pain lanced through him. A raw, searing pain in his memory like metal on an exposed nerve. The place where his memory stopped, the place where his present should be.

He sucked cold air into his lungs. But even it felt dirty. The metallic tang of exhaust fumes stuck to the molecules of life.

He jammed his hands into his pockets and walked quickly into the darkness, down the hill towards the fence.

There was no time to waste. He was close. He could feel it.

He slowly traced a path around the perimeter fence, refamiliarising himself with the layout, finding the occasional difference where the fence had been renewed, where a gate had been taken out.

Eventually he came to a place where the fence had been pulled down by kids wanting a short cut home. He stepped over the bent mesh, onto the stony path behind.

Now it was just a matter of waiting until the moment was right.

He sank into the darkness, and waited, knowing the time was coming quickly.

146

# 26

Jim looked up as the woman pushed through the revolving doors. He quickly put his paper down and glanced at the security monitor – he was supposed to look at it every couple of minutes, but the leader article on Forest's chances of being relegated had kept him engrossed for half an hour.

'Can I help you?' he asked, carefully placing the paper out of sight.

The woman pulled her leopard-skin coat around her and smiled.

'We're still safe in your hands I see,' she said, nodding towards where he had hidden the paper.

'I beg your pardon?'

'I said, I see we're still safe in your hands,' she replied seriously as she approached him.

He didn't know what to say.

'Jim,' she said, leaning on his desk. 'It's me!'

He looked at her unsurely.

'Alex?'

'Come on, it's only been a week, Jim. Don't say you've forgotten me already?'

'Sorry, I didn't recognise you. You look, er . . .'

'Beautiful?' she asked, stepping back and putting out her hands. She was wearing her grubby 501s, a tiny, faded blue T-shirt under the fur coat, and her hair was tousled and unwashed; it pleased her no end.

'Like you've been dragged through a hedge backwards,' he said sternly.

'Jim!'

'Anyway,' he said, squinting at her, 'how come you're here? I was told you'd had an accident.' He paused, then added gruffly, 'I was worried about you.'

Alex took her sunglasses off and turned the bruised side of her face towards him.

'I did, look. Except it wasn't an accident. I was mugged.' She had decided in advance this was the best excuse.

Jim frowned and shook his head.

'They should hang the bastards,' he said darkly.

'If they catch them, I hope they will,' she smiled. 'Anyway, don't worry. I'm OK.' She glanced at the clock on the wall above his head. 'Look, I need to get on. I'll see you later.'

'Are you here if anyone asks?' he shouted after her.

''Course not!'


Forester was behind the bench again when she walked into the computer room. And he was still talking to someone on the phone. She wondered if he had been there all week.

'All the new version had done is make it worse,' he shouted. She had never heard him angry before – his voice was an odd strangled falsetto.

She waited until he had finished.

'Have you got a minute, Forester?' she asked the bench.

He bolted up like a jack-in-a-box, and nearly smacked his head on a shelf.

'Alex. Are you alright?' he asked stiffly. 'What happened to you?'

She explained, touched by his concern. It took a while to get him around to the subject she was interested in.

'So tell me,' she said casually, 'how would you go about undeleting something?'

'Oh, that's easy,' he said, then paused. 'But I don't really know how to explain it. It's just something you . . . you know, do.'

She looked bemused, and tried to think of another tack.

'OK, OK. Let's take it from the top. What exactly is undeleting, then, when it's at home?'

'Ah.' Forester looked happier. 'It's what you do when you've

148

accidentally deleted a file, and want to get it back.'

Alex nodded.

'Right. OK. But when you delete something it's gone, right?'

'Well, it has, sort of. Do you know what a FAT is?'

'No,' she replied nervously.

'The FAT is where an index to all the files is kept. When you delete a file, you don't actually delete the contents, you just remove the reference to it from the FAT. So as far as the system is concerned, it's gone. But then it's still there as well, if you see what I mean – until something else gets saved over it, that is.'

'Uh-huh.' She nodded slowly. 'So how do you get it back?'

'You use an undelete program,' he said, as if it were very, very obvious.

'And you've got one, right?'

'Of course,' he said, as if it were a matter of personal pride.

'So if I use this program, I can get deleted files back?'

'As long as no one has copied anything else on there meanwhile.'

Bingo, she thought. That wasn't too bad. Now she knew what Jill had wanted to do; undelete the files on Fisher's wiped portable to see what was there.

It was as simple as that. As long as no one had used Fisher's portable she should be OK.

She bit her lip.

There were only two slight obstacles: firstly, the portable was locked away in the Kallman Institute, and – perhaps most difficult – she had to get Forester to explain how the undelete program worked in a manner she could understand.


It was raining when she left the building, and the sky was already dark, even though it was only just after one. It was going to be one of those days, she thought, when it never really got light. Cars hissed by on the wet tarmac, their headlights already on.

She crossed the road at the pedestrian crossing, and headed up to the deli at the end of the row of shops. It was one of her favourite places, a throwback to a time when the road had been doing better business.

She went in, shutting the door carefully behind her, and patted the damp out of her clothes.

She took her coat off, slung it over one of the tall stools by the window, and went over to the counter.

'Hel-lo?' she shouted through to the back.

She smiled as Mario grumpily shuffled through.

'Waddayawant?' he asked gruffly.

'Hi, Alex,' she said sweetly, bouncing on her toes. 'How are you? Haven't seen you in ages. Oh, very well, thank you.'

He squinted at her.

'Alex?'

'Yup.'

His face broke into a wide smile. 'Alex. I miss you. Where you been?' He looked at her closely. 'And what you do to yourself?'

'I, er . . . I walked into something,' she said sheepishly.

He looked at her sternly as if he were weighing her up.

'You don't look so good. You sure that's what happened?'

'Yes.' She nodded, smiling. 'Don't worry.'

'But you OK?'

'Yeah. I'll live.'

'Good. Then you go and sit down, and I bring you something. What you like?'

'I'd like a cappuccino, please, with lots of chocolate on top. A big one.'

'My pleasure.' He bowed slightly then shuffled off.

She sat down and looked out of the window, watching the cars slide by into town. The rain was falling harder and the streams of water on the glass distorted the view. She lit a cigarette and let her mind wander.

'There you are,' Mario said, making her jump as he dropped her coffee down and slid a plate in front of her.

'What's that?' she asked, looking at the huge flaky wedge on the plate.

'*Panatone* for you. Is nice. It will fatten you up some.'

'Thanks,' she laughed. 'You sound like my mother.'

He grunted and set off back to the kitchen with a shrug.

'Someone got to look after you.'

She shook her head, smiling, and turned back around. She ran her fingers through the condensation on the window while she sipped her coffee and worked out what to do next.

She knew she had to get to the portable at the Institute as soon as possible. Accidentally deleting the file on Jill's computer was a stroke of luck – it gave her some breathing space. But she was sure they would come looking for Fisher's portable sooner or later. And there was always a chance someone else might start to use it.

The question was, how would she get in?

She took a deep pull on her cigarette, and went through her options. The Institute was far too well secured to think about breaking in, especially after the murder, and the chance of finding the door gaping open like Jill's was fairly remote. She shook her head. For the moment she was stuck; she needed time to think about it.

She stubbed out her cigarette and took a bite of the *panatone*. It was delicious. She felt her stomach gurgle and realised she hadn't eaten all day.

She looked out of the window again, focusing on nothing in particular, and tried to think of what else she could be doing, but nothing immediately came to mind.

Then, as she finished off the crumbs and scooped the last of the froth out of her cup with her finger, an idea began to seep into her mind; her subconscious had obviously been churning away without her. Of course! she thought, as it struck her. There was something else. Now she knew that her attacker was a doorman. Maybe she could find out who he was – and who he was working for.

Suddenly a stream of ideas gushed into her head as the new avenue opened up.

And she knew exactly where to start.

She got up and shouted through to Mario, 'How much do I owe you, Mario?'

'No problem,' he shouted back.

'Come on, Mario,' she protested as he came through. 'You need to make a living. How much?'

'It's on the house. Because you are sick,' he said gruffly. 'As long as you come back sooner next time.'

'OK.' She pulled open the door. 'I owe you one.'

She jogged down to the pelican crossing and went back to the station.

'Most of them are bloody idiots,' Jim said indignantly when she asked him what he knew about doormen. 'All brawn, and no brains.'

'Sorry. I just thought ... y'know ... that you might know a bit about it. That was all,' she said casually.

She knew Jim loved to be asked for advice.

'Well, yes. As it happens I do know a bit about it.' He took his half-lensed reading glasses off. 'I've obviously come across a few of them in my time.'

Once he had made sure she knew the distinction between the highly honourable profession of being a security guard and the lowly status of doormen – and run through it three times – he warmed to the subject.

'They don't actually work for the clubs, you know. They just get hired. They'll all work for some agency or other.' He glanced around, and leant forward. 'Some of the younger lads who work for us sometimes do a bit of moonlighting,' he added seriously. 'But keep it quiet.'

Alex looked around the foyer. She wasn't sure why he was whispering – there was no one else around.

'Why?'

'Because it's against company policy.' He sat up straight. ''Course, never done it myself.'

Somehow Alex wasn't surprised; she just couldn't really see Jim breaking up fights and hurling people out into the street.

She stopped herself smiling at the thought of it.

'So do you know the names of any of these agencies?' she asked hopefully.

'Sorry.' He crossed his arms.

'Ah well,' she said, shrugging. 'I just thought ...'

'But I know a gym where a lot of them go.' He frowned, and paused for a moment. 'Now what's it called?'

# 27

Alex hauled herself onto the kerb, glancing around to see if anyone was about. She was OK; most of the shopfronts were boarded up, and the wide pavement in front of the big dilapidated thirties row was deserted.

She turned around and tried to see what she looked like in the window of her car. She had Amy's wig on again, and more make-up than she had used in her life. It all looked fine when she had checked herself in the rear-view mirror, but now she was out in the open she wasn't so sure.

It would have to do, she thought, dabbing at her pancake foundation. She certainly didn't look like herself, and that was what was most important.

She hitched her sports bag onto her shoulder, and ran her fingers through the thick red tresses of the wig as she turned and looked for the entrance to the gym.

The building was a big four-storey pile, its former glory given away by a series of ornate trimmings on the dark, soot-stained brick. Now the ground floor was divided up and contained a couple of vacant units with flyposters covering the empty windows and a mesh-fronted minicab office.

She looked up at the first floor. Lights blazed out of the big windows, and she could see the top halves of a couple of beefy men lifting free weights.

She walked across the uneven pavement, sorely tempted to follow the spicy smell wafting from an Indian restaurant somewhere down the road.

She pulled open the heavy chipboard door and went up the

stairs. The reception was dimly lit and smelt damp. She went to the counter and rang the bell, glancing at the handwritten adverts for poppers and cheap aftershave pasted to the glass as she waited.

A thin man shuffled to the counter.

'Can I help you?' he asked without much enthusiasm.

'Yes. I'd like to join,' she said, smiling.

He looked at her suspiciously.

'Are you sure you've got the right place?'

'Definitely. How much is it?'

'Look, perhaps you should go and have a look first. Have a go if you want. If you still want to join when you come back, ring the bell.'

He coughed hard into his hand and shuffled off without waiting for her answer.

'Thanks,' Alex shouted after him.

She adjusted the wig slightly, then headed towards the double doors down the dark, glossily painted corridor.

The weight room looked as if it had originally been used for dance lessons; it was huge, spanning the whole building, with windows on both sides. She heaved the sports bag off her shoulder, dropped it on the floor, and sat down on one of the long benches against the mirrored wall.

Nearby a huge black man was bench-pressing and making noises as if he was about to die. He was lifting the full pile of weights and his partner was pushing down on them to add more pressure.

'Go on,' his partner shouted, a haze of saliva falling towards the first man's chest. 'Hurt youself.' He had a slightly camp accent and a moustache that in most places would suggest he was gay – but not here.

She glanced over to the edge of the room where a couple of women were working together. They were the only women in an otherwise male domain.

She guessed they were probably both still in their teens. They were scraggy-looking with pale, unhealthy skin and greasy hair scraped away from their faces, pulled tight into jutting ponytails on the top of their heads; it obviously wasn't meant to look pretty. It was the hard but knocked-about look she saw in a lot of women in the inner city; women not yet twenty, but already old.

They were both wrapped up in what they were doing. Alex shuffled closer to hear them talk. They were white, but if she had shut her eyes she wouldn't have known it. They were talking in a weird cocktail of West Indian brogue and inner-city slang. It sounded comical, but she knew they were serious. Their accent said it all: don't mess with me – or else.

She slipped back out, paying the surprised-looking man the five pounds' subscription, and went into the locker room.

Time to go native, she thought, rubbing her eyes and leaving a shadow of mascara underneath. She took out a tissue and dabbed at her eye make-up until most of it was gone. Then she went to work on her lips. By the time she had finished her face was a uniform pasty white. She pulled her hair into a bunch and tied it with an elastic band.

She walked cautiously into the weight room half an hour later, and glanced around. She was glad to see the two women had gone. She went straight over to an empty machine in the corner. There was a poster on the wall with an illustration of how it worked. She scanned it briefly, then sat down; she'd had a go on a similar device the last time she had been in a gym, some time way back in the mists of time.

She hooked her arms behind the padded swing arms, and looked around the room. There were about a dozen large men all engrossed in various kinds of personal torture; none of them was paying a blind bit of attention to her. Good, she thought. It might take a little while to get the hang of it. She flexed her arms and pushed hard.

Nothing happened.

She felt her ribs strain and sweat prickle under her arms.

She took a deep breath and tried again, feeling the tendons in her neck stand out as she strained, but it wouldn't budge; not even slightly.

She unhooked her arms and got up, furtively looking about to make sure no one had noticed. She went around the back of the machine, squatted down, and looked at the pile of weights – the pin was wedged below the bottom weight.

She had been trying to lift the whole stack. No wonder, she

thought, coaxing the pin out with some difficulty, and replacing it near the top.

She sat down again and took a deep breath. This time she managed to move the bars slightly; just a fractional jerk before the weights clanked down again. She blew the air our of her lungs and slumped forward, feeling her ribs complaining bitterly and gooey sweat trickling down her chest. She glanced about quickly, and skulked around the back again, this time taking the pin out altogether.

She sat down firmly, took a deep breath, and managed to bring her arms all the way together. Good, she thought, as she pressed the armrests against each other. It was all a matter of finding your level. The first two weren't too bad. She did eight more before running out of steam.

She got up, feeling her head spin slightly, and walked over to another machine.

By the time she got to the third machine – something for her abs, whatever they were – she was beginning to hallucinate and the muscles in her arms had turned to jelly. She stared blankly at the menacing-looking pile of weights and decided to switch to a leg exercise.

Just as she was squeezing her thighs under the leg-raiser bar, and wondering how on earth she was going to casually approach anyone – let alone speak to them – without passing out, someone spoke to her.

'Are you OK?' a voice laughed.

It took her a second to register that it was speaking to her.

She turned her head stiffly, forcing a blank look onto her face. There was a tall, blonde man standing by her side. He was leaner than most of the others, with a pleasant smile that surprised her.

'I beg your pardon?' she said, trying to keep her face expressionless.

'Bloo-dy hell,' he said, sounding bemused.

'*What?*'

'It's just that you don't sound quite like what I was expecting, that's all. What are you, a Seven Series or something?'

'A what?'

'It's a joke.'

'Look, I'm sorry, but I haven't got a clue what you're talking about,' she said, turning back to the machine. 'I think you've got the wrong person.'

'C'mon, don't get uppity. Why not stop pretending and give up? I mean, it's not like you're here to work out is it?'

'Oh yeah,' she said, jerking her head back towards him. 'What makes you so sure about that?'

'Call it an educated guess.' He looked at her for a second, then smiled. 'Look, I'm sorry, alright? I shouldn't go jumping to conclusions. I guess you do look a bit classier than the rest.'

'What rest?' she asked, breathing in deeply.

'So go on, tell me. What are you up to?'

'I'm ... er ... I'm looking for someone,' she explained meekly, feeling her head swim.

'So I *am* right. Let me guess; something big, black and brawny, right?'

'Pardon?' She shook her head and tried to concentrate.

He crossed his arms and grinned. 'Look, it doesn't take a genius. People only come here for two things; men to push, women to pull. And BMWs all. It fair breaks a white boy's heart sometimes ... Anyway, I thought I'd put you out of your misery, sweetheart. Most of the guys you're looking for don't come in till later, so you're wasting your time at the moment.'

Alex got up stiffly. 'I'm afraid you've got me wrong, OK.' She could feel her face blazing, and felt a little faint.

She set off towards the door. She suddenly felt very light-headed and could feel the veins under her eyes throbbing.

'Hey,' he shouted after her. 'I'm sorry, OK?'

She stopped and slowly turned towards him, realising there was no point in running away. She couldn't see straight for starters.

'I'm really sorry,' he said, raising his hands apologetically. 'You just looked ... I don't know ... lost, I suppose. I didn't mean to piss you off, OK?'

Alex felt herself relax and let herself smile – she had let that old fight-or-flight feeling take over again. She took a deep breath. 'All right. No problem. I guess I was feeling pretty stupid. Maybe I just didn't need it pointing out, that was all.'

'You're right,' he agreed, and started to turn back to the machine. 'Anyway, I'll see you around.'

'There's just one thing.' She stepped forward.

He stopped and looked at her.

'What's a BMW?'

He smiled broadly and shook his head. 'Black Man's Woman. And round here . . .' He nodded at the room. 'They're normally well used and knackered, and had one too many drivers, if you know what I mean.'

'Charming!'

'But true.'

Alex looked at him for a second, then stepped towards him. It wasn't how she had planned it, but at least it had broken the ice.

'Alex,' she said, offering her hand.

'Pleased to meet you, Alex,' he said, looking slightly surprised. 'I'm Martin.'

'Listen.' She nodded towards the benches by the door. 'I need to sit down or I'm going to pass out.'

They went over to the bench and slumped down with their backs to the mirror.

'Can I ask you something?' she asked.

'Fire away.'

She'd had various plans about how to pitch the question. But at that moment she just couldn't be bothered to mess around.

'You wouldn't be a doorman, would you?'

He looked at her for a second.

'Er, yeah, I suppose so. I mean, yes. How did you know?'

'Call it an educated guess.'

'Do I look like one?'

'Not sure. I'm not sure what a typical doorman looks like, to be honest.'

He screwed his mouth up. 'I'm as typical as any of them, I suppose.' He shrugged. 'No one actually plans to be a doorman. It's the sort of thing you do when you can't think of anything else.'

She stretched her legs, beginning to feel a little better.

'So what are you going to be when you grow up?' she asked, rubbing her neck.

He looked at her and smiled. 'So now who's asking a lot of questions?'

'People in glass houses.' She grinned.

'OK. OK, I dunno. Actor, pop star, hod carrier. Haven't a clue.'

'Listen,' Alex said, looking around, 'is there anywhere I can get a drink around here? I think I need to get some liquid inside me.'

'There's a bar upstairs.' He nodded at the door. 'It's small and dingy, and run by a woman who looks half dead, but,' he said, raising his finger, 'it's very near, which I guess is a major plus point as far as you're concerned.'

He got up. 'Come on.'

Alex followed him out of the room, walking stiffly up the stairs behind him.

'I think you oversold it.' She looked around the empty, dimly lit space when they got there.

'I don't know,' he said, heading to the bar. 'It has a certain charm at times.'

He brought her a pint glass of orange squash.

'Thanks.' She took a long pull. 'That's better.' She patted some of the condensation off the glass onto her face. 'I can't believe you're onto that already.' She nodded at the beer he was sipping. 'Doesn't it go straight to your head?'

'Nah.'

'How come? I mean, there isn't even any alcohol in this and it's making me feel woozy.'

'Because I'm fit and you're not, that's why, and anyway, I've been off the weights a while. I was on my way out when I saw you.'

'I suppose it's one way of attracting a man's eye,' she said, shrugging as she finished off the glass. 'So, how long have you been working the doors?'

'A couple of years.'

'And before that?'

He snorted as he remembered. 'I was training to be a PE teacher, but I jacked it in.'

'How come?'

'Too dangerous.' He grinned.

'So you plumped for the comfy world of bouncing instead?'

He looked at her out of the corner of his eye, and smiled. 'It's a very sensitive discipline.'

'I bet.'

'To be honest, it was the only thing I could find to do that didn't involve sitting behind a desk.' He looked at her empty glass. 'Ready for a beer now?'

'Please.'

He got up. Alex followed him with her eyes as he strode to the bar. He had a lean, fit-looking body that tapered down to slim hips and long legs.

'So tell me,' he asked when he returned. 'What do you do?'

She smiled and took a sip from the bottle of cold Pils he had bought her.

'Well?'

'All right, then, since you asked.'

She gave him a quick rundown, glossing over the embarrassing bits and steering well clear of the Fisher story. He seemed genuinely interested, gently probing her with questions, and she ended up telling him more than she had expected. She stopped halfway through and looked at him, feeling slightly uneasy.

'What?' he said, drawing back slightly.

'Nothing.' She shook her head.

She told herself to be careful; the last time she had talked to a strange man she had received a good kicking for her troubles. But she had a gut feeling about him which she was relying on – although her instincts hadn't always been completely reliable when it came to men.

'So what's the name of the programme you're on now?' he asked when she had finished.

'*Midlands Report East*. Do you watch it?'

'Er, no, not really. I find that local stuff a bit, er . . .'

'Sad?' she offered.

'Er, yeah, a bit.' He looked uncomfortable.

'Yeah, well, you'd be right.'

He took a swig from his bottle, and looked at her for a moment.

'So what are you looking for now, Alex?' he asked, leaning back in his chair.

She stared at him for a moment. She wasn't quite sure how to come out with it without laying herself on the line. Maybe her gut feeling was playing up again. So far she had kept the subject of O'Neill and his cronies out of the picture. For all she knew they could be personal friends. But her instincts told her otherwise.

Big risk, Al, she thought. She looked at him and frowned, trying to put some logic around her instincts. But she was running out of ways forward.

She took a deep breath, and pitched in.

He listened intently, frowning and occasionally asking her to run over something again, making sure he understood what she meant.

'So which club was it?' he asked.

'Xero.'

'Ah,' he said thoughtfully. 'I should have guessed. That kind of explains it.'

'Explains what?'

'Why you got a kicking.' He looked at her seriously. 'You were very lucky.'

'It didn't feel that way.'

'Take my word for it. You were.'

'How come?'

'Because Xero's door is run by Dobson, which is unusual in the city centre,' he said, shifting in his seat. 'And Dobson always means trouble.'

'Go on.'

'Look, there's two outfits who've been running the doors in town for years. There's Barry Arnold, who I work for, and another bloke called Winston Roberts. They're certainly not saints or anything, but basically they're above board. Nothing too rough, no psychos, that sort of thing. Roberts tends to cover the black pubs and most of the late-night clubs, and Barry does most of the rest.'

Alex took out her cigarettes, and offered one.

'No thanks.'

'It all sounds a bit mafioso to me.'

'Not really. It just takes a certain type of person to handle muscle, that's all. You've got to employ tough-looking characters who can handle themselves, but the last thing you want is a bunch of nutters who start laying into the punters. It takes a

161

lot of experience to spot the right kind of person. And manage them.'

He drummed his fingers on the table, while he thought.

'Most attempts to set up new outfits are run by some knuckle-head who hasn't got a clue. They employ people looking for an excuse to throw their weight about. Then someone gets hurt, the place closes down, and that's the end of it. People don't go into town to get kicked in by the door staff. That's why most of the pubs and clubs stick with the old firms.'

'So where does Dobson come in?' she asked, blowing the smoke away from him.

'Dobson used to work for Barry. It was before my time, but people say he was a complete twat. Had a thing about students. Dobson set up when Barry sacked him. But he's lasted because of the sort of things they do. He runs places the others won't touch, like the blues clubs out in Radford and Hyson Green. He also goes in for a bit of protection. A lot of the dealers use him to carry out grudge attacks.'

He looked at her seriously. 'He's an animal, Alex. Take my word for it. I've seen what he can do.'

His eyes shone bright blue as he spoke. He took a sip of his beer and continued.

'Dobson fancies himself as some kind of white Yardie. Wher-ever his boys go, people get hurt. And I mean badly hurt.'

'Lovely,' Alex murmured. 'So how come his people are working at Xero?'

'Because Xero's run by a bunch of fly-by-night wankers, that's why. A lot of people reckon they can run clubs. They think it's just a case of getting a good sound system and a DJ, and they're away. The people at Xero are trying to do it on the cheap, so Dobson's boys are an obvious bet.'

He squinted at her. 'You're lucky you only got a beating. One of our guys lost an eye when he fell out with one of them. And got his face cut up.'

'That's very reassuring.'

'Look, Alex,' he said gravely. 'You were lucky you picked this gym. The people here are basically OK. Dobson's lot go to some hole up in Hyson Green. If you'd gone there decked out like that, a cut on the face would be the least of your worries.'

Alex smiled, but he shook his head.

'I'm not being funny. Don't go looking for them, Alex. You'll get hurt. Try some other route. If someone's paying them to keep you off, either stay off, or make very sure you don't let Dobson know you're still looking. OK?'

'OK.' She nodded. 'It's just that I don't know where to go next.'

He looked at his watch.

'Look, I'll give it some thought, if you want. A fresh mind might throw something up. And I'll keep my ear out to see if I can pick up what's happening. But right now I've got to go. My cat will be starving.'

He's got a cat, she thought. Nice guy, nice smile, a body to die for, and a cat!

'Fine,' she agreed casually. 'That'd be good.'

Martin walked her outside, and watched while she started the engine.

'Take care,' he said, as she slipped into first gear.

'Don't worry,' she smiled. 'See you later.'

She wound up the window, and glanced in the mirror.

'Oh no,' she murmured, catching her reflection. She had forgotten what she looked like.

She jerked her foot off the clutch and screeched off with a slight spin of the front wheels. Just her luck, she thought, as she glanced in the rear-view mirror and saw him turn back towards the gym.

# 28

Harry parted the blinds with his fingers and looked out.

'What the hell's gone wrong with this place?' he said, shaking his head. 'I can't believe that something like that can happen in a country that claims to be civilised.' He walked back to his desk and sat down.

He actually looked concerned, Alex thought as she stared at him. He really looked genuinely concerned. She was amazed. She didn't think he had it in him.

'It's why we moved out to the country,' he said, rocking back in his chair and looking at nothing in particular. 'I was scared shitless about the kids when we lived in town. I mean, it was boring as hell out there, but at least they could go out on their own.'

He looked wistfully at the picture on his desk. Alex had never seen him like this before. She knew that Harry's wife had left him and taken the kids up north somewhere. But it had happened long before she had joined the station. She had heard Harry shouting at his wife on the phone sometimes, complaining he never got to see them, but he had never actually spoken to her about it. She smiled and tried to look encouraging.

'Are you sure you should be back?' Harry shifted his gaze back to her. 'If you need more time off, just take it.'

'No, I'm OK,' Alex said assertively. 'I need to get back on the rollercoaster. It's meant to be the best way to get over these things. Get right back in the saddle.'

Harry thought for a second.

'OK, but you realise we're going to have to keep you off the screen for a few days?'

'Why?'

He kept the same quiet tone – it was calm and reassuring, almost like an affectionate father. 'Because you look like you've been in the ring with Prince Naseem, that's why. I think we need to let that shiner subside a little. Don't you?'

'Yeah, I suppose so,' she conceded reluctantly. 'So what do I do meanwhile?'

'Research?'

'Research? What for?' she asked warily.

Harry raised his hands apologetically.

'Now that things have died down a bit with our own little serial killer friend, Mike'll need some other things to cover. Maybe you could dig out a couple of stories?'

She was about to protest. The thought of having to work with Mike wasn't what she needed; just thinking about him wound her up. She could feel the colour rising in her face.

'Look, Alex.' He smiled at her. 'You're a bright girl. Think about it. I'm sure you can do the job and still have fun.'

She let her breath out slowly as she understood what he meant. Of course!

She would be able to choose what subjects Mike covered. What, where and who, in fact. She had to stop her mind whirring through all the possibilities. It was almost too good to be true. She could already think of one particularly nice little number: a pig farm which was crying out to be covered. The pig shit was building up in the ground, seeping into the water table and polluting it. She could see Mike grim-faced, up to his knees in excrement, talking to the farmer. She had been avoiding it for weeks.

She looked at Harry, trying to work him out. Had he done it deliberately? Was he actually being nice?

'Fine,' she said sweetly. 'When do I start?'

'Whenever you're ready.'

'OK, brilliant.'

She stopped halfway across the office, and looked back through Harry's open door. He was still sitting quietly, staring at the picture on his desk. She hesitated, wondering if she should go back.

Then, as she bit her lip and wavered, he picked up the phone and punched a number, cradling the handset on his shoulder while he grabbed for his cigarettes.

'Sara,' he shouted, while he pulled one out of the pack, 'where the fuck is that proposal I asked you for?' There was a slight pause. 'I don't give a fuck,' he roared, tapping the cigarette on the desk. 'Just get it in here now, sweetheart, or you're back on the streets.'

Good call, she thought, spinning around quickly before he saw her, and heading for the lifts – she was glad she knew where she stood with Harry again.

# 29

Alex put her feet on her desk and smiled. Alex one, Mike nil, she thought happily, as she screwed up a sheet of paper and threw it at the bin.

It went straight in. Things were definitely on the up.

She leaned back in her chair and shut her eyes, stretching her arms and savouring the memory. A broad grin – easily as wide as the drug-induced number she'd had in the club – stretched across her face.

No chance – those were his words. He had shouted them at her a number of times when she had shown him the outline for the pig piece.

'But it's a good piece, Mikey,' she had said pleasantly, all big eyes and coy looks. 'It's like being paid to talk to your friends.'

'I know what you're up to, you silly bitch,' he hissed, coming up close. 'But you can go and fuck yourself. I'm not interested. You go and sit in the shit if it's that good.'

But Harry had backed her up. At least he had after she had gone into his office and winced slightly when she spoke, rubbing her side and making sure her bruise was on full display. It was a cheap trick, but then nobody else played by the rules.

She was learning.

Mike, so to speak, was in the shit.

She put her hands behind her head and yawned. It had been a good piece. It had gone out the previous evening and she had enjoyed every minute of it. She was a little disappointed they had taken out the bit where one of the pigs had goosed him. But nothing was perfect. And it would stay on the shelf and come out to haunt him one day. It went some way to setting the record straight.

But she knew that giving Mike the runaround was really only wasting time. She let the image of him grimly stalking off after the shoot run through her mind one more time, then opened her eyes.

Success was the only lasting form of revenge, she thought, as she swung her feet down and pulled her legs under the desk. Not pratting around being petty. She wanted to finalise Mike's schedule for the next couple of weeks, then turn her attention to her real work.

When she had finished the final draft, she waved Liz over, and sent her to take it down to Harry.

She drank the last of her coffee, then picked the Styrofoam cup apart while she racked her brains.

She had hoped the time out would have given her some ideas. But she was still drawing a blank. She tried shutting her eyes and breathing deeply. But nothing came. She had a fluttery feeling deep in her pelvis that she was getting nowhere; that it was all running away from her.

She drummed her fingers on the desk, and stared at the misty city through the blinds.

She was still sitting at her desk, making a half-hearted attempt to look busy, when the receptionist put through a call; she hadn't bothered to take the name.

It took her a second to realise who it was.

'Martin!' she exclaimed when it clicked. 'How did you get my number?'

'You work for a TV station. It's not exactly difficult to find, you know. You don't mind, do you?'

'Er, no,' she said cautiously. 'It's just I wasn't expecting you to. Anyway, what can I do for you?'

'Look, I'm in a pay-phone so I'll get straight to the point. I've got an idea I thought you might be interested in.'

'Fire away,' she said, sitting up in her chair. 'It's one more than I've had. I hope it's good.'

'I think so.'

'Go on, then, put me out of my misery.'

He paused. 'Er . . . look, it might be easier if I tell you face to

168

face. It may take a while to sink in and I haven't got much money. What about lunch?'

'OK,' she said, smiling, not sure of his motives, but pleased anyway. 'You're on. I'll get the station to pay.' She looked at her watch. 'Half an hour?'

'Sure. Where?'

She gave him directions to Mario's, then put the phone down, smiling. Things were definitely on the up. She quickly cleared her desk, switched the phone over to voicemail and went to the ladies' to sort out her make-up.

She arrived at Mario's first.

'I didn't know you smoked so much,' Mario said, pushing a coffee in front of her as she lit a cigarette from the butt of her first one. 'You should eat something.'

'I'm waiting for someone.'

He raised an eyebrow. 'A man?'

She nodded.

'You make me jealous.' He shuffled back to the counter, rubbing his hands on his apron. 'He better treat you right or I see to him.'

'You might want to have a look at him before you make any promises,' Alex laughed.

Mario snorted and disappeared.

Martin walked straight past her when he came in and headed for an empty table.

'Hey, gringo. Over here,' she said, waving her hand.

He still didn't recognise her.

'Good grief, Alex?' he exclaimed, gawking at her. 'Is that you?'

He stepped up to the table and stared. 'Wow. You look a million times better. This your real hair, then?' he asked, putting a hand out to touch it, then changing his mind.

'Yes,' she smiled. 'Well, mainly. I mean, I had to help nature out a bit with the colour, but basically it's all me.'

He sat down and looked at her.

'Good one.'

'What?'

'Good shiner. You look like one of them women in those domestic violence posters. You know the ones?'

169

She gave him a sickly smile; she preferred the bit about how nice she looked.

'Cheers,' she said, allowing her cigarette smoke to blow his way.

'No need to get tetchy. Anyway, it's only temporary. It'll go away, and the rest is . . .'

'Yeah, yeah. Makes me a flawed masterpiece, right?' she said, grinning. 'I know.'

'Something like that.'

Mario came out to take their order, and gave Martin a non-committal once-over. Alex gave him a told-you-so look and ordered a couple of grilled mozzarella and spinach sandwiches – which always made Mario happy. As he walked proudly back to the kitchen she shook her head affectionately.

'Men,' she muttered, stubbing out her B&H.

'What?' Martin asked.

'Nothing.' She turned back to him. 'Why don't you tell me your big idea.'

'So,' Martin asked when he had finished. 'What do you think?'

Alex stared at him with wide eyes.

'It could work,' he said defensively.

She shook her head; nothing would come out of her mouth.

'What's wrong?'

'That's your idea?' she managed to say, when she realised he was waiting for her to speak. 'Tell me you're not serious.'

He looked hurt.

'You don't like it?'

She blew the air out of her cheeks and shook her head.

'It's not that I don't like it, it's . . .' She didn't know how to respond. 'OK,' she said after a pause. 'Let me get this straight. You want me to pretend to be some kind of drug rep or something; waltz in there and tart about a bit. Then you go loco, and while they're trying to section you, I just pop out the back and nick the portable while no one's looking. That's your plan?'

'Yes.'

'Martin, it's ridiculous.'

'Not if we do it properly . . . Anyway,' he challenged, raising his chin, 'if you have a better idea, fire away, love.'

She looked out of the steamed-up window at the murky shapes of the traffic outside.

'It hasn't a chance of working.' She shook her head.

'Why not?'

'Because . . . well, they'll recognise my voice, for starters.'

'You're just putting obstacles in the way, that's all. If you really want to get hold of that thing, then it can work. You can put on an accent.'

'Who do you think I am?' she said, smiling. 'Rory Bremner?'

'Look, it will work if you want it to.' He leant towards her. 'You must be able to do some kind of accent. You're on TV!'

'Well, I can't,' she said adamantly.

'I don't believe you. Where else have you lived?'

'Everywhere. I've had a very romantic life.'

'There you go, then, you'll have picked bits up. You're bound to have done.'

She wasn't convinced.

'I think it can work,' he insisted, when she didn't reply. 'And if you have different ideas, then shoot. Otherwise this is the best you've got.'

She looked at him, shook her head and pulled her cigarettes out again. She knew he'd already cast himself as the hero.

'All right,' she conceded, as Mario dropped their sandwiches on the table. 'I suppose you've got more chance of getting your head busted than me. Why not?' She grinned at him. 'And it's not like I have any other options.'

# 30

The bus heaved slowly up the hill, grinding down a gear as the slope got steeper. Laura sighed and looked out of the window, staring at her reflection and chewing her lip. There was no one else left on the top deck and the stops were getting further apart as they reached the edge of the city, so she hoped they might start to speed up – in fact she prayed that they started to speed up. She was late. In fact, she was very late. The breezy confidence she had exuded in the pub had gone, and all she could think about was her parents sitting tight-lipped in the front room waiting for her to get back.

She was on a tight curfew while she revised for her retakes.

Why didn't they understand? she thought, unhappily watching the traffic lights change to red ahead. She had been working hard, and she had needed a break. She deserved a break, for God's sake. She squeezed her hands between her knees and tried not to think about her father.

'Come on,' she muttered, when the bus started to move again.

She rummaged in her pocket, then pulled her full blonde hair back into a ponytail with the elastic band she had found.

She had told her parents that she was going to work in the library and that she would be back before eight. Oh God, she thought, it was nearly eleven. *And* she was pissed. She had washed her make-up off in the pub, and made Nikki take her slinky shirt home in case her mum looked in her bag. But there was no way she was going to be able to pull it off.

She rubbed the condensation off the window and looked outside. Her stop wasn't far ahead. She pressed the bell strip, and swung herself up.

The bus lurched as she started down the stairs, and she banged her knee on the wall.

'Shit,' she muttered. It wouldn't help if she was limping when she got back.

She scowled at the bus as it pulled away. She bet the driver was looking in his mirror, and she wanted to make sure he knew she thought he was a tosser for making her trip on the stairs.

She turned as it rattled into the night. The streetlights were a long way apart on the empty road and the apron of tarmac between the kerb and the shops was dark and gloomy. She looked at the row of darkened shopfronts, realising how quiet it was now the bus had gone. The only noise was the hiss of the breeze in the trees.

She bit her lip, not sure which way to go. She could either turn right and walk all the way up to the main entrance of the estate, or cut up the alley by the shops, taking the thin path by the school. The first route would take ages, but the second meant she had to walk down the pitch-black path on her own.

Oh God, she thought. What was she going to do!

She knew that taking the path was asking for trouble. It was a four-hundred-yard shuffle in the dark. Four hundred yards on her own.

But she was late!

She took a deep breath and tried to keep calm. You're just being silly, she thought. Acting like a little girl. Wasn't that what her parents always said when she asked them to treat her like a grown-up? She had been down that alley hundreds of times when it was light. There was no problem.

'Right,' she muttered, nodding and gritting her teeth.

She walked quickly across the tarmac, and with a last glance over her shoulder disappeared into the dark alley; a gangly figure suddenly swallowed up and gone.

She couldn't believe how dark it was after the yellow light of the street. She tried to walk as quickly as possible but the surface was uneven under her high-heeled shoes, and she kept turning her ankle.

'Shit,' she hissed, as she stumbled.

The path got stonier as the shops gave way to the thick black hedge. On the right, behind a chain-mesh fence, the school play-

173

ing fields fell away like a dark slick towards the faraway outlines
of the buildings. She staggered on the uneven surface, hugging
her puffa jacket around her.

Why hadn't she gone home earlier?

She realised she was breathing so hard she couldn't hear if
anyone was behind her. Maybe there was someone there.

She didn't want to look back.

She tried to speed up. Her parents were suddenly low on her
list of worries. In fact, if they magically appeared that very
second she'd be more than happy. What had she been thinking
of? They had been told at school not to travel alone and to carry
rape alarms, but then it had seemed like a laugh. The muscles in
her groin contracted in spasm.

Then she saw the yellow glow where the farm lane intersected
with the path ahead. She had forgotten about that. She felt herself
shudder, a sudden uncontrollable shiver. She didn't want to be
exposed by the gooey yellow light. But then she didn't want to
go back either.

She had to keep going.

As she stepped out from behind the hedge, the oily light
crawled across her skin. She turned her head stiffly and glanced
up the lane. The ruts of the old farm track were exaggerated
in the thick glow. The whole landscape looked nightmarishly
surreal.

She heard her breath come out in a sharp pant.

'Oh no,' she cried silently.

Because under the solitary streetlight was a silhouette. The
dark outline of a man.

She turned and stumbled. Then she was back in darkness, running blindly towards home.

She heard a voice behind her and gravel crunching.

Now her panic was focused. She felt naked – naked and lit up
by some invisible spotlight. Oh God, she thought, kicking off
her shoes. Oh God. Oh God, oh God. Please don't let him hurt
me. She put her head down and ran as fast as she could, oblivious
to the pain as the sharp stones tore at her feet and the hedge
slapped icy cold branches in her face.

And then she fell.

She went down on her hands, flat on her face.

She twisted herself around, blinded by sweat and dust from the path. She didn't want him to get her from behind. Shove her face onto the ground as he did it. She had to turn over. Then she could see him. Maybe if he saw her he would stop. Maybe . . . She heaved herself over, grazing her knees. And suddenly she felt something pull at her shirt.

She felt her body lifted off the ground. She jerkily moved her right hand up, and something coiled around her wrist, snaking around her forearm.

She felt his breath, and his hands across her body.

She wanted to cry, but nothing came out.

Then he let go of her, and for a second she didn't know what was happening. He had pulled back, she thought, her brain moving slightly faster than events. He had pulled back while he prepared.

Just as she felt the warm sting as she wet herself, he grabbed her flailing wrist. Hard.

'Calm down,' he said quietly. 'It's alright. Don't panic. I'm not going to hurt you!'

'Thank you,' she replied, not knowing why, feeling the fuse wire cut into her wrists as he bound her hands.

# 31

'I need you at the station now, Alex.' Harry's voice rattled in her ear.

She tried to focus on the clock by her bed.

'It's five thirty in the morning, Harry. Give me a break.'

'Just get here, OK? Things have just gone ape-shit.'

She struggled to wake up. She had spent the evening before with Martin, fine-tuning his plan, and it had been well past midnight when she had gone to bed.

'What things?'

'The happy-hooker killer, that's what. He's taken some girl hostage. And sent a note to brag about it.'

'You what?'

'Later, Alex. Right now I've got a million other things I need to do. Be here in half an hour.'

The line went dead.

Alex groaned as she pulled off the duvet. It was freezing. She stiffly swung her legs onto the floor, and sat on the edge of her bed with her head in her hands; she felt awful. As well as working through Martin's plan – eventually coming up with something that she had to admit might work – they had also managed to get through three bottles of wine.

She walked sleepily through to the bathroom and splashed cold water on her face.

The station was in uproar when she got in; it was more like six thirty on an election night than six thirty in the morning. She had three calls on hold before she took her coat off. It really wasn't what she needed. She cradled the receiver on her shoulder while she rummaged in her bag for some Nurofen.

She read through the brief on her desk.

A fourteen-year-old girl had gone missing. She had last been seen getting off a bus on her way home on Wednesday night. But she had never made it. The police were already looking for her when they received a parcel: it contained photocopies of press shots of each of the prostitutes that had been killed, each numbered in the corner. With it was a Polaroid of the missing girl – Laura Metcalfe – with *5?* felt-tipped in the corner, and a single sheet of paper with two words written on it in the girl's handwriting. It simply said: 'Save me!'

'Dear God,' Alex murmured, reading it again.

Pinned to the back of the brief were copies of the day's front pages. The first had a single bold headline:

*Deep throat killer takes girl*

Underneath was a numbered picture of each of the dead girls, finishing with a picture of Laura doctored to look like the other mugshots, with *5?* stamped in the corner.

So now he's got a name, Alex thought grimly. She had known all along it would happen sooner or later. But instead of the familiar rush of confused emotions – anger, frustration, envy – and the twitchy feeling that she was missing out, she felt something different. A single clear sensation ran through her, making her shiver and screw up her face. It rose up in the back of her throat like bile; the sour, caustic taste of revulsion.

She flicked through the rest of the pages. All the second editions had adopted the name. Even the qualities had started to use it, sarcastically at first, but soon losing the sense or irony. A star had been born, and they were fighting for the reader's attention.

She put the pages down and slowly rubbed her eyes, trying not to see the images running through her head. It came back in a jumble, snapshots from her dreams, half remembered from the depth of night. This time she was on the ground, running. The images unwound in slow motion, jumpy and grainy like a badly spliced newsreel. She saw a girl, just a blur – a smear on the celluloid – zigzagging across the white sand like a scared gazelle.

And then she saw the dark shape of the jackal. A hunched nightmare behind her, gradually running her down.

She stood up uncertainly, her head spinning, and walked quickly to the toilets and threw up.

# 32

Harris stopped in the middle of the incident room and looked around. The office was packed full of people frantically tapping at keyboards and making calls – but he felt a strange emptiness in the atmosphere.

He panned across the banks of uniforms and plainclothes. They were all keeping busy, but there was a tautness to their faces and a jerkiness to their movements. He imagined it was what a First World War trench had been like before a big push.

'They putting you back in charge, then, sir?' a voice said behind him.

He turned around and saw Steve Pearson smiling from behind his headset on one of the call-lines.

'Let's keep our minds on the task in hand, shall we, DC Pearson?' he replied briskly.

'Sorry, sir.'

He scanned the faces that had turned to look at him. They were tired and drawn – and there was more than a hint of desperation in the air. He cleared his throat loudly. 'Come on, people,' he said, his voice booming across the office. 'I know this is a big challenge we're all facing. But I also know that you're all more than up to it, alright? So let's show them how it's done, shall we?'

He felt the atmosphere relax slightly. 'Chop-chop,' he said, smiling at them. 'Let's go to work.'

He glanced back at Pearson and nodded at the light flashing in front of him.

'I think you've got a call, DC Pearson. Let's not keep them waiting.'

He turned around and strode towards Hague's office.

'You wanted to see me, sir,' he said, shutting the door behind him.

Hague glanced up from the report he was reading.

'Yes. Yes, sit down. I won't be a minute.' He went back to studying the report.

Harris sat down.

Hague turned the page, muttered 'Fuck,' then lobbed the report onto the desk.

'Oh Christ, what a mess,' he said, running his fingers through his hair. There were dark shadows under his eyes, and his normally impeccable suit looked as if he had slept in it. He looked at Harris and frowned. 'I'd like to canvas your views on our next step, Harris. Any ideas?'

'What does Professor Miller say, sir?'

'Are you taking the piss?' Hague hissed.

'No, sir,' Harris said impassively. 'I just noticed you were reading his report.'

Hague twisted his head in the direction of the report. 'This?' he said, picking it up. 'Let's just say that as the shit hits the fan Professor Miller seems to be increasingly good at diagnosing the problem – at length – but less good when it comes to coming up with solutions.'

He tapped the front page.

'Professor Miller believes our killer is probably suffering from an inability to reconcile the fundamental ambiguity inherent in the virgin–whore dichotomy. This has triggered a psychosexual reaction that has now led him to look for a target at the other extreme of the virgin–whore spectrum.' He shut the report and slung it towards the bin. 'And it goes on. He doesn't, however, tell us how we might find the bastard. Although he *does* think the girl is probably in grave danger.'

'I see, sir.'

'Doesn't he think the fact that the cunt has sent us half her scalp might have alerted us to that?' He rubbed his hand over his hair again and rolled his eyes. 'Look, Harris, we haven't got time to mess around. What's your opinion on this latest development?'

'I don't know yet, sir.'

'Well, have a guess.'

'I think we need to step back and see if we can make some new connections before jumping to any conclusions, sir.'

'We haven't got time to step back.'

'I'm not saying we should procrastinate. But I think there's a lot of mileage in trying to identify any patterns that might be particular to this situation rather than then trying to fit the situation with something off the shelf. We're way off the pace, sir, but it's what we need to do.'

'And how would you approach it?'

'Well, we're suffering from an acute lack of forensic evidence, sir. But we've got a lot of very experienced detectives on the ground. I think the first step should be to try brainstorming a few ideas with them. See what comes out of it.'

'Good. Then get on to it.'

'Sorry, sir?'

'Look, Harris. Out backs are against the wall so we need to spread the load if we're going to get anywhere. You know the men better than I do.'

'Yes, sir.'

'We've got a press conference at two which gives you four hours to get the men together and firm up enough ideas to handle questions.'


Harris strode out into the middle of the incident room and clapped his hands.

'Listen up,' he shouted. 'I want everybody from DS upwards in Conference Room One in half an hour. And I want you to bring some ideas about how we tackle this problem, OK?'

He looked around at the faces. 'We're up against it here, people, so don't be shy, I want to hear any ideas.'

He set off towards his office.

'I only hope it's not too late,' he said to himself as he pushed open the door.

# 33

Alex jerked the car to a halt outside the gym, pulling on the handbrake while it was still moving.

'Come on,' she hissed, trying to put the crook-lock on while she twisted around for her bag; she was very late.

She jumped out of the car and jogged to the front door.

'Sor-ry,' she gasped as she pushed her way into the weight room, dropping her sports bag on the floor like a dead weight.

'You don't look so good,' Martin said, seeming concerned.

'I've had a . . . bad day so far,' she said, gulping in breath. 'I was lucky to be able to get away.'

'Are you still up for it?'

She looked at him and nodded.

'Yep. Let's go get 'em.'

'OK. Great. I asked Brian on reception if we can use the changing rooms upstairs and he was fine about it. They only get used for dance classes, and since they haven't had any of those for years, there'll be no problem – so you can leave your stuff there if you want. It'll be safe as houses, because that's where he stores his porn mags.'

'Lovely,' Alex said, pulling a face. 'That sounds nice.'

She changed into an anonymous blue suit that she hadn't worn for years, and rummaged in her bag for Amy's wig; it was the one she had used first, a lush, beautiful red. She carefully smoothed it down and secured it with a headband.

She stared at herself in the blotchy mirror bolted to the wall. She felt very strange; like a grown-up version of a kid dressing up in her mother's clothing. But instead of seeing a little princess

182

in big shoes with copies of her mother's *Good Housekeeping* and *She* spread open behind her, she saw a pale, tired-looking woman with too much make-up; a woman who looked like life hadn't quite worked out right, standing uncertainly in a dusty room that smelt of mildew – the fluffy pink frock had been replaced by a tight-fitting suit, the big shoes with slim high heels, and instead of a couple of women's journals open on the bed behind her she was surrounded by piles of faded magazines with names like *Big Jugs* and *Slags*.

She lit a cigarette and looked at herself again. How far she had come, she thought, a tight, humourless smile on her face. She sucked in a huge lungful of smoke, blew it at the mirror, then switched out the light and went to look for Martin.

'Wow. Big hair,' Martin said when he saw her.

'Better than normal?' she smiled tiredly.

'Well . . . no. But I've got this thing about redheads. And that's a stunner.'

'You can borrow it some time.'

'Thanks. So what do you think?' he said, opening his arms. She looked him up and down.

'Isn't the Sellotape in the middle of the glasses taking it a bit far?'

'Attention to detail, Alex.' He tapped his nose and grinned. 'It's what sorts the men from the boys.'

'I'll take your word for it. Where did you get the parka?'

'Oxfam. I got the shoes there as well.'

Alex looked at his feet. He was wearing plastic sandals over tartan socks.

'Well, you certainly look off your head,' she conceded.

'I'll take that as a compliment . . . So,' he grinned, 'let's rock'n'roll.'

Alex watched Martin disappear around the corner to the Institute. She could feel the sweat prickling at the bottom of her back; her hangover was being washed away by a tidal wave of adrenaline. But it was giving a final kick before it went. She coughed dryly, thinking for a second that she might throw up again.

She took a deep breath and opened the car door. She had done another spade job with the make-up, and was wearing her old glasses, but she felt transparent. She was sure they would see through her disguise in seconds.

Inside, the receptionist took her name without batting an eyelid, and buzzed through to Anne, while Alex nervously flattened the creases in her skirt.

'She's busy,' the receptionist said, after listening on the phone. 'What company did you say you were from?'

'Smith Kline Beecham,' Alex said in a smooth Home Counties accent – sure she was sounding false.

The receptionist repeated the name into the phone. There was a pause and then she looked up.

'Can you take a seat, please. Someone will see you in a minute.'

Alex remained standing. She was too nervous to sit still; she shuffled from foot to foot, pretending to read the health promotion posters on the wall.

She was staring at a poster on schizophrenia when someone spoke behind her.

'Miss Griffiths?'

It took a moment to register that she was being spoken to.

She forced her mouth into a smile and turned around. The voice belonged to a dumpy teenager in a white coat.

'I'll take you to Mrs Dolby's office.' She waved towards the waiting-room doors. 'Follow me.'

They walked briskly down the corridor and through the swing-doors that led into the main waiting area. The room was packed, and a motley assortment of agitated and unhappy-looking people stared as they entered. Alex glanced quickly around, but she couldn't see Martin. She felt her eyes smart. Despite the *No Smoking* signs the air was thick with cigarette smoke.

She accidentally caught the eye of a man sitting nearby who was hugging his legs and staring at her open-mouthed. As soon as she looked at him, he thrust his hand onto his crotch and giggled. She jerked her gaze away and hurried after her guide.

They were nearly at the door when she heard the first crash. The dumpy woman, who was slightly ahead of her, spun around so quickly she nearly fell over. Alex followed her gaze.

It was Martin.

Bang on time.

He was standing on a low table by the wall, staring wildly around him, with his arms out sideways. The people nearby shrank back in horror.

'You nailed me to a post,' he shrieked. The whole room – including Alex – jumped when he spoke.

'You nailed me to a fuck-ing post, you bastards!' he yelled. 'But I didn't mind. I'm good that way.'

He jumped off the table, sending magazines spilling onto the floor. People began to scatter, and a couple fell backward over chairs.

'Judas!' he boomed, waving at the crowd. He sprang forward, snatched up a chair, and sent it flying towards the wall.

People started to back-pedal away from him. Panic was beginning to take hold, and chairs went over in the rush towards the swing-doors. A clot of people, all trying to get out at the same time, fell over in a heap.

'Jude-arse!'

Suddenly the door on the other side of the room flew open, and Alex saw Anne rush out with two nervous-looking men in tow. She was relieved; they had none of the bulky menace that the orderlies had in *One Flew Over the Cuckoo's Nest*.

Martin should be alright.

It was now or never.

She walked quickly to the edge of the room, and glanced around. No one was paying any attention to her. All eyes were locked on Martin, who was waving the broken chair around wildly.

'I am the anti-christ! I am an anar-chist!' he started to sing. He flung the chair down and started to pogo up and down.

Alex tore her gaze away from him, glanced quickly around, then pushed through the swinging door that Anne had just come through.

It brought her out in a sterile-looking corridor. She jogged along, her heels skidding on the polished floor, and looked at the nameplates on the doors: *Treatment Room A, Store Room, Dr G Stanhope*.

The doors swinging behind her batted soundbites up from the waiting room.

She heard someone trying to reason with Martin in a level

tone, but she couldn't make out the words. But then Martin's voice boomed up the corridor loud and clear.

'You think – that I think – that I'm Jesus Christ,' he hollered. 'What do you think I am, nuts?'

There was another drone of reasoning, this time more confused.

'He's dead, you idiot. Where as I am very much alive.'

Then she heard Anne, trying to sound calm and reassuring.

'I'm the king of rock'n'roll, you silly bint,' Martin shrieked. 'Not the king of the fucking Jews.'

He was loving it, she thought, shaking her head in disbelief.

Martin started to sing 'Love me Tender' in a deep boom. Alex tried to shut his voice out of her head. She passed Anne's office and then a couple of doctors' waiting rooms.

Then she saw what she was looking for.

*Dr I. Fisher.*

She glanced over her shoulder, then twisted the handle and stumbled into the dark office. She groped for the light switch, and the office sprang into sharp focus.

She tried to keep calm; with the door shut she couldn't hear anything from outside. The only sound was from the large aquarium against the wall. She wished she could hear Martin – at least then she would know what was happening.

She didn't know where to start. The room was a tip. Every inch seemed to be covered with something. There were boxes and piles of magazines everywhere, and huge piles of computer print-outs on the shelves.

As she stepped forward she knocked over a chair, spilling copies of *The Lancet* onto the floor.

'Come on,' she whispered to herself. A twitchy feeling was buzzing away in her pelvis.

She took a few tentative pokes at one of the piles on the top of Fisher's desk, then realised radical action was needed. She took a deep breath and swiped the whole lot onto the floor. She found a fax machine dangling over the edge, suspended on its cable. But there was no portable PC.

She moved around the office, shifting piles and prising open boxes.

It felt as if she were moving in slow motion. Every second

186

seemed to last an hour. She was convinced they were about to burst in and find her.

Where on earth was it? she thought, glancing desperately around the room. Maybe it wasn't there.

She noticed a dead fish floating on the surface of the aquarium. She watched for a moment as the bubbles bounced it around. Then she tore her gaze away from it; her attention was getting caught by everything except what she was there for.

Then she saw it; on the top of a filing cabinet in the corner, just visible behind a pile of print-outs, was a little grey box with a recharge wire plugged into it.

She almost sprang across the room.

She swept her hand across the surface to get the dust off it and picked it up. Its only distinguishing features were the TOSHIBA logo and a small red light glowing at the edge, but that was enough.

That had to be it.

She swung the bag off her shoulder, snatched the small transformer from the wall, and bundled the whole lot in.

Then she strode quickly across the room, snapped off the light, and was back in the corridor. She paused briefly; she couldn't hear any noise coming from the waiting room.

'Oh shit,' she mouthed as she walked tentatively towards the swing-door. Maybe they'd managed to restrain him.

She took a deep breath, then pushed the door ajar slightly.

Now she could hear voices. Quiet voices, trying to sound calm. She craned her neck and looked through the gap.

The room had emptied. A little group of staff huddled at the double doors to reception. Alex followed their gaze.

Martin was standing completely still in the corner, smiling and watching as the two men edged towards him; they each had a hand out in front of them and seemed to be trying to look assertive but non-confrontational at the same time – which was probably hard as Martin was brandishing a broken chair leg. Anne Dolby was standing behind them, talking in a low voice.

Alex edged through the door and walked slowly across the back of the room furthest away from them, keeping her eyes on Anne's back until she passed her. Then she switched her gaze to the double doors.

187

The little cluster dispersed as she approached them, their attention held by Martin. Just as she was about to leave the room she heard Anne's voice.

'Miss Griffiths!'

Alex stopped and turned but remained silent. Anne was staring at her coldly.

'Can you hang on a minute.'

Alex got ready to bolt, but as Anne stepped forward Martin suddenly sprang into action behind her.

'Come on,' he yelled, flailing the chair leg around. The two men backed off rapidly, and one of them fell over an upturned chair. Anne spun back around.

'Come on, you bastards,' Martin yelled, kicking a metal bin after one of the men. 'I'll be in goal.'

Anne raised both her hands, but didn't say anything; it looked as if she didn't know what to do.

'I'll take the lot of you on,' Martin shrieked. 'I'll be Seaman.' His voice was high-pitched, and even Alex was convinced he was out of his mind.

'Come on, then, see what you can do.' He stepped forward and Anne shrunk back slightly. 'Come on, love, try and put one past me. Give it your best shot. *Come on*!'

Alex turned and walked quickly out through reception.

She darted into the dark side street they had left the car in. Martin's battered old Escort was parked by a boarded-up warehouse, as far away from any lights as possible.

She went up to the passenger door, and bounced on her toes.

Martin had the key.

She dug her hands into her pockets, and looked down to the end of the street where he should appear. She shivered. The sweat had cooled under her shirt and she could feel a cold damp spot on her back. What if they had overpowered him? she thought, clamping her teeth together. How long should she wait?

But then she heard a noise and Martin careered around the corner, the sound of his feet echoing off the warehouse front.

By the time he reached the car, she was shivering uncontrollably, her breath coming out in spasms. She took her hands out of her pockets and rubbed them together as he stopped.

He looked triumphantly at her.

'Well?'

'Just – open – the – car,' she said numbly. 'Then you can smile.'

She hopped from foot to foot as he fumbled with the lock, resisting the urge to grab the keys and try for herself.

'Please hurry up,' she pleaded as Martin opened her door. Suddenly she was very scared.

The engine was already turning when she fell into her seat. It was turning – but it wasn't catching.

'What's wrong?'

'Don't worry,' Martin said, pulling out the choke. 'It's just cold.'

She looked in the wing mirror, but all she could see was darkness. Martin tried a couple more times, but nothing happened.

'Bloody Dagenham dustbin,' he exclaimed, letting go of the key. He hit the steering wheel and glanced in the mirror.

'Oh shit.' He grabbed the key again. 'Push your lock down.'

Alex twisted around, slammed down the button and looked over her shoulder. She could see the outlines of three people running towards them.

'Come on, you bastard,' Martin shouted as the engine coughed.

Then it caught.

He pumped the pedal and, as the engine howled, let out the clutch. They leapt forward and away.

'That was close,' Martin muttered, as he pulled the car around the corner at the end.

'It's OK,' Alex said, looking hard in the mirror. 'I think we've made it.'

His face broke into a wide smile as he changed gear. 'Am I a genius or what?' he grinned.

She hugged her coat around her. She had the shivering under control, but she was still freezing.

'Yes,' she conceded after a pause. 'You're a bloody genius. Mad as a bat, but a genius no doubt. Now get me home before I die of hypothermia.'

He drove through town and stopped outside her flat.

'Thanks, Martin,' she said, as she unfastened her seat belt. 'I'll give you a call tomorrow. Tell you what I've found.'

She turned around and caught him staring at her intently.

'What?' she asked warily.

He leant over to her, put his hand around her neck, and pulled her towards him. 'That was brilliant.'

The sudden movement caught her off guard.

'No!' she said, recoiling and putting her hand up.

'I'm sorry,' he said, pulling away. 'I was only going to kiss you on the cheek.'

'Oh,' she said, putting her hand down. She looked away. 'Look, I'm sorry. It's just that I'm a bit wary.'

'No problem.' He frowned. 'It was my fault.'

'No, it's not that ... You just caught me out, that's all. I'm sorry.' She looked at him and smiled. 'Come here.' She leant over and pecked him on the cheek. 'It was you who were brilliant. Thanks.'

He nodded and grinned. 'I know.'

They looked at each other for a long moment, and Alex felt her stomach flutter.

'I ...' she started, but couldn't think of anything else to say.

'I know,' he smiled. 'You need to spend some time with that little grey box, right?' He leant over her and opened the door. 'Go on. Off you go. Give me a call when you're done.'

'OK,' she said, not moving.

'Go on!'

She got out of the car.

'Look, once I've got this thing sorted, why don't we celebrate?' she said, raising her eyebrows. 'Y'know. Have a drink or something?'

'Sounds great to me.'

'Really? Good.'

She got out and watched him drive away, then turned towards the house.

She looked up and felt herself shudder as she approached the pitch-black alley. She stopped and pulled a small can from her bag; it was a CS gas canister. She wasn't sure if it would work – it had sat in a drawer for two years since she had brought it back from a holiday in France – but it made her feel better.

She glanced up the road where Martin had disappeared.

She'd be OK.

She walked tentatively down the side of the house then lunged around the corner, pointing the can in the air.

It was dark there, and . . .

She was sure she saw a quick, flickering movement. She stumbled as she stepped back. There was something there. She panned the can around in front of her, but she couldn't see anything.

Then she heard a rattling by the fence and saw the outline of a frightened tomcat shoot up the wall.

She took a deep breath, and tried to smile.

She bolted the door behind her, pulled off the wig and scratched her head, running her fingers through her damp, greasy, flattened hair.

Her whole body ached, and her back cracked when she stretched. She felt completely exhausted.

But she had the PC, which made it all worth it.

She went into the kitchen, turned on one of the gas rings and tried to defrost her hands.

When she was warm enough to move her fingers, she made some tea, went through to the bedroom and changed, dumping her suit in a pile in the corner.

She put the portable down on the living-room floor, and pushed the transformer into the wall socket.

'Dr Fisher, I presume,' she said as the PC whirred into life. 'Now let's see what you've got to hide.'

She took a sip of her tea and broke off a huge piece of Dairy Milk, stuffing it into her mouth whole. Then she slotted in the disk Forester had given her and went to work.

# 34

Lenny's nose was already broken. Dobson wanted to drive it right into his face, but he stopped himself.

'What do I pay you for, Lenny?' he said, punctuating each word with a slap on the face. 'To do what I say. That's what. Not to get stitched up by some jumped-up bitch with an attitude.'

Lenny's head lolled forward.

'Oh, for fuck's sake,' Dobson said, rolling his eyes. 'Let him go.'

The two men on either side let go of his arms and he slumped forward. Dobson turned around as Lenny slipped off the chair and hit the floor.

Leroy stared at him coolly.

'I don't think anyone realises just how much is tied up in this,' Dobson spat. 'It's not just my reputation that we're talking about here. Although that is important. There's a fuck of a lot money at stake. So how come this bitch is in my face again, Leroy? How come we didn't know that that faggot Fisher had a fucking computer? I thought we had this wrapped?'

Leroy's face was expressionless.

'We only know what they tell us, Frank. That was their problem.'

'Well, now it's our problem, homeboy, because if they go down, we go down, so we need to get it back fast.'

'Don't worry, Frank . . .'

'You can call me Frank when you bring that bitch in with a pole up her arse, OK? Until then it's Mr Dobson again. You understand me, Leroy? You understand? . . . You heading down the pecking order fast, boy. I don't want to hear no excuses!'

Leroy nodded slowly.

'Now tell me something I don't know.'

'All we know is that the bitch walked in there and took off with a computer while some guy stirred it up.'

'Who?'

'Not completely sure. But we know where to start.'

'How come?'

'Word is that one of Arnold's men's been asking questions. So that's what we're chasing.'

'Who?' Dobson hissed.

'Don't know yet, Fra . . . Mr Dobson. But we're on to it. We got stuff on the sicko who runs the gym down there, so we'll squeeze him. We'll make him talk. No problem.'

'Just find him.'

'What d'you want us to do when we got him?'

Dobson stepped closer to him. They were about the same height. Their noses were only about two inches apart. Leroy didn't move a muscle.

'I don't give a fuck,' Dobson spat. 'Cut his dick off and shove it in his mouth, for all I care. That's what I pay you for, Leroy. You remember that. If he knows something, get it out of him. If not, it's all the same. If he's asking questions, take him out.'

Dobson spun round as Lenny moaned and tried to turn over. He strode across the room and kicked him hard in the ribs.

'Cunt,' he shouted. 'Cunt, cunt, cunt.'

Each time Dobson's boot slammed into him, Lenny's back arched upward as if he had been electrocuted.

'You're bleeding on my carpet, you stupid cunt,' Dobson yelled, a haze of saliva falling across Lenny's stricken body. 'See what you're doing?'

He half-heartedly kicked him one more time then looked at the two men standing impassively against the wall. 'Get him out of here,' he said. 'Take him down to the hospital and dump him in the carpark. He's making me feel sick.'

The two men started to pull Lenny up off the floor.

'Think yourself lucky, Lenny,' Dobson warned darkly. 'I'm a generous man. You been dissin' me. But I'm giving you a chance. Take a day off. Clean yourself up. But if you're not at work at the weekend you're in big trouble, my friend. You hear me?'

Lenny wasn't hearing anything. As the two men dragged him towards the door his head hung limply and his feet trailed on the ground; a thick coil of bloody phlegm had started to come out of his mouth.

'Get him out,' Dobson said calmly. He turned back to Leroy, who was still standing watching with his arms crossed.

'That's what happens when you use white boys,' Dobson smiled. 'They fuck up.'

Leroy's expression didn't change. Dobson was forty, white, and his muscle was beginning to turn to fat. He was originally from Coventry, but his accent was more West Indian than West Midlands. Dobson thought he was a twenty-five-year-old Jamaican. He would have been ridiculous – if he hadn't been so dangerous. Leroy knew to take him very seriously indeed.

'Make me happy, Leroy. Bring that bitch in. I don't care what you have to do to get her. Just do it. I want her. I want whoever's helping her. And I want that fucking computer. Just do what it takes.'

He strode to the door.

'And get someone in to clean up that fucking carpet.'

# 35

Alex closed her eyes and tried to stretch the tension out of her neck. She was getting nowhere, she thought, stifling a yawn. She glanced at her watch. It was no good, she was going to have to call Forester. She stretched over to the TV, turned the sound down, then picked up the phone.

The ten o'clock news was just starting. She punched the station's number, watching the newsreader's mouth move silently. She knew what would come on next, she thought, cradling the handset on her shoulder while she waited for the line to connect. The picture switched to a video of the red-light district. The camera swept along a darkened roadside, a blur of red and black. Then it slowed and started to linger on the lone figures standing in the pools of light from the flaring streetlights, composites of peroxide white and shiny black leather turning away to hide their faces. She had watched the same item on the six o'clock news and knew it was Mike doing the voice-over. He had spoken gravely as the camera rested on a young girl standing topless under a streetlight, chewing gum and wiggling her hips at the traffic. She couldn't have been more than fourteen.

Then the picture switched to a still image of Laura Metcalfe.

'Is Forester there?' she asked when night security answered.

'What department's he in?'

'He's the bloke who lives in the computer room.'

'Oh, him. Yes, he's here. I'll see if I can get him. Hang on.'

The line went dead for a second. Then she heard the hum of the computer room, and Forester clearing his throat in the background. The screen was filled with the earnest face of a spokeswoman from Women against Violence against Women. She got ten seconds before the camera was snuffling about again in the pink fleshy light of the red-light district.

'Hello, IT Services,' Forester answered formally.

'Very professional, Forester,' she laughed. 'Have you been on a course or something?'

'Yes, actually,' he said, recognising her. 'Sir made me go on it. He seems to think that being polite will bring down costs or some such twaddle. Can't see it myself, but y'know. Anyway . . .' He put on his best professional voice again. 'What can I do for you?'

Alex had been struggling with the computer for hours. She had managed to retrieve hundreds of files, but whatever she did she couldn't actually get the thing to work again. It was beginning to drive her mad.

'Sure, bring it in,' Forester said, when she told him. 'I'm not too busy at the moment.'

'So why are you still there?'

'Oh, y'know, there's always something to do,' he replied vaguely.

Alex put the phone down, and wondered if Forester actually had anywhere else to live. Maybe he had a sleeping bag down the back of the bench.

She bundled the PC into the flight bag, and went to get her car keys.

The temperature had dropped below freezing outside. The moon shone brightly in the cloudless sky, bathing the back of the house with a milky light that made crystals of frost on the bricks glitter.

Alex crunched down the alley and out onto the road. What a beautiful night, she thought, craning her neck and looking at the stars. She blew steam into the air and watched it catch the light.

She put her hands in her pockets and set off towards her car, walking slowly down the pavement, letting the cold air clear her head. Three hours in front of the screen had left her with a dull headache.

She yawned and felt the cold air on the back of her throat.

A car door slammed up ahead.

She glanced up, squinting to improve her vision; her eyes

196

weren't focusing too well after staring at the screen. She could see two men about a hundred yards ahead. One of them was locking a car. She couldn't really make them out, but for some reason her stomach twitched with fear.

She kept walking.

She was breathing fast and shallowly with her mouth open, a short nervous pant. The cold air scoured the back of her throat.

The man finished locking the door and stood up, and the twitch became a wave. The streetlights weren't bright enough to show their features. But she could see both their outlines. They were broad-shouldered and tall – very tall – standing way above the tops of the cars.

She listened to her instincts – and knew that they were coming for her.

She fought the urge to bolt. She wanted to turn and run, but she knew that would be suicide; she was no runner. The car was the only option. And that meant she had to keep walking. It was about thirty yards up the road. Thirty yards in the wrong direction. Towards them.

She looked at the two figures. They were still just silhouettes. If she walked calmly to the car, they might not notice her. She would get there long before they did. If she ran they would know it was her.

She was beginning to shake again. She dug her hands further into her pockets and put her head down. From a distance it would look as if she were staring at the pavement. Her eyes were locked on the two figures. They were walking quickly.

It was the longest walk of her life. Each step seemed to take forever, her feet jarring on the hard stone paving slabs. And with each step the figures seemed to get bigger.

She glanced up as she reached the car. She could just about make out their faces, the dark shadows of their eye sockets, one face pale and pasty, the other black. She dropped her head quickly so they wouldn't recognise her, and her gaze streaked across the wing of her car. The exposed metal shone a deep black where the acid had stripped away the paint. She dug into her coat for her keys. Where were they? She rummaged through her bag quickly.

'Gotcha,' she muttered as she pulled them out.

She glanced back up the road. And her heart almost stopped. They had started to run.

There was perhaps thirty yards between them and the car. No more. Their bomber jackets filled with air as they hurtled towards her, the light catching on leather and white cotton. But there was still no definition to their faces. They were just two monsters tearing down the road to get her.

For a moment she was rooted to the ground. Not more than a microsecond passed before she scrambled her muscles into action, but in that moment the two figures seemed to double in size.

She crashed against the bonnet as she ran around to the driver's door. She steadied the key in her hand. And it went straight in. She snatched open the door, jamming herself into the driving seat, her coat catching on something as she tried to pull the door shut.

She yanked it free. Come on, she thought.

Come on, come on, come on!

She shot a glance at the left-side mirror as she struggled with the crook-lock. They were close. Their heads were cut off by the top of the mirror, but the images were large.

The engine caught first time. Something flickered in the corner of her eye. She told herself not to look up.

But she did.

All she could see was a belt and the crotch area of black jeans in the side window.

'Come on!' she pleaded.

Her hand was shaking. She missed the first attempt to slot into first. Then she got it. Her right foot fumbled for the accelerator. There was a crash against the door. The engine howled. She pushed the accelerator down slightly, and eased up on the clutch.

The engine stuttered.

For a split second – a silent moment that stretched on for far too long – she thought the engine was going to die. Her mind was already constructing vivid images of being dragged onto the road when the car lurched forward. She managed to jerk the wheel, forcing the little red Mazda out into the middle of the road. As she took off something ripped into the soft-top. The material made a zipping noise as a blade split it open.

But she was away.

She accelerated fast, moving up through the gears and making third before looking in the mirror. She could see them running behind her, but they were dropping back into the night. She blew the air out of her lungs, and glanced at the torn material flapping in the wind above her head.

It was time to run.

She didn't stop when she reached the end of the road. She pulled straight out onto the main drag with a quick glance, cutting up a double-decker as it struggled up the bus lane. She slammed the gear lever into second. The front of the bus dipped in her rear-view mirror as it braked. She floored the accelerator, and pulled away up the hill.

The lights were changing as she hurtled down the open road to the station. She went through on red, nearly taking out an old couple as they stepped onto the road. Then she was on the ramp and into the underground carpark.

She swiped her card and waited impatiently while the barrier rose. Being stationary again made her suddenly feel vulnerable.

The quick and the dead, she thought, shooting under the barrier as it was still rising. She had to keep moving.

The carpark was empty. She zigzagged through the pillars, and parked right by the lift doors.

She got out and inspected the damage. She was feeling calmer than she had expected; she knew what she had to do. Get the computer sorted and get the hell out. She ran her finger across the edge of the jagged slash in the roof. It was clean, made by something extremely sharp. She dug into her bag and pulled out her cigarettes, then walked quickly to the lift.

She held the smoke in her lungs until she was in the lift, then blew it out as the doors closed. She took another pull, and for no reason in particular blew it at the security camera.

'Shouldn't take long,' Forester said, jabbing the arrow key. 'You missed a couple of config files, that's all.'

'Thanks, Forester,' she murmured, absorbed in her thoughts. She shook her head and tried to concentrate. She needed somewhere to go. Fast.

She left him and jogged up to her office.

The lights were off and the room was illuminated by the grey light coming through the blinds. She walked over to the window, and looked down at the main road. She tried not to get too close to the glass.

The road was empty. A few cars shot by, but nothing was stationary. The front of the deli and the shops on the other side of the wide road were dark. The only sign of life was a group of people going into the pub on the corner.

She left the light off and went to her desk. It was a no-smoking office, but she lit another cigarette, hoping the smoke detectors weren't too sensitive.

She punched Amy's number and waited.

'Can I speak to Amy, please?' she asked when the phone was answered.

'I'm afraid she's away,' a stoned-sounding male voice replied. 'She's gone to her gran's funeral or something.'

She recognised Doug – one of the two deadheads who had rooms in Amy's house.

'Hi, Doug. It's Alex here. Do you know when she'll be back?'

'Er, no . . . I dunno . . . not really. Probably a couple of days? These things can be pretty heavy.'

'Yeah, right.' She chewed her lip. 'OK, never mind. Thanks anyway.'

She slowly put the phone down, and looked out of the window at the dark sky, wondering what to do.

'Martin,' she muttered, fumbling in her bag for his number.

She punched Martin's number and watched the bright pin-prick of an aeroplane trace a course across the sky. 'Please be in.'

'Piss!' she muttered as she heard an answer machine kick in.

'. . . I'm afraid I can't take your call at the moment, but if you leave a message I'll call you back.'

She was about to put the phone down, but decided against it.

'Hi, Martin,' she said after the tone. 'It's Alex. I . . .'

'Alex!' Martin's voice cut in. 'Sorry, I was expecting a call from my mother and I wasn't in the mood. How's it going?'

She told him what had happened.

'Bloody hell,' he said when she had finished. 'D'you think they know it was you today?'

'What do you think?' she replied, hearing the sharpness in her voice. 'That they were there for my unpaid poll tax?'

'OK, OK. I was only asking.'

'Look, I'm sorry. I'm sorry. I'm just rattled.'

'Don't worry . . . Are you OK?'

'Yeah,' she said, starting to feel a little better. 'Yeah, I think so.'

'So what are you going to do?'

'Well . . . I've called Amy but she's away. And I need some-where to stay, so . . .'

'You can come here if you want.'

'Oh, well, you know. I don't know.'

'Come on. Don't worry. I've got a spare room.'

'I . . . actually, yes, please. It sounds like a good idea.'

She jotted his address down; it wasn't far from Amy's.

'I'll be there in about half an hour.'

She cut the line, then called Amy's house again, telling Doug she needed to come around to pick up some things.

Forester was standing by the printer when she returned to the computer room.

'Hi,' he exclaimed when he saw her. 'It's working. It wasn't a big problem. Just a corrupt config file. I rebuilt it from one of ours.'

'Thanks, Forester. Thanks a lot.'

'And I've dumped all the data files onto hard copy for you.' He scooped a pile of paper off the printer. 'It's easier to read them that way.'

He handed the pile to her.

'Great.' She stopped hopping from foot to foot and smiled. 'You're a star. If you ever need a customer reference, I'm your woman.'

While she bundled the PC back into the bag, Forester hovered around in the background.

'Alex?' He wouldn't quite catch her eye.

'Uh-huh?' she asked, glancing up at him. He looked nervous.

'Would you . . . Would you . . . Look, it doesn't matter.' He hitched up his trousers.

'Would I what?'

'I just wondered if maybe you . . . we could maybe, you know, have a drink or something?' he stammered, looking at his shoes. 'I mean, you know, just a drink, maybe over the road at the Smugglers or something.'

She zipped up the bag and looked at him. His gaze was locked on the floor.

'I'd love to.'

'Really?' he said, looking up wide-eyed.

'Yes. But not now.'

'Oh.' His gaze fell to his feet again. 'I see.'

'Look, Forester,' she said, making him look up, 'I'm not fobbing you off. I've got to meet someone else tonight. But we'll do it another time. OK?'

'Fine,' he said, smiling faintly.

'Right. It's a deal. Now you leave these damned computers alone and go home.'

'OK,' he nodded. 'As soon as the back-up's finished.'

She left him squatting next to a huge grey box on the floor and headed for the lift.

The cold air rushed in as the doors rattled slowly open. She hitched the bag onto her shoulder and stepped out.

The sides of the carpark were covered with metal bars intended to stop intruders getting through the gaps. They were hopeless; the station lost about a car a week. But the bars did catch the wind. They creaked as the breeze moaned through the murky space.

She hurried towards her car.

When she turned on her headlights they lit up the space in front of her, but made the rest of the carpark fall into complete darkness. She turned the heating dial around to full.

She snaked the car back through the pillars, her lights catching on the luminous yellow stripes on the blotchy concrete.

She kept the car rolling as she waited for the barrier to rise. Then she accelerated up the ramp and out onto the main road.

The city was empty.

She drove over to Amy's house as quickly as she dared, trying to time it so that she didn't have to stop at any lights.

Then, with a bag full of Amy's clothes on the passenger seat, she wove her way carefully through the back streets towards Martin's house, her knuckles white on the wheel, attempting to ignore the howl of the wind through the gash above her head.

# 36

Alex opened her eyes as the fire crackled and the cat stirred on her stomach. She looked around; Martin had gone. She must have dropped off for a second, she thought, pushing herself up on the sofa.

The cat jumped onto the carpet and padded into the kitchen.

She looked around the small front room. It was packed full of grand but slightly dilapidated furniture; there was an overstuffed leather sofa, a huge dark sideboard, and a wonderful gilt-edged mirror above the fireplace. The house was tucked away at the end of a terrace by the canal. She stretched and yawned, feeling safe. Martin was burning peat on the fire, which filled the house with a rich, earthy smell. She was finding it hard not to doze off.

'There you go,' Martin said, coming in from the kitchen and setting a cup down on the table.

Alex started to get up. .

'Stay where you are,' he insisted. 'I'll use the chair.'

She pulled herself up anyway, and took the cup.

'So is your life always this exciting?' he asked, settling into the chair.

'I wish. My nerves are shot to pieces.'

'Maybe you should have something stronger.' He put his cup down. 'Can I get you anything?'

'Yeah, that would be nice.'

'What d'you fancy?'

'Oh, I don't know. Whatever.'

He went back into the kitchen, and came back with two big glasses of red wine.

'So what happens next?' he asked, handing her the glass.

'What with?'

'Your big adventure. What's your next move?'

'Oh, I don't know,' Alex said dreamily. 'Maybe this stuff will give me inspiration.'

'I doubt it. It's more likely to send you to sleep.'

They lapsed into silence. She could hear the old clock ticking on the wall behind her.

She pushed herself up and looked at Martin. He was stroking the cat under its chin.

'How long have you lived here?'

'In this house?'

She nodded.

'About ten years.'

'Wow. Long time.'

'I bought it with a friend when I left college.' He picked up a tin by the fire, and started to make a roll-up.

'I didn't know you smoked.'

'Not often. Would you like one?'

'Thanks. If you'll make it for me.'

She watched him while he concentrated. He stuck his tongue out while he worked.

'What happened to the friend?' she asked.

He looked over at her and smiled.

'Are you interrogating me, Miss Brierley?' He handed her the roll-up.

'Thanks . . . No. I'm just interested.'

'I bought it with this girl I was at college with,' he explained, starting to roll another. 'But it didn't work out.'

Alex lit the thin cigarette and blew the smoke towards the fire. 'So what happened?'

'So she left, and I bought her out.' He shrugged. 'It was as simple as that.'

'Were you close?'

'At the time, yes. But that was then.'

'Sorry.'

'Don't be. It's OK,' he said, sticking the finished cigarette in his mouth and settling back into the chair. 'It was a long time ago.'

He stretched over for the matches.

'So . . . how come you can manage to stay so calm at a time like this, Alex?'

'You're changing the subject,' she smiled.

'No I'm not. Now I'm just interested,' he said, lighting his cigarette.

'OK,' she said, raising her hands. 'I ask too many questions.'

'No you don't. That's not why I asked. I want to know.'

'What?'

'Tell me how you keep your head together while all this is happening.'

She thought about it for a moment.

'I'm not,' she explained. 'I follow the swan's example. Calm on the surface but thrashing away like a bastard under the surface.'

'I don't believe you.'

'It's true.' She laughed, 'I'll be honest with you. I've never been as scared as I am at the moment.'

'What, *now*?' he said with mock dismay.

'No.' She looked at him, shaking her head. 'You know what I mean. With this whole thing. Not knowing who is out to get you is awful. Especially when you know what they can do.'

'So why do you keep at it?'

'Because it's the only way to bring it to an end.' She shrugged.

'Is that all?'

'Yeah. I mean, mostly. To start with I was just looking for a story that might get me a better job, y'know. But now . . . now . . . It's like I've got something to prove. I mean, I've got to get to the bottom of it so I can go home without worrying about getting acid chucked in my face. But it's not that simple. It's more like . . .'

She stopped and looked at the fire.

'What?' he asked, staring at her.

'Nothing,' she said quietly, watching the dancing flames. She took a deep pull on her cigarette and closed her eyes.

He looked at her for a moment, as if he were trying to weigh something up.

'What is it, Alex?'

She turned to him and shook her head.

'It's nothing. I mean, it's nothing in particular, if that's what you're getting at.' She shrugged. 'Well, y'know, the usual things . . . Look, basically I want to prove I can do this for myself, that's all.'

He stared at her. 'And?'

She chewed her lip, and looked up at the ceiling. 'Look, Martin, it's just too complicated, OK?' she said eventually.

'We've got all night.'

She took a deep pull on her cigarette and blew the smoke towards the fire.

'Maybe I'll tell you when you grow up, OK!' She smiled, pulled her legs up and hugged them, and stared at the glowing embers.

'So who was it?' he asked quietly.

'Who was what?'

'There's always a who there somewhere. Who was it that you were thinking about when you suddenly got sad?'

'Oh, come on,' she laughed. 'It's nobody in particular. Just the whole world. You know what it's like.'

'Yeah, I do . . . But there's usually someone in particular.'

He looked at her hard.

'Oh, give me a break,' she said. Then she looked down. 'But yeah, there was somebody. Although it's not like you think. It's way more complicated than that.' She smiled sadly and shook her head. 'Look, can we change the subject. *Please?*'

'OK. OK, I'm sorry. Session over.'

She downed the rest of the glass. 'Thank God. I thought I was going to have to go home and take my chances.'

'Another?'

'Definitely.'

She relit her roll-up while he was gone, took a long pull then threw it into the fire. She watched as the flames quickly ate it up, then turned away and lay back on the sofa.

'So tell me what's on the wee computer,' he said when he came back.

'Oh, all sorts of crap.' She pushed herself up onto her elbow. 'I'm having a hard time understanding it at the moment. I think I've found what Jill was looking for, but there's pages of it. It's going to take a while. Maybe when I look at it tomorrow it'll be clearer.' She frowned. 'And there's some kind of database on there, but God knows how it works. The print-out from it looks like nothing on earth. How are you with computers?'

'Never used one before.'

'I thought you might say that.'

'Isn't there anyone you can ask?'

'Well, there's a guy down at the station who knows how to make them work, so he should be able to help me actually get at the data I need. But to be honest that's only half the problem. What I really need is someone who can help me interpret the information.'

'What sort of person?'

'I don't know – a doctor, or a medic or something, I suppose.'

'Don't you know anybody who knows about that stuff?'

'Nobody . . .' she started to say, then stopped as a thought struck her. The doctor at the hospital the day after Fisher had been killed. The cute one. 'Yeah, maybe . . .' she said slowly.

She leant over and pulled her Filofax out of her bag. She had taken his number. What was his name? She dug about.

There it was. Steve Hill.

'What time is it?'

'Just after two.'

'Oh . . . Maybe I'll leave it until the morning.'

'I think so. You look like you need to sleep.'

'You're probably right.'

He took her to a small bedroom at the back of the house. It had a big queen-sized bed under a sloping roof, and a huge chest of drawers. Other than that it was empty. The blinds were pulled down over the sash window.

'*Voilà*,' Martin said, as he clicked on the light.

'Nice!' She turned around and looked at him. 'Thanks, Martin.' She smiled.

'For what?'

She glanced up at the ceiling. 'Look . . .' She shook her head. 'I'm not very good at the heartfelt stuff. But . . .' She rolled her eyes. 'But if you hadn't been there today I couldn't have pulled it off, OK?' She glanced at him. 'Thanks.'

'It always makes you feel better to know you're not going to die alone.'

208

She hesitated, then put her hand on his shoulder and kissed him on the cheek.

'Goodnight.'

'If you hear howling out the back it's only the cats,' he said as he left.

'Let's hope so,' she murmured as she sat heavily on the bed.

She was out within twenty seconds of hitting the sheets, falling into a deep dream-filled sleep.

# 37

A glint of moonlight caught his eyes as she finally stopped moving. Otherwise the room was shrouded in darkness. He gently let go of her shoulders and raised his hand to his mouth, sucking the smarting flesh where she had bitten him. It had taken longer than he had expected for the temazepam to kick in.

He shifted his weight on the bed to get a better look at her. A thin yellow light from the window fell across her skin, lighting up her face. She looked so peaceful lying against the starched white sheets – but also so fragile.

He felt the first flutter of panic.

'You'll be safe with me,' he murmured, trying to ignore the rising feeling. His skin suddenly felt cold and clammy.

He reached out with a shaking hand, and flattened her hair over the matted, bloody patch on the side of her head.

'I won't . . .' he started to say, but suddenly it felt as if he couldn't breathe. He panted to try to relieve the tightness in his chest.

'I'll . . . I'll look after you.'

He grimaced, feeling the tightness wrap around him and clamp his chest. He squeezed his eyes shut, the sinews in his neck standing out like knotted rope, trying to force the hollow feeling back down. He dug his fingers into his thighs as the crippling emptiness tried to open out inside him, and gradually – very slowly – he began to feel the tension disperse.

He wasn't sure how long he'd had his eyes closed when he opened them again, but the moon had shifted in the sky slightly, casting a fuller yellow light across her face.

He pulled the sheets down slightly, exposing her delicate shoulders and smooth skin. He ran his fingers down her neck, feeling her windpipe with his thumb. It all seemed so fragile. Just a thin membrane between life and death.

He felt the churning in his stomach again, the empty feeling of helplessness dancing through him.

His eyes flooded with tears.

He leant forward, hooking his long fingers underneath her, and lifted her up. Her head lolled back as he pulled her towards him. Then he hugged her closely. On the bed she had looked perfect, but lifeless and dead. But now, although she still felt like a rag doll in his arms, he could feel the warmth of her body through her silky skin, and the flutter of her shallow breathing on his neck.

He pressed his face against her skin, his eyes tightly shut and his mouth pulled back, mouthing a silent, agonising scream.

'Dear God,' he whimpered, saliva dropping from his mouth and snaking down her shoulder. 'Please make it end.'

He dug his fingers into the tight flesh of her shoulders, almost crushing her as he held her. Then slowly he let go, placing her carefully back on the sheets.

He looked at her lying still. Her skin seemed to be glowing, clear as crystal, radiating back the cold moonlight mixed with the golden warmth of her body.

He ran the back of his index finger down her cheekbone, tracing the curve of her face.

'Not long now,' he said, smiling. 'Soon . . . soon it will all be over.' He looked at the window, and the cold white moon.

'Soon there will be no death,' he whispered. 'No sorrow, or crying or pain.'

The edge of his mouth turned up in a crooked smile, and all the pain and doubt left his face. Suddenly the life left his eyes.

'Soon,' he murmured, looking down again, 'it will be over.'

# 38

Alex was suddenly aware that someone was up above her; a darkness in the hazy white sky. She tried to open her eyes.

'Wha . . .?' she murmured deep in her sleep.

Something was near her, too near. But she didn't know what. A mist of milky white light blew through her head.

She felt something touch her skin.

'What?' she croaked, opening her eyes wide. She looked around, startled, not sure where she was, and saw Martin standing over her.

'What are you doing?' she mumbled, hearing her voice waver as she drew back into her pillow.

'Erm . . .' He looked embarrassed and held up a cup. 'I just brought you a cup of tea.'

'Oh,' she said cautiously, pulling the sheets up around her. 'Thanks. What time is it?'

'Seven.'

'Seven!'

'I've got to drive a van over to Mansfield this morning. Put some stuff into storage.'

She squinted at him. 'What stuff?'

'Just stuff,' he said, pausing then smiling. He looked at her closely. 'Anyway. Do you always look this good in the morning?'

She pulled her head under the sheets. 'I'm not a morning person. Go away.'

She heard him laugh. 'Will you be alright? I've got to go.'

'Yeah, I think I'll manage, thank you.'

'Well, be careful.'

'Thanks,' she replied sarcastically.

She waited for him to leave, then crawled out of bed. She looked in the mirror. It was worse than she had imagined. She had bags under her eyes like a basset hound's.

'Great.' She set off to find the bathroom.

It took her half an hour to come round. She made herself a large pot of tea and sat in a stupor in front of the cold fire. Now that it had gone out the cat was nowhere to be seen. She glanced at the clock and suddenly remembered Steve Hill.

She leafed through her Filofax until she found Steve's number, then pulled the phone over. While she was waiting for the line to connect she scooped Martin's tobacco tin off the hearth and started to roll a cigarette. She let the phone ring about twenty times.

She was just about to put the receiver down when he answered.

'Oh, yeah,' he said grumpily when she explained who it was. 'I remember. Tall and blonde, right?'

'And incredibly attractive,' she added brightly.

'Yeah, of course. Look, I'm sorry. I'm on nights and I'd just nodded off, so can we make this quick?'

'Oh, right . . . Sorry.'

She briefly outlined what she wanted.

'Fine. Whatever.' He sounded as if he was already halfway back to sleep. 'Meet me at Queens at six. I'll be in the staff canteen having breakfast.'

'Breakfast? At six?'

'Work it out for yourself,' he said groggily, before putting the phone down.

She frowned as the line clunked in her ear. She hoped he would remember he had spoken to her; he had sounded like she felt.

She held onto the handset, and punched the station number.

'Hi, Celia,' she said to Harry's secretary. 'Look, I'm afraid I'm not feeling too good today, I think I need to stay at home. Can you tell Harry I won't be in?'

'OK, I'll try, but I think he wants to speak to you. Can you hang on a minute?'

She was on hold before she could complain.

'No can do, Alex,' Harry bellowed as soon as he came on. 'I need you down here pronto. There are camera teams crawling all over town. We need to get people on the streets.'

'But, Harry . . .'

'But Harry nothing. I've got the walking wounded down here at the moment, so there's no reason you shouldn't join them. You don't sound too bad to me. I'll see you in my office in half an hour.'

'Thanks for the sympathy,' she muttered at the dead line.

She slumped on the sofa and smoked the rest of the roll-up, then hauled herself up and went upstairs to get dressed.

She pulled on her crumpled clothes, unsure of which was worse, old knickers or none at all. She decided old knickers were a safer bet, and set off.

Harry was sitting at his desk reading when she arrived.

'Ah, Alex,' he said, when he finally looked up. 'So glad you could make it. How are you?'

'I feel awful.'

'Well, you look no worse than usual. Anyway, I'm very short of time, sweetheart, so sit down and listen.'

She felt the heat rise in her cheeks as he spoke. Harry had pulled some pretty shitty stunts in his time, she thought, but this really took the piss. A pink mist began to swirl behind her eyes. The beating, the killings, Mike – they were all whipped up into a whirlwind in her head.

By the time he had finished her head felt as if it was going to explode. It was all too much.

'So,' she said slowly, 'up to now four women have been killed, some poor kid has just been kidnapped, and now the killer has sent a lock of her hair which he has just yanked out.' She heard her voice begin to rise. 'And *you* . . . you want me to go and talk to someone about a tortoise with three legs.'

'Three legs and a wheel,' Harry added seriously.

'And why on earth would you want me to do that, Harry?'

He looked at her disapprovingly.

'Because it's a gem, sweetheart, that's why. Think about it. Some kiddy runs over his tortoise on his bike; poor old tortoise loses its back leg; kiddy's beside himself with woe. Then bingo,

214

in steps good old Grandad who fashions an artificial leg with a wheel for little Touché . . .'

'He was a turtle,' Alex said darkly.

'Whatever. Anyway, it's a beaut. I can just see him skating around the back yard now. It'll have them in tears. It's exactly what we need. Too much scaremongering and they'll start to turn off, and whoops, there go the revenues. It's just as important as the serious stuff, Alex. Maybe more.'

'Yeah, well, you can get someone else to do it.' She started to get up.

'Yeah, right,' he said, putting his glasses back on. 'Have it wrapped up before it gets dark.'

She stopped and looked at him. He was already scribbling something onto a schedule.

'No way, Harry,' she insisted, stepping towards his desk. She was suddenly so angry she didn't know what to do. 'If you want that story then get your fat arse out of there and do it yourself.'

He looked up.

'I'll pretend I didn't hear that, sweetheart,' he said, taking his glasses off again. Colour had rushed into his cheeks. 'Now get the fuck . . .'

Alex stood her ground and shook her head. 'No, you get the fuck out of it, Harry,' she said, putting both hands on his desk. She could feel the muscles in her arms shaking with fury. 'I've had enough. You can sit on the bloody tortoise and twist for all I care. I've had it.'

She spun around, and stalked towards the door.

'What are you saying?' he hollered after her.

She stopped in the doorway, shut her eyes and took a deep breath. Then she turned around slowly.

'You can stick your job, Harry,' she explained calmly. 'That's what I'm saying.'

She saw his eyes flash.

'See you,' she added quietly, then spun around on her heels.

'I'll take that as a formal resignation, then, shall I?' he screamed after her.

'Take it how you want,' Alex shouted over her shoulder. 'Up the arse, for all I care. I'm out of here.'

She heard someone giggling nervously across the office.

215

'Have your desk cleared in ten minutes,' he yelled as she cut through the open-plan space.

She closed her eyes as the lift descended and tried to calm down.

'Very cool, Al,' she muttered to herself. 'Very cool indeed! There goes your income, your references, everything. Nothing like burning all your boats.

'Piss,' she hissed, staring at the ceiling. She had done it again. Once she got fired up, it just all flowed out of her mouth. She couldn't stop it. When would she learn?

But then it was going to happen some time.

She walked slowly into the office. She'd known it would be empty. She had seen it happen before. Someone would have called down ahead of her. It was an unwritten rule that no one spoke to you if you had to clear your desk. It was like getting too close to a leper; you would probably be alright, but it wasn't worth the risk. She knew that the coffee room would suddenly be very full of people washing mugs.

There would be no fond farewells.

She carefully emptied the contents of her personal drawer into an M&S carrier bag, then looked around the office. She had spent three years in and out of the stupid place and now she felt . . . nothing.

She looked across the empty desk where Mike sat; still nothing.

She wandered across towards the window, letting her fingers drag across the surface of Mike's desk as she passed it. She stopped by the huge plate-glass window, and dug her cigarettes out of her bag. It was weird, she thought, looking out at the dull grey cityscape. What they had been doing in that office and what went on outside were like two different worlds. While they produced Technicolor videos of the red-light district, high-gloss reproductions of the still shots of the victims, and conducted interviews in clean, brightly lit spaces, out there was just flat and grey. And out there somewhere he – whoever he might be – had slowly and methodically killed four girls, then taken another, ripping out a clump of her hair to prove what he had done.

All they had ever done in the station was deal with what had happened, how it had happened, whipping everyone up into a frenzy of fear.

She panned her gaze out towards the suburbs.

The real question was why?

Why had he kidnapped her instead of doing what he had done to the rest? She shivered, remembering a name from her childhood; Lesley Whittle – a girl kidnapped and eventually killed by the Black Panther in the seventies.

Something told her that they were running out of time fast.

She turned, glancing one last time out of the window, then walked back to the lift, stubbing her cigarette out on Mike's chair as she left.

# 39

Harris placed his head in his hands and slowly massaged his fingers across his brow. He had been sitting at his desk for over ten hours, and it felt as if he'd got nowhere. He pushed the papers aside and sat up, trying to stretch the stiffness out of his spine. He wasn't sure what to do next – eat, sleep, get pissed – but he knew he had to stop trying to scour the mass of reports and stats in front of him. Otherwise he would go mad. It was like searching for a ghost.

There was a knock at the door.

'Yeah,' he said, stretching his arms.

Grigson pushed open the door, and came in carrying a pot of filter coffee and two mugs. He looked pasty and tired.

'I didn't think there was much point in fucking about so I brought the whole lot.'

'You'll get in trouble,' Harris said, smiling.

'So what're they going to do, arrest me?' He filled the two mugs, then carefully placed the pot on a coaster and sat down on the swivel chair opposite. 'Mind if I smoke?'

'Christ, no,' Harris said, waving his hand. 'Cancer's the least of my worries at the moment.'

Grigson smiled and tapped out a Rothmans.

'You got anywhere?' he asked, exhaling smoke through his nose as he spoke.

'Nope.' Harris shut his eyes and stretched his neck. 'What about you?'

'Nothing. The boys are working hard, but we're still just clutching at straws. We haven't got anything to get a handle on.

We've looked at every fucking calendar there is – haulage shift patterns, festival guides, star charts, you name it. Nothing. We just haven't got enough information.'

'What about Scotland Yard?'

'They've been running searches for days, but no one's come up. Not even close.'

'Shit,' Harris said, looking up at the ceiling. He shut his eyes. 'He's going to kill her, Dave, you know that?'

'Yes.'

Harris opened his eyes and continued staring at the ceiling. He let his breath out slowly. 'Bastard,' he said, almost to himself.

'I beg your pardon, sir?'

Harris looked back at him and smiled. 'Nothing.' He bent over and pulled a bottle of Bells out of his bottom drawer. He unscrewed the top and tipped three-quarters of an inch into his mug.

'You want some?' he asked, glancing at Grigson.

'Well, you know how it is, sir.'

'Look,' Harris said, 'I'll be straight with you. I reckon we've got a couple of days left, tops, and I'm all out of ideas. So if Hague wants to sack me for having a drink on the premises then let him sack me. I'm prepared to take the risk. Meanwhile I need inspiration.'

Grigson smiled and pushed his mug across the desk. 'OK.'

'We need to find what makes him tick, Dave. Otherwise she's dead. Simple as that. And we're running out of time fast.'

# 40

Alex wriggled out of her skirt and kicked it into a crumpled heap in the corner. She stood in her bra and pants, and let her mind wander for a moment, trailing her fingers over the soft down on her stomach; it was as if a part of her life had broken off and started to drift away. It was an odd feeling.

The air in the room moved as the breeze outside rattled the sash window, breathing cold, crisp air through the gaps between the old wood. She felt her belly tighten and the hairs on her arms bristle. She shook her head and smiled, then sat down heavily on the bed and pulled on a pair of Amy's 501s and a big V-neck sweater.

Martin's cat stirred as the bed bounced, lazily looking up to see what was happening.

She looked at her watch; she only had slightly over an hour before she had to meet Steve. She needed to get a move on.

She opened up the portable and switched it on, then reached for the phone an dialled the station.

She told the receptionist that she was Forester's sister and that it was urgent.

'Sally?' he said, when he picked up. 'What's wrong?'

'Sorry, Forester, it's me,' Alex explained quickly.

'Ah.'

'Ah what?'

'Ah, I heard what happened, Al . . . er . . . I mean, Sally.'

'Yeah, well, you know, these things happen. Look, I'll have to tell you about it some other time. Right now I need some urgent technical support. Can you tell me how on earth to get

220

into this database, please? For old times' sake.'

He talked her through it. It took quite a while, but she realised he was doing his best to pitch it at her level. Eventually it began to click and she understood how to navigate through the screens.

'Thanks, Forester,' she said warmly when they had finished.

'No problem,' he said, adding unhappily, 'Look, couldn't you just apologise or something . . .'

'No, I don't think so. I think it's too late for that.'

'But surely it can't be that bad. I mean . . .'

'Look, Forester,' she explained as tenderly possible, 'I'm sorry, but if you don't mind, I'd rather not talk about it just at the moment. I need a little time to get over it, OK?'

'OK.'

'Thanks.' She paused. 'You take care of yourself.'

She shook her head as she put the phone down, thinking about the little things that would drift away with the station: Forester, Jim, the two grand old cleaning ladies she met when she worked late – all gone.

She pulled her legs up onto the bed and twisted round, tickling the cat's back as she made herself comfortable. Then she settled down to find out which of the records that Forester had printed she should give to Steve.

She trawled through the database for ten minutes until she found the screen that she wanted. Then she typed in *Numen* and waited.

Gotcha, she thought, as it came back with a full screen of information. There it all was: compound, patient numbers and how many patients had been completed.

She checked the patient numbers against the paper print-outs. They were all there. She blew the air out of her lungs, and started to feel better.

She smiled, thinking of Harry's scarlet face.

She turned the PC off and carefully placed it on the floor, making sure the recharge cable was in. Forester had explained that it would run only for a couple of hours on the battery, so she should recharge it whenever she could. She made sure the little light was glowing then packed the papers into the bag and set off.

Steve was mopping egg yolk off his plate with some bread

when she rushed into the canteen. The traffic had been a lot heavier than she had expected and she was ten minutes late.

'When did you last sleep?' she asked as he ushered her into the seat opposite him. She could feel the sweat prickling in the small of her back.

'You don't look so good yourself,' he replied with his mouth full.

'Thanks.'

'Anyway, I've got an excuse. I only managed to get a couple of hours after my morning call,' he said sarcastically.

He jammed the dripping bread into his mouth. 'S'cuse me,' he mumbled, 'but I'm on in twenty minutes.'

'It's OK. I used to interview livestock for a living.'

He smiled, then swilled down the mouthful with some tea. 'Very funny. So . . . what can I do for you?'

She ran through what was going on as quickly as she could.

'You haven't missed anything?' Steve asked, looking a lot more alert than when she had started. 'Like a world war or something?'

'No. That's about the size of it.'

'And you're sure about all of this?'

'Yes.' She nodded. 'Most of it. I mean, what do you think these panda eyes are all about?'

'Right,' he said, nodding dumbly.

Alex pushed the papers across the table while he fumbled in his pocket for his glasses.

'I knew Fisher was off the wall. But nothing like this.'

He looked down the first page.

'There's a lot here. I'll scan through them now. But I'll need more time.' He put on his glasses and started to flick through the pages.

'You need to focus on the pages at the back,' he said after a couple of minutes. 'That's where the information on any side effects will be. It's most likely the drug is doing something they hadn't bargained for.

'Look,' he said, straightening up. 'This could take a long time. Can I hang on to these? I can have a look at them in the grave-yard shift after midnight.'

'OK.' She nodded warily. 'I suppose so.' She didn't really want them out of her sight.

He started to tidy them into a pile.

'So what's a smart compound then?' she asked innocently.

'Why?' he said, banging the ends of the pages to square them up.

'Because that's what the compound was called in Fisher's database.'

Steve frowned and gazed into space for a moment.

'No,' he muttered. Then he nodded to himself. 'But then Fisher would be the ideal man.'

'For what?' Alex asked, reminding him she was still there.

He took his glasses off and rubbed his eyes. 'Look, I'm a doctor, so I'm trained to deal with hard facts, which means that what I'm about to tell you doesn't hold much water as far as I'm concerned. But I did read an article somewhere about the concept of self-dosing compounds. The gist of it was that instead of developing drugs as we do now – to hit certain predefined targets – it may be possible to develop compounds that would react differently depending on what they found in the body.'

'What's that mean?'

'In other words, it would regulate its own action depending on the severity of the condition. It was a nice idea. But it was a little short on detail. Like how they actually would work. I wrote it off as sci-fi to be honest.'

He ran his finger around his plate.

'I don't understand,' she said, shaking her head. 'What would be the big deal?'

'The big deal, Alex,' he said, licking his finger, 'would be that doctors wouldn't have to worry about over- or under-dosing their patients. The drug would work it out for them. Hence smart. If it was possible it would be very, very popular – whatever the illness. But for psychiatric drugs it would change everything. Medication would suddenly be a far safer option.'

He took a long pull on his mug of tea. 'In the case of an antidepressant, for instance, it would mean the same drug could be used for mild and severe cases. The medic wouldn't have to worry if the condition changed or swung. It would mean that he could ensure that extreme cases were sufficiently dosed without

223

the fear of doping up the milder cases and leaving them in cloud-cuckoo-land.'

'Wow!'

'Yes, wow,' he said. 'But then I don't believe it's possible. There's no evidence that anything like this has ever worked before.'

'But if it was possible?'

'If it was possible, then Fisher would be the obvious person to work with it. Anyway, what's more important here is that if my gut feeling about these forms is correct, whatever they are up to is at a very early, and therefore risky, stage. That's what you should be interested in.'

'How come?'

'Because since there are no official records, it could mean they're trying to pretest on people. It's speculation, but it does seem to fit what you've told me. And if they are doing that it means they're using his patients as guinea pigs.'

'I thought they had animals for that sort of thing. Why would anyone chance it on humans if it's so risky?'

'Because there's only so much you can test on rats and dogs. And it's especially difficult with psychiatric drugs, because animals don't share the same characteristics as people. Only a minor subset. If they wanted to rush through the development of a drug to get it to the market faster, then that is how they would do it. But it's a big if! If they are, and they get caught out, it would put them out of business and every doctor working for them in prison.'

Steve looked at his watch. 'Look, I've got to go, Alex. What if I call you tomorrow morning when I come off shift? Tell you what I've found.' He picked up his napkin and wiped his mouth. 'Meanwhile, take what I said with a pinch of salt. Like I said, it's all very pie in the sky. You would be best just to work your way through the AE pages at the back with an open mind. That's where you'll find anything.'

'The what?'

'Sorry. Adverse event pages. If there are any clues, that's where they'll be.'

His pager started to bleep. 'Got to go.' He jumped up and gulped down the last of his tea.

'Yeah, right,' Alex said, waving vaguely. 'I'll see you later.'

That had to be it, she thought, fumbling in her bag for her cigarettes. That was why they were going to such lengths to cover up their tracks. Numen were testing on Fisher's patients – and something had gone wrong.

What on earth were they working on, she thought, to go to such lengths?

'Miss,' someone shouted from behind the counter. 'This is a no-smoking area.'

She looked around the canteen. It had emptied and a couple of elderly staff were shuffling around, clearing up the plates.

'Sorry,' she said, waving her hand.

She got up and left, trying to work out what could have gone so wrong that it was worth killing for.

# 41

The street was packed full of cars when Alex returned. She drove slowly down the narrow, dark road until she saw a space just up from Martin's house.

She got out with the implications of what Steve had said spinning through her head. She had thought about it all the way from the hospital. And now she was convinced. First Fisher dead. Then Jill. They must have been testing something – and something must have gone wrong. It made sense. And now they were involved in a major damage limitation exercise.

So their one serious problem was her; because the key to the whole thing was dangling on her shoulder. The information in the PC would be enough to piece the whole thing together. That and the blister pack of drugs would seal it. If they got hold of the portable – and got rid of her – they were home and dry.

And they knew it.

She shuddered and looked over her shoulder.

They would have been to her flat by now. She was certain of that. It was the obvious thing to do. She just hoped they hadn't found the pack. But then they would have had to be lucky; she had hidden it under a broken floorboard behind her water tank.

She walked slowly towards Martin's house.

A series of voices were yelling at her in her head: common sense told her to give up, to go to the police, make herself safe, while another fading tone told her that this was her last big chance to get the story she deserved. But they were only background noises. They were drowned out by another sound, a voice she couldn't ignore which came right from the bottom of her soul, a primal scream that told her that something was happening she didn't yet understand, but that this was her chance to put things right.

She stopped and rubbed her eyes, trying to work out what to do. And as she did, something else told her to look up; that suddenly she was in danger.

She squinted down the dark road, unable to believe what she was seeing.

It was almost as if just by thinking about it she had summoned some demon from hell.

'Oh God!' she murmured.

Right on cue a dark figure had began to run towards her.

She looked around. There was no way she could get back to the car. She clawed at her bag and fumbled for the CS gas canister. She could hear feet hitting the ground hard. He was close. Her hands scrambled in her bag, but she couldn't seem to find the can.

'Alex,' someone shouted.

She looked up.

As the figure ran into the thin pool of yellow light, she realised who it was.

'Martin?' she exclaimed, unable to work out what was going on. 'What's happening?'

'Not now, Alex.' He gulped for air. 'No time. Where's your car?'

'Why?'

'Alex,' he said loudly as he stepped forward, 'we're in trouble, OK? So just take me to your car.'

Her body automatically recoiled from his touch. All she could do was nod.

They jogged to the car.

'Where to?' she asked, as she reversed quickly up the road.

'The police,' he said, his voice tight.

'Why?'

'Alex, just drive us to the police station.'

She slewed the car across the road to turn around.

'Look, what's going on?' she asked, jamming the gears into reverse.

227

'My house has just been trashed, alright? So just get us out of here.'

'OK.'

She hammered up the cluttered street and screeched out into the main road, with a flick of the back wheels. She floored the accelerator, heading towards the city, and glanced in the mirror.

'It's OK,' she said, changing up. 'There's no one there.'

'Good.'

Alex glanced in the mirror again and bit her lip. Then, with a sudden jerk of the wheel, she took a sharp right, shooting up the ramp onto the new concrete bridge over the canal and into the retail park on the other side.

'What are you doing?' Martin shouted, as the bright lights of a drive-through McDonald's flashed by.

'What do you mean?'

'I mean, where the hell are you going, Alex? I'm nervous enough without you going weird on me.'

She didn't say anything, concentrating on the thin road as it curved back to link up with the southbound route out of the city.

'Alex!'

'What?'

'Where are we going?'

'I don't know!'

'Then turn around for Christ's sake and get us to the police station.'

'No!' She jerked the wheel again, taking the lights out onto the dual carriageway on amber.

'Al-ex!' he shouted, hammering his fist against the dashboard.

She slammed on the brakes, feeling the seat belt clamp her to the seat. The car shuddered as they slowed down rapidly.

'Thank God,' Martin mumbled, closing his eyes.

She ground the car to a halt by the side of the road, and stared through the windscreen, gripping the wheel hard. The light from the high overheads made her eyes sparkle.

'I can't give this up,' she said quietly. 'Not now.'

'Why not?'

'Because I can't.'

'I don't understand.'

'I've just got to finish what I've started. I've got to . . .' She turned towards him and smiled. 'I'm sorry.'

'What for?'

'For getting you involved.'

'It was my choice.'

'Yeah, I know, but I didn't tell you you were dealing with a complete fuck-up, did I?' She stared back through the windscreen. 'Look, if you want to get out, you can. But I'm not going to the police. Not now.'

She turned back and looked at him.

'No.' He shook his head slowly. 'I'm coming with you.'

'Good,' she said quietly.

She jerked the gear lever into first, let the clutch out, and skidded the car off the gravel.

The overhead lights filled the vehicle with a gooey yellow light, occasionally flecked with sharp reds and blues from the signs outside the big retail sheds that flanked the road. Then they were in darkness as they shot up the ramp onto the concrete overpass that took the dual carriageway looping away south from the city towards the open countryside.

They drove in silence for about twenty minutes, the wind roaring through the gash in the roof.

'So what happened?' she asked eventually, staring intently at the dark road ahead.

'They were in my house,' he said, looking out of the window. His voice sounded faraway.

He ran his hand across his forehead.

'They must have already been in the house. I was lucky.' He paused. 'The van is too wide to park in the street so I took it around the back. There's some cleared land there, and I parked it off the road.' He shook his head. 'I noticed the light as I came down the hill. I thought it was you at first, but then I saw them as I was coming in the back yard, and . . .' He dropped his head and rubbed his eyes. 'I thought they had you, Alex. I thought they . . .'

She had to strain to keep her eyes on the road. Suddenly she wanted to touch him.

'Go on,' she said quietly.

He looked up again and stared straight ahead. 'Anyway, I had the jump on them. There's a pile of old planks behind the back door so I used one of them. I got the first one before he knew what was happening. The other one was a bit more difficult, but he went down eventually.'

'Are they, y'know, still alive?'

'Yeah, I reckon. I kept away from their heads. God knows why.'

'Good God. Is that when I arrived?'

He nodded.

'I could have got there first,' she said slowly. She checked in the mirror. Away from the city lights all she could see was an oily blank; there was nothing behind them.

She slowed down and turned off the main road, cutting into the mesh of tiny roads that ran across the rolling plain of the Vale of Belvoir.

She wound her way down half a dozen small lanes, heading deep into the rich arable land. All she could see was the little patch of tarmac picked out by the headlights in front of her. She drove carefully, concentrating on the unmarked narrow road, unsure of where she was heading.

Then suddenly the lights flashed across a sign for a hump-backed bridge. She slowed down, squinting into the darkness. She could see the road rising ahead and a grey sprawl of gravel by the road. It was a lay-by just before the narrow bridge.

She slowed down, pulling the car around in a tight U-turn onto the gravel, and stopped with a crunch.

They sat in silence for some time. The night air was cold, and all around was pitch black and deadly quiet.

'So, come on, what's all this about, Alex?' Martin asked eventually.

'Sorry?' Alex replied, snapping out of her daze.

'What's going on in your head?'

She stared out of the front window, her breath billowing in the cold air.

'Come on, Ali,' he said softly. 'Tell me what's wrong.'

She looked down for a second.

'Don't call me that,' she whispered.

'Why not?'

'It just doesn't sound right.'

'Why?'

230

'It's not me.' She ran her fingers around the wheel. She felt lost.

'What's wrong with you, Alex? Please tell me.'

'With me?' she snorted. 'Everything.'

'Oh, come on.'

She looked up suddenly, her eyes flashing.

'You don't know anything, Martin.'

'I know,' he said evenly, holding her stare. 'That's why I'm asking.'

She lowered her head again and went quiet.

A heavy silence filled the car.

'OK,' Martin said quietly when a few minutes had passed, 'this isn't going to get us anywhere.' He turned to her and smiled. 'So . . . what next?'

'What?' she mumbled.

'Well, here we are in the beautiful countryside. Granted it's a bit cold due to your extra ventilation, but other than that it's lovely. It was nice of you to bring me here.'

'No problem.'

'So unless you convince me otherwise I'll assume you've brought me out here to take advantage of me.'

She smiled, snorting slightly, and looked up. 'In your dreams, sunshine.'

'So?'

'So . . .' She bit her lip and stared into the darkness. She thought for a moment. 'So . . . this is what I think we shouldn't do. We don't go to my flat. Or your house. In fact we don't go anywhere near the city until I've had a chance to trawl through the database properly. I think I know what I'm looking for now. Then I'll call Steve tomorrow, and see what he's got.'

'What did he say?'

She ran through what Steve had told her.

'My mother always told me not to get involved with blondes,' he said when she had finished. 'I wish I'd listened.'

'I could always wear the wig.'

'No way. That would be worse. At least we're out here. The redhead would have me driving around in the city somewhere. For now I'm happier here.' He peered out of the window. 'So, where are we going to stay?'

231

'I think we're here.'

'Nice.' He looked around the tiny space. 'I hope you don't snore.'

They lapsed into silence again and Alex let her mind wander.

She shifted stiffly as she felt his gaze on her, and twisted to look at him. He was smiling.

'So who used to call you Ali, then?'

She rolled her eyes.

'You don't let up, do you?'

'Never.'

'None of your business.' She smiled.

'Come on.'

'It was just this bloke I used to go out with once. We were together for a long time.' She shrugged. 'But you know how it is.'

'So is *he* what's behind all this?'

'Look, Martin,' she said, staring at the gash in the roof, 'I'll be straight with you . . . I don't completely understand why I'm doing this if I'm honest, but . . .' She paused and shut her eyes, her breath steaming slowly from her mouth. 'I just need to sort this thing out, OK? It's just something I have to do.'

'Why?' he asked quietly.

'To feel better about myself.'

'He must have messed you about pretty badly is all I can say.'

She turned her head slowly, the light from the stars lighting up her face.

'It wasn't him,' she said, smiling thinly.

'Then who was it?'

She stared at him for a long moment then looked away.

'Me.'

She closed her eyes and shivered.

'Look, why don't you be a sweetheart and go and sort out the roof,' she said, stretching her neck. 'It's the price you pay for being a nosy bastard.'

'OK,' he laughed, shaking his head.

She gave him the key. 'There's a tarpaulin in the boot.'

It took her a long time to fall asleep, and when she did, she kept waking. It was freezing cold and she couldn't get comfortable.

Eventually she gave up completely. She squinted at her watch in the darkness; it was five o'clock. She shifted her weight, trying to relieve the numbness in her backside, and looked out of the window.

The darkness seemed complete at first, but as she stared into it she began to see some definition; the stark outlines of trees jutting into the air, the edges of the hedgerows, and the road snaking away like a little matt-black stream disappearing into the darkness of the plain.

She followed the road with her eyes. Where it disappeared into the night, there was the slightest glow of red on the horizon. At first she thought it was the first glimmer of light. But then she realised it was the glow of the city lights far, far away on the horizon.

The thin, wavering light triggered a distant memory. She let her memory unwind, playing back images from the past.

'What are you thinking?' Martin asked suddenly, his voice loud and close.

She jumped.

'Sorry,' he said a little more quietly.

She looked around.

'I just remembered a dream I used to have when I was a kid,' she murmured. 'When things were going wrong I used to day-dream I was belting down the road in my dad's old Cortina. All around was dark, and at the edges of the road were all the things I was trying to escape from. But I was too fast for them. All the time I was speeding down the road, a deep red glow would build on the horizon. And I knew things would get better.'

'What was it?'

'I don't know, but I always thought it was heaven.'

'So what happened when you got there?'

'Don't know.' She shrugged. 'I never did. I always woke up before I arrived. All I needed to know was that it was there. Then I knew things would be alright.'

He put his hand on her shoulder.

'What made you think of that?'

The touch was comforting. She leant her head towards him.

'I was looking at the road out there, and I noticed the glow of the city lights on the horizon.'

She looked out of the window; a faint trace of red was smeared across the clouds.

'It doesn't work any more, though.'

'Why not?'

She smiled and pulled her legs up slightly, still staring out of the window. 'You know, when I was at college I went to this lecture about the concentration camps. And there were so many dreadful things that happened in those places. But for some reason one of the things that really hit me was that at one of the camps they called the road to the gas chambers Himmel-strasse – Heaven Street. Can you believe that?'

She shook her head.

'Is that what changed things?' Martin asked. 'When you heard that?'

'No,' she said, smiling and shaking her head. 'No. I mean, terrible as that was, it's only really history to me. I mean, I didn't experience it. But it came back to me one day when I was sitting alone looking at the sky above, and . . .' She shut her eyes. 'And I felt dreadful. So utterly, utterly dreadful. It felt like everything had gone wrong in the world. And . . .' She blew the air out of her lungs, opened her eyes and stared at him. 'And up above the sky was blood red. Redder than I had ever seen it, but it didn't make any difference. I knew that things weren't alright. At all.' Her voice was almost a whisper.

'Why?'

She shook her head and shivered, looking at the horizon again. She wiped a tear off her cheek.

'I can't tell you,' she said in a small voice.

'OK, OK,' he said, softly. 'Don't worry.'

She shuddered. 'I'm cold. Do you mind if I start the engine?'

'Go ahead.'

They sat in silence while the engine started to warm the inside of the car.

Eventually a cold thin light started to diffuse through the sky, smudges of high cloud showing against a grainy grey background. Alex watched as the sky brightened into a huge gauzy canopy above the flat grey landscape.

'I need to stretch my legs,' she said, opening the door.

She got out and walked around in stiff circles. As the sky

brightened the land slowly opened up around her; over the low hedges on both sides of the narrow road huge flat fields were revealed in the milky light.

She walked up the road and onto the steep bridge, stopping at the brow. She looked over the stone parapet. The bridge crossed a narrow, overgrown canal, and was the only elevation for miles; she could see hedgerows criss-crossing the plain away into the distance, breaking the land up into huge brown squares of freshly ploughed soil. In the middle distance the spire of a church punctured the white sky, and far away on the hazy horizon, where the land began to rise, she could just see the jutting outline of Belvoir Castle. She slowly scanned the empty landscape, drawing crisp fresh air deep into her lungs, then turned and walked back to the car.

'Ready to roll?' she asked when she got back in.

He nodded.

She pulled the car around off the gravel, and drove up and over the bridge, away from the city and deeper into the flat country.

The road ran straight for about three miles, a thin black line with a wide ditch on either side running between two dense hedgerows. Alex hummed silently as they drove, occasionally glancing at the flocks of birds that took off as they passed, banking high into the sky over the fields.

'Aha,' she said, breaking the silence as she saw the tower of a church ahead.

'What?'

'I think we're about to re-enter civilisation,' she replied as the hedgrow gave way to a cluster of trees. The road curved sharply then suddenly emerged onto the main street of a village. She slowed down.

A row of small Georgian redbrick houses nestled together down either side of the road, with the church rising up behind them. She drove carefully down the main street, slowing down further as it opened out onto a green; in the middle was a small pond under a couple of huge oak trees. The green was surrounded by a series of cute, interlocking redbrick buildings with tiny white sash windows and black slate roofs.

She pulled the car up outside a small building that had a sign outside; it was a general store – a newsagent's, grocer and post office all rolled into one.

'I think we're here,' Alex said, turning off the engine.

'Looks good to me.'

They both got out.

'I'll go and see if I can get something to eat,' Martin said, walking towards the shop door.

'OK.'

Alex walked slowly around the green, watching as a couple of ducks sluggishly crossed the road.

On the far side she found the end of a short lane running between two cottages.

She wandered down past the back of the churchyard to a row of neat rectangular buildings at the end; one was a village hall, another an infants' school, and the third a tiny library. They were all of a similar design; tidy little shoe boxes of grey and red brick with steep serrated eaves, high windows down each side and an oval picture window above the front door. Beyond them the fields disappeared into a hazy oblivion.

Martin was waiting when she got back.

'There's another store in the next village that sells fresh food and coffee for the hunting brigade,' he said.

'Good. And I think I've found our bolthole.'

'Where?'

'There's a dinky little library down there.' She nodded at the end of the road.

'Great. We'll come back.'

'No.' She lobbed him the keys. 'Do you mind? I need the fresh air. I'll take the PC and wait outside, if that's OK with you?'

He saluted her formerly.

'I shall go and get provisions. I may be some time.'

'Don't say that,' she grinned. 'Remember what happened to Oates?'

'No.'

'Suffice to say he didn't come back,' she said, raising her eyebrows. 'So be careful.'

She slung the bag on her shoulder and set off towards the library, trying to ignore Martin as he crunched the gears behind her.

The day was still cold, but the sky had turned a clear bright blue.

She paced up and down outside the library until an elderly janitor opened the door suspiciously.

'We're closed,' he said cautiously.

'Fine,' she said, smiling. It was a beautiful day, and the air tasted fresh and clean; she was more than happy to wait. 'When do you open?'

'You can come in if you want.'

'Doesn't that make you open now?' she asked brightly.

'No,' he replied stubbornly. 'Because you can't take any books out.'

'Oh, I see.'

She followed him in.

The building had the quiet air of a classroom when all the children have gone. She sat down at a long table by the window, and looked around.

'I'm only outside,' the janitor said, as he shuffled out. She took it as warning not to try to steal any books.

'OK,' she called after him amicably.

The walls were covered with children's paintings. There were globes and groups of multicoloured smiling children and lots of whales and dolphins. They were all big and bold, and uniformly optimistic. She glanced around the room, then unzipped the bag and set up the PC on the big desk by the window. According to Forester she had about two hours of battery power – that would be just about enough.

She powered up the PC and was soon engrossed in the records.

# 42

Steve put his bleeper on the desk and rubbed his hand across his face. He looked at the pile of papers Alex had left him. It was well past midnight, and he was knackered; they were the last thing he wanted to look at. He decided he needed a coffee.

He walked slowly back from the vending machine, rubbing the muscles in his neck. He knew he wouldn't be able to sleep. He had gone beyond that, into the dead zone where you can't sleep but can't stay awake either.

He slumped back down and looked at the pile of paper again. At least they would keep his mind busy, he thought. He took a sip of the acrid liquid and picked up the first page.

Sixty minutes later he was wide awake.

He didn't hear his bleeper at first. He was too engrossed in what was in front of him. Eventually the steady beep pierced his mind. He looked at his watch; it was one thirty.

He shook his head. It was all beginning to make some kind of sense, but something still didn't quite add up. He picked up the bleeper and looked at the number. It was no good; he had to go.

He stacked the papers carefully and locked them in his drawer. Then he jogged sluggishly down to the wards.

It was one of those nights when the anxiety of one patient infected the rest, spreading through the ward until the whole place was a mire of unease; it kept him busy right through to the end of the shift.

By the time he got back to his office sunlight was flooding through the window. He pulled off his coat and threw it over the chair; he was exhausted and all he wanted to do was get out of the hospital and go home. He only just remembered to shove the papers into his briefcase before leaving.

He drove home against the early morning traffic. It was a beautifully clear day, and the low sun caught on the windscreen of the stationary cars on the other side of the road. It was one of the few benefits of night duty – watching the ordinary joes queuing up to get into the city – and it made him feel slightly better.

As he pulled his battered MGB onto the gravel drive outside his house he began to think about what he had read earlier.

He sat quietly at the pine table in the kitchen and flicked through the sheets, while the coffee dripped through the filter. He shook his head as he tried to work out what it all meant. Fisher was testing an antipsychotic drug alright, but it wasn't like anything he had ever come across, and he couldn't quite fathom out what had been going on. But he knew there was something there, something lurking in that pile of data and strange adverse reactions. He just couldn't see it yet.

He poured himself a coffee, and returned to the sheets. The data really needed pumping through a stats package for him to see any trend. He tried to memorise the most frequent problems; there were a lot!

He carefully sifted out all the back pages and spread a few across the table, then ran his eyes across the text, looking for patterns.

He was on to the third set when he saw it.

His eyes locked on a page at the edge of the table. He picked it up and looked more closely; patient number sixty-two. Withdrawal due to serious side effects.

He rummaged through the pile and found the supporting pages.

He carefully read down the page and whistled. The patient was showing abnormally strong mood swings, resulting in extremely violent outbursts. Fisher had taken him off the drug, then referred him back to one of his own clinics.

Steve looked out of the window, and tried to pull back some facts from his memory. There had been a log somewhere in the pile. He put the forms down and rifled through the other pages until he found it.

Thirty minutes later, he was still staring ashen-faced at the papers, his eyes fixed on one page in particular. But he was no longer looking at the text. That had long since sunk in.

He looked up, and tried to tell himself it couldn't be true. But he knew it was. If there was one thing he knew about Fisher, it was that he was always deadly serious. It had to be true.

'Holy Mary, Mother of God,' he muttered to himself.

What had they done?

No wonder they were keen to cover it up.

He walked slowly over to the phone, trying to remember what he had done with the number Alex had given him. He had to speak to her.

She was in trouble alright. And now he knew just how much; more than she could ever believe. He could see why they had killed Fisher. There was no way he would have been able to keep quiet. The implications were just too big. And then the walls would have come tumbling down. That was why they had killed him. Then the other girl.

'My God,' he muttered, still unable to take it in fully.

They had taken a big risk, and the million-to-one option had come up. That was why they were mopping up so fast.

He had to speak to her. He panned around the kitchen; where had he put that bit of paper?

He grabbed the telephone directory from under the stairs, ripped through the pages, then ran his finger down the names. *Bridle, Brier, Brierley.*

There it was! There was only one A in the part of town where Alex had said she lived.

He punched the number, and waited.

But when it finally clicked through he got the unobtainable tone.

He tried three more times, but each time he got the same tone. He called the operator.

'She must have left it off the hook,' she explained when she had tried the line for him. 'I can't hear any voices and she isn't responding to the tone. Sorry.'

'Thanks,' he said, and hung up.

He had to tell her.

He slammed the handset down.

There was only one thing for it. He pulled his jacket off the hook and headed for the car.

If he had stopped and thought about it he would have realised he was in danger as well. And maybe he would have been more cautious. Maybe. But all he could think about was what he had just read in Fisher's transcript. He had to find Alex. And quickly.

If he had stopped and thought more he might have saved his life. But he didn't. He went outside, got into his MGB and hurtled towards Alex's flat.

Like a fly to a light bulb.

He only had an hour left to live.

# 43

Alex's eyes were beginning to ache. She glanced at the clock as she stretched her spine. She wondered where Martin was; he'd been gone a while.

She got up and rubbed her back; she was stiff and finding it difficult to concentrate. She was about halfway through the forms, and she still hadn't found anything. It would help if she knew what she was looking for.

She looked at the clock again. Maybe Steve had come up with something? she thought. He should be home.

She yawned and stretched; it was no good, she needed a rest. She packed the PC into the bag, slung it on her shoulder, and wandered out.

As she walked up the lane she could hear the noise of a tractor somewhere in the fields and the squawks of the flocks of geese above as they flew over on their migration south.

There was an old red phone box over by a pub. She walked slowly down the main road, squinting against the sun, and watched as a light aircraft buzzed over, the sun catching its tiny fuselage.

She stepped outside the telephone box and fished around in her pocket for change. Then she heaved the door open. It was the first phone box she had been into in ages that didn't sport graffiti or fliers advertising girls. She punched the number and waited for it to connect.

She drummed her fingers on the shelf while she waited. She let it ring twenty-five times, but he didn't answer. She looked at her watch.

Damn, she thought. He must be asleep; dead to the world.

She went back to the library and set up the PC again. She had taken Steve's advice, and focused on the back pages. There had been a lot of minor side effects, but so far nothing that jumped out at her. She hit Return again, and pulled up another page.

She looked up again ten minutes later. There was still no sign of Martin.

The light shone warmly on her back through the big window. She wiggled her shoulders, and sighed. She could see the fields through the glass. A tractor plodded along half a mile away, slowly churning the soil with a flock of seagulls in tow. The bright light accentuated the autumn colours. It was all rich browns and sky blue. She yawned.

She turned back to the screen, and scrolled down to the next page. It was no good. She pushed the tiny computer away, and rested her head on her arms. The sun felt nice on her back.


Martin opened the car door and gingerly hooked his arm out. He placed the cups on the roof one at a time. As he pushed himself out of the driver's seat the whole car bounced and one of the cups fell over.

'Bugger,' he muttered, grabbing it before all the coffee spilled across the roof.

He clasped the paper bag under his arm and walked awkwardly towards the library with a cup in each hand.

Alex was asleep when he arrived. He put the cups on the desk, and wondered if he should wake her.

'Alex,' he whispered.

'Whadissit?' she mumbled.

'Coffee.'

'What? . . . Oh, great.' She lifted her head out of her arms. Her eyes were pink and half closed.

'Oh dear.' Martin smiled. 'You look, er . . . a little fatigued . . . Here, have this.' He handed her the full cup.

'Cheers,' she said sleepily. She stretched her shoulders, and pulled a pained expression.

'How's it going?' he asked.

'Not well. I'm knackered.'

'Shall I have a go?'

'Thanks,' she said gratefully. 'But it'd probably take more time to explain how you use this thing than it would to do it myself. I'll be OK. Why don't you take a walk around or something?'

'Sounds like I've got the good end of the deal.'

Alex took a bite out of the tea cake he had given her and hit the Return key.

Martin went outside and walked into the village. There wasn't much to see. Just a post office, a pub, and a cute little church among the cluster of houses. The road they had come in on ran straight through the middle and out the other side. He walked a little way out into the countryside and lingered by the canal, watching the fish under the surface.

Alex was sitting bolt upright when he pushed his way back through the door. Her fingers fluttered across the keyboard.

'Alex?' he said, sitting down.

She ignored him, and hit a couple more keys. Her eyes were locked on the screen.

'Jesus,' she murmured, shaking her head.

'Alex?'

She looked up, her eyes wide and strained.

'I think I've found it,' she said hoarsely. 'There's a patient here that Fisher pulled off the trial for some reason. It sounds like it was pretty serious.'

'Why, what happened?'

'I'm not sure yet. Give me a minute.'

Martin went over and leafed through an old newspaper.

She tapped the space bar. The machine bleeped as she hit the key and a red light flashed in the corner. She glanced at it. It was the Battery Low Light.

She selected the log file and tried to open it.

There was a click. Then the machine made one long bleep, and the screen went dead.

Alex banged the Return key, but nothing happened.

'Damn,' she exclaimed, hitting the space bar hard.

'What's happened?'

'The battery's dead,' she replied slowly.

'What about the thing you plug into the wall? They must have a socket here somewhere.'

'I'm sure they have,' she said, looking at him. 'Problem is, the transformer and the cable are sitting in your spare room.'

'Oh.'

'Oh, indeed.'

He smiled thinly, and rubbed the side of his head.

'Oh, well. I never did like the country,' she said, forcing herself to smile.

'And I was just getting the hang of it.'

'Well, I'm afraid we're going to have to cut the holiday short.'

The sky had lost its sparkle when they got out; a cold white haze had started to diffuse into the air. Alex shivered. She could already feel her stomach muscles tightening.

'I'll just give Steve a call,' she said when they got to the car. She handed the bag to Martin. 'You never know, he might just save us the journey.'

Martin watched as she jogged back down the street to the phone box, pulling the sleeves of her jumper over her hands as she ran.

'Well?' he asked, when she slid back into the car.

'Not there,' Alex replied. 'I don't know. Maybe he's working a long shift or something. So . . .' She snapped on the seat belt. 'I'm afraid we're going to have to go back and find out for ourselves.'

They drove slowly through the village. As they passed the last house the plain opened up in front of them. A freezing haze hung across the fields. Up ahead the huge open space melted away into a blanket of milky-white sky.

Alex pumped the accelerator and headed back towards the city.

# 44

Steve coughed as the blood ran down his throat. He couldn't see because it was in his eyes. He wanted to lean his head forward, but they wouldn't let him. Someone kept pulling him up.

'Come on, Dr Kildare,' the voice said levelly. 'Just tell us where the bitch is and we let you go.'

'I do-on't kn-ow,' he managed to stutter. He tried to clear his throat.

'Well, tell us where we can find out, then.'

'I do-n't know. That's why I'm here.'

Leroy rolled his eyes.

'OK, OK. Well, what about you tell us the names of some of her friends, then. Maybe they be some more use.'

'I don't know her friends.'

Leroy squatted down in front of him. He lowered his head and looked into Steve's bloodshot eyes.

'What do you think we are, stupid?' he said slowly.

He stood up and stretched his back, then looked over at Lenny; both his eyes were black and he had sticking plaster over his broken nose. He hadn't liked what Dobson had done to him; it hadn't been his fault.

'OK.' Leroy shrugged with a thin smile. 'I guess it's payback time.'

Lenny stepped up behind the chair and cracked his knuckles.

Steve's neck snapped back, pain searing into his brain. He tried to shake his head, but something slammed into his face again. Bright lights flashed in his head, and he could feel a broken tooth hanging from his gum.

'Do-on't,' he pleaded weakly, gulping in breath in spasms. 'Please. I don't – know – anything.'

'Yeah, right,' Leroy said sarcastically, 'but I know – and you know – that you're lying. You come here, you don't know this, you don't know that, you don't even know why you're fucking here. You're treating us like bitches, man. You know that? Now I'm running out of patience. Just tell me something I need to know, or you'll wish you were never born.'

Steve knew there was nothing he could tell them. Nothing that would make them go away. He started to sob. 'I'm – not a – blood-dee hero – I'd tell you if I knew. But I do-on't.'

'That's all we need,' Leroy grinned. 'A faggot doctor.'

He stepped forward.

'Shut up,' he shouted, inches away from Steve's face. Steve convulsed as saliva splattered against his skin, mixing with his blood.

'Tell me how we find her. You've got the fucking papers with you, you dickhead. We *know* that you know. So why don't you just cut this crap and make it easy for yourself?'

Steve couldn't speak. His throat was choked with saliva and blood. And there was nothing he could say.

'You a hymie?' Leroy yelled in his ear. 'I bet you fucking are. You think the world will miss a faggot hymie doctor? Huh?'

Steve's mouth was moving but nothing was coming out.

'Oh, for fuck's sake,' Leroy said, rolling his eyes. He stood up and wiped a spot of blood off his Tommy Hilfiger jacket with a look of distaste.

Steve died ten long minutes later.

And they were still none the wiser.

# 45

Alex looked up the street towards Martin's house. It was getting dark. As they had driven through the city the sky had started to fade, curdling from cream through yellow to a thick fleshy pink. Now the sun had dropped behind the rooftops, casting long shadows on the tarmac.

'Come on,' Martin said. 'Let's get this over with.'

Alex shivered and quickly followed him down the street.

He took a deep breath outside his house, then gently pushed open the front door and went in.

'Oh God,' Alex murmured, as she stepped into his front room behind him.

It looked as if a bomb had gone off. There was stuff everywhere – the furniture had been ripped open, spewing stuffing all over the place, the big old clock lay shattered in front of the fireplace, and the floor was covered with the rubble of broken glass and objects tipped out of drawers.

Martin bent down and picked up a small picture frame with shattered glass.

'Oh, Martin, I'm sorry,' she said, putting her hand on his arm.

'It's OK. It's only stuff.'

He tossed the frame into the empty fireplace and went through to the kitchen.

Alex stepped over to the fireplace and glanced at the upturned picture. It was a holiday snap of a happy-looking blonde woman on a beach somewhere. The cracked glass made her smile look crushed and obscured her eyes.

She started to bend down to pick it up, then changed her mind.

As she went into the kitchen she tried not to think about what her flat would look like. Whatever they had done she could only hope they hadn't unearthed the blister pack. The contents would be traceable to the manufacturer; Jill had explained that. Without it the only evidence was on the computer. She wanted something hard to make it stick.

She saw Martin through the kitchen window. He was standing in the back yard with his head bowed.

She walked over to the open door, suddenly realising he was cradling something in his arms.

'Oh no,' she whispered.

It was his cat. They had killed his cat – probably just for the hell of it.

She stepped out into the yard.

'Are you OK?' she asked quietly, putting her hand on his shoulder.

'Sure.' He nodded slowly. 'He was only a cat, after all. I mean, people are being killed, right?'

'It doesn't stop it hurting.'

'Yeah.' He looked around, forcing himself to smile. 'Did you find it?'

'No, not yet.'

'Then get on with it. I . . . I, er . . . just need a minute, OK?'

'OK.'

She turned around, glancing at him out of the corner of her eye, then went upstairs.

As she pushed open the door to the spare room a cloud of feathers danced across the floor in front of her. The thick mattress had been cut open, the springs jutting up like splintered bones through broken skin.

She dropped to her knees and looked under the bed; the transformer was sitting there with the cables still attached. She dragged it out, put the plug in the wall socket, and powered up the PC.

She started to move quickly through the screens – her fingers brushing the surface of the keys – until she found the one she wanted; the first page of the log file for patient sixty-two.

Five minutes later she was reading it for a second time, her mouth slightly open.

'Good God,' she gasped as she paged down.

When she had finished the whole log again she stared at the screen for a moment – the awesome implications making her head spin. Then she got up and went downstairs.

'Martin,' she called quietly from the kitchen door.

He turned around. All the colour was gone from her face.

She shook her head. 'I know ... I know what happened, and ...'

'Go on.'

'I know why Fisher was killed ... and ... and it's incredible.'

'What's happened?' he asked, gently placing the body of the cat on the ground.

'I'd think you'd better come in.'

She ran her hands through her hair, and looked down at the screen as if she couldn't believe it herself.

'That's only the half of it. There's more. It's ... it's just ... incredible.'

She took a deep breath and glanced at the ceiling.

'Fisher was definitely running a trial for Numen. All the evidence is on here.' She nodded at the PC. 'And ... and ... well, there's a section at the back of each patient's records where any side effects are recorded. There are tons of them.'

'And that's bad, right?'

'No. Steve said to expect that. They always get a lot of minor side effects. And that's what most of them are. Slight headaches, that sort of thing. But then I got to patient sixty-two.' She looked up at Martin. 'His were way, way more serious. Really off the wall. He was withdrawn from the trial.'

'So?'

'So, he was withdrawn because he was suffering from severe mood swings. Big ones that nearly always ended in violence. Fisher wasn't sure if they were due to the drug or not. But he took him off just in case.'

Her head was swimming. She was coming to the part she couldn't believe.

'There's a series of transcripts on here. I think Fisher's kept them as patient notes so he could type them up somewhere later. There's a huge one for this patient. It's written in doctor-speak, but there's some stuff in there that anyone could understand.'

250

She stopped again.

'Go on,' Martin said impatiently.

Alex looked bewildered. She stared into space, and shook her head.

'It says . . . that the patient claimed to have killed someone.'

Martin thought for a moment.

'Yeah. But don't these type of people say that sort of thing all the time? You know, delusions of grandeur and all that.'

'Yeah, probably. But this is different. There's a whole history on him. About problems with his family and stuff. He'd had violent outbreaks before, completely out of control and always against women. Young women. Fisher transcribed exactly what he said, and it's far from pleasant reading. It's all in there, Martin.' She pointed at the screen as if it might bite her. 'This isn't make-believe. It's what Fisher said, his interpretation. And what he said was he suddenly realised he was treating someone who really was killing people. Young women. And . . . that means it could only be one person. Think about it.'

He stared at her as it sank in.

'Bloody hell!'

'Exactly,' she said levelly. 'The Deep Throat killer.'

'That can't be right.'

'I know. I said it was amazing. But it's all here. It's . . . all here . . .' She trailed off.

'Are you sure?'

She nodded.

'Very sure. That's why Fisher's dead. He must have told Numen and they panicked. Then Jill found out, so they killed her too. They'll have hundreds of millions of pounds invested in this. If it gets out that they were trying to buck the system, they're dead in the water. They're out of business. And whoever's running this goes down for a long time. God knows why they were prepared to take such a risk. But now they're trying to cover the whole thing up, and they've nearly managed it. All they need is this computer, and they're off scot-free.'

'And me and you.'

She looked at him and smiled.

'Yeah, and me and you.'

'Good God . . .' Martin slowly blew out his breath, shaking

251

his head. 'So,' he said eventually, nodding at the screen. 'Who is he?'

'What? His name? I don't know yet. I came straight down as soon as I found out . . . hang on.' She clicked into another screen then typed *62* and hit Return.

The disk hummed as it trawled the datafile.

There was a brief pause. A silence. Then the screen filled with information.

She squinted to read the letters:

```
NAME:     MASON, DAVID.
DOB:      31/10/65
SEX:      MALE
TYPE:     CAUCASIAN
```

She let the breath trickle out of her mouth. It all looked so innocent, she thought. Just a normal name, living in a run-down but quiet suburb on the edge of town.

She looked at the screen in silence.

'David Mason,' she heard herself say, but her mind was running way ahead; she had his address.

'That's where she'll be,' she whispered.

She looked up sharply.

'Where's your phone?'

'It got ripped out.'

'Shit,' she muttered, starting to get up. 'In that case we need to get this address to the police. *Now!*'

'But I thought . . .'

'That was then, Martin. Now we know. It's over. It's all here, and . . .' She stared at him, her eyes wide and blazing. 'We know where he is. That's where he'll have that girl. And . . . there isn't long left.'

'How do you know that?'

'I just do . . . Come on.'

Martin stood by the kerb as she walked around to the driver's door. She looked across the roof at him. The streetlights had just come on and bathed him in soft orange.

'I owe you for this,' she said.

She was just about to put the key into the lock when a feeling

252

of utter dread swept through her. The key froze in her hand. A millisecond before the shattering noise ripped into the cold evening air, she knew – with absolute certainty – that their luck had just run out.

She started to move her head, and suddenly things seemed to slow down.

She glanced over at Martin and saw him turning towards the noise – a screech of brakes that reverberated off the terraces, tearing at her eardrums.

Her skin prickled; she already knew who it was. She shot a look up the road. A huge black BMW was hurtling towards her.

They had found them.

'Alex!' Martin yelled.

She didn't know which way to turn. Everything seemed to be happening in a jumble – snapshots, images unwinding in slow motion, jumpy and grainy like a badly spliced newsreel. She looked across at Martin. He had started to run around the car. She heard the engine rev nearby.

She turned towards it. As the car bore down on her, the yellow light glinting off its tinted windows, the front dipped and the back end reared up; a hunched dark shape coming towards her. The brake lights blazed a deep blood red on the cloud of exhaust and burning rubber swirling under the back wheels. Alex fumbled with her keys but could not take her eyes off the jack-knifing car.

'Oh my God,' she murmured as the door opened and a figure leapt out.

He was like a silhouette. His image fused with the glossy black car and the dark shadows falling across the road. The only definition was the piercing whites of his eyes, and the glint of the gun in his hand, sparkling yellow in the sodium light.

Even though it all seemed to be happening so slowly, it was all happening too fast.

'Alex!' Martin shouted. 'Move.'

She spun her head back to the door, and managed to twist the key.

'Alex!'

She looked back at the figure. She could see the gun move as he tightened the muscles in his hand, the barrel locked on to her.

253

She saw the flash as the gunpowder exploded in the barrel, the gun bucking in his hands. She felt completely powerless. Only her mind could react quickly enough. Her body was left behind. The noise crackled in her ears. It was loud, far louder than she had expected.

Then Martin was in front of her.

Things slowed down even more – almost to a standstill. Martin twitched in front of her as the bullet hit him. She saw his blood as it arced slowly through the air, and felt it splatter softly on her face. Then the light changed as he fell away. The view opened up in front of her and she could see the gunman again.

She heard a noise like a jet engine erupt deep in her head. It rose to a scream, and sent signals shooting through her nerves. She had to move. The gun would go off again. And the next bullet would smack into her.

Her muscles sprang into life. Everything jolted and suddenly everything was real again. She was in the seat as Martin hit the road. She saw him go down heavily at the edge of her vision, crumbling motionless into the concrete. She wanted to do something, but her instincts told her to run; if she stayed she would be killed as well. She had to get away.

She could still see him as she put the key in the ignition, a pool of blood expanding outwards around his head.

She was sure he was dead.

Everything seemed to happen automatically, her instinct to survive guiding her. She turned the key as the gun fired again. The noise boomed dully inside the car as the engine turned. She didn't know where the bullet landed – only that it had missed.

Then she had the car out in the street. She floored the accelerator and screeched forward, her door still open. The gunman dived out of the way as her door connected with the side of the black car, slamming shut.

She glanced in the mirror as she took the corner onto the main road. And saw the headlights. They were coming after her.

She skidded out into the wide road towards the city centre, flicking on the headlights as she straightened up. The dashboard burst into life, and she saw the petrol gauge at the bottom of her field of vision.

Oh no, she thought. When had she last filled up?

254

She looked down at the gauge in panic; the needle was just bouncing above red.

Enough; just enough.

The engine screamed as she accelerated down the empty road towards the city.

She glanced in her mirror and saw the BMW's headlights blazing behind her; two white eyes piercing the night, running her down.

She was heading fast towards a roundabout. The BMW was so close its headlights had disappeared below her field of vision; all she could see was a smooth black windscreen, the light from the overheads slipping off the opaque glass.

She stared wildly ahead as the roundabout raced towards her. There were cars sweeping across in front of her. She jabbed the gear lever into third.

There was no way she was going to stop.

An estate car skidded sideways as she pulled out in front of it. She heard the blare of horns then, with a flick of the back end, she was out onto the long drag into the city centre.

Car showrooms and retail warehouses swept past darkly at the sides of the road.

She looked in the mirror. Nothing else had cleared the roundabout.

She took the set of lights at the end of the road well after they had turned red, only just controlling the car as she turned into the city centre ring road. She jerked the car around the back of a taxi that loomed up in front of her.

And suddenly there were figures in the road ahead of her. She stabbed the brakes, slewing the car across the four lanes and just missing them.

She shook her head and glanced in the mirror, seeing a woman shooing a little group across the road behind her. They were kids – and they were in some kind of fancy dress.

Then she noticed the bus stops along the side of the station; they were swarming with little witches and monsters.

It was Hallowe'en, she realised. It was Hallowe'en and it was nearly over.

She slowed down slightly, and pulled back across the road. The police station was just on the other side of the city centre.

If she wasn't careful she would crash before she got there.

The road doubled back around the rear of the bus station, then swept up around the bottom of the city centre. As she took the corner she saw a car veer crazily across the slip road on the other side. It was going the wrong way around the system, she realised. Cutting the corner.

'Stupid bastard,' she muttered, pulling across a lane to avoid it as it came out in front of her; probably a joy-rider.

Then she saw the colour.

It was black; a big oily-black BMW. It suddenly switched lanes, pulling way over to the far side of the road then racing back towards her.

'Oh no,' she mouthed silently. It was going to ram her.

She jammed her foot on the brake pedal. The brakes locked and the car skidded sideways. She stopped side-on with the black car.

For Christ's sake don't stall, she thought. Not now.

She crashed the lever into first, and let her foot off the clutch. As she shot forward the wheel twisted violently in her hands. She swerved around the boot of the black car, seeing its wheels throwing up smoke as it tried to reverse into her.

Then she jerked the wheel again, careering the car back across the lanes, the force flinging her against the door.

She hurtled through the traffic lights ahead, not even seeing what colour they were; the light from the overheads, the filling station by the road, all blurred into one. Wind howled through the gash in the roof. It didn't matter. She wasn't going to stop.

The headlights were in her mirror again.

She hurtled around the inner ring road, zigzagging through the light traffic, flicking the back of the car to try get them off her tail. But she couldn't.

Then the black car started to pull out, and she knew they were going to try to get up beside her. The wind dragged at her hair as the gap in the roof began to open up. She floored her right foot – but the big car began to inch forward, slowly crawling up alongside.

She knew if it drew level she was dead.

She looked up ahead, and saw a tiny side road coming in from the left; it would take her right into the city centre.

It was her only chance.

She set the muscles in her shoulders, ready to make the turn. The car was nearly at her side. As their wing mirrors connected, she jerked the wheel. For a moment she thought she was going to turn over. The brakes screamed and she felt the right-hand wheels rise.

Then she was in the side street, thumping back down on the suspension and jolting along. She grazed the side of a parked car, then pulled straight.

'Oh God,' she muttered, clenching her legs and feeling her wet hands slide on the wheel.

She looked up ahead and felt her stomach churn – she had made a big mistake. It wasn't the road she had thought it was. This one was zoned off at the end with a barrier that could be lifted for fire engines.

She slowed down.

The barrier was down and locked.

She wondered if she should get out and run. But then she would be a sitting duck if they saw her. It was a dark, empty road, and a long run to the safety of the crowds in the square. She had to stay with the car.

She stopped in front of the barrier.

*Maybe* . . .

She glanced in the mirror.

She saw two lights as a car turned into the end of the street. There were two hundred yards between them. But she knew it was them.

She inched forward. The low-slung Mazda was just about small enough to go under. She feathered the pedal and felt the metal scrape across the roof.

She looked in the mirror again – the two lights were hurtling towards her.

They weren't going to stop!

Then her head hit the headrest hard, and the little car lurched forward, tearing the material from the roof. She shook her head, and groped for the clutch with her foot. She was through, and the engine was still running.

She looked in the mirror. The black car had rammed her then ploughed into the barrier, tearing the roof off like a sardine can lid. It was jammed under the buckled girder arm, its windscreen caved in.

It looked dead, she thought, feeling the tension relax in her chest. That was all she stopped to see.

She bumped across the pedestrian precinct, and out the other side.

She pulled onto the apron of concrete outside the police station two minutes later, stopping right outside the front door.

'Oi,' a young policeman shouted, as she got out, 'you can't park there.'

She headed towards the door.

'It's an emergency,' she hissed, swinging the bag onto her shoulder.

'I don't care. You can't park there.' He stepped forward to try to block her way.

'So arrest me,' she said, avoiding his hand. 'I'll meet you inside.'

She pushed open the door, momentarily blinded by the bright lights, then strode up to the reception desk.

'Call an ambulance,' she blurted at the woman behind the glass.

'What's happened?' the woman asked calmly.

'Someone's been shot.'

'OK.'

The woman was efficient; she quickly took Martin's address and put through an emergency call for an ambulance. Then she called someone else and talked quietly into her headset.

'There's a door behind you.' She nodded over Alex's shoulder. 'Pull the handle when the buzzer goes. I'll meet you on the other side.'

As Alex turned she saw three little witches sitting morosely on the chairs at the edge of the waiting room. She glanced at them; they were only about eight years old – they looked scared and unsure.

A warning signal went off in her head. Something that had lurked in her mind since she had read the transcript tried to surface. But whatever it was wouldn't connect.

What was it? She ran through what she had read.

Fisher had traced the start of Mason's problems back to the

258

age of ten, when his younger sister had had an accident. She had fallen off a wall when they were playing on a disused railway cutting, banging her head hard as she fell. She had swallowed her tongue when she landed and the oxygen deprivation had left her in a coma.

She was like that for two years.

The family had been very close up until then, but from then on everything had changed; suddenly his parents had other things on their mind. David hadn't understood; he was too young. He just thought they were ignoring him. They had probably done their best to give him their attention, but things were different; their daughter was on a life-support machine. There was only so much time they could give him.

Then she had died, and his parents – unable to cope with their grief together – had split up soon afterwards. From then on Mason had turned in on himself, as he was shunted back and forth between parents with new partners and surrogate families. For long periods he wouldn't talk to anyone, and when he did he lashed out at those around him; blaming them for what had happened. But deep down he really blamed his dead sister. If she hadn't fallen, if she hadn't taken their attention away, and finally if she hadn't died, things would have been different. It was her fault.

But there was also something else – a fundamental paradox in the situation that he never resolved. He had wanted her to die when she was on the life-support machine so he could have his parents back, but then if she hadn't died they might still be together. He could never come to terms with that; part of him wanted her dead, and the other half wanted to save her – but both halves hated her with an equal venom. It pushed him over the edge.

Alex stopped in the middle of the room and looked at the children. She was missing something really obvious. What was it about them? She racked her brains.

She turned around as the buzzer on the door sounded. The woman pushed it open and smiled warmly.

'Step this way, Ms Brierley. Someone's on the way to talk to you.'

259

As Alex stepped through the door, she suddenly felt her body go numb.

She knew what it was.

She felt a twitchy feeling run through her as her mind unknotted.

Fisher had found out that Mason's violent outbursts frequently occurred on dates that had been important to his family; Christmas and school holidays, for instance. The days when he had felt most abandoned. The last killing had been on his father's birthday.

That was it!

It had been on the database screen. Mason's birthday. It was Hallowe'en. October thirty-first. Mason's birthday was today.

'Jesus Christ!' she whispered.

'I beg your pardon?' the woman said, turning towards her.

Alex stared at her blankly.

Mason had told Fisher the reason he had killed prostitutes was because he had access to them – what he meant was access on the day he wanted. Now she realised why he was doing it. All the girls he had killed had been young. He was stuck in a loop – rerunning through his confused fantasy to kill his sister as the loneliness bit in.

And today was Mason's birthday.

If ever he was going to kill someone it was tonight. That girl. That poor little girl lost somewhere in the dark.

If he was going to do it, he was going to do it soon – very soon.

'I need to talk to someone now,' Alex said. 'It's very, very important.'

# 46

Alex ran her hands through her hair, feeling her hand tremble.

'Is it OK if I smoke?' she asked the constable in the corner.

'Sure. Go ahead.'

'Have you got an ashtray?'

'Don't worry, love. Just tap it on the floor.'

She looked at the door.

'How long's this going to take?' she asked.

'Like I said, they shouldn't be long. Don't worry.'

She flicked her lighter, then shook it in frustration when the flame wouldn't catch.

The constable got up and ambled towards her. He was a squat man of about forty, with a quiet, honest voice. He was tailor-made for the job of keeping people calm.

'There you go, love,' he said, holding his lighter in front of her. She dipped the end of her B&H into the flame.

'Thanks.' She straightened up and pulled deeply.

The door suddenly swung open, a WPC holding it, while a man in a light grey suit walked in.

'Ms Brierley,' he said crisply, sitting down in front of her. 'DI Harris.' He held out his hand.

She shook it with a brief flick of the wrist. He had a cool, calm air of authority about him.

'Can you tell me how Martin is?' Alex asked sharply.

Harris frowned and looked at the WPC standing by his side.

'The shooting victim,' she explained. 'The ambulance took him over to Queens.'

'Is he . . . is he alive?' Alex asked shakily. 'I need to know.'

261

'I'm afraid we have no information on his condition at the moment,' the WPC said formally.

Harris leant back in his chair.

'Then find out,' he ordered.

He turned back to Alex.

'Oh, and get Ms Brierley an ashtray while you're at it.' He shook his head and smiled. 'Would you like some tea?'

She managed a tight smile.

'No thanks.'

'Fine ... OK.' He glanced at his notes. 'Right, I need to get a few things straight. So you're a reporter. . . .'

'Look,' Alex said slowly. 'I need to know what's going on, OK? I've been here for hours, and no one seems to know what's happening. Have you got him?'

He glanced up at her.

'Who?'

She leaned forward, her eyes suddenly blazing. 'David Mason. Who the hell do you think?'

He closed his eyes for a second, and when he opened them he looked tired.

'I'm sorry. It's been a long day.' He pinched his nose and blinked slowly. 'Please accept my apologies.'

'Sure. No problem,' Alex said, sitting back in her chair. 'It's been a long day for me too.'

He stared at her and smiled. 'Yes. We've got him.'

'And the girl?'

'She's very poorly, but ... she's still alive. We caught him just as he was leaving his house. She was in the boot of the car – and she'd been there a while.' He rubbed his hand across his face. 'She's got mild hypothermia and she'll need some surgery for tendon damage. But I think she'll be OK. Physically at least.'

'Thank God,' Alex said, putting her head in her hands. She suddenly felt a huge pressure lift inside her; exhaustion coursed through her body. 'Thank God.'

She scraped her fingers slowly through her hair; trying to control the flood of feelings that suddenly swamped her. It was as if a wall had come tumbling down at the back of her mind somewhere and all of a sudden she was feeling everything at once – a cocktail of conflicting emotions cascading through her head.

She felt her head spin and for a moment it was as if she was falling through open space.

And then she was crying thick big, teardrops plopping on the table.

'Are you OK?' Harris asked, sounding uncomfortable.

'Yeah.'

'Do you need a minute?'

'No.' She shut her eyes tightly, trying to block out the images in her head.

She could see that girl as clearly as if she were her own.

'No,' she said, forcing the tears to stop and sniffing hard. 'No. I'll be OK. It's just that . . .' Her voice trailed off. 'It's nothing.'

She rubbed her eyes with her knuckles, then looked up, and smiled sadly.

'Do you think he understood the consequences of his actions?'

'I'm sorry?'

'What I mean is, do you think Mason really is a monster, planning and calculating? In control. Did he really know what he was doing? Or did he just sort of slip into it, one step at a time, without really knowing?'

'Look,' Harris said, shifting in his seat. 'I'll be honest with you. I really don't know. And I don't even want to try. You can come up with as many theories as you like, but they never really get close. What you have to come to terms with is that it happens sometimes, and it always will do. All we can do is try and minimise it.'

'Right,' she said, shaking her head. She stared into space for a moment. 'Do you know what really amazes me?' she murmured.

'What?'

'That it doesn't happen more often. All those fucked-up people out there . . .'

'Look, Alex,' Harris said gravely, 'don't go down that route. It'll get you nowhere. Trust me. I've been there. Just thank the Lord that it doesn't.'

Alex picked up her cigarettes, flicked away the trail of ash, and took a long pull.

'I want to see him,' she said slowly.

'I'm afraid that's not possible.'

'Look . . . he wouldn't be here if it wasn't for me, OK? So I

263

want to see him. I *need* to see him. You owe me that. . . . Please.'

Harris placed his chin carefully on his fingers and looked at her solemnly.

'OK,' he said slowly after a pause. 'Once we've got things wrapped here I'll see what I can do, alright?'

Alex looked at him uncertainly.

'You have my word.'

'Thank you.' She nodded slowly.

'OK, so . . . why don't you run me through what you know about the Kallman Institute first.'

When Alex had finished, Harris clicked off the tape recorder and started to scribble down some notes. He wrote hunched up with his face bent close to the paper, crossing out words and replacing them carefully with new ones. Alex could see the bald patch on top of his head as he worked.

'Thanks.' He sounded tired. 'So we need to get hold of that blister pack. That's the key to the whole thing.'

Alex nodded.

'Are you up to going back to your flat?'

'Not really.' She shrugged. 'But I guess I'll have to go there some time, so it might as well be now.'

# 47

Alex kept her eyes on the stocky outline of the policeman ahead of her as they crunched blindly down the side of the house. Suddenly she didn't want to go into her flat. She remembered a scene from *Klute* where the police were searching a murdered woman's house, and came across a pair of her unused knickers covered with the killer's semen.

Men had a nasty habit of leaving their mark, she thought unhappily. She shook her head, and tried not to think about it.

'I've a feeling it's not going to be too pretty in here,' she said grimly as they pushed open the front door. She forced herself to smile. 'I don't suppose there's any chance of you boys helping me clean up while you're here, is there?'

Detective Sergeant Grigson smiled. 'I'll see what I can do.'

They picked their way carefully down the hall, their torch beams scanning the floor, catching on splintered wood and ripped carpet. There were three policemen with her – two sturdy uniforms and Grigson – but she still felt uneasy.

'Don't worry,' Grigson said, as they approached the kitchen door.

'Fine,' Alex replied. 'After you, then.'

'Where's the light?'

'On the wall on the left inside the door.'

He carefully pushed open the door and groped around on the wall.

'It's not working,' he said after a few seconds.

'Maybe I forgot to put a shilling in the meter.'

'Really?'

'Joke.'

Alex followed Grigson through the door, while the other two continued down the hall. She felt her breath catch in her throat as he panned the torch around; she had expected the place to be in a mess – but she was still shocked. They had torn the kitchen to pieces. The beam bobbed across exposed floorboards and wires hanging out where fittings had been removed.

'Where's the bathroom?' Grigson asked, pulling hard on his cigarette. She heard a dry crackle and saw the bright orange tip flare in the dark.

'Down at the end of the corridor.'

'Come on.'

They stumbled out into the hall.

Grigson twisted the bathroom door handle and shoved, but it wouldn't open.

'Kick it down if you want,' Alex said after he had given it a few tentative shoves. 'It's not going to make a lot of difference.'

He stepped back slightly, cracked his shoulders, then put his full weight into the door. It flew open on the third attempt. He staggered in and the torch beam shot along the floor, leaving the hall in darkness. Alex felt the hair on the back of her neck prickle and quickly followed him in.

'Oh God,' she murmured as he moved the beam around the room.

The pedestal sink had been wrenched off the wall and water was gushing from the ruptured pipe, sinking through the gaps in the exposed floorboards. The side of the bath had been prised off and the toilet cistern was in bits. And there was stuff everywhere. They had even emptied her tampons out of the boxes, just like they had at Jill's.

But it was the gaping hole by the water tank that held her gaze.

Where the loose plank had been there was now only a gaping hole. They had removed the floorboards on either side.

The blister pack was long gone.

She slumped against the wall. She knew that without the pack they were in trouble. She wasn't sure how the computer data would stand up on its own. There would be no physical evidence to link the trial to Numen. And if they couldn't get Numen, they wouldn't find who it was that had been after her; she had been depending on that.

Her stomach contracted as she thought about it, and for a second she thought she was going to throw up.

'Excuse me, sir,' one of the PCs called from another room. 'I think you should come through here.'

Grigson turned sharply, his torch beam suddenly scampering towards the door. Alex shook herself into action and followed quickly; she didn't want to be left alone in the dark.

'Do you know who it is?' Grigson asked her, as the three beams illuminated the body tied to the chair in the middle of the living room.

It was male, she could see that. He was well built and fairly young. But she couldn't tell who it was. She could see where the ropes bit into his biceps. And the blood matted in his hair. But she couldn't see his face; his head was slumped forward.

'No,' she replied shakily. 'I don't think so.'

Grigson stepped forward and carefully lifted the head, focusing the beam of his torch on the side of his face.

'Oh no,' she gasped.

She could see only pale, pasty skin and the left eye bruised shut. The other side of the face was in shadow. But she already thought she knew who it was.

He moved the beam, illuminating the whole face, and she felt herself convulse.

She tried to stop herself looking. But she couldn't drag her gaze away from the other socket, the empty space where his eye should have been.

She felt the bile rise in her throat.

Even like that, with his lips pulled back in an awful grimace, she recognised him.

It was Steve.

His hair was plastered to his head with matted blood, but there was no mistaking him.

She felt her legs go weak.

She put one of her hands against the wall.

'Oh no,' she cried, hearing her voice die in her throat. Then she threw up, dipping her head and retching into the corner.

267

# 48

The bright scene on the other side off the glass looked like a movie from the little dark room.

Alex walked up to the glass.

'Can he see me?' she asked, staring into the interview room.

'No, don't worry. He can't.'

She put her fingers on the glass. That was him, she thought, looking at the pale figure behind the table. That was really him.

As she ran her fingers down the warm surface he suddenly looked up.

'Are you sure he can't see me?' She stepped back uncertainly as he looked straight at her.

'Absolutely. It's a one-way mirror.'

He stared with such intensity that one of the men interviewing him turned around to see what was there, then frowned; all that was there was a mirror.

She turned her back to the glass and looked at Harris through the gloom. His face was illuminated by the room behind her, the rest of him in darkness.

'Can you give me a minute?' she asked, frowning.

He hesitated. 'OK . . . I'll just be down the corridor.'

'Thanks.'

She turned back when Harris had gone and gazed into the stark white room again. She stared at the pale hunched figure on the other side of the table. There he was, she thought – the reality behind the story. Just sitting there. And he didn't look like a monster, or an animal, or a warped, evil presence. In fact he didn't look like any of the soundbites that had been used to describe him. He just looked . . . *normal*. Just a regular-looking guy sitting quietly being interviewed, his translucent skin and sandy red hair bleached out by the bright light in the room.

She wasn't surprised.

But what was inside? she thought, staring as he earnestly answered a question. She stepped right up to the glass.

What was going on inside his head?

She slowly let the air out of her lungs, and as her breath briefly fogged on the glass, he looked up again, lifting his head then dragging his eyes up until they stared straight at her.

She felt her mind clench as she gazed into his watery blue eyes.

What was underneath?

He looked towards her curiously, and slowly his face broke into a wide, open smile. It was a look of sudden understanding and recognition, an expression without malice or danger, that beckoned her in.

She felt something stir inside her.

What she saw on his face was – quite simply – the sweet innocent smile of a child; nothing more, nothing less.

Then he looked down and she felt her head empty. She shut her eyes.

'Dear God, forgive him,' she murmured. 'He didn't know what he was doing . . . None of us did.'

She breathed slowly and carefully for a few moments, then, with a final glance at the thin figure huddled at the desk, turned and left the room. As she did he looked up again.

None of the three men in the room saw his eyes flit across the mirror, or saw his mouth move.

'Thank you,' he mouthed silently, as the door shut behind her. 'Thank you.'

# 49

There were twelve beds in the ward, arranged neatly in two rows down each side. Some had curtains pulled around them, allowing a little privacy during visiting. The air buzzed with anxious chatter – there was either too much to say in too little time, or not enough to fill the awkward hour.

Alex walked slowly down the middle, glancing up towards the far end of the ward.

He hadn't seen her, she thought, smiling.

He was gazing out of the window, staring at the birds arcing away through the cold grey sky.

'What's a nice boy like you doing in a place like this?' she asked brightly, lobbing a bag of grapes on the bed beside him.

Martin turned around stiffly.

'Alex,' he exclaimed, a smile breaking out on his face.

'The one and only,' she grinned back.

'It's good to see you.'

'Likewise. So . . . is that it?' she said, nodding at the sling and the neat bandaging on his shoulder. 'Is that all you've got to show?'

'What? Oh, this . . . yeah. Are you disappointed?'

She glanced at the huge bunch of flowers in her hand.

'Too right I am, I mean, I was at least expecting a drip or something, and maybe one of those little machines that beeps. I wouldn't have got you such a big bunch if I'd known.'

He smiled and shook his head.

'Only joking.' She handed him the flowers.

'Thank you.'

She bent down, pretending she was about to peck him on the cheek. 'How are you feeling?' she asked.

'OK.'

'Good.' She ignored his cheek, and kissed him firmly on the lips.

When she pulled away he looked shocked.

'Good grief,' he muttered, his lips covered with her lipstick. 'What was that for?'

'You saved my life,' she said, raising her eyebrow. 'Remember?'

She sat down carefully on the edge of the bed.

'I thought you'd been killed, you dolt. Why did you do that?'

He shrugged and shook his head slightly.

'I haven't the faintest idea.'

She put her hand out and brushed his cheek.

'I thought you were dead,' she said, shaking her head.

'Well, I'm not.'

She focused on the wall behind his head, and she suddenly knew she was about to cry.

'Oh God,' she said, rolling her brimming eyes. She tried to push it down, but it swept across her. Her voice sounded hollow when she spoke.

'I'm sorry,' she mumbled, feeling a drop run off her nose.

He put his hand on her arm.

'Ohhh . . .' she moaned, throwing her head back, and trying to contain the tears. 'This isn't me.'

'It rather suits you.' He rubbed her arm before pulling his hand away.

'Thanks,' she smiled. She sniffed and looked at him. 'I didn't want to leave you there. I really didn't. It's just that . . . Look, I'm sorry, OK?'

'I know.' He took her hand. 'But if you'd hung about then we'd both be dead. That's what they were there to do. You took them away, Alex. That's why I'm still here. That makes us even.'

She nodded and felt another tear drip off the end of her nose. She shut her eyes and squeezed his hand.

'We're quits,' he said gently.

It was too much. She put her head in her hands and sobbed quietly. It all just came out. Her head bobbed slowly.

271

'What's wrong, Alex?'

She shook her head slowly.

'I thought you were dead,' she repeated through her tears. 'All the time I was in the police station, all I could think of was you on the ground. You were so still. No one seemed to know what had happened to you. I thought you were dead, you idiot.'

He ruffled her hair with his hand. 'Well, I'm not.'

She looked up and saw him smiling. It caused a fresh wave of tears to fill her eyes. She stared at the ceiling until she had them under control.

When she looked back he was grinning.

'What are you laughing at?'

'Let's just say you don't exactly look like Demi Moore in *Ghost* at the moment.'

'That's right, kick me while I'm down.'

'Sorry.' He smiled and shook his head slowly. 'You're quite a girl, Alex, you know that?'

'Yeah, yeah,' she said, sniffing up the last of her tears and swallowing them. 'Don't try and compliment your way out of a corner.'

He shook his head again. 'And you're impossible. You pull this off, and you still can't take a compliment.'

'Yeah, well, maybe I haven't pulled it off.' She looked out of the window. November had brought a freezing slab of grey sky with it. It hung like an icy blanket over the city.

'There's a strong chance that Numen might get away with it.'

'What?'

'They're saying that the data on the computer was from a post-marketing trial Fisher was doing for them.'

'What's that mean?'

'It means that they know that we haven't got the actual drug, so instead of denying any involvement with Fisher they're saying they were testing out another drug – one that they know is safe.'

'But what about Mason?'

'They'll be able to prove it wasn't anything to do with their drug.'

'But surely they can't get away with it?'

'I don't know. Maybe not. Probably not. I don't know. But meanwhile they're still out there somewhere. It's unfinished business. It could take them ages to sort it out. If only I had hidden that pack somewhere better!'

'You're too hard on yourself, Alex. If you hadn't found out about Mason he would still be out there cutting women open.'

'I know that. It's just that I feel like it's me who has come out of this worst. So the killer is caught. The streets are safe to walk again for everyone except me.'

'But Numen are off the hook. It would be idiotic to draw attention to themselves by having something happen to you. It's in their interests for you to remain safe.'

'Sure, that's the logic. I've been through it a million times. But I just can't convince myself.'

'So what are you going to do?'

She shrugged and looked at him for a moment. He was propped up against the pillows. Apart from the bandages he was the picture of health.

'Go back to London, I suppose.'

The flicker of a frown showed on his face for a moment. He looked as if he was about to say something, but he stopped himself.

'It's what I've wanted to do for ages. To get away and start again. I've been asked to write my story for the *Sunday Times*. But this way it doesn't taste so good. It feels like I'm running away again.'

'You'll be OK, Alex,' Martin said, forcing himself to smile. 'Once you get down there, it'll all seem a million miles away.'

'Yeah, maybe.' She nodded. 'I hope so.'

'So what are you going to say about Mason?'

'God knows. It's a weird one. They reckon he had two personalities fighting inside him. It went right back to his sister's death. Part of him blamed her for taking his parents away from him, and leaving him alone. But the other part just wanted her to be alright again. It was something he couldn't reconcile and it has split his personality right down the middle. One side of him was killing the girls, while the other was actually trying to save them. Isn't that a blast?' She shrugged. 'But who knows what he was really doing. I think initially he was just incredibly lonely. The first killing was probably an accident. But once it had happened and the media started covering it, the rejected part of him had found a way of getting attention. Each time he did it, that part of him became more powerful. It made him feel wanted.' She snorted. 'Life imitating art, you might say. That's if you call newscasting an art.

'Meanwhile the other part just kept going through the same futile attempt to save the dying woman. Just as it had when he had watched his sister choke on her tongue. When the doctor got there he performed an emergency tracheotomy, but it was too late. The damage had been done. It wasn't Mason's fault. He was only a kid. But he had the guilt. Every time he looked at the women dying at his feet, that part of him suddenly tried to do what he thought he should have done then. He would cut open their windpipe and try to stop them dying.' She shook her head. 'An impotent act to try to cover up his guilt.'

'It's a good story.'

'Yeah,' she replied dryly. 'And it'll make that side of him happy, wherever they put him.'

'Come on, Alex. Give yourself a break.'

'Sorry,' she said, getting off the bed. 'I didn't mean to burden you with all this.'

She looked down the ward. People were starting to leave.

'Look's like it's time to go.'

'When are you planning to leave?' he asked, as she pecked him on the cheek.

'Couple of days. There's a few things I've got to sort out first,' She stopped, tapping her fingers with her teeth while she thought. 'I don't suppose you'd be interested in adopting a cat,' she asked.

'He or a she?'

'He.'

He thought for a moment.

'Is he like you?'

'Far nicer.'

'OK,' he nodded. 'Yeah. Why not?'

'Great. That's a weight off my mind. It's nice to know he's going to a good home.' She glanced over her shoulder, the ward was all but empty. 'I'll bring him around to see you when you're back home.'

'That'd be good. Hopefully things will be in better shape when I get back. A couple of friends have been sorting the house out, so – fingers crossed – it should be habitable.'

'I'll give you a call.' She made a move to go.

'Look,' he said quickly, 'can we go out before you leave? You know, dinner or something.'

She looked at the bandages. 'What, dine out on hospital food?'

'No. They say I'll be out of here the day after tomorrow. How about it?'

'Yeah. That'd be lovely,' she said, nodding. She looked up the ward again. 'Right, I'd better shoot.'

He smiled sadly at her and shook his head slowly.

'What's wrong?' she asked, stepping back up to the bed.

'It's nothing,' he smiled. 'Honest. It's just that visiting hour seems to go very quickly when you're here.' He pulled his hand away and looked up the ward. 'Go on. You need to go.'

'Are you sure?'

'Yeah.'

'OK,' she said. 'I'll see you later.'

She turned around at the door. A nurse was pulling the curtains back, and she could see him staring blankly out of the window. The sky had brightened, but it was still a flat icy grey.

She turned back before he saw her, and headed for the lifts.

# 50

'Alex!' Jim said, as she strode out of the lift. 'Are you back to stay?'

'No, I'm just here to pick up a few things. And Harry said he wanted to see me. God knows what he wants, but I thought I'd pop my head in. Is there anything for me?'

'Er, yeah. There's a couple of letters, and, er . . .' He stopped and shrugged sheepishly. 'There was a parcel delivered a couple of weeks ago when you were off sick. I, er . . . sort of forgot about it. It's in the post room. I'll . . .'

'Alex!' a voice boomed behind her.

She recognised it immediately. It was Ashley James, one of the anchormen from Birmingham. He was one of the last people she wanted to see.

'I'll pick them up on the way out,' she said quickly.

When she turned around Ashley was homing in with his best smile on.

'Great to see you,' he boomed, taking her hand. He was a well-toned fifty-year-old, with a boil-in-the-bag personality and an all-year-round tan. The housewives loved him.

'Ash,' she said without much enthusiasm. He had never spoken to her like that before. It was usually a curt nod and a grunt if she was lucky.

'Alex, Alex, Alex,' he smiled, patting the back of her hand. 'You've suddenly become the jewel in our crown. You look great.'

She was getting the full works. The double-handed handshake meant he had decided she was going places. She could see how people fell for it if they had never met him before.

She carefully extricated her hand.

'I want to hear all about it, Alex,' he said, showing a perfect set of teeth. 'What about dinner?'

'Thanks, but I'm in a bit of a hurry, Ash. You know? Maybe another time.' She started to step around him.

'No problem. I understand. Tomorrow?' he asked confidently. He treated her to his best on-screen smile.

'Sorry.' She started to head for the lift. 'I'm pretty tied up just at the moment.'

She punched the button.

'Fine. Give me a call.'

'Sure,' she said, without looking at him.

It took her quite a while to get to Harry's office. All the people who had disappeared off the face of the earth when she was clearing her desk had suddenly come out of the woodwork. She avoided them but stopped and chatted with Dave and Ted Connor, before freeing herself and knocking politely on Harry's door.

Harry darted her a glance as she shut the door behind her.

'Sorry,' he said curtly into the receiver. 'I've got a guest. I'll call you later.'

He put the phone down, and shot out his hand.

'Alex,' he smiled warmly. 'It's good to see you.'

'Likewise,' Alex replied, sitting down in the chair he was waving at.

The next five minutes were bliss.

She enjoyed watching him squirm; every last second of it. She had never seen him look so uncomfortable. Not even when he was trying to pass his kidney stones. Obviously someone at head office had told him he had to hang on to her. And judging by his increasing agitation, it sounded like they didn't want no for an answer.

'Company car, Harry? What can I say?' she said when he upped his offer.

'So you'll take it?' he asked tightly. He had managed to fix a smile on his face, but it was beginning to look ridiculous.

'Nope. But it was nice of you to ask!'

'Think about it, Alex. It's a once-in-a-lifetime chance. You'll get to cover the kind of stories you've always wanted to out in the field and act as cover for the news anchor in Birmingham. It's a brilliant offer.'

'Maybe it is, but it's not me any more. I've suddenly realised I don't want to spend the rest of my life smiling, and bantering with the weather girl. There must be better things to do.'

'So we'll find you something in research.'

'Thanks, but no thanks, Harry.' She pushed her chair back. 'It's just too late. Thanks for asking, though.' She smiled at him, her eyes crinkling around the edges.

'Take care, Harry,' she said softly.

She got up and left him with the same idiotic grin fixed on his face.

She walked briskly across the office, ignoring the little cluster of people who were milling around, trying to look busy.

It was time to go.

As the lift rattled down to the underground carpark she closed her eyes and stretched her neck. It had felt strange being in the office, like going back in time.

The lift hit the bottom of the shaft with a clunk, bouncing slightly, as the doors slowly rattled open. Cold air rushed in through the gap with a roar.

Behind was darkness.

She swallowed hard before stepping out.

'There's no one there, Al,' she muttered. 'You're going to have to get used to this.'

She stepped out onto the concrete, the cold seeping through her coat.

She felt her eyes water. The carpark was deserted. She could see vehicles sitting darkly between the pillars. But there was no one there.

Or no one she could see.

She pulled her coat around her. The station above seemed like a million miles away.

She heard the doors start to close behind her.

'Come on, Al,' she repeated to herself as she stepped into the first pool of darkness.

Her heels made a loud click on the concrete floor, the noise echoing away between the stained supporting pillars. Her car was sitting in a deep pit of shadow on the far side of the carpark. She clutched the keys in her pocket and walked quickly towards it.

The lift doors thundered shut with a bang.

A slight moan from the bars at the edge of the carpark drifted through the air.

She was almost there when she heard the noise. Something clanked at the other end of the carpark, sending a sharp noise echoing off the concrete walls. She clenched her fists and felt the keys cutting into her sweaty palm.

She shot a glance over her shoulder.

There was a movement on the far side of the carpark; the only movement in the still, dark space. The fire door by the lift was swinging open, the bright light from the stairwell fluttering through the gap.

There was another bang as the heavy door smacked against the concrete wall. The light seemed to bob as a silhouette obscured the source. Then it flooded out again as the figure moved swiftly through the open door. She couldn't make him out across the gloomy space. But he was in a hurry.

She fumbled with the keys in her pocket.

'Alex!' Her name boomed against the walls. It sounded like a voice from the dead.

She pulled the keys out.

'Alex!' The words ricocheted around her.

As the key went into the lock, the voice registered. She slowly let go of the fob, and turned.

The figure was rushing towards her. She tried to look calm as it approached. She pushed her shoulders back, and waited.

'I hope I didn't make you jump,' he croaked, gasping for air. She could see the sweat beading on his forehead.

It was Jim.

Alex forced herself to smile.

She put her hand on the car behind to steady herself. Jim couldn't have looked less threatening; five foot six, pot belly and receding grey hair.

'You forgot to pick up your post,' he panted. He had a large parcel and a couple of envelopes in his hand.

She rolled her eyes.

'Sorry, Jim. I had other things on my mind.'

'You look like you've seen a ghost,' he said as he handed them to her.

'Yeah,' she replied, managing to smile. 'I feel like it too.'

She watched as he waddled back across the carpark.

How long would it be before she didn't panic every time she heard a noise when she was on her own? she thought, as he disappeared through the door.

She slid into her car and threw the parcel onto the passenger seat with her bag. She was looking forward to getting away from the station and back to the safe warmth of her hotel room; she had checked into the Royal for a couple of days until her flat was sorted out.

She would open the package when she got back.

She turned on the engine, and rummaged in her bag for her cigarettes.

'Damn,' she muttered, peering into the empty packet.

She flicked on the headlights, took a deep breath, and carefully wove the car through the pillars.


She picked up a packet of Marlboro in the lobby and took the lift to the tenth floor.

She gripped the cigarettes in her teeth while she released the lock with her room card, pushed the door open, and managed to turn the main light on with her shoulder.

The room lit up, and she could see her reflection in the window.

She quickly went to shut the curtains. She felt naked with the wide expanse of glass open to the world. She yanked the thick curtains shut and felt a little better. But her stomach was still hollow and aching. She lobbed the parcel onto the bed without looking at it.

Her clothes had been picked up by the cleaner and folded across the chair, and the mountain of cigarette butts were gone from the ashtray. The room felt antiseptic.

She shut her eyes and let herself fall forward onto the bed.

'Shit,' she murmured, burying her face in the pillow.

She lay with her eyes closed and tried to think. She had been through it a million times. There was nothing else she could do. She would just have to take her life one day at a time, and try to forget Numen. And hope they forgot her.

The warmth of the room started to make her feel a little better. The lifts were working hard, and the hum seeping through the pillow made her feel sleepy.

She rolled over and rubbed her eyes, realising she was lying on the parcel from the station.

She lifted herself up on her elbows and pulled it out. It was a fat Jiffy bag wrapped with lots of brown tape, marked Private & Confidential. She ripped it open and emptied the contents onto her chest. A couple of sheets came out first, then a huge bundle of paper flopped out and landed on her stomach.

She pushed herself up against the wall, and peered into the envelope. There was something wedged in the end. She stuck her fingers in and fished out two thin unmarked white boxes. She turned them over, then dropped them by her side.

She yawned and looked at the top sheet. It was a photocopy of a letter. She quickly scanned the top of the page, trying to take it all in at once.

Then the name jumped out at her.

It took a moment to sink in. Her mind recoiled as it hit home. She blew the air out of her lungs and whistled.

'Holy moley.'

It was a photocopy of a letter from Ian Fisher to Numen Biotechnology.

She sat bolt upright, and scanned down the page. Her eyes darted across the letters as she leafed through the other pages. They were all from Fisher to Numen. Her hands were trembling as she skimmed through the pile.

A couple of pages had fallen onto the bed. She picked them up. The top one was printed in a rough typeface on a cheap printer.

It was from Jill:

*Dear Alex,*
*Hopefully I will have spoken to you by now. Enclosed is*
*what I found in Fisher's filing cabinet and it's dynamite.*
*It certainly proves he was running a trial for Numen. The*
*early letters are fairly formal, but later he starts getting*
*edgy. He doesn't exactly say why, but judging by his tone*

*it was something pretty serious. The replies from Numen*
*weren't there so I don't know what they said back.*

*There's a couple of drug packs in the parcel. I found*
*the inventory in his cabinet. The other blister pack I sent*
*you turned out to be a placebo, so it's no good. These*
*packets have the active compound in. If Numen are*
*developing a drug, they will have a patent out on the*
*compound. If we get these analysed and they match up*
*with one of Numen's patents, then we've made the*
*connection. Now all I need to know is what went wrong.*

*I'll keep looking around, and be in touch.*
*See you soon.*
*Jill.*

Alex clawed open one of the packs, and tipped it up. Two blister
packs fell onto her lap. She let out a low whistle.

'Jill,' she whispered. 'Why didn't you call me?'

She shook her head, and started to look through the pages.

After ten minutes she knew she had them. Jack O'Neill and
his cowboys could do whatever they liked. This would bury them
alive. She could feel the edges of her mouth pulling into a smile.

She finished reading the notes, and wriggled across the bed
towards the phone. Then she stopped.

Not yet!

It felt as if a huge weight had been lifted off her. She wanted
to savour it. She rolled on her back and laughed. Then she stood
up, and sat straight back down again. She didn't know what to
do first.

She went to the mini-bar and pulled out a can of Stella. The
computer would register some outrageous amount to her bill but
she didn't care. This was her moment.

She would soon be free from the vultures.

She cracked open the tin and took a long pull. The cold liquid
fizzed nicely inside her mouth, and the tension started to ebb out
of her muscles.

She belched happily, and went into the bathroom, turning on
the taps full blast.

She didn't want to call Harris yet. That could wait.

She turned on MTV while she got undressed. Some rap band

282

were doing their worst, but even they sounded beautiful at that moment. She could hear the water thundering into the bath through the open door.

Beer, hot water, and the taste of victory. What a combination!

She wanted to let it sink in for a while. Then she would call Harris, and set the dogs on Numen.

She lay in the bath for a long time. The scent of bath oil blended with the steam and filled the air. She arched her back and breathed in slowly.

The rest of the evening would be spent giving statements, and waiting for things to happen. But for a while she was at complete peace with herself.

An hour later, she pulled the car out of the carpark and headed for the central police station. She glanced briefly in the mirror.

But suddenly she knew that no one would be there.

# 51

The clock on the council chambers was sounding the last stroke of eight as Alex started up the hill. She stopped and took a last deep pull on her cigarette, then threw it into a shop doorway. It was a crisp, cold evening. The paving stones were a frosty white and beginning to glisten. She blew the smoke out, and watched it billow in front of her and catch the light.

She ambled over to Jigsaw, and looked in the window while she dug around in her bag. It was freezing, and she only had a thin coat on, but the cold air seemed to evaporate as it touched her skin. She found the bottle she was looking for and dabbed some No. 5 behind her ear. She could see herself in the window. For once her hair looked right. She stroked a little perfume through it, then set off towards the restaurant.

She walked slowly up the stone-paved street, glancing in the windows. It was a nice area of refurbished Edwardian shops and restaurants running into the Gothic splendour of the old lace-making area, now a haven for the off-beat and trendy.

She saw Martin before he saw her. She let the waitress help her out of her coat, and watched him across the tables. He was scrutinising a menu. He'd had his hair cut, she thought. It looked good.

She set off towards him.

There were three wooden steps down from the bar. She was wearing her best Emma Hope high heels and she stumbled slightly on the top step.

'Piss!' she hissed under her breath.

That was not the impression she had wanted to make. But

when she looked up he was still bent over the menu.

He glanced up just as she got to the table. He was wearing a black wool jacket with a crisp open-necked white shirt. The shoulder stuck up slightly over his bandaged arm.

She slid in opposite him. 'Of all the restaurants in all the world.' She grinned.

He smiled back and watched her sit down. 'And you have to walk into this one looking like that. You look beautiful.'

She couldn't think of a reply.

'Thanks,' she said meekly, trying to sound as if people said it to her all the time.

She put both elbows on the table and raised her eyebrows.

'So what's on the menu?'

'Too much. What do you think?'

She glanced down at the handwritten card in front of her.

'I had blackened salmon last time I was here. It's really good.'

Martin looked up as the waitress arrived at the table.

'Champagne?' she asked, holding the bottle up for him to look at the label.

'Er, no. I don't think so,' he said, leaning back so he could look at her. The waitress looked confused.

'I ordered it,' Alex explained quickly. Martin shot her an enquiring glance.

'We're celebrating, right? So this is my treat. OK?'

'Fine.' He shrugged. 'Why not?'

The waitress carefully popped the cork, and poured out two glasses.

Alex twirled the glass in her fingers, and watched the bubbles rise. When she looked up at Martin she realised he was waiting for her. She raised the glass towards him.

'To . . .' She wasn't sure what to say. 'To the future, I suppose.'

They clinked their glasses and took a sip.

The restaurant was about half full. The low hum of conversation was overlaid with mellow jazz from the CD behind the bar.

'Would you share a starter with me?' she asked, screwing up her mouth as she looked at the menu. 'A whole one's usually a bit much.'

285

'Sure.' He nodded and smiled. 'Do you do this a lot?'

'Not often enough,' she replied, emptying her glass. 'And never with the right people.'

She refilled their glasses. The alcohol had softened her focus, and the whole restaurant had taken on a warm orange glow.

'So have you finally nailed Numen?' Martin asked when the waitress had taken their order.

'Christ, I hope so. I've spent the last God knows how many days stuck in that bloody police station. But I think we've got it wrapped up at last.'

'Does that include Dobson?'

'Yeah. It'll take a bit of time to sort through the mess, but they're all up to their necks. They analysed the tablets in the blister packs and Jill was right. Numen had filed a patent on that compound earlier this year. That was all it needed.'

The char-grill at the far side of the restaurant suddenly blazed as something was poured over it. They both looked around. The smell of barbecuing meat wafted towards them.

She shut her eyes. 'God, I'm starving.'

Martin was looking perplexed when she turned back.

'So why did they do it?'

'Simple. Money.'

'OK, so why has no one else done it if there's so much money involved?'

'Maybe they have, I don't know. But it's probably not worth the risk. The whole business rides on reputation. Someone at Numen was obviously very confident that this one was going to work. But there was probably more to it than that. It sounds like the directors at Numen rather oversold the potential of the new compound to Kogai when they were being taken over. Kogai paid such a lot for the company because they thought the drug was in a later stage of development. I think they were in the dark about the whole thing. They assume the people they were dealing with were bound to be honest. Probably because they were doctors. They thought the compound was only about a year away from the market, and when it hit they could start printing money. Kogai put the old Numen directors on a percentage to make sure they delivered. That's why they were so desperate to get it to the market. Desperate enough to risk breaking the rules. They figured

286

they could put the supporting documentation together if the trials were successful. If not, then they could have erased all the records. It would have been fine if David Mason hadn't started killing people.'

Martin frowned.

'Yeah, but surely it was just a matter of time before it made someone else go loco?'

Alex shook her head.

'Actually no, probably not. The irony of this whole thing is that although the drug certainly didn't help Mason, it probably wasn't to blame. He was just a maddo, as they say medically. But they would have had a hard time convincing the authorities, considering they were running an illegal trial with him on it. The adverse publicity would have killed any chance the drug had of being marketed, even though it probably works very well. They had five hundred million pounds riding on it. It was a big risk to take. But the directors only got their cut if it hit the market when they said it would.'

'You mean, if they'd done things properly they'd have been allowed to sell the thing?'

'I think so.' She took a sip from her glass. 'It's a funny business. It's all about big risks and even bigger gains. A lot of things can happen with these things. Especially when you're into psychiatric drugs. That's why they have to test them so rigorously. Because the frightening thing is that they quite often don't know how or why the drugs actually work. They just know that they do. That's what the trials are about. They prove the things work, even though they don't actually know how. That's a bit spooky.'

The waitress arrived with laden plates.

Alex's sported six medallions of grilled lamb with an arty swirl of red sauce. She dropped her nose to the plate and sniffed.

'Hmm. Smells good enough to eat.'

'So you feel safe again?' Martin asked as a plate of char-grilled salmon was placed in front of him.

Alex straightened up and thought about his question. 'Yeah. Yeah, I do. Or at least as safe as I ever did.'

She looked at the empty bottle. 'You fancy some more champers?'

287

'Why not?'

She called the waitress over.

'When are you going to London?' Martin asked, as she filled his glass.

'Tomorrow.'

She saw him flinch.

'Really? Why so soon?'

'Because I'll feel better down there.' She shrugged. 'It's out of the way. And I might as well get started. The *Sunday Times* have asked me to deliver five thousand words by next week. I've never done anything like that before, so I need to get going. But the main thing is I need to move on. It's time to leave. There's nothing keeping me here now.'

He looked at her silently, and she suddenly knew what he was going to say.

'You could stay with me,' he said awkwardly.

She shook her head slowly, then realised what he meant.

'Oh, Martin . . .' she said, looking at the table.

'You'd be safe with me.'

She moved her hand across the white cloth, and put her fingers over his. She could feel the tension.

'I know I would. I'd just about convinced myself that I would never meet anyone I liked again, Martin. Just got used to the fact. I've spent years getting tangled up with idiots because I was looking too hard, and now when I decide to strike out, you have to turn up. Life can be a bitch . . .'

'You don't have to go, Alex,' he said quietly. 'You could stay here and write. London's only a couple of hours away.'

She shook her head.

'No. I can't. I need to start again. Do it properly this time. I've got to go to prove something to myself. If I stayed here I'd blame you every time anything started to go wrong. It wouldn't be fair.'

'I'm prepared to take that risk.'

'But I can't,' Alex said softly. 'I've thought about this for so long. I've got to give it a try.'

'You've got to stop running one day, Alex. Why not now?'

She shook her head and smiled.

'I'm not running any more.'

'Oh yeah?'

'No.'

He paused and looked at her. The char-grill crackled and the sound of laughter reverberated around the room.

He stared at her for a long time, the warm light glinting off his pupils. She twisted the glass in her hand, half enjoying and half embarrassed by his intense gaze.

He leant forward.

'It was a kid, wasn't it?' he asked quietly.

She looked up sharply. 'What do you mean?'

'It was a child. That's what's been cutting you up, isn't it?'

Suddenly the background noise seemed to blur. She felt her vision jump, and a soft yellow glow fill the room.

'What do you mean?'

'Look, it doesn't matter.'

She stared at him, her eyes suddenly dark and blazing.

'Yes, it matters.'

'You lost a child, didn't you?'

She looked at him for a long time, a faint smile ghosting across her face.

'Yes.'

She shook her head and ran her fingers through her hair. 'You don't give up, do you?'

'You've got to let it go.'

She put her hands on the table and stared at her fingers.

'Yes, it was a child.'

'What happened?'

She shut her eyes. Another jumble of images swamped her, but this time they began to take shape.

'I . . . I had an abortion.'

'What happened?'

If ever there was a time she should have cried it was then. But suddenly everything seemed so clear. She threw her head back and stretched her neck. 'It was just after I got to the station . . . just as things were falling apart with Rob. It was just such a mess . . . Everything was spinning out of control, and . . .'

She looked down at the table. 'And I'd been in town a couple of weeks, and things weren't going too well, and . . . and I slept with someone. It was simple as that.'

She shook her head.

'I got drunk and I'd been feeling shit, and for a moment it all just seemed fine and dandy.'

She squeezed her eyes tightly shut again as the memory welled up.

'Are you OK?' Martin touched her hand.

'Yeah, yeah,' she said, opening her eyes and smiling sadly. She looked at him for a moment.

'It was Mike,' she said, shaking her head.

'You mean . . .'

'Yeah, exactly.'

'How come?'

'He did a good job on me. He probably knew I was feeling sad and vulnerable. I mean, he seemed so cool and charming and everything, and I just fell for it. It wasn't even like he was that bad, and I don't remember much of it, but . . . but I got pregnant.'

'Did you tell him?'

'God, no.'

'Why not?'

'Because he's a bastard, that's why!' She looked at him defiantly. 'He proved that the next day. It was like nothing had happened – except *everybody* knew. So I . . . I had an abortion.'

'On your own?'

'Yes.' She looked away; she couldn't look at him.

'And Rob?'

'It was too late with Rob.'

'That must have been awful.'

She shut her eyes again and nodded.

'It was.'

'You did the right thing.'

'I know,' she said, barely audible.

'So why's it cutting you up so much?'

'Because I didn't deal with it properly. I didn't deal with it at all. I just got on with it, pretended everything was OK. But . . . but it's like your body doesn't know what's happened, you know? It gets confused. It still acted like a mother for a while; I felt like a mother for a while.'

She stared into space.

'And I never said goodbye.'

290

He took her hand and squeezed it.

'Alex . . . *Alex*.'

'What?' she murmured, looking down at the table again.

'You did the best you could. That's all you could do.'

'Yeah . . . maybe . . . I guess.' She looked up at him and smiled. 'So now you know. Satisfied?'

He shook his head sadly.

'Let it go, Alex.' He stared into her eyes. 'You've paid the price.'

'Yeah.' She nodded. 'It feels like that.'

The moon was high over the city when they left. They walked slowly down to the square together. The Christmas lights were already twinkling in the shop windows.

A few people were waiting for taxis, and a crowd of drunken girls giggled as they clattered between bars, but the square was quiet. A couple of skateboarders were trying kick-flips from the fountains.

She took his hand as they walked by the grand old council chambers.

'What do you want to do now?' she asked.

'I don't know. Whatever you want.'

She looked at the sky. It was big and clear. The stars were dotted brightly across a deep blue background. She suddenly knew that what she was feeling was right.

She kept looking at the sky as she spoke.

'I'd like to go back to the hotel,' she said quietly. 'And I'd like you to stay with me tonight. That's what I want.'

He stopped. She swivelled her head towards him, unable to read his expression.

'No,' he said, smiling.

She looked down at her feet.

He stepped forward and put his hands on her arms.

'No . . . because if we're going to do this, let's do it properly. Come and stay with me tonight. At my house. Not some hotel room, that could be any place. I want to treat you right.'

She met his gaze and smiled. The light seemed to make his eyes dance.

'OK.' It came out as a whisper.

It was the only thing she could say before he kissed her.

The fire was still smouldering when they got back.

They sat on the sofa for a long time. She kissed him awkwardly at first. But it soon felt natural. She ran her fingers across the back of his neck, and dug her tongue deep into his mouth.

Eventually, as the fire burned down, the last log crackling and breaking, they stirred. Alex got up silently, and stood in front of him. She looked down at him on the sofa, then put out her hands and pulled him up. She kissed him again, a long, lingering kiss with her eyes tightly closed, kicking off her shoes as she dragged her nails slowly across his neck, then she turned and led him upstairs.

She lay in the bed in the dark for a long time afterwards, unable to say anything. She pulled the sheet over her and looked at the creamy moon through the window. She could see the outline of a bare tree against the dark blue sky.

It had been a long, long time since she had felt like that.

They had let the sheets fall away and she hadn't minded him seeing her. He had made her feel attractive when he looked at her. The light through the lace curtain had cast patterns across their skin as they moved.

She heard the match burst and looked at him as it flared into life.

'What are you doing?'

'What do you think?' he said with the cigarette bobbing in his mouth.

'I thought you didn't.'

He glanced down at her. 'This is different. This is a ritual I've never been involved in. I just want to make the moment last. Do you want to share it?'

She nodded happily, and squeezed his forearm. The tobacco crackled as he sucked on the filter. She let her head fall onto his shoulder, and he lifted his arm around her, stroking the side of her face.

'Will I ever see you again?' he asked quietly.

She pushed herself up and took the cigarette from his hand.

'Yeah, maybe. As long as we can do that again.'

'So you only want me for my body?'

'No, but put it like this. It's a nice bonus.'

She handed the cigarette back and let herself slump down against his arm again.

She woke in the middle of the night, disorientated and unsure where she was. But when she heard the steady ebb and flow of his breathing she remembered. She put her hand out and touched his back, and he muttered slightly in his sleep.

She sat up carefully, keeping the sheet pulled around her. They hadn't shut the curtains and she could still see the moon against the dark sky. The bottom of the glass had started to crystallise with frost.

What are you doing, Al? she thought, looking at him. His head was half under the covers. It was all a lot of people wanted. And it was far more than most people ever got. Did she have to throw it away?

She shook her head.

She looked out of the window at the clear, dark sky, and for the first time in a long time – perhaps ever – she felt at peace. She shut her eyes and for a few seconds her head completely cleared. And she realised that sometimes you don't actually know how bad things have been until they start to get better.

She opened her eyes again, suddenly feeling the space around her that she existed in. At last she had forced herself to step right up to the edge of the open wound in her head, and stare straight in – and at last she knew what it was that she had been so scared of.

It was herself.

She had spent a lifetime running away, jumping from one thing to another, telling herself that she knew where she was going. But all she had been doing was running scared. Running away from anything that pinned her down, from the gnawing regret that stalked her just out of sight like the killer in the night, waiting for the right moment. Scared of the crippling feeling of inadequacy that drove her to keep doing things she didn't want to do. And she had been running so fast – so blindly – she hadn't actually got anywhere. She was still carrying all the old baggage she so desperately wanted to leave behind.

And she knew that she needed to let go.

293

Make peace with herself, then move on. She needed to leave it all behind – the frustration, the anger, everything. To leave the fear behind – and get on with a life that fitted. To stop running blindly and open her eyes to the bright light of possibility.

She softly got out of bed, the crisp sheets sliding delicately across her skin, and walked over to the window. The cold air made her skin feel tight and clean. She could see her reflection in the glass. Just a dark outline, the shimmer of her A-line slip clinging to her body. And she liked what she saw. She ran her hand through her hair and smiled.

It was time to go.

She put her clothes on quietly, taking her time, then padded softly out, pulling the door silently shut behind her.

She found Jasper sleeping on the rug in front of the dying embers of the fire.

She stroked him on the back of the head. 'Take care of him, won't you, sweetie.' She smiled as his ears twitched. 'OK?'

He yawned and stretched, but didn't wake.

'You always had your priorities sorted, didn't you, Jasp,' she said, smiling and running her hand down his back. She got up.

'Take care.'

She walked slowly through the empty streets, enjoying the cold, clear night, and the silence in her head. She looked at the star-peppered sky and smiled, knowing there was one more thing she had to do before she left.

# 52

The bells from the church nearby were ringing, the noise sounding louder and clearer than usual through the wide-open windows.

Alex checked the flat one last time. She walked slowly through the empty rooms making sure she hadn't forgotten anything. The carpets had been ruined in the flood and had been stripped out, leaving stained wood and exposed pipes. The whole flat felt soulless and lifeless.

When she had finished she went into the kitchen, picked up the phone and carefully punched Martin's number.

It rang five times before he answered.

'Martin?' she said, sounding hollow.

Then she heard the crackle as the ansaphone kicked in. She let half the message run before she cut the line.

'Maybe another time,' she whispered as the dial tone purred into life in her ear. 'Maybe in another life.'

'Thanks,' she said quietly into the receiver as the line went dead.

Then she placed the handset back into the cradle.

The pigeon slime in the alley had turned into a hard, thick crust in the cold. It crunched under her boots.

She threw her garment bag on top of the boxes in the boot, and tried to shut the lid, but it bounced open again. She had to get up on the bumper and sit heavily on it before she could coax it shut.

The sky was cloudless and a crisp, clear blue. But it was already beginning to darken slightly, and the temperature was

295

dropping fast. She wanted to get on the road. She jumped off the bumper and sprang onto the pavement in a single movement.

She drove slowly through the city centre. She had expected to feel some emotion. Some pang of self-doubt as she left. But there was nothing there. Just a strange numbness, and the growing fizz of excitement in the bottom of her stomach.

She pulled onto the long loop road that swept south out of the city. The sky was beginning to show pink on the horizon, and the dark shapes of migrating birds flapped low across the river.

She drove down the dual carriageway out of the city, taking the overpass across the river and onto the long road down to the motorway south. As the light began to die on the horizon, a cold white strip formed in the sky ahead of her.

A few miles south of the city, about halfway between the city limits and the giant power station that sat by the motorway, she saw the sign she was looking for.

She slowed down and turned left onto a small road that dipped away into the country; frozen fields stretched away around her. She drove carefully, scanning the meandering road as it wove between the rolling fields.

As she drove past a patch of high trees she found what she was looking for.

She turned left into a tiny lane that banked steeply down between two thick, high hedges and was only wide enough for a single vehicle. She drove slowly until the lane stopped abruptly in front of a small church. She turned the car around in the gravelled space in front of the gate and stopped.

She turned the engine off and got out. The church sat in a tiny overgrown yard, hemmed in between the lane and a small river behind. Tall, thin trees rose all around.

She shuddered; it was a long time since she had been down this way. The last time was just after she had come back from the hospital, when the pain inside her, both physical and mental, was so bad she'd had to get out. She had just got into her car and driven anywhere.

And this is where she had ended up.

She walked through the arched wooden gate. Night was beginning to fall and the temperature was dropping rapidly; a crisp, clean autumn smell hung in the cold air. It was almost exactly three years since she had last been there. But this time the sky was a hazy pink, and a cool breeze blew across her skin. Then the air had felt thick and charged. Clouds had scudded across the sky, and the wind had ripped at her hair.

She had sat on a flat gravestone in the corner by a gnarled dead tree, not knowing what to do, feeling more alone than she had thought was possible. It was as if she had come to the end of the world. The old graveyard had looked like a bombsite from Armageddon, the blackened stubs of the headstones poking out of the ground like accusing fingers. And the sky had been bright, so bright that everything had become a silhouette.

She had sat on the headstone and wept, and above her the sky burned red. Redder than it had ever been before. And when she had looked up it was a deep blood red, a seething blanket of hate above her head.

But now . . . now it was just empty. A blank wide-open space slowly turning pink.

She walked slowly through the graveyard and stopped at the low wall at the bottom. She put her elbows on the wall and looked at the river on the other side. It was a narrow, slow-moving strip of water, clear as crystal.

She could see the stones on the bottom, tiny fish flickering under the surface, and the tops of the apples, fallen from the trees upstream, bobbing slowly along in the water.

She opened the carrier bag she had brought with her.

It was full of things she had bought over the years for her baby. A whole load in the few weeks after she had come back from the hospital, wandering dazed through Boots, looking at the other mothers. Then little bits and pieces she had picked up when it felt like a birthday or she was just thinking about her.

And it *was* a her.

She knew that.

She looked at the little toys – a tiny dinosaur and a bear – and smiled.

It was time to go.

She swung the bag and watched it arc through the air, falling into the water with a splash. It sat on the surface for a moment, then gradually sank as it meandered downstream.

She watched it until it disappeared.

'Goodbye,' she murmured, watching the ripples on the surface. 'I'll see you.'

She started to turn, watching the last fragments of light shimmer off the surface as it became still again, then walked slowly back to her car.

She rubbed the tears from her eyes – she hadn't even known they were there – and smiled.

Finally it was time.

She had spent the last three years praying for someone to spot her and offer her a job on one of the networks. Any job would have done. And now she had more offers than she needed, and she had turned them all down. She had amazed herself at first. But she knew it was the best decision of her life.

She wasn't sure exactly what she would do when she had finished the article. She would take it one step at a time. No master plan. Or no master plan beyond knowing that controlling her own destiny was everything. She wanted to write her own future. Control the words and she could control the show.

She slipped back into the car and sat quietly, watching the sky change colour through the trees, the pink darkening to a deep red. The sun had dropped somewhere behind the horizon, a fierce light flaring in the background.

She twisted the key, gunned the engine and headed back up the lane, turning right, onto the thin, deserted road.

She drove quickly, wanting to get back out onto the open road before night fell; the sky was darkening rapidly around her and a strip of light burnt on the horizon away on her left.

She pulled the car back out onto the main road, heading up the hill south-west towards the setting sun. She looked in the mirror but all she could see was a blank space behind her.

There was nothing there.

Then, as she swept over the brow of the hill, the sinking sun burst into view. She shielded her eyes and felt the car dip down and away.

This it is, she thought. This really is it.

Up ahead the shimmering road snaked towards the bright light on the horizon.

She floored the accelerator, the engine noise filling the interior, and hurtled into the blazing light; a glinting shape disappearing quickly into the blood red sky.